When Life Happened

When Life Happened

by
JEWEL E. ANN

Copyright © 2017 by Jewel E. Ann
ISBN: 978-0-9990482-2-1
Print Edition

Cover Designer: © Sarah Hansen, Okay Creations
Formatting: BB eBooks

Dedication

For Logan, Carter, and Asher
Love without condition
Forgive without apology
Make every day your favorite day

Chapter One

THE SMALLEST ROOM belonged to the biggest loser. Nothing said pathetic like blue polka-dot bedding on a white trundle bed surrounded by four walls pinned with rock-band posters and famous volleyball players.

"Take the bed, Parker. You can put it in one of the spare rooms."

"I don't want the bed, Mom."

"Why not? You've slept in it since you were four."

Parker turned off the light and carried the last of her belongings down the stairs. "Do you see how you just answered your own question?"

There was no pride sleeping in her childhood bed at age twenty-six, just like there wasn't any pride in the string of temporary jobs and a useless college education. Parker Cruse hadn't planned on wearing the boomerang label, nor had she planned on her high-school sweetheart cheating on her with Piper—her twin sister.

"Once a conniving slut, always a conniving slut." She wore the devil's smirk, scrutinizing the photo of the happy couple.

The day the cheaters exchanged vows, Parker stopped planning. She also stopped talking to her sister. Piper's choice, not hers. Mixing a strong laxative into the bride's coffee the morning of her wedding irreparably damaged their relationship.

"Your sister is not a slut, nor is she conniving. It's been two years since the wedding. I think it's time you call her."

Ignoring her mom's peace efforts and biased assessment of her twin, Parker made a final inspection of the silver-framed, eight-by-ten wedding photo on the dark-stained mantel. She ran her finger along the wood.

"When's the last time you dusted?"

"Parker."

"Mom," Parker mocked, brushing the dust off her finger.

"I'm serious. Piper is your sister. I hate that you both can't put the past behind and start anew."

A month's worth of dust covered the photo as well.

"I'm serious too. You used to scold us for not helping out around the house, but now that I'm *willing* to help out, you feel 'judged' every time I pick up a dust cloth or vacuum."

"Stop changing the subject."

Parker traced her finger along the mantle again.

S h a m e

"Parker!" Janey Cruse smacked her daughter on the butt and erased the graffiti with her hand. "Now I'm going to have to take everything off the mantle and dust it. You're worse than those idiots who write 'wash me' on the back windows of dirty cars."

Worse? Not really. She *was* one of those idiots who wrote "wash me" on the back windows of dirty cars.

Parker took the wedding photo from the mantle and inspected her sister's light brown hair styled in long waves down her back like their mom's. Scorned and unforgiving, Parker had cut hers off to shoulder-length, flattened the life out of it, and dyed it three shades darker because she was *done* being an identical twin.

"The photographer did a superb job of photoshopping the train of her dress." Parker shook her head and whistled softly. "We must have worked for over an hour trying to get all that shit off the satin and lace."

"Parker, it's not funny."

"No." She turned toward her mom, wearing an exaggerated toothy grin. "It's really not."

"You ruined her wedding."

With a shrug, she traced her finger along the dusty photo.

Traitor

"Well, nobody died."

"Parker."

"Mom." She drew out Janey's name, thwarting her mom's effort to have a serious conversation.

Three quick honks echoed from the drive. Janey frowned at the photo when Parker returned it to its spot. She grabbed the gray wicker laundry basket and made her way to the back door across the patterned linoleum scuffed and scratched from years of heavy traffic.

"That's what she said to me." Dropping the basket at the door for her dad to load into the truck, she faced her mom again. "When I walked in on them, in my bed, *naked*—"

"Parker, I don't need to know—"

A bit of laughter fell flat into simmering, painful amusement. The dishwasher clanked and gurgled, jabbing at Parker's nerves as much as her mom's peace-making attempts.

Even then, years later, it still stung. "What? The details? You don't need to know that sweet, innocent Piper had her mouth around my boyfriend's—"

"Parker!" Janey clenched her fist at her chest like reaching for an invisible string of pearls.

With absolute certainty, Parker knew her parents had had sex *once* in their married life. They'd slept in separate bedrooms for as long as her memory could recall. Janey never understood what "the big deal" was about sex. On the rare occasion that she even said the word, her face contorted with disgust.

"This it?"

"Yes," Parker replied to her dad without turning away from her mom's sour-grapes face.

He grabbed the basket. A few seconds later a gust of wind whacked the screen door shut.

"Fine. No more details, except this one. When I told Piper she ruined my life, that I turned down two different volleyball scholarships so I could attend the same college as Caleb ... she said, 'Sorry, Parker, I really am, but *nobody died.*'"

"Sweetie..." Janey tilted her head to the side, voice soft "...that wasn't a good reason to do that to her on her wedding day."

A lava of anger spread along Parker's skin until her cheeks burned. "I did what I did because of her stupid toast at the rehearsal dinner!"

"It was a lovely toast."

"Fucking hell, Mom!"

"Parker." She *tsk-tsked* her with a disapproving head shake. "You're too intelligent to use such language."

Years of pent-up anger clawed to the surface. Parker ran her hands through her hair and tucked it behind her ears while grumbling. "Let me refresh your memory. It went something like this: 'I'd like to thank Parker for being oblivious to the love blooming between Caleb and me, then graciously stepping aside so we could be together.' That wasn't a lovely toast. It was a verbal slap in the face, and it was horrifically embarrassing and degrading."

Janey moved closer and rested her hand on Parker's cheek. "Piper called me yesterday. She and Caleb are moving back home next month." Her lips pulled into a sympathetic smile. "Your sister is pregnant."

They would name their child something like Gullible or Oblivious and say they named it after Parker.

"Well, good thing I'm moving out so they can come visit you and Dad without running into me." Keeping resolute confidence after that statement deserved an award considering her "move" was *way* across the road into her grandparents' old farmhouse. An impressive show of independence for a college-educated twenty-something. If Piper and Caleb accurately named their child after her, it would have to be Pathetic Loser.

"You riding over with me or walking?" her dad asked. "I drove Old Blue over earlier and parked it in the garage. You'll want to get a garage door opener soon. Definitely before winter."

Parker turned and pushed a half smile through her stubborn frown. "I'll ride. It might make it feel more official. As for the garage door opener, it's not a high priority. I can open and shut the door just fine."

"I'm going to miss you, sweetie."

Bart Cruse rolled his eyes at his wife's comment. "Jeez, woman! She's going to be across the road. A hundred yards."

Another affirmation of Parker's loser status.

"Crack the windows. You've done all that painting, and even though the base paint had no VOCs, there were VOCs in the tints. And don't forget to check the smoke alarm batteries."

"Yes, Mom." She gave her a thumbs-up and followed her

dad out the door.

"And the carbon monoxide detector too! I'm afraid you'll forget about it when you turn on the furnace this winter!"

Bart chuckled as the loose gravel of their drive crunched beneath his boots. "See what I've been dealing with for the past thirty-five years?"

Parker squinted as a sudden gust kicked up dirt when she hopped in the truck. "She just expresses most of her love in the form of worry. It's still love." She slammed the door.

He mumbled something, but it wasn't any term of endearment.

PARKER'S NEW INDEPENDENCE may have been in the hundred-yard shadow of her parents' house—separated by opposing gravel drives and a two-lane country road—but it qualified as freedom.

Different house.

Different lot.

A new start.

She and her father had spent the better part of spring fixing the old place up on the inside. They refinished the dark wood floors of the two-story farmhouse, painted the cabinets white, and replaced the laminate countertops in the kitchen and two bathrooms with granite. Parker covered almost every wall with a shade of blue to make it her own. It may have had a few VOCs lingering, but Parker preferred a new-paint smell to the previous musty odor that clung to every surface.

Parker spent every last dime she'd saved since college to make the renovations. Utilities would be a challenge until she found a job. The thermostat sat at eighty-two, and she'd drop it to sixty-five in the winter. She wasn't homeless or living with her parents; that's all that mattered.

While cooking her first official dinner in *her* house, someone's fist rapped against the front door. With a hundred percent certainty, she knew Janey Cruse, professional worrywart, was at her door.

Mommy Dearest couldn't stay away for a full three hours. No parties or orgies were in Parker's immediate future, but she wanted to keep her options open and parents from dropping in at will.

She flipped off the gas burner and lifted her grilled cheese off the griddle pan. "Hot! Ouch!" It landed on her plate, total luck. Parker sucked her burnt finger tips as she inched closer to the door, barely able to contain her giggles.

"Yes. Yes! YES! Oh, give it to me! Harder! Faster! Oh … god … more tongue!" Parker moaned and yelled before covering her mouth to silence the laughter. Satan knew her by name, of that she felt confident.

She needed a front door camera to see the look on her mom's face. It went on her list of things to get before the garage door opener. After a few seconds, she shimmied out of her shorts and top, wearing only her panties and bra. It was mean, but Parker loved a good joke. She opened the door to relieve Janey of her impending heart attack or stroke.

"Sorry, you caught me in the middle of—oh shit!" Parker jumped behind the door as the aged, wooden steps creaked beneath the man retreating down them; he glanced back at her.

"You're not my mom." She winced while peeking around the door as the words shrieked from her throat.

He bit his lips together and hummed. "I think you should be relieved I'm not your mom."

Her nose wrinkled as sweaty embarrassment beaded along her skin. "Sadly, I'm not."

"My ... um ..." He adjusted his red Cubs cap on his head, exposing his matted dark hair for a brief moment before pulling it lower to hide his eyes. He had a handsome face and tall, lean body that wore his dark jeans and a gray tee perfectly.

"My dog got out of our yard. I think he's behind your shed. I just didn't want to roam around your property without letting you know my intentions. You know ... people guarding their property with guns. But, I, uh ... doubt you have a gun on you at the moment." He kept his gaze lowered like a real gentleman.

"I'm..." keeping his chin down, he jerked his head to the side "...your neighbor to the south, Gus Westman."

"Sure. Yeah. Let me ... uh ... slip my clothes back on, and I'll help you look for him."

Gus shook his head. "No need. I'll let you get back to your *thing*."

She left the door cracked an inch and grabbed her clothes. "It's not what it sounded like. I was just faking an orgasm," Parker yelled from behind the door. Tugging her shorts up her legs, she rolled her eyes. "Not what I meant," she whispered to herself, pulling her shirt on.

"None of my business. I'm ... going to look for Rags."

"Be right out!" After shoving her feet into faded navy Chuck Taylor's, she grabbed her sandwich from the kitchen and hustled out the front door. "Rags? Is that his name?"

"Yeah." Gus glanced over his shoulder as she ran to catch up, his embarrassment evident in his nervous smile and difficulty maintaining eye contact.

"Sheepdog, right?"

Gus nodded as the tangled weeds and grass rustled and cracked releasing a warm, earthy smell while they trudged toward the shed.

"Thought so. I've seen him in your yard. I'm Parker, by the way."

Another quick sideways glance. "Nice to meet you. I've met your dad. He said you were going to be moving into the farmhouse."

"My dad didn't mention he'd met you. We watched, *admired*, your house being built last summer. I've seen your Westman Electric van, but I didn't realize you were the owner. Grilled cheese?" Tearing apart her gooey sandwich, she offered him half.

"No. I'm good."

"It's Havarti and pepper jack." Surely a bite of the greatest cheese combination to ever be melted between two pieces of sourdough could erase all memory of the naked girl who answered the door.

"Really, I'm good, but thank you."

With a shrug, she took a bite. "There he is!" She pointed to the corner of the shed.

"Rags!" Gus yelled. "Come. Now!"

The white and gray dog hung its head in a moped posture and inched toward them.

"Fuck," Gus grumbled.

"Oh man. I'm very sorry." In case the bra and panties didn't prove her lack of manners, mumbling over a mouthful of sandwich did the job. "I need to get those cockleburs dug out."

There must have been over a hundred burrs tangled in the dog's thick coat.

"She's going to kill us both, buddy." Gus tugged the bill of his cap down a bit as if it could shield him from trouble.

Rags sat in front of him, tongue out, almost smiling.

"Your wife?"

Gus nodded.

"You're going to have to shear him like an actual sheep."

"Yeah." He released a long sigh, rubbing his temples.

"My grandparents used to have two golden retrievers. When they'd get into the cockleburs, the only choice was to get out the shearers. I think they're still in the shed."

"Really?" For the first time, Gus's brown eyes with flecks of gold met Parker's and held her gaze for more than a few seconds. He grinned. Not a creepy man's grin but more of a boy's grin. The you-just-got-me-out-of-trouble grin.

Parker felt it in places inappropriate to feel a married man's grin.

"I don't want to keep you from your company." He jerked his head toward her house.

She laughed. "No company. I really did think you were my mom. It was a joke. She doesn't believe in sex."

He narrowed one eye.

"True story. There's no other way to say it."

When the skepticism faded from his face, he cleared his throat. "Let's get this done, Rags. We're both going to be sleeping in the dog house."

Chapter Two

T HE DOOR HINGES squeaked as they stepped into the shed
attached to the garage. Parker's canvas shoes scraped along
the dirt-stained concrete floor. A mix of mulched grass on the
lawnmower blades, rusted tools, and dust hung in the air.

Unlike his wife and most other people he knew, Gus loved
the smell of the country. For him, every breath of Iowa air felt
like hard work, good people, and the true heart of the land.

Parker tapped her finger on her bottom lip, surveying the
entire shed filled with garden tools, dirty flower pots, stray
tools, and an old bike. Neatly-wound extension cords hung
from nails on the wall, and coffee cans and mason jars filled
with odds and ends lined shelves—a little bit of everything and
everything in its spot.

It was more organized than any place Gus had ever seen.
That said a lot considering he married an overachieving
perfectionist.

"Hmm ... I think ..." Parker walked to the far wall.

Gus couldn't remember the last time he'd given a woman,
who wasn't his wife, a second glance. He married a stunning,
petite, blonde, who fulfilled his every fantasy. No need for
second glances. Like everything else in life—needs changed. He
had no idea he *needed* to let his eyes have a second glance until
they kept wandering in the direction of Parker's long legs—tan,

defined, and marred with a few scars that for some reason made them quite sexy.

He'd been out in the heat too long that day; it was possible the nearly one-hundred-degree temperatures fried his brain. That and his wife left two weeks earlier on a business trip.

"Here they are. I hope these still work." She lifted onto her toes to grab the shearers off the top shelf.

Eyes that had a mind of their own homed in on those legs, especially her tight calves. Gus didn't go to strip clubs with his friends or even Hooters for lunch. Aside from a few internet searches gone wrong—or right, depending on how one looked at it—he didn't even watch porn. That's how lucky he was in the sex department.

But living the saint's life for five years of marriage earned him a pass, so he thought.

"You're staring at my legs."

His gaze flicked up to Parker's frown as she turned, holding the shearers in her hand. Times had changed. Even before he got married, Gus couldn't remember a woman ever calling him out on something like staring at her legs.

"I'm ..."

She sighed, lips twisted to the side. "Pretty ugly, huh?"

He gulped down the saliva in his mouth instead of letting it drool down his chin. "Uh ..."

"Volleyball. ACL surgery twice." Bending down, she traced the scars with her finger.

Gus smiled. Of course those defined legs could only be those of an athlete. Had she been a few inches shorter, they would have seemed stocky, but Parker had to be just under six foot, and nothing about her looked stocky.

On a blink, he forced his gaze away from her body, focusing over her shoulder to the horseshoe nailed to the wall. "You should flip that around." He nodded toward it. "Like a U. Otherwise, the luck runs out the open heel part."

The wind sighed under the eaves like the god of infidelity whispering in his ear. *Get your shit done and get out!*

Parker narrowed her eyes then glanced over her shoulder. "Well, son of a bitch. That explains a lot." She set the clippers on the workbench, retrieved a hammer from the drawer, removed the nail from the horseshoe, flipped it, and hammered it back to the wall. "I'm not usually one to buy into superstitions, but if you knew the luck I've had …" She pushed out a long breath while returning the hammer to the drawer.

Gus rubbed his scruffy chin while shaking his head. His face hurt from grinning so much. She'd answered her door, almost naked, so naturally his focus had been drawn to her body, but the girl next door had a peculiar personality that he found quite likable.

When she returned her attention to him, he moved his hand from his chin to his mouth, wiping the smile from it. "I sprained an ankle, pulled my groin, and strained my hamstring, but never anything that required surgery." He hoped she didn't notice his abrupt digression back to the original topic.

She plugged in the shearers. "What did you play?"

"Everything—football, basketball, track, and baseball."

She whistled and patted her leg. "Come here, Rags."

Rags backed into a corner.

"Get over here." Gus grabbed his collar, but the stubborn mutt refused to move.

Parker whistled again and held out her hand. Rags shot off toward her.

She grinned, shooting Gus a quick look. "Turkey jerky."

"You always have turkey jerky in your pocket?"

"Of course. Don't you?" The clippers hummed to life. She wasted no time shearing the bur-tangled fur off Rags, feeding him small pieces of turkey jerky every thirty seconds or so to keep him still.

Genius.

"Actually, I don't carry dried meat in my pockets. Usually just a pack of gum," he said over the hum of the clippers.

"Willard Farm, fifteen miles south of here. Best jerky around. We get all of our meat and eggs from him. Or at least I will when I get a job again. I'm sort of between jobs. Four years of college and the best I've done so far has been a string of temp jobs. I'm totally winning at life these days." She glanced up with the goofiest toothy grin spread across her face.

Most women failed at not taking themselves so seriously, brushing off a bit of bad luck and getting on with life—at least that's what Gus thought about the succeed-or-die woman in his life. He should not have expected anything less than a laid-back attitude from the half-naked girl who answered the door and carried turkey jerky in her pocket for no other reason than just because.

Rags licked her free hand then she pulled it away to finish what would be a state fair-record shearing time. Desperate for more, he licked her legs near the frayed edge of her denim shorts. Gus needed his wife to return home immediately. Envying a dog licking another woman's legs crossed a line that required more than a day pass for second glances.

"There." Pride beamed along her face as she admired her grooming skills. "Sorry..." she ruffled his head "...no more treats for you."

Gus wanted a treat. He, too, had been good. The second

that thought entered his mind, he cleared his throat and stepped toward Rags. "Thank you for saving us from the wrath of his mom. I seem to spend a lot of time with him in the proverbial dog house."

"I can see that about both of you." She grinned and shot him a wink. She gave them freely.

He couldn't remember the last time his wife smiled in a way that didn't seem forced. And never had he been the recipient of a flirty wink from her.

"Here, let me help you clean that up."

As he reveled in genuine smiles and winks, Parker made haste with the hand broom and dust pan. Gus felt like a gawking idiot for standing there so long.

"Just grab the trash bin over there for me."

He scooted the metal bin right next to the pile of burs and fur on the floor. "I've never seen a shed this organized."

Parker dumped the fur into the trash; then she looked around the shed lined with every imaginable tool neatly in its place on a hook or shelf. Not a cobweb in sight. "I dig organization. My grandfather used to do his woodworking in here, but it was a disaster. After he died, my dad and I cleaned everything up and organized his stuff so it makes sense. I get an odd high from it. Not like germaphobe OCD shit, just good old-fashioned organization. Ya know?"

Gus nodded slowly, mesmerized by the life that bled from every inch of her. And that smile … fucking perfect.

"You have kids?" She had a way of making the moment real again.

He needed that, so did his dick. "No. Just Rags."

"Oh. Sorry, I can't really guess your age with that hat covering…" she squinted at his head "…maybe some gray hair or a big bald spot on top?"

She kicked him in the nuts with her wit while keeping a smile plastered on her face and a twinkle in her dangerous blue eyes.

Gus removed his hat and leaned forward. "No gray yet and no bald spot. But thanks for making me feel old. Do I want to know your age?"

"You mean, do you want to know if you should feel like a dirty old man for checking out my legs earlier or just guilty because you're married?"

He pressed his fist to his mouth to hide his grin. "God-damn, you sure know how to bust a guy's balls."

"Just giving ya shit. Take your dog home, slip into your plaid Lands' End slippers and cardigan, and enjoy your prune juice without worrying about such trivial things as inappropriately looking at the legs of a minor."

Gus chuckled, the kind that started deep in his belly, the kind that felt so damn good. "You're trouble."

She wound the cord around the shearers and lifted onto her toes again to put them back on the top shelf. "Stop looking at my legs and ass, old man."

"Tell the *young girl* thank you, Rags. I want to get home and settled into my easy chair before Masterpiece Theater starts."

Still on her tippy toes, Parker glanced over her shoulder, cracking a grin. "Good night, Mr. Westman."

He herded Rags to the door. "For the love of god, call me Gus. My father is Mr. Westman."

"What is he, like ... one hundred?"

Gus turned, relishing the feeling of a genuine smile on his face. It hadn't been there in a long time.

"Oh, hey?"

He grabbed the door right before it shut. "Yeah?"

"I need a few outlets moved. Do you do small jobs?"

"Not so much, but I'll do it for you."

She brushed dog fur off her shirt and shorts. "I'd appreciate it. No hurry. Whenever it fits into your schedule."

"I'll come by in the morning."

Parker waved him off. "No. Not on the weekend. That's probably your time off. Seriously, no hurry. I'm good with extension cords for now."

"I'll be by around nine," he said while walking away so she wouldn't have a chance to argue anymore.

"WAIT A MINUTE, buddy." Gus grabbed the wrist of his sidekick for the day a second before his pudgy little finger pushed the yellowed doorbell button.

"Why?"

Gus ruffled the mop of blond hair hanging in the boy's innocent brown eyes, looking a bit like Rags. "We're early. Let's just hang out here on the porch for a few minutes."

They sat on the top porch step, watching the birds and squirrels flitter and skitter about as Parker belted out the second verse to Taylor Swift's "Shake it Off."

"I like this song."

Gus chuckled. "Yeah? Sounds like she does too."

Maroon 5's "Moves Like Jagger" followed Taylor. Parker also knew every word to that song. Glancing at the clock on his phone, Gus's mouth twisted into a grin with a slight head shake while the nine-year-old boy bobbed his floppy-haired noggin, his foot tapping to the beat. At 8:55 the concert ended.

They waited the final five minutes to make sure there would not be an encore performance.

When they felt satisfied the curtain was down and the stage lights were off for good, the boy rang the doorbell as Gus stood a few feet back inspecting the empty flower boxes beneath the windows and hanging planters at each corner waiting to be filled.

"Just a minute!"

Before Gus could stop him, the eager finger pushed the yellowed button one more time.

"I said just a minute, not just a second." Parker swung open the door, breathless, sweaty, and instantly grinning at the impatient culprit. "Oh, wow! I thought you said you didn't have kids."

Gus tried and failed at not homing in on her short gray dress that looked like something one might wear playing tennis. "No. This is my nephew, Brady. Brady, this is Parker." He wanted kids, a gaggle of them running amuck and suiting up for little league, but his wife adopted a job instead.

"Hi, Brady." Parker bent down to his eye level and smiled until her nose wrinkled. "I do believe you are the most handsome little boy I have ever met."

He grinned and shook his head as if to see her better through his long, disheveled bangs. "Hi."

"You're out of breath." Gus attempted to control his lingering amusement by rubbing his lips together.

Parker slicked back a few stray hairs then tightened her ponytail. "Yeah, I was tramping."

Gus covered Brady's ears. "Excuse me?"

She shook her head. "Sorry, rebounding … jumping … mini trampoline."

"Ah, I see."

Brady shoved Gus's hands away from his head.

"Come in." She held open the door as Brady stepped in first followed by Gus.

"Here, buddy, carry this." Handing Brady his tool belt, Gus brought in a fancy-looking tool bag.

Her living room consisted of bare blue walls, a blue futon, a red bean bag, and a mini trampoline amid newly refinished dark wood floors. No knickknacks, pictures, scented candles, or anything else that gave a house the feel of home—except the smell of coffee.

"Male bonding, huh? I hope you two have more planned today than moving my outlets."

"Little league game," Gus said.

"Is that what they call geriatric baseball? Must be a Parks and Rec thing you're doing. Huh, Gus?"

The gift of her contagious smile was worth the sacrifice of being the object of her amusement.

Scratching his chin, Gus pursed his lips. "Fun little jabs in front of my nephew. That's not really fair, is it?"

"How so?" Mischief danced in the blue depths of her eyes.

"I have to be a role model, which prevents me from saying anything back to you."

"What could you possibly say back to me?" She tapped her chin with her finger as her eyes rolled to the ceiling.

"Nothing, I suppose. Except maybe a bit about your karaoke performance."

She nodded slowly, eyes flitting between Gus and Brady. "You were here early."

"A bit." Gus simpered.

"Define 'a bit.'"

"Taylor Swift early."

Her narrowed eyes grew wide with surprise. "And you ... what? Stood at the door listening to me?"

"We sat on the top step." Brady inspected the room, oblivious to any wrongdoing. "Uncle Gus said we were early."

Parker pulled her hair out of its ponytail, slipped the band on her wrist, and combed through her dark, tangled strands still damp with sweat. "It's not polite to eavesdrop."

Gus met her expectant gaze with a shrug. "We didn't have our ears pressed to the door. I'm sure anyone driving by with their windows down heard you."

"And?" She set her gaze on Brady. "How did I sound?"

Brady's grin reached his eyes. "Really good. I like that song."

"Smart boy." Parker held out her fist, and Brady bumped it with his.

"Where's your breaker box? I need to get this done before Brady decides he likes you better than me." Gus ruffled Brady's hair.

"Downstairs." Parker nodded toward the door to her right.

"I'll be back, buddy." He followed Parker down the rickety stairs. A musty smell enveloped them in the chilly, damp dungeon with mildew cracks snaking across the concrete floor. "Definitely has the odor of an old farmhouse."

"Yeah, I don't plan to come down here unless there's a tornado." She wrinkled her nose, giving him a quick glance over her shoulder.

"Parker." He laughed. "These aren't breakers; they're fuses." He brushed away a few cobwebs.

"Same thing. Right?"

Gus removed his hat then put it on backward, leaning closer to the old panel. "Yes and no."

"You don't know what to do with it, do you? I can call my dad or—"

Slowly, he turned his head, giving her a playful scowl. "Or what? An electrician?" Something about her made it impossible to distinguish the snarky woman with an evil grin from the innocent girl who forwent the opportunity to think before speaking.

Still, Gus enjoyed the way she squirmed, twisting her lips and looking at her nails. "Something like that."

"Humor me and pretend for today that I'm a real electrician."

"If you insist." With her chin tucked to her chest, she glanced up at him with a playful batting of her eyelashes, a grin dominating her face.

Gus knew some guy would fall hard for Parker. Marry her—feeling like he owned the world for having found her. After all, she was gorgeous, sexy, playful, and fun—so much fun. Then she'd one-eighty on him. Flirting? Gone. Sexy? Nope, not for the husband. At least, that had been his experience with fun, beautiful women. Bait-and-switch.

He returned his attention to the fuse box. "I'm a little surprised with the work you and your dad did in this place that you didn't have the wiring redone. It's old and dangerous. This fuse panel increases your risk of fire by at least three times."

"Don't tell my mom. She has enough to worry about."

"I'm serious."

She sighed. "Fine. As soon as I get a job again, hopefully soon, I'll start saving for new wiring. You have anyone you recommend?"

"I know a guy." Gus grinned, but not like an electrician

grinned at their customer; it felt more like the smile of a little kid hitting his first home run. In twenty-four hours, the girl next door had managed to remind him how miserable he was in his marriage, how much fun it was to flirt, and how much trouble she could cause in his life.

"So you're not going to move my outlets today?"

"It would be smart to wait until everything gets rewired."

"How much are we talking?" She crossed her arms over her chest.

"A few grand."

Her eyes nearly sprang from their sockets. "Really? Well, that's not happening for a while. For now, why don't I pay you to move the outlets. What do you charge an hour?"

"Fifty dollars."

"Alrighty then." She returned a sharp nod. "You know ... I think the extension cords are working just fine."

"Relax, I didn't say I was going to charge you anything. I'll move them until I can find time to rewire your house at a *neighborly rate.*"

"What's the neighborly rate?"

"Depends on the neighbor."

She pointed a finger at him. "You know ... I did shear Rags for you. Maybe we can make an even trade?"

He barked out a laugh. "An 'even' trade? Since when does it cost several grand to buzz down a dog?"

"No! Not that." She shoved his shoulder.

He wanted to shove her back—as in *up against the wall.* Swallowing hard, he blinked to erase the vision from his mind. That wasn't him. Those thoughts weren't his. Yet, he let them in his mind, and they felt real as they spurred parts of him to life in unwanted ways.

"I'm talking about moving the outlets, not rewiring my house. I don't want to feel like I owe you."

"That's fair." He turned back to the fuse panel. "I'm going to flip the switch to all the electricity while I do this. It will be easiest. Are you good for a little bit without it?"

"Yes." She headed up the stairs. "But let me open this door. Otherwise, it's going to be pitch black down here when you flip it."

The door hinges groaned when she opened it. "Okay."

He flipped it and navigated the creaky stairs.

"Just don't forget to turn me on before you leave."

The toe of Gus's boot snagged on the edge of the stair, and he caught himself with the rail. Had she been reading his mind?

"Sorry." Parker cupped a hand over her mouth, muffling her laugh. "Gah! That sounded so wrong."

"Nah … the switch." He cleared his throat. "I got what you meant." The perfect chance to give her shit presented itself, and he choked because his dick began to have an involuntary response to her.

"Brady? Let's get this done before your game."

Brady, having taken a seat on a chair in the kitchen, jumped to attention.

"So, Mr. Brady, why are you hanging out with Uncle Gus today?" She grabbed a cookie from an old ceramic cookie jar shaped like a chicken and held it up as if to ask Gus permission to offer it to Brady.

Gus nodded.

"Thank you." Brady took the cookie and shoved half of it in his mouth.

Parker led them up the stairs.

"My sister got called into work, and Brady's dad is out of town."

"Grandpa's sick. A pain in his ass," Brady said matter-of-factly through his mouthful of cookie.

"Brady!" Gus tugged on the little boy's ear until he giggled.

"Grandma said so. She said until he got better, he was a pain in her ass too."

Halfway down the hall, Parker glanced over her shoulder; a smile tugged the corner of her mouth upward. Gus pinched his upper lip between his teeth and rolled his eyes.

"My dad's hemorrhoids have flared up. My dear sister needs to refrain from using speaker phone when they call. Innocent ears."

"It's okay. My mom talks like an uncensored child all the time." She winked at Brady then pointed to the outlet by the window. "Can you move that about five feet to the right?" Then she pointed to an outlet below her television mounted to the wall opposite her bed. "Can you move that one so it's hidden behind the TV?"

"Yes and yes." Gus inspected the outlets.

"You can watch my baseball game today."

"Oh …" Parker looked between Gus and Brady.

"Um … I'm sure Parker is busy, buddy."

"Yeah, I've got like a bunch of stuff … to do …" She shook her head. "Not busy at all actually."

Gus looked up from his tool bag. "Well, if Brady invited you and you want to go, then …" He shrugged. That was his excuse if anyone asked. *He* didn't invite the neighbor lady, Brady did. Who was he to say she couldn't go to a little league game open to the public? Parker would be there; other men and women would be there. No big deal.

"Sure. I love baseball."

Of course she loved baseball. Gus loved baseball. His absent wife did not like baseball. Gus questioned if his wife still liked *him*.

"Great ... just ... great." His enthusiasm faded after the first great, settling into an uneasy pang of guilt in his gut.

Chapter Three

PARKER NEEDED A life. The endless tailspin had to end. Step one: shake off her past, gather her bearings, and stop being totally available at the last minute for a little league game.

Plans on a Saturday? Nope.

Just moved out of my trundle bed.

If Amazon Prime offered a life, she would have one-clicked the hell out of it and selected recurring monthly delivery.

However, Parker couldn't resist Brady's cuteness, and she found herself looking forward to watching him. Life or no life. In a way she couldn't comprehend, she looked forward to hanging out with Gus as well. He was married. That wasn't a problem. Parker was the victim of cheating. She could never be a homewrecker.

Friends. Maybe they could be friends, the kind of friends who teased each other about stupid shit like shearing dogs, karaoke, and old age. It had been quite a while since she'd had a friend.

"You made it." Gus scooted over. "Here, you can sit in my spot, so you don't burn your legs on these hot-as-hell metal bleachers."

Parker tugged at the legs of her shorts, but they were way too short to protect her skin from the metal. "Thanks." She sat next to him. "So no other family came to watch Brady today?"

"Not today. Usually, everyone is here."

"Well, good thing I came to cheer him on too."

Gus grunted a small laugh. Parker couldn't decipher its meaning, so she focused on the game.

"The back of their shirts say Westman Electric. Someone sprang for some serious sponsorship."

Gus rubbed his hand over his mouth, trying to hide his grin. "Brady's up to bat." He pointed to number eight in his batter's helmet, tapping the bottom of his cleats with the bat like a pro.

"Let's go, Brady!" Parker clapped and bounced up and down.

Gus shot her a look with a single peaked brow.

"What? Don't you know how to cheer on your guy?"

With a soft chuckle, he shook his head.

Brady knocked it deep into left field on the first pitch.

"Attaboy! Woo hoo! Nice hit, Brady!" The bleachers shook beneath Parker jumping up and down.

Brady stopped at third base.

"Jeez, old man, how'd you even climb this high in the bleachers? Look alive!" Parker tugged on the bill of Gus's Cubs cap.

"August? Who's your friend?"

They both turned to the couple up behind them a few rows. The tan blonde kept her head down, focused on her phone while the equally tan man beside her dragged his hawkish gaze over Parker. He had a nearly-bald head with patchy peeling skin and crooked teeth peeking out between cracked lips. That weirded Parker out a bit.

"Matt, this is Parker." Gus let her name hang in the air.

She waited to see if he would define her role in his life—

neighbor, fake sister, cousin, friend. Nope. Just Parker, said in a way that did funny things to certain parts of her body in a very un-friend-like way.

"Nice to meet you, Matt." She shook his hand and turned back to the game. "Go, Brady, go!"

Brady slid into home right as the catcher caught the ball from the first baseman.

"Out!" the ump yelled.

"What?" Parker shot to her feet, hands in the air and then they dropped to her head, and she tugged her hair. "Are you kidding me? Are you blind?"

"Parker," Gus tried to interrupt.

"Get this guy some glasses! Brady was there like … a week before that ball hit the catcher's glove. What the—"

"Ma'am?" A middle-aged gentleman with jeans and a red polo shirt crooked his finger at Parker.

"Me?" She pointed to herself.

He nodded.

Parker climbed down the bleachers and hopped off the last one, standing an inch taller than the man with Brady's team's logo on his baseball cap.

"Do you have a child on this team?" he asked.

"No. Why?"

The man nodded toward the back of the bleachers. She followed him.

"We have a good conduct policy for these games. Parents are expected to follow the rules of good sportsmanship same as the kids."

"Well, thank goodness I'm not a parent, huh?"

He sighed. "While we cannot penalize the child for the actions of a non-family member, we can ask that you leave the ballpark."

"You're kicking me out? For what? Being a spectator? I'm pretty sure yelling at referees and umpires in sports dates back many years. It's part of the game."

"These are nine and ten-year-old boys. This isn't an MLB game with a crowd of drunk spectators. We expect the people in the bleachers to be role models for our young players."

"Is there a problem?" Gus walked around the corner, hands in the pockets of his shorts.

"No, sir." The spectator police gave Gus a reassuring smile. "Just informing this young lady of our good conduct rules."

"Do you know who this man is?" Parker jabbed her thumb in Gus's direction. "He's Gus Westman as in *Westman Electric*, the man who sponsored the shirts for the team. And I'm his friend. So if you kick me out it's like you're kicking him out, and who kicks their top sponsor out of the game?"

Gus leaned close to Parker's ear. "See the name of the orthodontist office on the scoreboard? I think they are the top sponsor."

"Listen, I'm only trying to keep everyone happy and a positive environment for the kids. If you can keep your comments to encouraging ones, then I'll let you stay."

"She'll obey the rules." Gus eyed Parker, daring her to say another word.

She blinked a few times. "Whatever."

"Come on." Gus turned. "Brady's pitching."

Mr. Rules nodded at Parker as she walked past him with a scowl on her face. She climbed the bleachers and sat next to Gus, who tugged on the bill of his hat as if the shadow cast by it could hide the amusement curling his lips.

"Let's go, Brady!" Gus yelled as if to shove his positivity in her face.

"So … I got thrown out of three volleyball games in high school for arguing with the ref." She watched Brady pitch.

"Ya don't say?" Gus chuckled.

"I know. Shocking. Jerky?"

Gus turned, eyeing the turkey jerky she pulled out of her pocket. "You have jerky in your pocket again?"

Parker shrugged as she ripped open the top of it with her teeth. "Smell it." She held it to his nose. "Would you rather have a bite of this or a stick of gum?"

Like a dog grabbing a treat, Gus snatched it with his teeth. Parker giggled and tore it away from him.

"Mmm, pretty good." He nodded, chewing it slowly.

"See, told ya." She nudged his knee with hers.

He stiffened. They were friends, that's all. Nudging came with playful banter. A man and a woman could be friends without it being sexual. Parker knew her limits and they were hard, uncrossable limits branded into her conscience since the day she walked in on her sister and Caleb.

"So you didn't splurge on advertising on the scoreboard. What's up with that?" Taking a bite of the jerky, Parker leaned in to nudge him with her shoulder but stopped short, thinking of the people behind them who only knew her as "Parker."

"Brady wanted the name on his shirt."

"You're a pretty cool uncle."

"The coolest." An impish smile twisted his lips as his gaze remained on the field.

Parker found his coyness adorable—in a platonic way.

"So … how is it you had no other plans today?"

She sighed a small laugh. "Well, when you're twenty-six with no job and no boyfriend, it leaves the old social calendar pretty bare. My friends are all getting married, having babies, or adulting with real jobs."

"What's your problem?"

"Wow!" She couldn't hold back. Her elbow landed in his ribs.

He shook with silent laughter.

"We've known each other for twenty-four hours and you're making assumptions that something is *wrong* with me?"

"Hey, you started it. The gloves came off when you started in on my age."

Twisting her lips, she nodded slowly. "I see. Oh, Gus Gus Gus … I haven't smiled this much in a long time." She winked at him. "I'm glad we're neighbors. You're so much more fun than my parents."

"And younger." He narrowed an eye at her. "Right?"

"A bit."

They returned their attention to the game as sparse claps accompanied hoots and "You've got this, Lance," and "Run, Simon!"

"Sooo … tell me about your wife."

Gus stiffened again the way he did when she nudged him with her knee. "She works a lot. Travels a lot."

Parker waited for him to elaborate, but he didn't.

"That's great. I guess. Must mean she's successful."

Gus grunted. "Yeah, she's definitely that."

"Is she out of town now?"

"Mmm-hmm."

Parker swatted at a fly probably detecting her jerky stash. "When does she return?"

"Tomorrow. I think." His reply lacked all enthusiasm.

Parker pointed to the dugout. "Brady's up to bat next." And that's all she said to Gus for the rest of the game.

Chapter Four

HUMIDITY AND NINETY-DEGREE temperatures usually didn't suffocate Des Moines, Iowa until late July. That summer, a week of mid-nineties and no rain blindsided June. Relief would eventually come in the form of severe thunderstorms leaving farmers thanking God for the rain and cursing him for the wind and tornado damage.

"You must be Parker?"

Parker turned toward the woman's voice and jumped up, brushing off the dirt plastered to her sweaty legs like a second skin. Her de-weeding expedition began at six that morning. The sun hovered around the noonish area in the clear sky.

"Hi. Yes, I am."

The petite woman with blond curls pulled into a bun—makeup flawless—held out her hand. Parker turned her hands palm side up, frowning at her soiled gloves. The woman's stark-white, sleeveless blouse and pleated dress shorts didn't stand a chance. Parker's wide-eyed stare tried to tell her as much.

"I'm Sabrina Westman. You met my husband and dog last week." Her awaiting hand held firm in the space between them.

"Yes! Pleasure to meet you." Parker peeled off her old gloves, revealing sweaty hands with dirt embedded under her fingernails. She shook Sabrina's hand. The last time she talked to Gus was at Brady's ballgame.

Sabrina may have tried to hide her flinch, but Parker saw it. After six hours in what felt like one hundred percent humidity, how could her hands be anything but disgustingly moist?

Sabrina held her sweat and dirt-smudged hand stiffly from her body like a cast. "I appreciate you taking care of Rags's bur issue."

"Oh, no problem. I felt really bad about it. The cockleburs are gone. I removed all of them early this morning. Not that it can erase what happened last week, but …" She shrugged.

"It's fine. Not your fault. I've been telling Gus to fix the fence gate for months. Obviously, he doesn't listen to me."

Parker nodded. Sabrina's husband had seen a complete stranger in her panties and bra. He heard Parker's fake orgasm charade. And they had had a few uncomfortable moments in her basement and at the baseball game. Asking Sabrina if he mentioned any of that didn't seem like a good idea, but she wanted to know how much confidence and dignity she could justify in Sabrina's presence.

"Anyway … he mentioned you were between jobs."

"Oh … he did?"

"Yes. He said you've been doing some temp work. Is that not correct?"

"Um … yeah. I'm waiting to hear back from a chiropractor in Waukee. She's looking for a full-time receptionist. I think I stand a good chance." Parker dreamed of using her four-year degree to secure a minimum-wage job with no degree or experience necessary and no chance for promotion.

"Gus said Rags took an instant liking to you."

Parker laughed, brushing more dirt off her legs. "It was the turkey jerky. I had to find a way to keep him occupied while fixing the cocklebur situation. I'm certain most dogs would take a liking to me if I had dried meat in my pocket."

"Gus also mentioned you have a lot of energy and that shed of yours is organized to ... and I quote, 'my wife's perfectionist standards.'" Sabrina smirked.

"I like things tidied up. I'm far from a perfectionist. I just like things ... neat."

Gus talked about her. She wondered if he'd mentioned her legs as well. Doubtful. A few harmless glances meant nothing. Had he nailed her to the barn door with his cock, Caleb and Piper style, that would have been another story. Parker had thought about him ... a little too much. The playful banter about his age had been more for her benefit. Finding the married neighbor guy attractive was not allowed, especially for Parker, president of the "I Hate Cheaters Club." Thinking of him as old, gray, and balding became her survival. And the platonic friendship? That was still in question.

"I'll get to the point." Sabrina glanced at her Apple Watch. "I need help. I had hoped Gus could be that help, but he's too busy." Her exaggerated eye roll contradicted her words. "I recently took over a large engineering firm, and I travel a lot. Thankfully, we don't have kids, but recently I've found it nearly impossible to keep up with certain things in my life."

"I get it." Parker didn't really get it. Twenty-six-year-olds having just left the nest for the second time couldn't possibly comprehend the demands of a job with experience necessary, demands beyond answering a phone, and traveling for a reason other than a getaway with friends. "Can I ask how old you are?"

Sabrina's brow pulled into an unspoken question.

"Sorry, I'm just curious how long it took you to…" *Move out of your parents' house. Get a real job. Find a man who's not a lying, cheating, bastard.* "…achieve such success."

Sabrina's shoulders pulled back as confidence curled her lips revealing her bleached teeth. No one naturally had teeth *that* white. "Thirty-eight."

"No shit. Wow! You don't look it at all." Parker made a mental note to invest in higher SPF sunblock and buy some whitening strips. She had twelve years to make something of herself and find a job that required fancy dry-clean-only clothes and an Apple Watch.

Sabrina's smile faded like she'd reached her smile limit for the day. "As I was saying … if you're interested, I'd like to hire you to be my personal assistant."

A job. Sabrina Westman offered her a *real* job. She traveled, so Parker would travel. She wore fancy white blouses, so Parker would wear them too. She wore an Apple Watch, of course Parker would need one too—so they could sync their calendars, message each other, and calculate how many steps they took to keep their professional asses in shape.

The opportunities reached infinity. Sabrina had to know some influential people. Working with her felt like a real chance to open the door to a job in communications that paid well. Parker prepared to dust off her four-year degree.

"Yes! I'd love to!"

"You would?"

Parker stood corrected. Sabrina managed to find one more smile for the day. The sun had melted her makeup, leaving red lipstick on her perfect teeth and black mascara smeared at the corners of her eyes. In a matter of minutes, the Iowa humidity transformed her from beauty queen to a whore after a blowjob.

"When do I start?" She failed at playing it cool.

"How does tomorrow sound?"

"Perfect!"

"Great. Seven at my house?"

"I'll be there."

THREE YEARS AFTER college, Parker had yet to procure a job that required something more than casual attire.

"Pathetic." She performed one last surgical scrub that resulted in little success. Her nails were trimmed and clean, but days in the dirt left the skin around them stained. If she didn't stop scrubbing them, they were going to bleed.

With less than twenty-four hours' notice, she had to choose between shopping for a few new outfits and getting a manicure. She decided to keep her hands balled into fists for the day and hoped Sabrina and her colleagues would focus on her new blue skirt and light gray, three-quarter-length-sleeve blouse. Of course, she went with closed-toe navy pumps until mani-pedi day.

The Westmans' modern, two-story house dwarfed Parker's century-old fixer-up farmhouse in every way. From the moment she stepped onto the marble tile in the impressive foyer, her neck strained to gawk at the blown-glass entry chandelier.

"Your home is simply amazing," she said in a weak voice. The grandeur of it took her breath away. "The outside is impressive, yet still conservative. But the inside ... this is ... wow."

"Thank you, my brother designed it," Sabrina said with her focus on the contents of her handbag. "Do you have a funeral or something today?"

"Uh ... no. Why do you ask?" She rubbed her hands down her skirt.

Sabrina pulled out her compact and applied another layer of red over her plump lips. "You seem a little overdressed for errands. That's all."

"Well, I didn't know what we had planned today." Parker tugged at the sleeves to her blouse and picked invisible lint from them.

Sabrina's red dress and silver heels were far from casual. Why was Parker's attire so out of place?

A laugh escaped Sabrina as she rubbed her lips together while snapping her compact shut and depositing it in a black handbag. "*We,* my dear, don't have plans today. *I* have a meeting then I'm flying to Hong Kong. I'll be gone for the next five days. On the kitchen counter is a list of things to do today. Give me your cell number, and I'll have my assistant, Brock, send you instructions for the rest of the week."

Her words sounded like Chinese, but the part Parker definitely could not have heard correctly was "my assistant, Brock."

"I ... I don't understand."

"August, I'm leaving. I'll text you when I land." She paused her busy hands for two seconds, eyes focused on the top of the staircase. "Lazy ass is probably still asleep." Sabrina's blue eyes did that familiar roll Parker had come to associate with most of her comments about her husband—August.

"Sabrina, I thought you hired *me* to be your assistant."

She pulled her suitcase to the front door. Parker followed her like a dog waiting for a nibble of turkey jerky.

"I did. Sorry ... I know we didn't have time to discuss payment. Will thirty dollars an hour work? You can use my car to run errands if you'd like. Ask August for his credit card if you need gas."

Thirty dollars an hour exceeded her expectations. And she should have been doing backflips, but ... Brock. Parker needed to know about Sabrina's *assistant* Brock.

"But you just told me your assistant Brock would email me."

She turned on her pointy heel. "Shoot, yes, I almost forgot to get your email and cell number." Sabrina pulled out her phone and handed it to Parker. "Add yourself as a contact while I take my suitcase out front since my lazy ass husband isn't—"

"Isn't what?"

Parker froze when a familiar deep voice sounded behind her. Shirtless Gus pushed past in a pair of jeans, no shoes or socks—also no balding gray hair, old-man gut, or anything remotely repulsive. And he smelled of lingering shampoo and soap.

Dammit!

The expected intimate goodbye between Mr. and Mrs. Westman surpassed chilly and settled into iceberg territory. The wall at Parker's back refused to camouflage her presence which added to the awkwardness.

Gus shook his head at Sabrina. She rolled her eyes at him. Parker kept her nose down, typing her info into the phone, trying not to stare at shirtless Gus because ... wife ... married ... off-limits. Someone needed to drag shirtless Gus up the stairs for a proper goodbye. Sabrina turned her nose up at the opportunity. In another life, one where she wasn't president of the "I Hate Cheaters Club," Parker would have volunteered.

"Here." Parker handed Sabrina's phone back to her, but she couldn't bring herself to press the assistant Brock subject anymore with the thick tension between Mr. and Mrs. Westman.

"Have a safe trip," Gus said as he came back into the house, leaning down to kiss the top of her head.

Sabrina only nodded. Not even a smile.

"Good morning, Parker." Gus offered a friendly grin as he brushed past her again.

Stealing a quick sniff, her lips twisted into a nervous smile. "Morning," she whispered as if acknowledging Gus broke an unspoken rule; Sabrina sure thought it did.

"Rags is out back. At least I hope he hasn't escaped out the broken gate again. Ask August if he's going to walk him. Otherwise, I need you to do it before you pick up the flowers for Rae."

"O—kay."

The door closed behind her as a black Lexus slowed to a stop in the circle drive, leaving Parker befuddled.

Sabrina thought she needed two assistants.

Flowers waited for Parker to deliver them to a woman named Rae.

Archenemies showed more affection toward each other than Gus and Sabrina.

Parker needed to ask Gus about walking Rags and possibly his credit card. Nothing about that felt awkward.

She slipped off her unnecessary heels then found the kitchen and the to-do list.

❧

Pick up flower order from Flowerama and deliver it to Rae with a bowl of chicken and rice soup from one of the local delis. Ask August for the address.

Drop off my dry cleaning that's in the hamper on the north side of my closet.

Pick up the dry cleaning. Transfer it to my wooden hangers and arrange in order.

Find out why they haven't treated the yard recently. The dandelions are out of control.

Buy and wrap three baby gifts and two wedding gifts – check registries.

Find out what August wants for his birthday – purchase, wrap, and text me what it is.

"What. The. Hell?" Parker whispered to herself. Sabrina didn't hire her as an assistant; she hired her for an errand girl. No dress clothes required. No traveling outside of a fifteen-mile area. No Apple Watch. No chance for promotion—ever.

Thirty dollars an hour. Parker could do it. *If* she could manage to extinguish her fiery ego, she would see that working for Sabrina beat the minimum-wage receptionist job at the chiropractor's office. Then again … they were offering free adjustments and spinal scans.

Chapter Five

GUS. HE SEEMED to be a major part of Parker figuring out how to accomplish the day's tasks. She needed to get going, which meant she needed to find him. Creeping up the stairs, she listened for any sign of him.

"Gus?" She flinched, startled by how loud her voice sounded in a house with such tall ceilings.

"Parker."

She tiptoed down the hallway toward the sound of his voice. Why was she creeping? She didn't know.

"Gus?" Her tone escalated to a warning. Shirtless Gus wrecked her composure. An accidental glimpse of naked Gus would have obliterated her fragile world.

"Parker."

She laughed as fully-clothed Gus stepped into view, taking a seat on the bench at the end of a mammoth bed adorned with a gazillion pillows in every shade of pink imaginable.

"Don't say my name like that. It's … weird."

He pulled on one white sock and then the other. "You said my name."

Maybe Gus abused Sabrina or drank too much or … something unimaginable that explained why his wife showed so little affection. Parker liked him and that sentiment held merit given their brief acquaintanceship and her distrust of men.

She clamped her mouth shut and swallowed hard when he looked up, catching her shameless visual assessment.

"That's..." she cleared her throat "...different. I was looking for you."

"You were looking at my legs." He stood.

Parker forbid her eyes from looking anywhere but straight into his eyes. But after a few seconds, she failed the stare-off.

"Pfft ... you're wearing old man jeans. Not the same. And I wasn't looking at them."

"You were. And how old do you think I am?"

She wasn't dangerous. *He* was the dangerous one.

"Your wife is twelve years older than I am, so I assume you're probably..." her lips twisted "...forty?"

Gus barked out a laugh. "Fucking little ballbuster. I'm six years younger than my wife."

Younger. Parker didn't see that coming, but it explained his lack of gray hair or flaccid skin.

"Still six years older than I am, so ... *old.*"

Gus grinned, not at all phased by her attempts to appear uninterested in him. "Well, you found me. Whatcha need?"

After a long blink, she held up the note Sabrina left. "I need to ask you a few questions."

He cracked another killer smile and slipped on his Cubs cap. "I'm all ears."

The note became the new safe zone for her eyes. "Are you going to walk Rags?"

"Why would I?"

She risked a quick glance up with a squinted eye. "Um ... I don't know. I'll do it."

"Why?"

"Because she told me to ask you and if you aren't going to

walk him, then I need to do it."

Amusement grew along Gus's face. "There's a half-acre-enclosed area for him. I never walk him. He chases birds and critters, then he passes out for the rest of the day."

"So ..."

"So, tell her I walked him if she asks."

"But you're not?"

He crossed his arms over his white T-shirt-clad chest. "No."

"And ... I don't need to?"

"No."

"Alrighty then. Next. I need Rae's address."

"Why?"

She sighed. "Are you going to ask me 'why' about everything I ask you?"

"Probably." He returned a half smile.

Pressing her lips together, Parker shook her head and returned her focus to the note. "I'm supposed to pick up flowers and then chicken and rice soup from a local deli and deliver them to Rae today."

"Unbelievable." He rolled his eyes to the ceiling and rested his hands on his hips. "I'll take care of it."

"Of which?"

"Everything."

"The whole list?"

"No." He started down the hall, leaving a trail of invisible aftershave. She chased after him and his scent.

"The flowers?"

"Rae." He rounded the corner at the bottom of the stairs.

"So you're going to pick up the flowers and get the soup?"

As soon as he reached the kitchen, he grabbed a cola from

the Sub-Zero refrigerator next to dark-stained custom cabinetry hanging above white granite countertops. After gulping half of it down, Gus returned his attention to Parker. "Rae is my grandmother. It's her birthday. She lives in assisted living. I'm not going to have some stranger deliver her flowers and soup."

Parker tried not to be offended by his words. After all, she *was* a stranger to his grandmother.

"I'm sorry." He sighed.

"No." She shook her head. "No reason to apologize. So, you'll take care of Rae. Great. What dry cleaner do you use?"

Gus quirked an eyebrow. "Do I look like a guy who sends shit to a dry cleaner?"

"I ..." Her nose wrinkled. "I feel like that's a trick question, so I'm not going to answer it. Let me rephrase my question. Do you know what dry cleaner Sabrina uses?"

He pursed his lips and jerked his head to the right and then to the left.

No. Fabulous.

"No problem. I'll map out all the dry cleaners in a five-mile radius."

She ignored his snickering.

"Who treats your lawn?"

"I treat the lawn."

Her head snapped up. "You don't hire a lawn care company?"

"Nope."

How Parker managed to get herself into awkward situations remained a mystery. She drew in a deep breath. "Well, in that case, I need to know the last time you treated the lawn, and I'll need you to take care of the dandelion overgrowth before Mrs. Westman returns in five days."

Gus wet his lips and rubbed them together to hide his grin. "Anything else, *Parker?*" Her name from his lips evoked mixed feelings. Everything about him evoked mixed feelings.

"Who do you know who's getting married in the next few months?"

"No one."

"Babies on the way?"

"Nope."

"Very helpful." She shot him a challenging look.

He shrugged and chugged the rest of his cola, tossed it in the pullout recycling bin under the counter, and headed to the back door. "Later."

"Wait!"

Bent over, tying his brown leather work boots, he glanced back at her. "Yes?"

"What do you want for your birthday?"

He finished tying them, stood erect again, and opened the door. "I want a pony."

A grown man wanting a pony. What the hell?

"When's your birthday?"

"Today."

The door slammed shut.

DES MOINES HAD more dry cleaners than one might have thought. As unhelpful as Gus's lack of knowledge had been to her, Parker couldn't deny that she wasn't someone who sent "shit" to the dry cleaner either. However, she found the right one, made the exchange, swapped hangers, and arranged them in order. The right order? Time would tell.

Like a bittersweet and unexpected gift, Assistant Brock

messaged her with a list of tedious crap to accomplish before Sabrina returned from China. Having his number, Parker messaged him back hoping he would have some insight to the upcoming nuptials and tiny people entering the world. Earning his coveted number one assistant position, he sent her names, dates, and links to registries. She was grateful and intimidated at the same time.

Since Gus promised to take care of the flowers and soup for Rae, that left her with some extra time to take Rags for a walk and deal with the dandelion situation that she felt confident the lawn care guy would choose to ignore.

Feeling good about her accomplishments for the day, she clocked out and walked home.

"Coming!" Parker called to the unexpected guest knocking at her door.

"Parker." Gus held up the birthday card she'd left for him on the counter. "'Happy Birthday. Enjoy. He's yours for twenty-four hours,'" he read her words.

"I was supposed to wrap him, but ... well, you can plainly see the dilemma I had." She tugged at her lip and shrugged.

"There's a pony in my backyard—my backyard that no longer has a single dandelion in it." Wide, whiskey eyes peered at her as his head jutted forward. "Explain."

"Come in." She stepped out of the way.

"I can't come in. I have a *pony* to attend to in my back-yard."

"I fixed the gate, so neither Rags or Romeo should get out."

"Romeo?"

"The pony. Supposedly, he's good with the mares."

"Whose pony is he?"

"A friend of a friend situation. A kid who graduated high school with me works at Prairie Meadows. He knows a lot of people who have horses. He found me a pony on short notice.

Just a loaner. Don't get too attached. They're picking Romeo up by the end of the day tomorrow."

Gus blinked over and over, lips parted, hands limp at his sides.

"He had surgery on his leg last year, so you can't ride him. I hope that's not going to ruin your birthday."

"Sabrina told you to get me a pony for my birthday?"

"No. She told me to ask you what you wanted. Buy it. Wrap it. And message her what I bought you. I asked, and you said—"

"A pony." He chuckled and shook his head. "I was—"

"Joking. Being an ass. Whatever. I get it. I'm not an idiot."

"But you did, in fact, get me a pony."

"Yes, because your wife hired me under false pretenses then left me with a ridiculously vague to-do list this morning, and then you…" Parker clenched her fists and stepped out the door, toe-to-toe with August Westman; he swallowed hard as she tilted her chin up to him. "…you were no help whatsoever. How can two people be so oblivious to what the other one is doing in their life?"

Score one for Parker. She grimaced the minute the words fell from her lips—a brilliant reflection of self-assessment.

"Oh shit." Her eyes pinched shut while her head shook side to side.

"You don't have to feel bad. It's true. Sabrina and I should—"

"No. It-it's not you. It's me. The 'oh shit' was me." Laughter and tears warred in her head. Parker's sister and boyfriend had been sleeping together, and she had no clue until she saw it—up close and way too personal. She knew exactly how two people could be so oblivious to what the other one was doing in their life. Parker's smile wilted as she whispered, "Thank you for inspiring a very humbling moment."

Gus took a step back and shoved his hands into his jeans' pockets. "Now I'm really lost."

"Forget it." She shook it off. "You share your birthday with your grandmother. That's cool. Did she enjoy the soup and flowers?"

Gus nodded slowly but his expression was still the confused look from seconds earlier. The crackling of a car pulling into the gravel drive stole his focus. He glanced back over his shoulder as a black Chevy Cruz came to a stop.

"That's my ride."

"Is something wrong with your truck."

She waved at her friend Mindy. "There's a lot wrong with Old Blue, but that's not why I have a ride for the night. I had a long first day at my new job, and I haven't been drunk in months. Thought I'd rectify that tonight. Mindy is four months pregnant which makes her the perfect designated driver, and she's dying to get out of the house since she spent three months at home hugging the toilet."

Gus gave Mindy a friendly wave. Parker grabbed her purse from the floor by the door then locked it behind her.

"You named your truck?"

"Nope. My grandfather did. I just inherited it. Thought changing the name would be weird. It's been called that forever."

"O-kay." He lifted his cap and scratched his head before pulling it back on. "Have a good time."

"Thanks. Happy Birthday, Gus. Enjoy your evening with Romeo and Rags."

"Uh-huh," he hummed as he walked down the porch steps.

Chapter Six

PARKER AND MINDY met three other friends from high school at a bar downtown in East Village. Choosing Caleb and his college of choice over her volleyball scholarship opportunities led to four years of sex on demand instead of making lifelong friends. When she moved back home after college, Parker reconnected with a few girls from high school.

"I've had too much to drink," Parker shouted over the loud music, the scuff of bar stools dragged along the wood floor, and patrons laughing and swearing. "And…" she closed her eyes for a moment, but the room continued to spin making her as dizzy as the cloying perfume mixed with the aroma of nachos and fried pickles "…I'm tired of shouting."

"Close your tabs. We're moving on!" Mindy motioned to the other girls, holding up her credit card. She fixed her short black hair in the mirror behind the bar that reflected a half-dozen neon beer signs.

Parker leaned toward her. Misjudging the distance, her lips pressed to Mindy's ear. "Moving on? No. We should go home."

Mindy's elbow landed in Parker's ribs. "You've had three drinks, you lightweight. I have five months of freedom left. We are not going home yet."

"I don't want to throw up. I don't like it."

Mindy laughed as they snaked their way through the crowded bar toward the door. "Let's go to the brewery on the corner. They don't have live music, so you shouldn't have to yell, and you can get some food to absorb all *three* drinks you've had."

"I'm not hungry."

She ignored Parker's whining and looped their arms together as they stepped out into the suffocating humidity.

"It's past my bedtime." Parker rested her head on Mindy's shoulder.

"It's ten o'clock. What are you? Sixty?" Gretchen giggled, blond hair matted to her sweaty face as she peeked over her shoulder at Parker. The girl must have danced ten songs in a row at the bar. A bar where no one else was dancing.

Upon opening the door to the brewery, Parker noticed half the noise level of the bar and smelled foods far more appealing than nachos and fried pickles—like French fries.

The waitress with a bust twice as big as her ass and streaks of red in her blond hair seated them in a U-shaped booth close to the bar.

"Just water for me." Parker's numb lips attempted a sober smile at the waitress.

"She'll also have a Coors Light, nachos supreme, and sweet potato fries with ranch dressing," Mindy handed the waitress their menus.

"I can't eat that—"

"You'll feel better once you do." She reassured Parker, who questioned what kind of mom Mindy would be.

The other girls ordered martinis and cheeseburgers as the whir of a blender sounded in the background. A margarita sounded good to Parker, rimmed with yummy salt and sugar.

By the time their food arrived, Parker had consumed *three* more drinks, and the world felt like a much happier place.

"This is *so* good," she mumbled through a mouthful of sweet potato fries. "I'm *so* hungry."

Mindy laughed. "Told ya."

The cold beer washed the salty food down. Everything tasted heavenly. Had she switched to water, then Mindy's food-absorbing-the-alcohol theory might have been correct. Instead, Mindy had to hush Parker every two seconds, reminding her that there was no longer any reason to shout.

"Cheers to an awesome night with awesome friends, awesome food, and awesome beer." Parker slurred her words and held up a bottle of beer. "Tonight has been ..."

The girls giggled as her brain quit mid-sentence.

"Awesome?" a male voice said from the booth next to theirs. "That's the word you were looking for, right? 'Tonight has been *awesome.*'"

More laughter from her friends erupted as Parker tried to find the source of the voice. The slow drip of alcohol into her bloodstream dulled her perception, leaving a numbing tingle.

Gretchen pointed behind them.

Parker scooted around and stood up on her knees, peeking at the group of guys in the booth behind them. "Au-gu-st Wa-Water-man. What are the chances?"

"Parker." He grinned, looking too sexy for his own good in a Captain America tee and his signature Cubs hat.

There must have been five or ten other guys in the booth with him. Ten if he had lots of friends. Five if the last beer messed with her brain.

"Happy Birf-day, Gus." Parker's head dipped into a sharp nod. At some point, her reflexes decided to take the night off.

Her neck failed to keep her head from bobbing around.

"Thank you, Parker."

Why did she love and hate hearing him say her name? Was that possible? Sober Parker didn't like it, but drunk Parker could have listened to him say it all night. She licked her lips as he tipped back his beer, keeping his eyes set on her.

"These are my friends." She jabbed her thumb over her shoulder. "Friends, say hi to Gus and his ..."

"Friends?" Gus once again offered to finish her sentence.

"Yes. That's the word. Gus likes ponies and dandelions in his yard."

"Hi," her friends chimed in the background.

Gus eyed her, wearing a twisted grin on his shadowed face. She thought he needed to let his head get some air, give the old Cubs cap a night off.

"Well, aren't you going to introduce me to *your friends?*" She beamed with pride having accurately completed a sentence without anyone's help.

The guys celebrating with Gus looked at him while he stayed focused on her. "Parker, these are my friends. Guys, this is my neighbor, Parker. She's incredibly talented at faking orgasms, shearing sheepdogs, karaoke, and stealing the dandelions from my yard."

The male versus female reaction to that introduction proved to be rather entertaining. Parker's friends threw their heads back in unrestrained laughter while Gus's friends bowed their heads, attempting to stifle their amusement.

"Fuck! If she's your neighbor, then I need to move to your neighborhood," one of the guys next to him mumbled, eliciting the second round of laughter.

"For the record..." Parker held up a finger "...it was my

first time shearing a sheepdog." She giggled. "But I'm sooo flattered Gus thinks I'm good at it. And..." she held up a second finger, but she wasn't counting anything "...I didn't steal the dandelions. I removed them one at a time under the direct order of my boss. Finally..." a third finger shot up "...I only fake orgasms when I'm home alone." Her fingers remained in the air as she ended with a resolute nod. "There you have it."

"Parker Cruse." Mindy pulled her arm. "Let's get you home."

A flicker of a smile passed Gus's lips as everyone else continued to laugh.

"I'm so tired." Parker turned around and deflated in the booth.

"Everyone needs to use the ladies' room before we get in my car. And no vomiting allowed." Mindy grabbed Parker's purse and tugged on her hand.

"You're going to be such a good mama." Parker rubbed Mindy's tummy as they played follow the leader to the ladies' room. Never before had she rubbed a pregnant woman's belly. Wasn't her thing. But enough alcohol made all kinds of embarrassing acts "her thing."

Mindy helped Parker steady herself as she relieved her bladder—so she wouldn't fall in the toilet—washed her hands, and made her stand outside the ladies' room. "Gretchen needs my help. I think her cell phone fell in the toilet." Mindy pushed Parker's shoulders back against the wall and pointed a finger at her face. "Don't move. Don't pass out. Don't vomit. Don't. Move. An. Inch."

"Yes, ma'am." Trying to focus on anything made her head hurt, so she closed her eyes.

"Open your eyes," Mindy said, finger still pointed at Parker's face.

"Okay. They're open."

Parker waited like a good girl ... and waited ... and got tired of waiting, so she slid along the wall to the door to the ladies' room and tugged it open.

"Mindy?"

A couple of guys gave her the stink eye. *She* wasn't the pervert in the ladies' room. *Why the looks?*

"There's no Mindy in here. You need me to call you a cab?" a guy decorated with tats and piercings asked as he grabbed a wad of paper towels and dried his hands.

"No. Mindy is my DD. I'm good. Oh wow!" Parker brushed her hand along a funny looking porcelain sink. "Haven't seen one like this before. Nice."

The guy laughed. "A urinal?" He chuckled some more. "I'd wash my hands if I were you."

She pulled her hand away and stiffly held her fingers out like Sabrina had done after she shook Parker's sweaty hand the day they met. "Ew ..."

"Parker?"

"Gus?" She turned.

"She with you?" pierced guy asked. "If so, make sure she washes her hands." He brushed past Gus.

Parker held up her hand. "High-five?"

Gus shook his head and steered her by her shoulders to the sink. "Wash them."

She held them under the water.

"Soap," he said.

She tried to focus on his reflection in the mirror to roll her eyes at him. Epic fail.

He handed her several paper towels.

"Aw, thanks, Gus." Parker sighed as he dried her hands

since she held the towels without actually drying them. "You'd be a good mom too, just like Mindy."

Without a response, he guided her out of the men's room.

"Parker!" Mindy pressed her hand to her chest. "What the hell were you doing? I told you to stay put." She eyed Gus with disgust. "Trying to take advantage of a drunk girl?"

Gus released Parker's shoulders and held up his hands in surrender. "Nope."

"He helped me wash my hands." Her bobblehead nodded. "I got a little too personal with a urinal."

"Let's go." Mindy grabbed Parker's hand and pulled on it.

Parker jerked it away and turned toward Gus. "Night, Birfday boy."

"Nigh—"

Before he could finish, Parker lifted onto her toes and pressed her lips to his. They were warm and soft and tasted like her favorite beer.

"Parker!" Mindy ripped her away from him.

Parker laughed. "What? It was a birthday kiss."

Mindy dragged her out of the brewery. When Parker glanced back, Gus rubbed his hand over his mouth.

"I thought you said his *wife* is your boss?" Mindy opened the car door and shoved Parker into the seat.

"What happened?" Gretchen's voice slurred from the backseat. The other two seemed to be passed out.

"Nothing," Mindy grumbled before slamming the door shut.

"I think Mama Mindy is going to ground me." Parker hummed a sigh, closed her eyes, and surrendered to the alcohol in her blood.

Chapter Seven

THE ALCOHOL DIDN'T kill Parker, but the memories and the embarrassment that accompanied them vied for the job of executioner.

"Feeling better?"

"Mom?" Morning aimed its flashlight in Parker's face. "Shut the curtains." She buried her head under the pillow.

"Mindy called me this morning. Said I might want to check on you. It could be alcohol poisoning. Was it worth it?"

"It's not alcohol poisoning. Just a good old-fashioned hangover. I'll live."

Janey jerked the pillow off her daughter's head. "Not if you don't grow up and start taking better care of yourself."

"It was one night." Her hand felt around. Finding the sheet wadded at her waist, Parker yanked it up over her head. It didn't block out much light.

"Don't you have to work today? How's your new job going? When did the neighbors get a pony? I don't think that's allowed in the covenant."

"The Stantons have a goat and chickens." Parker's pulse claimed a front row seat in her head—loud and strong as she sat up, eyes squinted.

"They were grandfathered in."

"Whatever." She stood, suppressing a grimace. "It's not

their pony and it will be gone by the end of the day."

"The guy, Mr. Gustafson, was outside brushing it this morning."

Parker laughed. Her head pounded. "Ouch. Stop making me laugh."

Showing no regard for her privacy, Janey followed her to the bathroom. "I wasn't trying to be funny."

"Gus. His name is Gus or August Westman, not Gustafson. You've watched *Grumpy Old Men* too many times. And ... hello? I'm peeing."

"I changed your diapers, Parker. And we're both women. What's the big deal?"

Parker couldn't wait, so she did her thing. Mothers didn't care about dignity. The go-to response for everything was "I changed your diapers" and that somehow gave them the right to an eternity of privacy invasion.

"You really shouldn't use antiperspirant."

"Stop reading the labels on my things."

"Parker, if you don't let your body sweat, then all the toxins stay trapped inside and ..." The woman who thought Parker still wore diapers frowned as she inspected her daughter's whitening toothpaste.

Parker flushed the toilet and nudged her mom aside with her hip so she could wash her hands. "The toxins stay trapped inside and what? Make me toxic."

"Are you pooping regularly?"

"Mom! Really?"

"I take magnesium before bed every night, and I have a good clean out in the morning. Your father?" Her nose wrinkled as she shuddered. "It smells like he gave birth to a rotting animal carcass that's been *up* there for days."

"Funny thing…" squeezing past her, Parker grabbed a white robe from the foot of her bed "…when I was younger you always asked me why I spent so much time at my friends' houses and they rarely came to our house. Well, I wasn't sure if I'd still have friends if you shared your bowel movement schedule."

Janey followed Parker down the stairs. "Don't be ridiculous. I would never—"

"Never what? Tell the lady making your burrito at Chipotle that you love the hot sauce, but it 'sure burns coming out the backside.'"

"Oh, Parker, she was close to my age. I'd imagine she's had a few cases of red hole herself."

A heavy dose of Mother did little to remedy Parker's hangover. Grabbing two Advil out of the cupboard, she washed them down with a tall glass of water. "Unbelievable." She laughed, looking out the window. "He's still brushing Romeo."

"Who's Romeo?"

"The pony." Parker turned and set the glass on the counter. "Well, as much as I'd love to continue this *shitty* conversation, I can't. Work calls." Specifically, an apology for her inappropriateness the previous night.

"Lots of water today, Parker."

She leaned down and kissed her mom on the cheek before heading back upstairs. "Yes, Mom."

AUGUST WESTMAN WOKE with a flurried mess of emotions. Loneliness and resentment had crept into his life. He lived with a dog that belonged to his wife and a wife that belonged to her job. At least that's what it felt like with Sabrina gone almost as much as she was there. And when they were together, they were still so far apart.

He'd worked hard to build his own business as one of the best and most respected electricians in the Des Moines area. His job became his life after Sabrina landed her dream job heading up an engineering firm. No more date nights. No more spontaneous getaways. No more coming home for lunch to his wife in lingerie.

Instead, he had a new neighbor. A *young* neighbor. And he had the feel of her lips pressed to his imprinted into his memory forever. On that particular morning, he also had a few hours left with his borrowed pony, so he decided to make the most of it.

"Shit. Be cool," he whispered to himself as Parker Cruse strutted her defined legs toward him, perky boobs bouncing with each step, and dark, pin-straight hair whipping around her neck.

"Morning." Gus cleared the frog from his throat, keeping his gaze on the long strokes he made along Romeo's back.

He'd hoped it wouldn't be too awkward, but his inability to make eye contact screamed awkward.

"Good morning." Parker tugged the bill of her cap down low while she squinted. A middle finger gesture to the sun. "Where'd you get the brush?"

"Sabrina's bathroom drawer." His lips quirked into a grin, but he still didn't look at her.

"What are you going to do with it when you're done?" Parker's hand glided along the smooth chestnut fur he'd just brushed.

"Tap it on the bottom of my boot a few times and put it back in her drawer." He grinned.

"Wow, I have to confess. When I first met your wife, I was a bit envious of her."

That unexpected comment earned her a quick look.

"Not..." she shook her head "...like I was envious because of you. Which I know might be hard to believe after the..." she bit her lower lip and wrinkled her nose "...kiss last night. It was because she's so put together and successful. But now I'm not envious of her because when she returns she's going to brush her hair with *that* brush and..." her words tumbled down a hill, gaining speed "...that's pretty shitty of you, but I've done worse things so I really can't judge you, but ... Gah! Please say something! I kissed you last night and it was stupid and wrong and a huge, drunken mistake on my part. I'm not that girl. I don't hit on married men. You have to—"

"You're forgiven. It's forgotten." He shrugged. Then true to his word, he banged the brush on the bottom of his boot.

"I'll tell Sabrina as soon as she gets home and apologize—"

He chuckled, shaking his head. "Not necessary."

"But—"

Gus turned and walked to the house. "You were drunk. It was my birthday."

"Your birthday?" She chased after him. "That's not an excuse."

"Fine." After washing his hands in the mudroom sink, he tugged the ties loose on his boots, toed them off, and headed toward the stairs with the dirty brush in hand. "You were drunk. I was the victim. Because you're my wife's employee and it was your first day, I won't file a sexual harassment suit this time."

"I'm sorry!"

He stopped midway up the stairs and turned. Parker's chest

heaved and her face flushed.

"I already said you're forgiven."

She curled her hair behind her ears and adjusted her baseball cap. "I know, but you never let me apologize, so I don't want you to think that I'm not sorry. I am. And I *really* need to tell Sabrina to clear my conscience. Even if she fires me."

"A real Girl Scout, aren't you, Parker?"

"No. I just don't approve of cheating."

"Cheating?" He laughed again. "That means you must have a boyfriend?"

"What? No."

"Then there was no cheating. I didn't kiss you."

"But you didn't stop me." Her voice escalated.

"You didn't give me any warning. I thought you were attempting to hug me for rescuing you from the men's room." After a few moments of silence—a stare-off—he shook his head and continued up the stairs. "Whatever. Tell her. Don't tell her. I don't care."

"Is she going to fire me?"

"She should." His voice echoed from the far end of the hall.

PARKER'S PHONE CHIMED with creepy timing. A message from Brock with her list for the day. She considered responding with "I kissed Gus. Sorry. I'll find another job," but it really didn't feel right to share that information with Brock or by any other means than face to face. It would be an agonizing four days carrying the guilt around. A fair punishment.

Dwelling on her fate accomplished nothing. Instead, she focused on another day of important stuff that only a highly-skilled assistant such as herself could do.

"What are you doing?"

She startled at the sound of Gus's voice. "Rating bananas."

He grabbed a cola from the fridge. "What does that mean? And why are you doing it?"

"I'm determining which ones you might still eat and which ones should be used for banana bread. And I'm doing it because it's on the list for today." She glanced at him over her shoulder.

"Sabrina doesn't bake." He frowned. "Well, she used to but she hasn't in years." His gaze met hers. "So why is she having you save ripe bananas?"

Parker's attention returned to the nine bananas under scrutiny. "The next thing on my list is making banana bread. A loaf for you and one that I'm supposed to deliver to your parents."

"You're kidding."

"Not kidding."

"This is ridiculous."

She held up three of the bananas that still had a bit of green at the tips. "Will you eat these?"

Over the short amount of time she'd known Gus, he'd been easy going about everything. Three bananas changed that.

"Rags," he called with an unfamiliar edge to his voice.

Their sheared friend raced into the kitchen through the doggy door in the mudroom, bringing with him the wonderful scent of an overheated dog on a humid day. Gus snatched the bananas like he was pissed off with her, or the bananas, or something. He peeled one and fed it to Rags. Then the second. Followed by the third.

Unblinking eyes dared Parker to say anything.

Her internal thoughts escaped as a whisper. "That's a ... lot of bananas for a dog."

Gus closed his eyes, a hint of regret pulling at his brow when he exhaled. "I have to get to work." He opened his eyes revealing the Gus she'd met a week earlier. "What do you need from me?"

"Need from you?"

"Yesterday you had a million questions for me."

She laughed a little. "And you were basically no help at all. If I have questions, I'll text Brock."

"You do that." Gus adjusted his cap and turned.

"Gus?"

He paused at the door. "Yeah?"

Her lips rubbed together as she second-guessed asking the question that wouldn't leave her head.

"Parker?"

"Uh ... it's just ... Why did you say Sabrina should fire me when I asked you if she would?"

He focused on the floor between them for a few seconds then lifted his gaze to hers. "If she loved me now like she loved me then, she'd fire your ass for touching something that's hers."

There were no words to say back to him. Gus spoke the truth. The only question left unanswered: How much did Sabrina love her husband?

BROCK HAD THE glamorous assisting job that probably included dining at ritzy restaurants, which required snazzy ties and suit jackets. Glamorous didn't describe Parker's new job, but she still liked it. While the lists were random and unpredictable, she never felt bored.

By the end of the day, she'd baked banana bread, delivered

a loaf to Gus's parents, stayed there and chatted with them for over an hour—super nice people—reserved a tent, booked a caterer and a local band for the Westmans' Fourth of July party, and researched several new nail salons because of a recent plantar wart incident at Sabrina's regular salon.

Gus shook his head as she walked up their blacktop drive with Rags a little after six that evening. Squirrels scampered across the grass looking for refuge in nearby trees while gnats buzzed around her head. For a brief moment she thought of Caleb and the life she'd imagined. In that brief moment, Gus became Caleb in the porch chair, legs spread wide, his hand clutched around a bottle of beer resting on his knee. Parker played his wife and that smile on his face conveyed complete adoration.

She released the tension in her hand, and Rags took off running, leash dragging behind him to the porch, to Gus—to Caleb. They greeted each other like all good dogs and their masters did.

"Parker." Gus's voice, not Caleb's, filled the thick evening air.

She blinked, refocusing on the reality in front of her. Gus wasn't her husband. Rags wasn't her dog. It wasn't her life. Twenty-six-year-old Parker Cruse didn't have a life.

"Did you hear me say he doesn't have to be walked?" He gave Rags a good scratching behind the ears.

"Yes." Parker plopped down into the glider next to Gus. "But he's a dog and they like new smells and different scenery. It's good for their senses and it wears them out mentally, not just physically."

"And Sabrina's paying you to walk him."

She grinned, staring at her childhood home across the street and over one lot. "And that. But I like him too."

Rags collapsed at her feet.

"He doesn't lie at my feet. He knows he's Sabrina's dog. Her brother gave him to her as a puppy—a birthday gift when she turned thirty because they never had pets growing up."

"But he likes you."

Gus took a pull of his beer then grinned. "Yes. I let him sleep with me when she's gone ... which is a lot. Pisses her off when she comes home to fur all over her side of the bed."

"I know. She's already instructed me to wash the sheets *twice* the morning she flies home."

Gus chuckled. "Of course she did." He held out his beer to Parker.

She stared at it.

"We've already exchanged germs."

"Shut up." She snatched the bottle and took a long gulp, followed by another, and another.

"Christ, woman! I said we've exchanged germs." He grabbed the empty bottle and shook it back and forth. "But that last swallow was all backwash. One hundred percent bodily fluids."

Parker giggled and suppressed a burp. "You backwash?" She shrugged. "I didn't notice. Most bodily fluids I've swallowed don't taste like beer." She slapped a hand over her mouth. "Oh shit." Her words muffled behind it.

Gus perked an eyebrow.

"I didn't mean it that way." She blushed to the tips of her ears, internally cursing her mom for passing along the oversharing gene.

"Do I want to know what 'most bodily fluids I've swallowed,' means?"

Folding at the waist, she covered her face with her hands and buried her embarrassment in her lap. "You must think I'm a tramp. I mean ... the fake orgasm, the kiss, and now this. Gah! How embarrassing." Shooting up from the chair, she held up her hand in a wave gesture but kept her body moving in the direction of home. "Have a pleasant evening, Mr. Westman. I'm going home to cut my tongue out."

Chapter Eight

AS PREDICTED, SEVERE weather rolled in that night knocking out power and claiming the lives of a few trees. Gus awoke a little after midnight to an empty spot beside him and incessant barking outside.

"Rags ..." Gus groaned knowing the dog outside arguing with Mother Nature couldn't hear him. "Stupid dog." He pulled on a pair of shorts and hurried downstairs, shoving his bare feet into his work boots at the last second before throwing open the back door. "Rags!"

The rain stopped but the wind continued to rustle the trees. The heavy branches of the old oak tree on Parker's side of the fence whined with each gust like an elderly man getting out of bed. Someone's crazy dog jumped against the gate and barked—over and over.

"Rags!"

"Rags!"

Gus stopped at the bottom of the deck stairs and listened.

Did someone else yell "Rags" too or was it an echo?

Something moved on the other side of the fence. Rags stopped barking. Squinting his eyes, Gus trudged through the marshy yard. "Rags?" He drew out his name with a softer voice, trying to listen at the same time.

Nothing.

The dog vanished, leaving Gus alone in the footprint of the storm. A lone light, half a football field away, disappeared as well, like a wish had been made and it was time to cut the cake. He didn't need another reason for Sabrina to be angry with him, so he unlatched the gate and sloshed that fifty yards to Parker's house.

After knocking and waiting several minutes, he took a chance on the doorbell. The porch light above him illuminated a second before the door eased open. A single, wide eye appeared and a couple feet lower a wet, black nose wedged in the crack.

"Gus?"

"Parker."

She opened the door the rest of the way and scratched her head. A soaked, oversized T-shirt clung to her body.

"Rags." Gus dropped his gaze to the naughty dog, anything to keep from staring at the peaks and valleys of the younger woman who was not his wife.

"He doesn't seem to like storms."

Gus nodded. "It would seem. Yet every time it storms, he runs outside and barks like he can chase it away."

Parker peeled the blue shirt away from her skin. Gus made a quick inspection to make sure the peaks were hidden before he made eye contact.

She crossed her legs and kept the wet shirt pinched between her fingers, holding it away from her body. "I thought maybe you didn't hear him. When I opened the gate, he practically knocked me over in a mad dash to my door."

Her eyes moved along his body, and at that moment he remembered the inappropriateness of his own attire for visiting his half-dressed neighbor in the middle of the night.

"I'd invite you in, but ..." Parker stared at his wet boots covered in clumps of mud and grass.

"No. Sorry, I'm a muddy mess, I just—"

"So was Rags." She gestured to her T-shirt, tugging the damp cotton. "I had to carry him up to the tub to wash his paws and in the process, I got a little wet."

August would not have been a man had he not imagined her peeling off that shirt, revealing her curvy body and taut nipples. He'd already seen their outline; it didn't take much to imagine them completely bared to him. And August would not have been married had he been the man who did anything more than *imagine.*

He crossed his hands over his crotch as his neglected cock made an attempt to set up camp right there on Parker's front porch. "Thank you for doing that. I'm so sorry he woke you. If it ever happens again, just call me." Gus jerked his head. "Rags, let's go."

The dog took two steps backward and heeled.

"Rags." Gus frowned.

Like flipping Gus the bird, Rags eased to all fours and ran up the stairs.

"Rags!"

Parker bit her lips together for a few seconds then snorted a laugh.

"You think this is funny?"

She covered her mouth with her hand as she shook her head, eyes wide and unblinking.

"Then why are you laughing?" Gus crossed his arms.

Her eyes homed in on his arms and then a bit lower, widening even more.

"Just ..." He turned sideways and shifted his weight to obscure her view of his erection. His mind knew he was married, happily or not, but he possessed an indiscernible dick when it came to a half-naked woman in a T-shirt. "Go get him, please."

It didn't matter how many attempts she made to keep her shirt from clinging to her body, he'd seen it and neither his analytical brain or rogue dick could un-see it. The more she messed with it, the harder he got.

"How am I supposed to make him go with you?"

"Parker! Jesus, woman! Just go get the damn dog so I can get to bed."

And lose the fucking erection.

"Okay." She held her hands up and backed up slowly. "I'm going."

On a sigh, he dropped his head with a slight shake. "I'm sorry, I—"

Thunder echoed in the distance.

"It's fine. I get it."

"I don't think you do."

Parker started up the stairs. "No, no, I think I do." Something in the tone of her voice confirmed that she *did* get it.

Gus grumbled and adjusted himself. Before he could fully ease *the tension* with thoughts of dirty baby diapers or colonoscopies, Parker returned in navy sweatpants and a dry T-shirt— no Rags.

"Sorry." Her nose wrinkled. "He won't come, and I'm too exhausted to wrestle him down the stairs. So unless you're going to take off your muddy boots and go get him yourself, I suggest we just let him stay here for the night."

"Fine." He rubbed the back of his neck. "Thanks and ... I'm sorry—"

"Gus, stop. It's no big deal. Guys can't control *that*." She shrugged.

He flinched. "What? No. I meant Rags, not ..." Gus rested his hands on his hips and dropped his head again. "Dammit! This shouldn't be so hard."

Parker cleared her throat. "It's still, um ... *hard?*"

"Not my..." he turned his back to her " ...what I mean is I wasn't talking about me. This conversation shouldn't be so difficult. That's the word I meant—difficult." Gus moved one muddy boot in front of the other and didn't look back. "Good night, Parker."

"Good night, Gus."

ASIDE FROM SOME tree limbs and a few pieces of siding, the storm did far less damage than Gus's encounter with Parker. His marriage had survived its first five years without a fight that lasted longer than a few hours, and those minor fights ended in long nights of incredible sex. He loved his wife. Temptation may have lurked in the distance, but it always stayed in his blind spot.

Until Sabrina found success in a career that seemed to take precedence over their marriage.

Until sex became a chore she did before leaving town, like checking off a task on her list.

Until "don't forget to walk the dog" replaced "I love you."

Until she made more money than he did.

Until a young, blue-eyed woman with dark hair and an infinity of perfect curves walked half-naked into his life.

Temptation no longer resided in his blind spot. She lived a hundred yards away.

"Rags! Slow down! I need to wipe your muddy paw—aw

fuck ..." Parker's voice faded into defeat as Rags bolted through the doggie door along with chunks of mud and grass stuck to his paws.

Instead of stopping him, Gus made his own mad dash to the back door, throwing his work gloves and stainless steel water bottle in the passenger seat of his van as he hopped in and shut the door. Dreaming of doing ungentlemanly things to the innocent neighbor girl made morning chitchat an equally bad thing.

"Gus?"

He backed out of the garage as she waved at him—a stop wave, not a goodbye wave. Unfortunately, vivid memories of her smell, her taste, and her warm flesh molded to his in his all-too-real dream meant anything she needed from him that day would have to come in the form of a text.

"Where are you going in such a hurry?" She jogged a few yards down the driveway as he stepped on the gas without looking back.

He rolled up his window, giving a quick wave before it completely shut. "I'm going to work where guys who burp and fart can keep my mind out of your pants, *Parker.*"

As he pulled into the driveway of his first job, a new construction project, he welcomed the sight of only one other vehicle—Abe's truck. They both were accepted into the same apprenticeship program after electrician school. Abe lacked the funds to start his own business, so he went to work for Gus. They became close friends.

"Good morning, sunshine," Abe greeted as the twang of country music played in the background from an old radio with a bent antenna.

Gus rolled his eyes. "Always so fucking perky." He took a

sip of his coffee that he grabbed on the way and stepped over the coiled wire and a pile of sawdust mixed with a few nails, empty chip bags, and a crushed water bottle.

"Just like your wife." Abe gave shit as good as anyone, and he could get away with saying things to Gus that would land any other guy on his ass.

"I'll take your word on that one."

Abe set a roll of wire on the dust-covered subflooring. "Uh oh, someone's not getting laid. Someone else banging your wife?"

Gus fastened his tool belt. "Yeah, her job." The high-pitched grind of a saw and methodic thudding of a nail gun sounded from next door. It was the symphony of Gus's days.

"Can't help ya there. Denise is a teacher. Doesn't make shit." He laughed. "But I suppose that means she's getting fucked by her job too."

"Can I ask you a question?" Gus stared at the floor plans, not wanting to look too distressed.

"Shoot."

"Your first wife."

"The bitch?"

Gus nodded. "The bitch. What made you cheat on her?"

"She was a bitch. Weren't you listening?"

Gus rolled up the plans and smacked Abe on the head. "Yes, I was listening. But I'm serious. When you're not being an ass, you're a good guy. I know you have morals. So at what point did you decide to have an affair with Denise? Did you know your marriage was over? Was it just too painful to keep your dick in your pants? Was it revenge? How did you rationalize it in your mind?"

Abe narrowed his eyes. "We discuss the Cubs and where

we're going for lunch. What's with all these crazy questions? Is your vision okay? Have you looked at your wife lately? I don't mean any disrespect, and I love Denise, but *I've* sure as hell looked at your wife. It's impossible not to so what's your problem?"

Gus ran wire, searching for words that made sense. "She feels like a trophy on my fireplace mantel. It wasn't like this before her new job. We had a marriage. We were a team, and I loved the game. Now it feels like we're just married. The game is over. And Sabrina is nothing more than …"

"A trophy on your mantel?"

Keeping his hands busy and his back to Abe, Gus nodded.

"Did you just have this epiphany or have you found a *new trophy?*"

With a grunt, Gus shook his head. "I don't want a trophy."

"I see," Abe chuckled, "only not really. But if we stick with the sports scenario, would it be safe to say you've found a new game?"

The image of Parker from the night before popped into Gus's mind. More accurately, it never left. "Forget I said anything. I'm just … off. When Sabrina gets home, I'm going to book us a vacation and not take no for an answer."

Chapter Nine

"SO WHY IS the dog here?" Janey asked.

"Jeez, Mom, I told you he stayed here last night after the storm, and when I finished at the Westmans' this afternoon, he followed me to the gate and wouldn't stop barking. So I brought him here until Gus gets home. I think he likes me." She cleared her throat. "The dog ... that is."

Janey sniffled with a wrinkled nose as Parker handed her a glass of iced tea. "He's already triggering my allergies. My throat and ears are a little itchy too."

"Good thing you don't live here, huh?" Parker grinned her signature clenched-teeth smile that she reserved for her mom.

"I suppose." Janey coughed after one sip of the tea. "Sugar? Really, Parker? You don't need sugar in your tea."

"My house. My tea."

Her mom took another sip that ended with a sour face. "What do you think of August Westman?"

Parker choked on her tea. "W-what do you mean?"

"Your dad thinks he's a nice guy, but he doesn't know him that well, and he says that about everyone. What do you think?"

She thought he was married. That's all she needed to think, all she needed to remember. Otherwise, thoughts of his tented shorts, toned legs, and the gaze that lingered on her breasts made everything south of her navel all warm and tingly.

"He's nice."

"You see much of him?"

Parker took another sip of tea and swallowed hard as she nodded. "I've seen *enough* of him."

"Since his wife's gone so much, you should offer to make him dinner sometime."

Rags cocked his head to the side as if he, too, thought it was a good idea. Parker sat in the kitchen chair across from her mom, bringing a knee to her chest with her heel propped on the edge of the seat. When she glanced out the window, the white Westman Electric van pulled onto the blacktop driveway next door. The idea of his nearness made her uneasy in an inappropriate yet thrilling way.

"Mom, I'm not sure making dinner for a married man while his wife is out of town is the best idea."

"Parker Joy." Janey sighed. "Why do your dirty thoughts always jump to sex? Get your mind out of the gutter, young lady. I raised you better than that."

"Sorry, I guess Caleb screwing Piper kinda left my mind in the gutter."

With a frown, Janey slowly shook her head. "That was different and you know it."

"Different? Yeah, you're probably right. I don't think Piper made him dinner first. Had she done that, then they probably wouldn't have had sex because she can't cook worth shit. They both would have been on the pot all night."

Before her mom could jump to Piper's defense, Rags barked at the knock on the door and ran toward it.

"That's probably Gus. I texted him about Rags. Please behave, Mom."

"What's that supposed to mean?"

Parker declined to answer before her bare feet slapped across the wood floor to the door. "Hey." She contoured her lips into a nervous smile.

"Parker." Gus narrowed his eyes at Rags. "Your mom is coming home tomorrow, mutt. She's not going to be happy to hear that you've been cheating on her." His last few words faltered like he wanted to reel them back in, but it was too late.

"Nobody is cheating on anybody." Parker pushed out an awkward laugh but fell short in her attempt to look nonchalant. Her cheeks heated.

She took a step back and nearly stumbled onto her butt, taking her mom with her. "Oh! Sorry, Mom. I didn't know you were *right* behind me."

Janey regained her footing and stepped in front of Parker. "Excuse my daughter's manners. I'm Janey, Parker's mom and your neighbor."

"Yes, hi, I'm Gus Westman. It's very nice to meet you."

They shook hands like adults past the age of thirty did. Parker wanted to stick her tongue out at her mom and run and hide under her bed from Gus and all talk of cheating.

"You too. I just told Parker she should make you dinner. She's an excellent cook. Her grandmother, who used to live here, taught her all of her culinary skills. Piper never wanted to learn."

"Mmm..." Gus nodded "...is Piper your other daughter?"

Janey turned back toward Parker, giving her a disapproving frown. "You didn't tell Gus that you have an identical twin?"

Parker shrugged. "Apparently not. It never came up, or maybe it just slipped my mind."

After holding a peaked eyebrow at Parker for a few seconds,

Janey turned back to Gus. "Parker makes homemade pasta with a delicious Bolognese."

"Oh yeah?" Gus's gaze shifted to Parker.

"Sure, when I have a stocked kitchen, which I do not. I'll make it another night and drop some off for you and Sabrina."

Gus's hopeful smile faded with the mention of his wife.

"Oh, make him your tuna with homemade dill spread. And don't tell me you don't have the ingredients for it; I looked in your refrigerator earlier."

"Of course you did." Parker gave her a stiff smile.

"It's fine. I have plenty to eat at home—"

"Don't be silly, Gus. Before we had the girls, Bart used to travel when he worked in sales. I remember how lonely it was eating by myself. Parker..." she turned back and pointed a finger "...don't take no for an answer. Nobody likes to feel like a charity case, nor do people like to eat alone."

"Mom—"

"Nice to meet you, Gus." She patted him on the arm as she brushed by him and out the door like she didn't contrive the most awkward situation for two people who had no business being alone together. "Good night, sweetie."

They both spoke at the same time.

"I'll make something at home."

"I'll get started on the tuna."

"You don't have to—" Gus shook his head.

Parker mirrored his gesture. "No, it's fine. I'm sure dinner alone does get lonely after a while. I haven't been on my own long enough to know that for sure, but ... it's fine. It's just dinner, right? And we're friends so ..." Her plan to be his friend hadn't materialized quite as she had imagined.

Gus nodded slowly, each nod gaining momentum like he

had to physically convince himself that the answer to her question was yes.

"Great! So…" she jabbed her thumb behind her "…I'll get started. There's beer in the fridge."

After mentally cursing her mom for the hundredth time in less than a fifteen minute time span, Parker busied herself with dinner.

"A twin. I never would have guessed." Gus took a swig of his beer as he leaned his hip against the counter next to her.

A laugh broke from her chest while she chopped the scallions. "I know. It's hard to believe I'm not a one-of-a-kind."

"Oh, I'm sure you're still one-of-a-kind."

She chuckled softly. "You could be right. I have twenty-twenty vision, yet I've been blind to so much in my life. That's definitely a *unique* condition."

Gus smirked with a curious lift of his eyebrow while he retrieved his phone from his pocket. "Perfectly blind. Do tell." His grin dissolved as he focused on his screen. "It's Sabrina."

"Oh…" Parker nodded toward the other room "…you can take it in there if you need some privacy."

"Hey." He brought the phone to his ear.

"Or stay here," Parker mouthed as she tucked her chin, returning her focus to the cutting board.

"Rags is fine. I am too if you're wondering." He ran his hand through his dark hair then stared up at the ceiling.

Parker stole a quick glance at him, enjoying the rare view of his head without his Cubs cap.

"I'm having dinner … with a friend."

Parker gulped back the ball of nerves that had wormed its way from her stomach to her throat. Gus said they were friends. He had to mean it. Why would he lie to Sabrina?

"No, not Abe. Yes, I have more than one friend. Are you only calling about your dog?"

Parker could hear Sabrina's voice, but she couldn't make out actual words. Almost a minute passed before Gus spoke.

"I think you should reschedule."

More silence.

"Because I think we need to take a vacation ... together."

Rags scratched at the door.

"I've got him," Parker whispered, looking for any excuse not to witness any more of their private conversation. She followed Rags outside. A few minutes later Gus stepped out the back door and sat on the top concrete step.

"She still planning on coming home in two days?" Parker asked without looking at Gus.

"Yup."

"I wasn't trying to eavesdrop, but I heard you mention a vacation. I'd be happy to watch Rags."

"No need."

"No vacation?"

He shook his head slowly, jaw clenched.

She whistled to Rags, who had started to wander toward the shed. He ran back to her without hesitation, like she'd been giving him orders for years.

"Sorry. Maybe when she sees how incredibly efficient her B-team assistant was while she's been gone she'll reconsider." Parker waited for Gus to look at her. When he did, she grinned, and he rewarded her with a one-sided grin of his own.

"B-team assistant?"

She shrugged. "I'm not exactly Brock."

Gus stood and opened the door for both Rags and Parker. "No. You're definitely not him."

Parker washed her hands and finished preparing dinner. "I'm a little surprised that ..." Her words hung in the air as she reconsidered saying them.

"That?" Gus stared out the window toward his house.

She set the plates on the table along with two new beers. "This is really not my business, but I can't help but think that it's a little strange ... Sabrina having a male personal assistant."

Gus glanced over his shoulder. "That's a little sexist, is it not?" He walked to the table and folded his tall body onto the old wooden chair that creaked under his weight.

"I know, but that's not what I mean. I'm just surprised you're okay with your wife having a male assistant that is with her more than you *and* travels everywhere with her. I take it you're not the jealous type?"

"Jealous? No. I'm not insecure either."

"You've never worried that she or they might ..."

Gus took a bite of his sandwich. "Cheat?" he mumbled with his mouth full.

Cringing, Parker nodded. "It happens."

Gus shrugged. "Not to everyone."

"To *a lot*," she whispered to herself.

"To a lot?" Gus leaned forward, turning his ear toward her. "Is that what you just said?"

Shoving a bite into her mouth, she bought herself a few extra seconds to ponder a response. "Yes." She wiped her lips with a white paper napkin.

With a stern face, he studied her then nodded. "I suppose it does."

She leaned back in her chair, tapping the side of her beer bottle. "Why do you think people cheat?"

The combination of a tense brow and a slight grin gave

Gus a look of both confusion and amusement.

"Why the look?"

He blew a long breath out of his nose. "Nothing. I just … didn't expect you to ask me that. I-I don't know how to answer that for sure. There's probably more than one answer."

"Yeah, I suppose." She took a slow sip of beer, contemplating the same question that kept her from letting go of the past.

"A friend of mine cheated on his first wife."

Parker's eyes met his. "Oh? Did you know about it before his wife found out?"

Gus nodded.

"But you didn't tell her?"

"Nope." He took another bite of his sandwich.

"Why not?"

"Wasn't my place."

Her head jerked back as her spine straightened. "Why not? Because he was your friend?"

"No." Gus wiped his mouth and took another swig of his beer. "Not my marriage. Not my business."

"So what if the wife had been the one cheating on your friend and you found out, would you have told him?"

"Nope."

"What the hell? Are you serious?"

"People see things when they're ready to see them, and they're blind to them when they're not ready to deal with reality. She wasn't ready for a divorce. She wasn't prepared to fight for her marriage. Had she been either, then she would have acknowledged the lack of attention he gave her, the odd hours he was gone with no accountability, and a million other obvious signs."

Parker's jaw dropped as she blinked slowly again and again.

She wanted to leap across the table and strangle him for making such ridiculous accusations. Her mind screamed, "I wasn't stupid and blind!" And yet she admitted her blindness to him a few minutes earlier.

Still, reflecting back, there were no signs. The what-did-I-miss scenario played in her head again as it had done so many times before over the previous years.

Gus grimaced. "Shit. Someone cheated on you."

Shifting her gaze from the past to him, she nodded.

"Fuck. I'm sorry."

"Don't be. I'm just ..." She shook her head. "I'm just trying to decide if what you said is true, but I don't see it. I think I would have wanted someone to tell me."

"Would it have changed the outcome?"

"I ... I don't ..."

"How did you find out?"

The image resided in her mind, not weathered by time.

Clear.

Heartbreaking.

Devastating.

Indescribable.

"I walked in on them in bed together."

Gus sucked in a hissing breath. "Oh shit."

"Mmm-hmm."

"It was irrefutable."

She canted her head to the side. "Irrefutable? It was the ultimate betrayal."

"Yes, but had someone else told you, there would have been this small part of you—the same part that made you blind to all the signs—that would have doubted them. But you saw it with your own eyes. Irrefutable."

No one had ever made Parker question herself like that. "So let me get this straight. If your wife were having an affair and someone else found out before you, you wouldn't want them to tell you?"

"Fuck no." He took another pull of his beer. "My wife. My life. None of their fucking business."

"Wow … just … wow. That's crazy. You'd rather look like a fool to the rest of the world."

"If someone has to tell me that my wife is cheating on me, then I'm already a fool. Telling me isn't going to change that. And what if something happened to her, some freak accident, and they knew I knew? I'd be in prison for murdering my cheating wife. No thank you. I'll stick with ignorance is bliss until I figure it out on my own."

Parker laughed. "Oh my god, that's the most ridiculous thing I have ever heard."

"Weirder things have happened." He gave her a pointed look.

"You're crazy." She stood and took their plates to the sink. "I don't think I'll ever get it … the cheating. If you love someone, your heart should always trump physical desire."

"We often hurt the ones we love the most … or the ones we *should* love the most."

He had no idea that his words cut into her very soul, the place she harbored such hatred for the person she'd loved the most since birth. Everyone thought she blamed Caleb. But he didn't live in her soul; that special place had always been reserved for Piper.

"Out of control hormones are no excuse." She rinsed the plates and set them beside the sink.

"Desire is very powerful."

Parker reached for the handle to the fridge. "I don't buy it."

Before she could make sense of what was happening, Gus whipped her around and pinned her to the refrigerator door with his body, chest to chest. He pressed his hands flat to the door on either side of her head as she flattened hers to it just below her hips.

She tried to speak as his eyes stripped every ounce of her confidence. His warm breath touched her lips as he licked his, hovering an inch above hers. When her mouth opened to protest or scream, nothing came out.

"Parker," he whispered in a deep, throaty voice.

The hammering in her chest and the weight of him against her made it difficult to breathe. Warmth flooded her body, yet goose bumps pimpled along her skin from the sound—the *feel*—of her name falling from his lips. He didn't move, but his pulse danced along every inch where his body connected to hers.

"Don't fucking think … just …" He pinched his eyes shut. "Tell me what you *feel* right now."

Scared.

Confused.

Angry.

Exhilarated.

Turned on.

Tears stung her eyes as he opened his.

"Tell. Me."

"I …" She slowly turned her head side to side.

"Are you scared?" The control he held in his voice seemed to slip with each word.

Parker felt his presence in places she didn't—shouldn't—want to feel it. Heavy in her breasts. Wet between her legs.

"Yes." Her voice shook.

"Why?" Gus's lips lingered close to hers. "Are you afraid of me?"

"I-I'm afraid…" she swallowed hard "…of myself."

"Why?" His right hand slid down an inch then moved to her face.

She closed her eyes as the back of his fingers brushed her cheek, down her neck, and along the bare skin of her arm. Her nipples hardened against his chest, betraying her.

"Because I'm …" She spoke in breaths, painful and laborious.

Gus shifted a few inches, wedging his knee between her legs; his thigh rubbed along the apex of her legs as his hand moved from her arm to the hem of her shirt.

As her breath hitched from the warmth of his fingers brushing her bare skin, her conscience wept, pleading with her to break the silence. She needed to tell him to stop. It was wrong. He was the devil, a drug, and she didn't want to be the sinner and the addict.

"You're what?" His hand moved up her shirt, stopping at the edge of her bra as his knee moved a fraction.

So. Fucking. Wrong.

"Confused," she whispered.

"And?" His fingers caressed her abdomen.

Her muscles clenched. "Gus …"

She looked up at him and blinked, sending tears running down her cheeks.

He pressed his knee into her until her hips involuntarily bucked against it. She grimaced and more tears filled her eyes as her body betrayed her again.

"Tell. Me." He gritted his teeth and stroked her again with

his leg, and again her pelvis rocked into it.

As she squeezed her eyes shut, her hands gripped his shirt, warring between the *need* to push him away and something else too terrifying to admit.

"It's ..." A deep and almost painful pressure settled between her legs. "D-desire. I feel..." she fisted his shirt tighter, an unrecognizable voice in her head begged him to move his leg again. Push it higher into her. Harder. Deeper. "...desire." The admission brought such guilt, but her body couldn't feel what her mind comprehended. Her body could only feel one thing at that moment.

Gus's head dipped lower until his breath enveloped her ear. "What are you going to do about it, *Parker?*" He remained static, hand idle at her belly, hard thigh stilled between her legs.

Even with him pressed against her body, she could have shoved him away, smacked him across the face, or screamed. He held her, but not tightly nor as a hostage. Gus ripped away her control then gave it back to her, yet she remained transfixed only by his words and the way they made her feel desperate and helpless to the moment.

"G-go home, Gus." She released his shirt, closed her eyes, and held her breath.

He vanished like a dream, leaving only the echo of the door screeching on its hinges and the shudder it gave her when it thwacked shut—an eerie reminder that it really happened.

Chapter Ten

T HE DISHES WERE clean. Day bled into night leaving a rustic sunset painted along the cornfield horizon. Parker's tears dried, but the memory of what Gus did poisoned her conscience. She would quit her job, of that there was no question. However, her plans of telling Sabrina about the drunken kiss at the bar seemed trivial after the incident in the kitchen.

It was sexual, intimate, suggestive, and inappropriate. Yet nothing happened. He baited her—taunted her—then vanished. All for what?

She couldn't wait for Sabrina to arrive before confronting Gus. Breaking into her emergency reserve of courage that she kept for Armageddon situations, Parker marched over to the Westmans' and pounded on the front door.

No answer.

Like an errant child, she rang the doorbell over and over, sending Rags into a frenzy.

No answer.

Gus was there. She'd watched his place without as much as a blink since he left her in a puddle on her kitchen floor. Determined to get answers, she stomped around back and went in through the unlocked door. Rags greeted her, but no Gus.

"Where is he?" she asked Rags.

Rags ran up the stairs. It wasn't the answer she wanted. At eight forty-five, she couldn't imagine him already in bed.

"Gus?" Her uneasiness over going to his bedroom diluted her attempt to sound mad.

The master bedroom door was open, but the bathroom door was shut, and the shower murmured behind it. She sat on the bench at the end of the bed and waited. As minutes passed and memories of earlier that night fed her anger, her patience dwindled to nothing.

With the twist of her wrist, the unlocked door opened in silence. She kept her head down not wanting to look at naked Gus behind the glass-walled shower.

"Why did you do that to me?" Her voice stayed firm and even, in spite of her heart pounding against her ribs.

"Fuck! What the hell are you doing, Parker?" Gus turned his back to her. "Get out!"

She crossed her arms over her chest, keeping her eyes on her flip-flop-clad feet. "Not until you answer my question."

"I'm in the shower *naked*."

"I'm not looking. Just answer me."

He shut off the water and grabbed a towel, rubbing it quickly through his hair before tying it around his waist as rivulets of water continued to race down his body.

"Go home, Parker. It doesn't matter." He sidestepped her to get to the walk-in closet bordered in dark wood drawers and racks of clothes hanging perfectly from matching wood and brass hangers.

"You're a dick. A cheater. A pathetic excuse for a husband." Parker followed him then whipped around and squeezed her eyes shut the moment he dropped his towel as if he'd given up on hiding his naked body from her.

"Yeah, I'm probably a dick." He slipped on gray sweat-pants, sans underwear. "But I'm not a cheater, and you have no idea what kind of husband I am."

"You ... you tried to seduce me." Anger fueled her fight, overriding how terrified she felt being feet from naked Gus.

He laughed. That fed her anger even more.

"I wasn't seducing you. I was making a point." He slipped on a white T-shirt.

"Bullshit. I was there."

"Precisely. Then you should know that I wasn't seducing you." He grabbed her shoulders and steered her away from the entrance to his closet.

She turned, relieved to find him dressed. "I *felt* you." Her eyes narrowed.

He smirked. "You did, did you?"

Heat spread up her neck and burned her cheeks. Discussing Gus's erection in his bedroom with Sabrina out of town qualified as the most inappropriate conversation she had ever had. "You're such an ass. Just tell me why?"

Twisting his lips to the side, he narrowed his eyes. "You're young. You think the world is so black and white. In your fairy-tale world, love is a magic wand spreading trails of glitter and granting happily ever afters."

Parker stepped closer, knowing the lion could pull her into his den. "I don't believe in fairytales."

"No?" He shrugged. "Then I guess I made my point."

"I don't get your stupid point!" Her fingernails dug into her hands as she clenched them.

Gus leaned forward, putting them at eye level. She held her ground, even though his proximity made her body tremble.

"Someone cheated on you. And you're so fucking mad

about it because you can't understand it. But love is an emotion that resides in your head and your proverbial heart. It has to be nurtured to grow or it dies. *But ... desire ... it's* instinctual. Physical. *Carnal.* And when it wants its way, your brain shuts down and the only heart you hear is that blood-pumping organ in your chest. A slave to your *desire,* readying your body to do *one* thing and one thing only ..." He leaned into her ear and whispered, "Get. Off."

August Westman proved he was the devil. Parker became the worst possible version of herself in his presence. He drugged her with his words, pulled her under with his confidence, and stole her innocence with a whisper.

Gus stood straight again. "Do you want me to treat you like a child, Parker? Like my wife's *B-team* assistant?"

She swallowed hard and shook her head.

"Truth?"

She nodded.

"I love my wife." His brow pulled tight as if saying those simple words somehow pained him. "She's brilliant, and beautiful, and sexy, and I'm committed to her in my head and my heart. But I miss her. Because even when she's here ... she's not really *here.* So when she hires this young girl that smiles all the damn time, and says the funniest things, and looks at me the way my wife used to look at me ..."

Parker could barely breathe and every small gasp of air she found was laced with his herbaceous soap and pheromones.

Gus sighed while shaking his head. "I-I can't think and my heart becomes that indiscriminate blood-pumping organ because I'm a man, and maybe that's no excuse, but I feel so ..." He ran his hands through his wet hair then interlaced them behind his neck. "I wanted to prove that you desired me at that moment and black turned into an ugly gray because you so desperately wanted that release. I wanted you to acknowledge that desire is a drug and no one is immune to its effect."

Gus made gray a terrible color. Parker preferred black and white—and blue.

"You've known me less than two weeks."

He shrugged. "And you've kissed me once and answered the door half-naked twice. I'm a decent guy, but I'm no saint."

"Gus, I …"

"Don't sweat it, Parker." He moved past her toward the stairs. "I'm not making you my mistress. I'm not cheating on Sabrina. I shouldn't have done what I did to you."

She chased after him.

"I'm sorry." He continued. "After she called me, I was frustrated with her. Then you went off about the whole cheating thing, and I was pissed at the world and needed to justify my feelings. I used you to do it, and that was shitty of me." He kept walking to the kitchen without looking back. "Let's forget it ever happened."

"What?" Parker couldn't believe he said that.

Gus tossed Rags a treat from his dog tin on the counter. Then he grabbed a cola from the fridge.

"Are you kidding me? *Forget* that it ever happened?" With eyes wild and hands flailing in the air, she stomped across the tile floor toward him, not stopping until they were toe-to-toe. She glared up at him as he took a casual swig of his cola, ignoring her in-your-face attitude like she was nothing more than a fly on his shoulder.

Rubbing his wet lips together, he eyed her with suspicion. "Yes, that's what I said."

"So we say *nothing* to Sabrina about the kiss or you getting me off in my kitchen."

Gus's head jerked back, eyes wide. "You got off on my—"

"No!" Taking a step back, she shook her head several times and tried to gain some composure. "I didn't actually … I just came close … or … what I mean is …" Her nose wrinkled as she fumbled her words. Embarrassment bloomed along her skin as it always did so easily around him. "Stop putting words in my mouth." She pointed a stiff finger at him.

He chuckled. "Parker—"

"Stop saying my name!" She hated how he made it sound so dirty.

He laughed, even more, holding up his hands in defeat. "Sorry, *Ms. Cruse,* I haven't put anything in your mouth … *yet.*"

She gasped. "Pervert! I'm telling Sabrina everything as soon as she gets home tomorrow. And when you're out on your horny, cheating, egotistical ASS, you'll have no one to blame but yourself." Riding a wave of adrenaline, she stormed to the back door.

"Jeez, I was joking. But make sure you tell my wife that you've made a habit of not wearing a bra around me, Ms. *Nipples.*"

Parker slammed the door and looked down at her fitted tank top that *had* a built-in bra. However, that extra layer of cotton didn't stand a chance of keeping her nipples in line around cocky Gus Westman and his rude comments that seemed to turn her on as much as they infuriated her. "Son of a bitch …"

PARKER FELL IN love with Caleb in one night. He offered to tutor her in calculus, and they stayed up until four in the morning discovering their shared love of country music, pickled eggs, Chuck Taylor Converse shoes, and *Grey's Anatomy*. By the following week, she discovered her new favorite past time involved making out with Caleb in his parents' basement while "studying" calculus.

It took ten days for Caleb to take her virginity. It should not have come as any surprise that in the same amount of time August Westman seduced her with his words, made her question her morals, and wreaked havoc on her body. Three changes of underwear in one day seemed extreme.

The following morning did nothing more than end a sleepless night. The better perspective she'd hoped for didn't come to fruition. Dressed conservatively in baggy capris, an oversized black Iowa Hawkeye tee, and a bra with extra padding in the nipple area, Parker went to work for her last day at the Westmans'.

She planned on quickly completing the ridiculous tasks Brock emailed her the previous night, finish the day with taking Rags for a long walk, and confess her adulterous sins to Sabrina as soon as she arrived home. Drowning her guilt in a bottle of wine would top off her evening before scouring the internet for job listings in the morning. With a little luck, the receptionist job at the chiropractor's office would still be available.

It pissed her off to see Gus's van still in the garage when she arrived, blowing her whole purpose of arriving a half hour later than usual.

"Good morning, Rags." Parker ruffled his fur and kissed the top of his head. "Did you forget to get your dad up and send him off to work?" She scooped a cupful of dog food out of the bin in the mudroom and dumped it in his food bowl then filled up his water dish.

Silence enveloped the house. Even as she tiptoed up the stairs, she couldn't hear any signs of Gus in the shower or getting ready for work. If his intention was to beg her not to say anything to Sabrina, then his efforts and late start to the day were going to be all for nothing.

"Oh, for Pete's sake," she whispered to herself upon seeing Gus facedown in bed with a pillow over his head and one leg hanging off the side. "Go to work, Mr. Westman." With a swift tug, she pulled the blankets and sheet off him, leaving him in nothing but a pair of black briefs. It threw her off for a second, but she sucked it up and focused on the task at hand.

"I've been instructed to change the bed sheets before your wife arrives." She yanked the pillow from his grasp and stripped off the pink pillowcase.

"What the fuck?" he mumbled into the mattress.

"Get up, or I'm going to throw your ass in the washing machine with your girly, emasculating, pink sheets. Why don't you grow a pair and tell Sabrina you're not going to sleep in a cloud of cotton candy."

He turned his head to the side and squinted open one eye. "Why don't you tell her?"

She grabbed the other pillow and stripped it too. "Because I already have enough to chat about with her."

He eased to sitting then unfolded his tall body, stretching his hands high above his head while yawning.

"Oh!" Parker jumped back.

Gus glanced down and chuckled. "When you're spilling your guts to my wife later, there's no need to add this to your cheating claims. It's called morning wood, Parker, and you can't take credit for it no matter how long you stare at it."

Her eyes snapped up to his, mouth open but unable to deny he busted her on that. "Shut up. I wasn't—"

Gus brushed past her to the bathroom. "You were. I don't mind. But really ... keep your mouth shut when you do it, or *something* might fill that open hole of yours."

She ripped the bottom sheet from the bed. "Why do you have to be such an asshole?"

"I don't." He turned on the shower.

Grumbling a few expletives, she wadded up the sheets and tossed them into the hallway. "Then why do it?" She folded the blankets and tossed the decor pillows back onto the bed.

His voice echoed from the shower. "Because you feel less guilty about what's happened if you hate me. So I'll let you, I'll even help you out ... because I'm a nice guy like that."

"Nice guy my ass," she mumbled to herself.

"I don't usually breach that hole, Parker ... not my thing ... but I could make an exception."

Her hand flew to her mouth, shocked that he heard her but even more shocked by his reply. The Gus who knocked on her door looking for his dog that had gotten into her cockleburs was not the same Gus making lewd comments to her. She didn't understand what had happened and it didn't matter. It was her last day with the Westmans.

Chapter Eleven

B REATHING BECAME IMPOSSIBLE with every step Parker took toward the Westmans' house on her way back from a long walk with Rags—her final duty as Sabrina's B-team assistant. Of course, Sabrina would fire her, but would she hate her?

"Here we go," Parker whispered to Rags as they turned the corner to the drive.

They went in through the back door. As she reached for Rags's leash to release him, she heard voices upstairs. She knew it was none of her business, but curiosity won over so she gave Rags a few treats and locked him in the mudroom so he wouldn't run upstairs and make his—and Parker's—presence known quite yet.

Tiptoeing toward the stairs, she stopped at the bottom and listened.

"You knew my job involved traveling," Sabrina said.

"I'm not complaining about your job or the traveling involved. I'm just saying we need to get away if this is going to work."

She laughed mockingly. "Work? What is that supposed to mean, August? Are you giving me an ultimatum? I took over the company less than nine months ago. I'm still earning everyone's respect. If I take off for leisure time with my husband, I'll look weak and unfocused. It's not fair of you to ask me to do this right now."

"So what? Our marriage is on hold until you earn the respect at work you think you deserve?"

"Jesus, August! Stop making it sound like my success is bad for our marriage. You hated it when I harped on you about going out with the guys every weekend. When's the last time I did that? You have freedom galore. I've hired a maid to clean up after you and an assistant to grocery shop and take care of everything else. All you have to do is wake up and go to work. That's it! Short of hiring someone to suck your dick, I've taken care of *everything*."

"Nice, Sabrina. You make me sound like a child. You treat our marriage like a business arrangement. You treat our sex life like a chore—"

"That's not true."

"It is true!"

Parker jumped as Gus's voice roared through the house.

"The last time we had sex you told me not to go down on you because you didn't *want* to have an orgasm because you needed to stay focused on your presentation for the following day. You said ... and I quote, 'But you do your thing, August, don't worry about me.' What the fuck kind of marriage is that?"

"You're right, August! I'm a terrible person for meeting my husband's needs. You're so fucking selfish. Do you have any idea how many women in my shoes would simply tell you they didn't have time for sex and would send you off to stroke your own cock? Can't you show me a little bit of gratitude for at least meeting you halfway?"

"I can't do this." Gus's voice broke in defeat.

"One more year, August. Give me one more year and I promise we'll take that trip, and have sex on the beach, and do all the things you think we're missing out on right now. This is my life, and I've worked too hard to get here to just give it up because my husband feels lonely."

"I'm not lonely."

"Well, you sure are acting needy."

"Fuck you."

Before Parker could make a run for it, Gus was jogging down the stairs. She tried to hide around the corner, but before she could get there, his eyes landed on her.

She bit her lower lip and grimaced. "Sorry ... I was—"

He cut her off with a firm shake of his head, jaw clenched, and murder or something even more intense than that in his eyes. Parker retreated backward toward the mudroom door as Gus's long strides gained on her.

"I have her primed and ready for your confession, Parker." Anger bled through his words.

She tried to swallow past the massive lump in her throat as he raged by her to the garage, leaving the mudroom door open. Before she could stop him, Rags bolted toward the stairs.

"But, Parker?"

As she turned toward his voice, he grabbed her arm, yanked her into the garage, and pinned her against the wall.

"If you're going to tell Sabrina about our kiss, it sure as fuck isn't going to be the lame, drunken kiss at the bar."

"Wha—"

He silenced her by smashing his mouth into hers, delivering a kiss that obliterated every thought in her head. When his tongue probed into her mouth, sliding against hers, she tried to push him away. He cradled her face to deepen the kiss even more and when he moaned, she did the unthinkable—the unforgivable: she laced her fingers through his hair and kissed him back.

Gray. A terrible color. The murky water where sinners thrived. Parker Cruse was a hypocrite. A cheater. And in need of another change of underwear.

Just as quickly and violently as he pulled her into his lips, he pushed her away. Mussed hair. Swollen lips. And breathless. "*Now* you have something to tell her."

Parker ghosted the pads of her fingers over her lips, legs shaky, heart ready to explode as Gus jumped into his van and screeched out of the driveway.

"*THOU SHALT NOT JUDGE.*"

Parker hid in the garage for fifteen minutes, rubbing her lips together, savoring the taste of Gus, fixing her hair, and waiting for her heart to snap out of cardiac arrest. How would she explain *that* kiss?

"August?" Sabrina called.

Parker froze.

"You can do this," she whispered to herself, making one last check of her hair in the side mirror of Sabrina's BMW.

"Hello?" Parker said with as much confidence as she could muster given the adulterous circumstances.

"Parker? I'm upstairs. Come up here, please."

On a deep breath, she climbed her way to the executioner.

Sabrina walked out of the bathroom in a white robe and towel around her head. "Oh, I'm so glad you're still here."

"You are?"

A floral mix of rose and lavender wafted from the bathroom.

She stepped into the closet and dropped her robe. Gus had a beautiful wife. Her body wasn't better than Parker's, just different. Parker had longer legs with more defined muscles and scars from playing sports over the years. In contrast, flawless, milky white skin covered every inch of Sabrina's petite frame. She looked like a life-sized doll: subtle but perfect curves, perfect nose, perfect lips, perfect eyebrows.

"I don't know where August went, he can be such a child, but I'm meeting some friends for drinks, and I need some help to get organized before work early in the morning." After slipping into a short, tight, black dress and heels, she gave Parker a smile that bordered on a grimace. "No rest for the weary."

"I guess not." Parker's words lost their momentum. She needed to tell Sabrina everything, but thoughts of the Westmans' fight, the kiss, and the way Sabrina hustled to go out with friends when she needed to work on her failing marriage left Parker a little dumbfounded.

It took Sabrina less than five minutes to dry her hair enough to pull it back into a tight bun and apply a bit of makeup. Parker envied how easily Sabrina looked amazing.

"I know you're probably ready to be done for the day, but could I beg you to unpack my suitcase and sort out my clothes? Most of them will need to go to the dry cleaners, but I have some undergarments that need to be hand washed."

"I need to discuss something with you."

"Is it life or death?" Sabrina shoved the contents of one purse into another one. She had a lot of purses. She had a lot of everything.

"I wouldn't say life or death, but—"

"Then it will have to wait. I already gave August more of my time than I had to give." Sabrina used her clutch purse to wave as she hurried toward the stairs. "Thank you, Parker. You're the best."

"I kissed your husband," Parker whispered, knowing there was no way Sabrina heard her.

The back door slammed shut, leaving behind Parker, Rags, and a million unspoken words.

"I'm going to hell." Parker continued her solo conversation. "Not because I kissed your husband…" she knelt on the floor by Sabrina's suitcase "…because I liked it."

It came as no surprise that the dirty contents of Sabrina's suitcase were packed as neatly as they surely had been the day she left. That's why she hired Parker. They both thrived on organization. The surprise came when Parker sorted the clothing.

"Whoa …"

When Sabrina said she had "undergarments" to be hand washed, Parker never imagined lacy lingerie, the impractical kind women wore for only one reason.

A wet nose tickled Parker's neck. "Hey, buddy."

Rags sniffed the pastel pink teddy as Parker held it from the edge as if she dared not touch it for many reasons. She tossed it onto the pile with the rest of the hand washables.

"Rags, no!"

He dropped to the floor and rolled in the pile of expensive silk and lace, desperate to either impart his scent onto her stuff or Sabrina's scent onto him.

"Rags, stop!" Parker tried to pull him away, but his random rolling and contortion of his body in every direction made it impossible to control him. Instead, she grabbed as many pieces of the lingerie as she could without ripping them out from underneath him.

"Drop it. Drop it! DROP IT!"

He had at least one teddy and two thongs hanging from his mouth as he sprinted down the stairs toward his doggy door. Were her clothes laced with crack? What was his deal?

A sliver of light that lingered in the western horizon allowed her to see the naughty canine running around the yard.

"Rags, come! Now!" She walked toward him with calculated steps as he crouched into down dog, ass in the air, tail wagging. "Please, drop … it." On the last step, she lunged for his collar, but he dodged her attempt and bolted to the left as she face planted into the grass. "Dammit, Rags!"

When she lifted her head all she could see was the outline of Rags using his paw to hold the garments to the ground while he shredded them with his teeth. Accepting defeat, she rolled over and sat up, stopping all movement the moment she felt something soft and squishy beneath her ass.

"Please don't tell me …" She leaned to the side and strained her neck around to look at her ass. "Shit." Closing her eyes, Parker shook her head, cursing the day that stupid dog and his owners came into her life.

"Canine hell is a real place, Rags. You've been warned." Easing to her feet, she looked in front of her for any more piles of poop. One pile of it plastered to her ass was enough for the night.

Gus and Sabrina were probably out drinking. Lucky them. Parker still had to deal with Sabrina's clothes—what was left of them—clean up the scraps of lingerie in the yard and change her pants.

"Playtime is over, demon dog."

Seemingly content with his mess, Rags allowed Parker to drag him to the garage by his collar. She attached his leash and tied it to the leg of Gus's workbench in the garage.

"Stay put while I clean up your mess."

After using a piece of cardboard from their recycling bin to scrape as much dog poop off her ass as possible, she went upstairs to quickly tidy up the suitcase mess, praying that the odor from her pants didn't linger. Then she grabbed a plastic shopping bag from under the sink and headed out to pick up the scraps of silk and lace in the yard. And because she was the unluckiest person on the face of the earth, as she picked up the last of the mess, the headlights to a white van blinded her as they rounded the corner of the drive to pull into the garage.

"I hate my life." She took the bag to the garbage bin on the side of the garage.

"Do I need to pack up my shit and get out?" Gus asked.

Parker let the lid to the garbage bin slam shut, and then she turned to him. "I don't know, Mr. Westman." Sarcasm dripped from her words. He'd kissed her. She'd kissed him back. But everything that happened after that overshadowed all awkwardness that she should have felt at that moment. "I didn't get a chance to tell Mrs. Westman about her despicable husband and her equally despicable B-team assistant because she didn't have time for me. And then your savage dog ran off with your wife's fancy *undergarments*, ripping them to shreds.

"Which by the way ... I know you like the ignorance-is-bliss life, but..." Parker cocked her head to the side and narrowed her eyes "...don't you find it suspicious that your wife packs sexy lingerie for a business trip that she takes *without* you?"

Gus shrugged and walked toward the back door. "She

doesn't own anything that's not sexy. Refuses to buy cotton. What the—" He freed Rags from the leg of the workbench. "Did you tie him to this?"

"Uh …" Parker grimaced for a second then pulled back her shoulders. "Yes. I did. After chasing him around the yard, I had to keep him out of trouble while I finished unpacking Sabrina's suitcase."

Gus shook his head and whistled. "Don't tell her you tied her baby to my workbench." He went into the house, and she followed him.

"Oh, for crying out loud. It was only for like … twenty minutes, and he had at least three feet of slack. That hardly qualifies as animal cruelty. Besides his 'mommy' barely gave her 'baby' a second glance before she marched out the door in her slutty dress and fuck-me heels."

Gus cracked open a beer while giving Parker a hard look, jaw set. "That's my wife you're talking about."

She laughed. "I don't think you can stick your tongue down my throat and press your erection to my belly then an hour later defend *your wife's* honor."

Gus swallowed back some strange emotion as his eyes averted to the side for a few seconds. "I love her," he whispered.

Caleb had once loved Parker too. Even after she caught him in bed with Piper, he swore he still loved her more than Piper. Thinking back, underneath all the anger and betrayal, there was a part of her that truly believed him.

"Then fight for her."

Caleb didn't fight for Parker. It probably would not have changed the outcome of their lives, but that's what people in love did. They fought for each other.

Gus grunted a painful chuckle. "How do you fight for

something that's already yours?"

"People aren't property, Gus. You can't possess her. You can fight for her attention and maybe even her heart, and that's enough to live out your 'til-death-do-us-part."

"I kissed you."

Biting her lips together, she nodded. "Total prick. I can give you womanly advice, but I can't make you less despicable."

He set his beer on the counter then stepped closer to her. "You kissed me back."

She no longer berated herself for the way his nearness sent chills along her spine and heat to other places that seemed to crave his touch. "You said it yourself. Desire is not love. We've known each other less than two weeks. I'm young and incredibly hot." Parker smirked. "You're old and my standards are clearly a bit too low, so we're physically attracted to each other. It's just biology. 'Carnal.' Nothing more."

"Old? You still think I'm—" He took a step closer and frowned as he sniffed several times. "Did you step in dog shit?"

Her confident grin waned. "Oh ... um ..." She retreated backward. "Not exactly."

Gus continued toward her.

"Good night!" She turned to make a quick exit.

"Parker? Did you shit your pants?"

She groaned, shaking her head, eyes closed. "No, I didn't shit my pants. Rags did."

Gus barked out a laugh. "Pray tell, how does a dog shit *your* pants?"

Whipping around, she folded her arms over her chest. "Ha ha. He didn't shit my pants. I sat in a pile of his poop."

"How did you not see—"

"Just ..." She held a flat hand up to him. "Shhh. Good

night, Mr. Westman."

"For the record, Parker, I don't find you all that 'incredibly hot' at the moment."

"Screw you, Gus, you hairy, gray-balled bastard." She stepped over Rags sprawled out on the mudroom floor and didn't look back.

Chapter Twelve

"WE NEED TO talk."

Sabrina jumped, pressing her hand to her heart. "Dammit, August! You scared me." She flipped on the bedroom light and stepped out of her heels. "Why are you sitting here in the dark?"

He leaned forward in the white, wingback chair by the window in their bedroom, resting his arms on his knees. His eyes squinted against the light; he'd sat there for two hours waiting for her to come home.

"I figured you wouldn't come up if you saw the light on."

She unzipped the side of her black dress while walking into the closet. "Don't be ridiculous. You make it sound like I'm avoiding you."

Gus rubbed the long day and two agonizing weeks out of his eyes. "Are you?"

She came out of the closet in a black nightie, rolled her eyes at him, then rounded the corner into the bathroom. "And I thought *I* had a lot to drink tonight. You're paranoid, August."

He stood, cocking his stiff neck to one side and then the other. Sabrina's designer chair was not made for comfort. "You've been gone for five days and when you get home the first thing you do is turn around and leave again to be with your friends." Gus leaned against the bathroom door frame, arms crossed over his bare chest, shorts low on his hips.

"And your point?" She tugged on her hair tie sending long blond waves spilling over her shoulders and down her back.

Abe was right—Gus had a wife that most men would kill to have as theirs.

"I remember a time when being apart for a mere eight hours had us ripping off each other's clothes and fucking like rabbits on the stairs or kitchen counter because we couldn't even make it to the bedroom."

"Sex. It's always about sex," Sabrina mumbled over her toothbrush and a mouthful of foam.

He moved behind her. When she bent over to spit, he slid his hands up her sides, pressing his erection against her ass.

"Gus …" she only called him that when they had sex, and she said it like a moan with a name.

"I miss my wife," he whispered in her ear as she set her toothbrush aside before pressing her hands flat to the granite.

"It's … late …" Her words were breathy as his hands cupped her breasts.

"Tell me you don't want this." He sucked and bit at her earlobe while rocking his pelvis into her.

"Gus …" Her eyes drifted shut.

He snaked his right hand up her silk nightie and down into the front of her lace panties. "If you're not wet for me, then I'll stop."

"I'm not … fuck … Gus …" Sabrina dropped her chin and moaned again as two of his fingers slid across her clit.

"Feels like I'm not stopping." He buried his nose into her hair then bit the back of her neck at the same time he thrust his fingers into her.

"I …" She panted as he fingered her. "I'm … tired."

Gus chuckled against her skin. She wasn't too tired to move her hips in rhythm to him fucking her with his fingers. His dick felt like it could explode, a lethal combination of needing a release and thoughts of Parker and the way she tasted.

"Please ..."

When he removed his fingers and spun her around, he couldn't tell if her plea was to keep going or stop. Her tense face and drunken eyes conveyed both pain and desire. The proof of her arousal on his fingers prevented him from stopping to ask questions.

He shoved down his shorts and briefs and kicked them to the side as he curled his fingers around her panties, sliding them down her legs. Their eyes met for a brief moment when he lifted her up. Before he had time to analyze the stranger looking back at him, he guided her legs around his waist and slid his cock inside of her.

They locked mouths, desperate and angry. She tasted like caramel and oak of her favorite chardonnay, and a hint of perfume lingered on her skin. He walked them to the bed where he pinned her beneath him. Gus's body made love to his wife while his mind fucked the girl next door.

"GOOD MORNING." GUS kissed his wife on the forehead as he set a tray of food by the bed. The previous night wasn't about sex. Sex was just the only way he knew how to get her out of her obsessive mind long enough to listen to him.

Sabrina squinted open her eyes. "What time is it?"

"Five-thirty."

"I'm going to be late." She sat up, brushing her hair out of her face.

"You have fifteen minutes before your alarm will go off. I'm claiming these fifteen minutes with you."

She sighed and a sad smile accompanied her sleepy eyes. "August, what's going on?"

He handed her a cup of coffee. "I feel like I'm competing with your career and I'm failing."

"Aug—"

"No. Let me finish."

She nodded, baring a flash of vulnerability as she brought the mug to her mouth, steam swirling above it.

"I won't ask you to take a vacation until you're ready. I won't ask you to be home for dinner every night. But I need something from you even if it's only fifteen minutes at the ass crack of dawn. And I need these fifteen minutes to feel like fifteen days—unhurried and uninterrupted. I want to feel like your husband, not your job."

He hated the conflict in her eyes.

"I think I gave you a lot longer than fifteen minutes last night." She playfully cocked an eyebrow, but Gus felt it was more like a distraction from the things he'd said than an actual compliment to what they shared the previous night.

Taking her coffee, he took a sip then set it back on the tray. "The sex was good." His hand slid up her thigh but stopped before reaching the top.

She tensed under his touch and rested her hand on his as if to make sure it wasn't going any farther. "The sex was good."

Gus nodded. "But the sex is always good." He wasn't an idiot. Gus knew how to please his wife, and he knew when her orgasms started and when they ended. He also knew that she was silently fighting him the previous night. She was turned on and it pissed her off. Why? He didn't know.

"You need your ego stroked this morning, August?"

He returned a half smile. Desperate to connect with the playful woman he married five years earlier. "I'll never say no to you stroking me."

The alarm clock on her phone chimed. "Your fifteen minutes is up." She threw off the covers and stood.

He grabbed her wrist as she began to walk off. She turned, confusion etched on her face.

"Are you happy?"

She scoffed. "Are you dying, August? Why the sudden sentimentality? The incessant I love you's. The neediness?"

"Incessant I love you's? Sorry, I'll tone that down." He released her wrist, grabbed the tray of uneaten food, and took it back to the kitchen.

Thirty minutes later, her heels clicked along the tile as she came into the kitchen. "Tell Parker if you see her that I'll have Brock send her a shopping list before noon. In the meantime, ask her to wash our bedsheets."

"She washed them yesterday morning per your request." Gus focused on his phone screen because he didn't even want to look at his wife by that point.

Sabrina flung her brown Gucci handbag over her shoulder. "Yes, but now they're dirty from all the … sweat and whatnot from last night."

"Wow … when did we start changing the sheets every time we had sex and *whatnot*?"

"Stop being so argumentative. Just pass along the message. And don't wait up, I'm taking a client to dinner tonight. Bye, baby." She blew Rags a kiss as she walked out the door.

"HEY, DEMON DOG!"

Gus chuckled at Parker's greeting for Rags. Apparently, she hadn't forgiven him for the previous day's incidents.

"Oh …" She stopped inside the door. "I thought you'd be gone by now."

Gus grabbed an apple from the wire basket on the counter and tossed it into the lunch sack by his Cubs hat. "As in gone to work or kicked to the curb?"

Parker frowned. "Work. How could you get kicked to the curb when I haven't said anything?"

"Good point. So no, I haven't gone to work yet. I have a meeting with a builder at nine."

"I see." She glanced at the clock on the microwave. "That's not for an hour and a half. Want me to make you some breakfast?"

"Already ate … before six this morning."

"Early riser." Parker scooped out a cupful of food for Rags and filled his bowl with fresh water. "I've always envied morning people. I get up early, but it's never easy." She opened the fridge and poured herself a glass of orange juice, which seemed fair since she was the one who freshly squeezed it for Sabrina the previous afternoon, yet Sabrina didn't drink a drop.

"Actually, I'm not really a morning person, but someone told me to 'fight for my wife,' so I made her breakfast in bed this morning."

"That was nice." Parker took a sip.

Gus returned a tight-lipped smile. "Yes, it really was. I also fucked my wife long and hard last night and so she's requested you change the sweat-stained, *dirty* sheets again."

Crash!

The glass shattered on the tile, splattering orange juice everywhere. Parker stood idle for a few seconds as if it hadn't yet registered that it was she who dropped it.

"Rags, get back." Gus ushered him into the mudroom and blocked the door so he couldn't get into the kitchen.

"Shit!" Parker jumped into action like her delayed brain finally caught up to what she had done. "I'm so sorry. I'll get this cleaned up. You go to work."

"It's fine." He grabbed a new roll of paper towels, a hand broom, and a dustpan.

She used the towels to absorb the juice as he swept the glass into a pile.

"What happened?" Gus asked.

"What does it look like? I dropped the glass of juice." She wouldn't look at him.

"No shit, Sherlock. I mean, why did you turn as white as that roll of paper towels two seconds before the glass slipped from your grip?"

"Wow! Really?" Still refusing to give him so much as a glance, she threw away the dirty towels and grabbed the mop from the mudroom while he finished sweeping up the glass.

"You're upset?" Gus dumped the glass into the trash and removed the bag from the bin, tying it at the top.

"No. Yes ... I don't know." Parker's brow furrowed as she focused on cleaning the sticky floor with hot water and the mop.

"You're jealous." He tried not to grin like it pleased him, but he failed.

"Fuck you," she whispered.

"You told me to 'show' my wife how much I still loved her. So I—"

"Yeah, yeah, I get it! Jeez, I don't need the details. I'm not even going to be here that much longer. As soon as Sabrina gives me more than two seconds of her time, I'm going to quit."

"You moving too?"

"What? No. Why would you think that?"

"Because you're quitting a good paying job for what? To get away from me? Yet your front door will still be a hundred yards from mine. My wife's dog will still find a way to get your attention, and I will still have to come rescue him—or you—depending on how you look at it."

Parker frowned, finally giving Gus a quick glance. Then she rinsed the mop out in the mudroom sink. "So you're saying the only way I can avoid you is to move?"

Gus peeked around the corner at her. "Yes."

"You move. Why should I have to move? My house has been here longer than yours."

He loved her sassy rationale and the way her spine straightened with confidence that wasn't entirely believable.

"You've lived there a couple of weeks." He chuckled.

She turned toward him but her furrowed brow did nothing to hide the glimmer in her eyes. As much as she wanted to be pissed off at him, her body wouldn't cooperate. "The house has been in my family for generations. My grandparents lived there, and so did their parents."

"I paid over three hundred thousand for my land alone."

Her head jerked back. "Are you insane?"

"I did it for love. To 'show' my wife how much I loved her."

Parker shoved him out of her way—not a brush by but an actual shove—even though he wasn't blocking her. "I pity the poor man who doesn't have *three hundred thousand dollars* to express his love to a woman." She laughed. "Or maybe I pity the woman whose man thinks three hundred thousand dollars can buy her love. I'm not sure. I'll get back to you on that."

"Will you? That would be great."

Sarcasm seemed to be the theme that morning.

"And while you're at it, would you mind telling me why you're so pissed off?"

"I'm not pissed off." Parker leaned against the counter, messing with her phone.

"You're pissed that I had sex with my wife."

She grunted. "Yeah, sure, that's it. I'm pissed that a guy that I've known for two weeks had sex with his *wife*. Makes total sense. How did you guess?"

"Because I'm pissed off too."

The muscles in her jaw tensed as she swallowed hard. "I was being sarcastic," she whispered without looking up.

"Well, I wasn't."

"I don't care."

Gus stepped closer. "Ask me why."

"I don't care."

Another step.

"I made love to my wife last night while thinking about my neighbor."

"Jesus, Gus …" Parker whispered, looking up slowly while shaking her head.

"The day before we met I would have said no fucking way was I that guy. A cheater? No. Fucking. Way. Then you happened and in an instant, I became a hypocrite and a cheater."

Parker returned a pleading look, staring at him like her

whole world was about to crumble to the ground. "My sister."

He narrowed his eyes. For a second he questioned whether he heard her right.

Her glazed-over gaze fell short of his, focusing on his shoulder or maybe something over it. "My boyfriend cheated on me with my sister."

No way did he see that coming.

"I hated her more than him. We are family—blood, yet we haven't spoken in two years, and I think I was prepared to never speak to her again. Until…" she shifted her eyes to meet his "…you said my name." She laughed, and it sounded like the most painful laugh he had ever heard.

"My. Name. How stupid is that? Honestly, I've never really liked it. But when *you* say it … I *feel* it in places I sure as hell shouldn't be feeling anything from a married man. I don't want to feel you. I don't want you in my head. I don't want to check myself in the mirror a hundred times before I walk over here in the morning. I don't want to envy your wife. And I don't want to know that you *fucked* her last night while thinking of me."

"Parker—"

She took a step to the side as he stepped toward her. "I'm *coveting* thy neighbor's husband! That's a sin, Gus. Like … a major one … I think. I've blamed the ruination of my life on cheating, but here I am having horrifically inappropriate thoughts about my neighbor. There's no way around it. I don't know how to stop it. My mind doesn't have an off button. Seriously … I'm going to Hell!"

"Parker—"

"STOP SAYING MY NAME!"

Swallowing his tongue, he retreated a few steps, giving the

rabid neighbor her space.

Her hand flew to her mouth, eyes wide. Rags dashed to her side, tail wagging. The nameless girl broke into laughter—complete hysteria. Not a good sign. "I ... I'm sorry." She fought for a breath, wiping tears from her eyes. "I haven't had sex in ... a *long time.* I just replaced the batteries in my vibrator before we met, and they already need to be replaced again. My friends tell me to set up an online dating profile, but I tell them that's just for people looking to hook up. But let's be honest, if my vibrator batteries are only lasting two weeks, it might be time for me to find a quick hookup before I end up with some silicone rash in my girl parts."

Winded breaths filled the air as they stared at each other. It took a few minutes for Gus to realize she'd stopped talking.

"August Westman ... you kissed the life out of me yesterday and then flaunted your sexual conquests in front of me this morning. I just finished telling you a bunch of random stuff that ended with the words 'silicone rash' and 'girl parts.' Say. Something."

"I fear this erection I have could last longer than four hours. So if your batteries are dead, then I could probably—"

"Not funny, Gus. I'm serious. The day we met we didn't do anything. How could you feel like a cheater the moment we met?" Parker shook her head.

"But I did do something. The moment you jumped behind the door and smiled in spite of your embarrassment, I broke my wedding vows. Like when I was nine and my mom took me to the eye doctor, and he held these lenses up to my eyes. I had no clue what I'd been missing, but it was total bliss. A whole new world. I didn't want to blink because I was afraid the clarity would vanish. I felt this euphoria from the tip of my nose to the end of my toes.

"When you smiled, I didn't want to blink because I knew the second I did, you'd still be there, and I'd still be in a fucking miserable marriage with another woman. I'm pissed off for the same reason you are."

Giving in or maybe feeding her curiosity, she glanced up. "Well, I just said I wasn't, but enlighten me, Mr. Westman."

"The woman I should desire feels like a stranger and the woman I *do* desire *is* a stranger. I want to do the right thing, but after last night, I don't even know what that is. And you ... you're so damn scared that you're becoming everything you thought you hated. Tortured by the emotions you can't control. Traumatized by your past. And so fucking afraid of the future because happiness has eluded you and now you're not sure you even deserve to be truly happy."

"I deserve to be happy. I *am* happy." Parker tipped her chin up.

A lopsided grin stole his lips. "You're happiness personified, like a warm bag of peanuts at the ballpark. I see it and it's so damn distracting, but I don't buy that you see it yourself." He pulled on his Cubs hat and grabbed his brown bag. "Let me be the bad guy with the fucked-up marriage. I won't drag you into it anymore, but I also won't ask you to keep quiet if your conscience is killing you. Good day, *Ms. Cruse.*"

Chapter Thirteen

"DO I SEEM happy to you?" Parker asked Mindy over lunch at a sub shop a block from Mindy's work.

"Everyone who doesn't have to pee a hundred times a day seems happy to me."

Parker grinned. "That girl I shared the womb with is also pregnant. Did I mention that?"

Wiping her mouth, Mindy laughed. "Piper is pregnant? Wow. Bet that stings a bit."

Parker picked off a piece of bread and tossed it in her mouth. "The pregnancy? No. The fact that they are moving back to Iowa? Yes."

"Shit! Are you serious?"

"Serious. And my mom came over last night to see how I felt about them living with me until the new house they're building is completed … in *five* months."

Mindy gasped. "No. Fucking. Way. What did you say?"

"I said no fucking way, but here's the kicker. Technically, the farmhouse and the land it's on is half Piper's. Our grandparents left it to both of us. Caleb makes an obscene amount of money, so they haven't asked for a check yet, but something tells me I'm either going to have to choke on my pride and let them live with me or sell the place when they demand Piper's share."

Parker blew a long breath out her nose. "And mark my word, Piper would love nothing better than to see me have to sell it and move back home ... which I will *not* do. I will live at a homeless shelter before I move back for the third time."

"When are they moving back?"

"Middle of July."

"That's a month away. You can work something out. Maybe you could fuck her husband ... you know ... for revenge. If she's half the hot mess I am, it won't take much for Caleb to jump into your bed."

Parker twisted her lips to keep from grinning while she leaned back and scratched her chin. "That would even the score, wouldn't it?"

Mindy giggled. "Yes, it totally would. Everyone in your family would disown you, and it would be quite the story to explain to your niece or nephew someday, but ..."

"Way to look at the bright side." Parker cracked a smile.

"Speaking of the bright side, how's the new job?"

"I'm getting ready to quit."

"What? You said it was the perfect job and the pay was insane for a job with no experience necessary. What happened?"

"I think the couple is having marital issues." Parker stared at the crumbs on her plate, fearing Mindy would see the bigger picture if they made eye contact.

"Lord, I hope it's not because of the kiss at the bar. If that's the case, I will totally stand up in your defense that it was nothing more than too much alcohol, *and* everyone who knows you also knows there is no way you would ever do anything with a married man."

Nope. Not Parker, president of the "I Hate Cheaters Club."

"Sabrina, the wife, travels a lot with her job. I think it's put a lot of stress on their marriage."

"I can see that. You know what else I can see?"

"What's that?"

"Back to your original question: Do I think you're happy? No. I don't. You need to get out more, have some fun, and find a sexy guy to crawl between your legs."

"I don't need—"

"Aaannnd … I know just the guy." Mindy grinned. "Mark. He's the newest doctor at our clinic."

"A podiatrist? No. I cannot date some guy who messes with nasty feet all day."

"Ankles too. That's not too nasty." Mindy failed to keep from giggling. "I know. It's a little gross. I'm glad I just answer the phone. But come on … one date. He's wet behind the ears, just out of school, and so eager to *please*."

"You think hooking up with some eager foot-fetish doctor will magically make me happy?"

"Do you have any better ideas?"

No. She didn't.

AFTER GOING A full week without running into Gus, Parker agreed to a date with the foot doctor. An hour before her date's arrival time, Sabrina messaged her finally offering the five minutes to chat. Parker threw on her strapless white dress that hugged her curves, stopping two inches above her knees. Then she slipped into black heels that showcased her calves.

"Wow, aren't you dressed to kill." Sabrina inspected Parker as she stepped into the foyer. "Please tell me you're not wasting that dress and those shoes on a girls' night out."

Parker rubbed her glossed lips together to contain her grin. "I have a date."

"First date?"

"Yes."

"Tell me about him?"

After weeks of wanting two seconds of Sabrina's time, she chose the worst possible moment to give it to Parker.

"He's a—"

"Sabrina, have you seen the—" Gus walked around the corner from the kitchen, stopping with a jerk to his whole body as his eyes homed in on Parker.

"Look at our little neighbor girl, all grown up and looking stunning. Don't you think, August?"

Parker looked anywhere but directly at Gus. High heels had never been an issue, but for some reason, her knees and ankles wobbled as she stood there under the scrutiny of the Westmans.

"Uh … yes. Wedding?"

"Don't be ridiculous, August. On a Thursday night? Really?" Sabrina rolled her eyes. "Men. What did you want to talk to me about?"

Gus kept his eyes on Parker. She could *feel* it. He didn't take Sabrina's hint to leave the room.

"It can wait a second. Did Gus need something?" Parker said.

"He can wait. Your date can't."

Parker gave in and shot Gus a quick glance. His jaw set, hands fisted, maybe in preparation for impact. He had no way of knowing what she wanted to discuss with Sabrina, but he sure had to have an idea.

"I'm giving you my two-weeks' notice." Parker's voice

trembled along with her knees and ankles.

"Oh? Why? Do you need more money?" Sabrina took a step closer, showing actual concern—probably for herself.

"No. You've been very generous. But I think it's time to find a job that's suited for my degree. As much as I'd love to walk your dog and bake banana bread all day, I think it's time to grow up and find a real job." She cleared her throat. "No offense."

Sabrina shook her head. "None taken. Have you secured another job?"

Parker gave Gus another quick look. His eyes roamed over her body, bringing on a need for an underwear change.

"N-no. Not yet."

"Well, don't feel the need to give me a two-weeks' notice, but also don't feel the need to quit until you've actually accepted another job. I'm sure you have living expenses. Why go without an income if you don't have to? And honestly, I'd be so grateful if you could stay until after our Fourth of July party."

Parker's teeth dug into her lower lip as she searched for the courage to say, "No, thank you," but Gus's eyes on her left her overheating and fuzzy in the head. "Okay. Thanks."

"Great! I'll leave you a list on the counter in the morning. Have a great time on your date." Sabrina lowered her voice. "And if you're a bit late in the morning, no big deal."

Parker thought she could hear Gus's teeth grinding together and the joints in his fingers popping under pressure.

"Thanks. I'd…" she retreated to the door "…better get going."

"Be responsible, *Parker*." Gus narrowed his eyes as a small smirk played across his lips.

The jerk had to say her name after he already had her worked up to a boiling point from his eyes alone.

She winked and flashed him a huge grin as she slowly pulled the door shut behind her. "No worries, Mr. Westman. I have plenty of extra-large condoms in my purse."

Click.

VIRGIN, DOE-EYED, PARKER Cruse would have felt some odd loyalty to her married neighbor. I-pick-all-the-wrong-fucking-men Parker felt zero loyalty. She also felt it necessary to not only let Dr. Mark Blair crawl between her legs on their first date but to distract him for an extra hour in the morning so he would happen to leave after Gus left for work, therefore seeing Dr. Mark's car in her driveway.

"Thanks for last night … and this morning." Mark palmed her ass under her large T-shirt and kissed the life out of her. He possessed some serious skills and the ginger hair, freckles, and killer smile didn't hurt either.

"Thank *you*." She rubbed her bruised lips together.

"So, can I call you sometime?" He fiddled with his key fob.

Mindy had been right. He was adorable and eager to please.

"I'd be disappointed if you didn't." A little disappointed. The foot thing still weirded her out a bit.

After a quick shower and a toasted English muffin with peanut butter, she skipped to the Westmans' feeling ten stories high on life.

"Morning, Rags." She kissed his head then opened his food bin.

"I already fed him."

"Shit!" She jumped. "Gus, what are you doing here? I saw

you … I mean … you're usually gone by now."

He leaned against the doorway, sipping coffee from a to-go cup. "I took the morning off to have the oil changed on my van and tires rotated. A guy from the station brought me home after I dropped it off."

"Oh. Um … okay." The corners of her lips quirked into a light smile when she turned to squeeze past him.

Gus didn't move an inch, making her ass brush against him as she tried to get by. "How was your date?"

With her back to him, she grinned, hating herself for wanting him to ask her that. "Fun. Casual. But definitely fun."

"Fun, huh?"

She pretended to look over the list Sabrina left on the counter. "Yeah. Mark is a doctor, and he's *young*, so lots of fun … lots of stamina. You know, that sort of thing."

"What kind of doctor?"

"Medical doctor."

Gus chuckled, leaning his back against the fridge. "I figured. What's his specialty?"

"Uh … I think legs."

"Legs? Never heard of that specialty."

"Well, you're not a doctor, so I'm sure you aren't familiar with *every* specialty."

"No, I'm not, but my sister is a neurologist. I'll have to ask her about the leg specialty."

She tossed the list on the counter and glared at him for the first time. "He's a podiatrist. There. Are you happy now?"

"Now? No, not now. But I might be in another twenty years if I need him to dig out my thick, yellow, fungal-infected, ingrown toenails."

"For your information, he's *amazing* in bed." Shoulders

back, chin up, Parker stepped closer to Gus, daring him to say another word.

The asshole smirked behind his coffee cup. "I bet Dr. Scholls really hammer-toed you to the headboard ... or did he prefer the footboard?"

"Wanna know how many orgasms I had? How many *extra large* condoms we used?" Something in the deepest depths of her brain warned her to stop talking, but she couldn't get the message through her stubbornness that flowed like a busted pipe without a shut-off valve.

The longer their standoff continued, the more Gus's features softened—surrendered. "I don't need to know your numbers, although I'm sure they're quite impressive. You *really* did look stunning last night, and I hope he was deserving of you."

Blink. Blink. Blink.

"But?"

Gus shook his head. "No buts. You're young and single. I'm old-er and married. One of us deserves to be happy. I choose you."

Her head jutted forward like she didn't hear him correctly. "You choose me? What? My happiness?"

"Yes."

It was sex, not happiness. A date, not marriage. Her ego bowed its head, embarrassed about the temper tantrum it had two minutes earlier, dukes up, ready to fight Gus.

"You deserve to be happy too." A hundred other fighting words waited their turn, but for some reason, the compassionate ones insisted on being heard first.

He breathed out a soft laugh. "My life is far from terrible. Even if my marriage has hit a rough spot, I have so much more than Sabrina to be thankful for."

"Stop it."

His head cocked to the side. "Stop what?"

"This!" Parker turned and ran her hands through her hair. "I shattered a glass of juice when you told me you had sex with your wife. Which is ridiculous because I *hate* cheaters and according to your own admission, you've been crossing the cheating line with me since day one. I should have celebrated your sex with Sabrina."

She laced her fingers on top of her head and stared out the window at Rags chasing a butterfly in the yard. "Why, why didn't I celebrate the sacred union of your love? I'm all for that ... like I'm *so* into that kind of beautiful monogamy. Yay monogamy!" Parker's hands shot above her head like her team scored a touchdown.

As quickly as her hands reached for the ceiling, they flopped back down to her sides, and she turned to face Gus again.

"Yay monogamy." He gave her a weak thumbs-up.

"I think things were better between us when I hated you a little."

"Despicable me?"

"Yes."

"I'm pretty sure I offered to be that person so you could feel better about yourself." He tossed his empty cup in the garbage. "In fact, I worked my ass off to be the guy you hated. And that's not easy for me because by nature I'm a pretty nice guy."

"Nice self-assessment." She rocked back and forth on her heels, staring at her toenails that she hid behind a dense layer of pink polish so Dr. Good Feet wouldn't inspect them too much.

"Do you think you'll leave her?"

"Sabrina?"

"Yes. And I'm not asking if you think you'll leave her for someone else, and definitely not me. We both know I have the leg doctor now. Who could compete with that?" Parker peeked up at him.

A crooked smile touched his lips, and it made her feel connected. That scared her. Gus was not someone she needed to feel any connection to, yet that's exactly what she felt every time they were in the same room.

"He basically treats fungus all day. Good catch, Parker."

"Thanks, Mr. Westman."

He glanced at his phone and sighed as tension drew his brow tight. "My parents have been married for forty years. Both sets of my grandparents made it past their sixtieth anniversaries. I think they all attributed the longevity of their marriages to passion. Live to love. Fight to keep the love. Make up to do it all over again. It's hard to love someone when they reject your love. It's hard to fight when they won't speak. And it's even harder to make up when you don't even know what you're fighting for."

Gus infuriated Parker ninety percent of the time. He spent the other ten percent breaking her heart. She found herself drawn to his imperfections and captivated by the man who wanted nothing more than to love a woman. It made her angry and incredibly envious of Sabrina.

After a minute or so of silence, Gus cleared his throat and glanced at his phone again. "You need to take me to the station to get my van. They're done servicing it."

"I *need* to?"

He grabbed the list off the counter and pointed to the top.

"See. Take Gus to pick up his van."

She snatched it from him. "That's not Sabrina's handwriting, and she doesn't call you Gus."

Gus nodded toward the door. "Come on. I'll buy you a tank of gas and a donut at the station. And for the record, Sabrina does call me Gus when we're being very ... monogamous."

"Fuck you, *August*."

"That's the spirit, *Parker*."

Chapter Fourteen

"HEY, GUS! YOUR van is parked out back. Pam has the keys and your bill," Stu, the owner of the station, said as he helped a young girl add air to her tires. He ended his days with as much grease on his blue pants and matching shirt as any of his employees.

"Thanks, Stu. I appreciate it. I'll be adding this tank of gas to my bill too." Gus grinned at Parker as he topped off the tank to Old Blue, a Chevrolet two-door pick-up truck. It wasn't as old as her farmhouse—but close.

"And a donut." She pulled her hair back into a ponytail.

"And a donut." Gus screwed on the gas cap. He couldn't remember the last time Sabrina ate a donut or anything fried or frosted. He couldn't say anything to guilt Parker, who had the attention of every guy in the station with her snug, white tank top and gray shorts—very short shorts. Nothing more than miles of tan legs and defined arms.

"Hey, Gus. How's it going?" The bell on the station door chimed as Pam called from the register. "Who's your friend?"

"Pam, this is Parker, my ride and Sabrina's assistant."

"*B*-team assistant," Parker mumbled, inspecting the re-maining donuts and the rotating display of hot food.

"Nice to meet you."

"You too." Parker shot her a quick smile before returning

her attention to the overcooked food and slim pick of donuts.

"Add the gas on pump six to my bill too, please."

"You got it. Anything else?"

"And a donut," Gus said.

"Two." Parker fished out *two* donuts with the clear tongs. "And a slice of sausage pizza."

"Anything else?" Gus eyed her, having trouble hiding his grin.

With the slice of pizza in one hand and the bakery bag pinched between her teeth, she grabbed a blue sports drink out of the cooler. "And this," she mumbled, holding up the bottle as she walked toward the register.

He tossed down his credit card, giving Parker a perked eyebrow. "You're an expensive ride."

She shrugged. "You're cutting into my lunch break."

Gus pressed the home button to his phone. "It's ten forty-five."

"I skipped breakfast and burned a lot of calories last night. Remember?"

Gus coughed into his fist, hiding his expression from Pam's curious eyes.

"Need a bag for your stuff, honey?" Pam asked.

"No thanks." Parker headed to the door, folding the piece of pizza in half and shoving a third of it into her mouth. "Gus, grab my donuts and drink. Thanks," she mumbled over a mouthful of pizza.

He gave Pam an awkward smile and followed Parker. "Thanks, Pam."

The door to her truck creaked when she opened it.

"I saw some WD-40 in your shed."

"Ugh! It's terrible isn't it?" She took the drink and bag

from him before hopping into the driver's seat. "It's been greased a million times. I think it's become grease resistant."

Gus rested his arms on the roof and leaned in slightly as she licked the oil from the cheese and sausage off her fingers. "I find it odd that your mom touts your culinary skills, yet you're fine with eating stale donuts and greasy, convenience store pizza."

She twisted off the cap to the sports drink and gulped half of it down, ending with a breathless sigh. "Don't tell my mom I ate this. I'd never hear the end of it. All the grease could make me sick, but damn it tastes so good now." A soft moan vibrated up her throat as she attacked the cake donut with white frosting and pink sprinkles. After swallowing, she took another few gulps of the blue liquid sugar. "I always pay at the pump, so this stuff doesn't tempt me."

"You do realize you're an adult now, right?"

"I know." She held the last bite of the donut up to his mouth.

He shook his head.

"Come on. It's amazing."

Continuing to shake his head, he chuckled. "So we're back to amazing again, like at the brewery the night of my birthday when everything was *amazing* to you."

She licked her sticky lips then wrinkled her nose. "I'm afraid your memory of that night is a little better than mine. Here, you have to."

He wasn't quick enough to dodge the bite of donut she smashed into his lips. Dry and *not* awesome, just as he suspected. "Thank you, Parker."

As she cackled with her head thrown back, he bent down, fisted the hem of her white tank top, and used it as a napkin—

trying desperately to ignore how soft and warm her skin felt when his knuckles grazed it.

"Hey! What the hell?"

"Oh…" he stood up " …sorry, but payback is a bitch, Parker."

Narrowing her eyes, she growled. "Enough with the 'Parker,' and you're right. Payback *is* a bitch."

Gus wiped the rest of his mouth with the hem of his shirt, not missing the quick glance she made when he pulled it up, exposing his abs. Another dick move to add to his growing list, but he wiped more than he needed because it had been too long since a woman looked at him the way Parker did—involuntarily wetting her lips.

"I don't get it. 'Parker' is your name. Ms. Cruse makes me sound like some sixty-year-old professor handing you the results to your final exam."

"Well, it's better than the way you say my first name."

"Which is how exactly?"

She rolled her eyes as if his question were that crazy, then fished out the second donut—chocolate glazed. "You know." Half the donut fit into her mouth, leaving Gus wondering what other large items she could accommodate.

He thanked God for his choice of jeans that morning, keeping his dick contained—painfully contained. "No. I don't know."

Parker put her hand over her filled-to-capacity mouth. "Dirty."

"Dirty?" He laughed.

She nodded, chewing slowly like he might be doing the Heimlich on her if she couldn't completely swallow. "Yes," she mumbled then swallowed twice. "It sounds dirty … or …

erotic when you say my name."

"Par-ker." He shrugged. "No. I don't think it sounds dirty or erotic." "P-ar-k-er." He rolled his eyes to the sky then shook his head. "Nope. You're crazy. I say it like everyone else says it."

"You don't. Trust me." She held the other half of her donut in her mouth as she fastened her seat belt. Then she took one more bite and tossed the last bite into the sack. "But I don't have time to argue with you. I have important chores to do for your wife, including finalizing things for your big Fourth of July extravaganza."

"Barbecue."

She mocked him with a laugh. "Oh, buddy, this is so much more than a barbecue. I've booked a local band, and even though it's not on the list, I might see if Romeo is available."

He grumbled, keeping his angry words indiscernible. "It's still a barbecue."

Parker laughed again. "There's no grill involved and no barbecue sauce. The menu looks more like a high tea. I was told nothing fried, nothing messy, nothing with too much onion or garlic, and nothing that's still stuck to a bone. Only bottled beer and white wine. Sangria will be served, but not allowed in the house, which seems doable since the tent that's getting set up in your backyard is nicer than a lot of starter homes."

Thoughts of murdering his wife had never crossed his mind ... until that moment. "I need to make a phone call. Thanks again for the ride."

A smile came warm and inviting from her lips, and for that brief moment her smile was all that mattered. *That's* what made him act the way he did, say things that were inappropriate, be reckless with his marriage. Feeling nothing but sunshine and bliss tempted him in ways he never imagined. Parker Cruse was all sunshine and bliss.

"Bye, Mr. Westman." She winked.

He shut her door and blinked, bringing him back to reality and his wife who had morphed into some hoity-toity hostess.

GUS WAITED UNTIL his van was parked outside the new construction house, right behind Abe's truck. Calling Sabrina en route might have landed him in the ditch or in the middle of a multi-car pileup. Twenty minutes later, he still couldn't keep the anger from shaking his hands.

"I've got like … two minutes, August. What do you need?"

"Mind telling me why our 'small barbecue' has turned into something fit for royalty?"

"God, August! Please tell me *this* isn't why you're calling me in the middle of the day."

"Barbecue, Sabrina. A grill or smoker, marshmallows, fire pit, lawn chairs, and beer in a can or maybe a keg with a stack of red cups. What the hell are you thinking? A tent? Sangria? We aren't those people!"

"Calm down. I'm not asking you to do anything more than show up—preferably in something that doesn't have some sports or brand-name logo plastered to the front of it, and *no* hat."

At that moment he vowed never to take off his Cubs cap or wear anything but T-shirts with big-ass logos.

"I'm not paying for a dime of this."

A condescending laugh trickled in his ear, like acid on his nerves. "That's why we opened separate checking accounts last year."

He held his middle finger up to the phone. "Yeah, we didn't need to separate our money when I had bigger paychecks."

"I don't have time for your insecurities right now. One of us has a job that doesn't leave time for pointless conversations about bruised egos. Goodbye, August."

He chucked his phone onto the dash. "Fuck!"

Tap. Tap. Tap.

Gus turned as Abe's knuckles rapped against the window. He shoved open the door, forcing Abe to retreat a few steps.

"Let me guess. A simple oil change and tire rotation turned into new brakes, new battery, and a bill three times what you were expecting."

"No." Gus slammed the door and stalked toward the house. "The love of my life has turned into an unrecognizable ..." He bit his tongue as words like bitch and wench ran through his mind. It wasn't Abe's business.

"Shit. That's why you asked me about my experience with cheating. You're not happy at home."

"It's just a rough patch." He inspected the work Abe had already done. In spite of his fondness of logo shirts and baseball caps, Gus prided himself on being a perfectionist with his job.

"A rough patch or have you fallen into a fucking canyon. The barren, unforgiving kind that indiscriminately takes lives before anyone can rescue you?"

As much as Gus wanted to blame Parker for the state of his marriage, he couldn't. He berated himself for trying to use her as an excuse to look for imperfections between him and his wife. But their problems existed before Parker—in only a bra and panties—answered her door. If he never laid eyes on those legs or saw that smile again, Sabrina would still be a bitch that grew out of nowhere.

Maybe she was on drugs. Maybe some parasite invaded her brain, changing her personality. Whatever it was, he couldn't live the rest of his life mourning the woman he married, despising the stranger in his bed, and pining for the girl next door.

"I don't need to be rescued."

"Famous last words, my friend … famous last words."

GUS FINISHED HIS day on autopilot, doing his best to ignore Abe and his concerned expressions. He arrived home to his parents' red Ford Escape parked in the circle drive and Parker roaming the yard with a five-gallon bucket. She still wore the *short* shorts and donut stained tank top from that morning. Sabrina's BMW parked in the garage came as the most shocking surprise.

He removed his boots in the mudroom and entered an empty kitchen. "Hello?"

"Out here, sweetie," his mom, Tessa, called from the screened-in porch.

"Who died?" Gus asked.

"No one, sweetie." Tessa smiled, tucking her graying, chin-length hair behind her ear. "We were out for a drive and thought we'd stop and say hi. We haven't seen Sabrina in weeks."

Gus eyed his wife, still in her perfectly-pressed dress and heels, sipping a glass of red wine. "I'm shocked you're home."

She shrugged. "I had a bit of a headache, so I came home early. I guess it's fate since I haven't spoken with your parents in a while."

Gus nodded slowly.

"You know I've got some weed killer that would work much faster on your dandelion problem than the young lady out there pulling them one at a time." His dad, Gerald, chuckled while watching Parker.

"She said those chemicals could be harmful to Rags, and I agree with her." Sabrina brought her wine glass to her lips, shooting Gus an evil glare like he'd been trying to kill their dog.

"So Parker pulling weeds is your happy hour entertainment?"

Gerald whistled, shaking his head. "That girl does not stop. Hard worker. Nice young lady too. Your mom and I thoroughly enjoyed chatting with her the day she brought us a loaf of banana bread. She can bake too. If your brother weren't hell-bent on dating high-maintenance airheads, I'd fix them up."

"Bran's just young and finding his way," Tessa defended their youngest son as she glided gently in the padded patio chair.

Gus, the middle child, had good work ethic. Tabitha, his older sister the neurosurgeon, had a near genius I.Q., but Bran, at twenty-five, had no interest in finding a purpose, a real job, or a relationship that lasted longer than one night.

It amused Gus to think of 'hardworking' Parker being all that different from Bran. Her résumé consisted of a string of temp jobs. And on a Friday night, she had nothing better to do than pick dandelions.

"She might be off the market anyway." Sabrina looked out at Parker. "From what she said, her date last night went really well. A young doctor."

"A podiatrist." Gus grunted.

His mom laughed. "August, podiatrists are medical doctors too."

"They sure are." Gerald nodded. "My last visit was with this new guy, Dr. Blair. Great sense of humor and my bunions have never been better."

"Dr. Blair? Is his first name Mark?" Sabrina asked.

"Yes, you know him?"

"No. But that's who Parker went out with last night."

"Oh lord …" Gus said under his breath.

"Parker?" Gerald called, adjusting his Hawkeye baseball cap—like father like son—except his hat covered up a ninety-percent bald head.

She glanced in their direction, brushing away a few stray hairs from her face with the back of her wrist.

"Dr. Blair is my doctor!"

Gus rolled his eyes.

"Great guy. Well done, young lady." He gave her a thumbs-up.

She gave him the A-okay sign and her signature smile. "Thanks, Mr. Westman, he sure is."

"Well, if you'll excuse me I'm going to lie down for a bit to get rid of this headache before dinner." Sabrina hugged his parents before shooting Gus a cold look on her way in the house.

"Feel better, dear," Tessa said.

"We'd better get going too, Mama." Gerald winked at Tessa.

She gave him an endearing smile. Sabrina used to look at Gus that way.

"We're looking forward to your Fourth of July party."

Tessa kissed Gus on the cheek.

He slipped his shoes on and followed them out to their Ford Escape. "I'm glad *you* are."

His dad patted him on the shoulder. "I heard. No barbecue. I see ya fighting it, but once you've been married for as long as your mother and me, you'll know just to say, 'Yes, ma'am.'"

Gus questioned if his marriage would last forty years as his parents' had. After recent events, he wondered if his marriage would last another forty days. "That's code for taking it up the backside, right?"

Tessa gave him a disapproving frown.

"No." Gerald shook his head to reassure his wife as she got in the car. After she closed her door, he grimaced at Gus. "Yes, it's code for that. Bye, young lady! Tell Dr. Blair hi, if you see him before I do."

Parker waved. "Sure thing."

After his parents drove off, Gus made his way to Parker. "Dandelions will not kill anyone. Stop pulling them." He reached down and picked one that she hadn't gotten to and blew on it.

"Stop!" She grabbed it from him. "You're blowing seeds everywhere which will make *more* dandelions."

He chuckled. "So."

"Even if I have to make up a fake job, as soon as this party is over, I'm quitting. But for now, I'd appreciate you not making my job harder."

He shoved his hands into his jeans' pockets. "About this party … I'll pay you double what she's paying you if you make it the Fourth of July celebration *I* want."

Parker glanced up from her squatted position. "Excuse

me?"

"She's paying you thirty an hour to plan this? I'll pay you sixty an hour, but everything is what I want."

She shook her head and returned her attention to the last patch of yard still marred with the forbidden yellow-flowered weed. "She'll fire me."

"Who cares? You're quitting anyway."

"Not the same thing. I'm not moving, which means I'll still occasionally see her and I won't have her pissed off at me from now to eternity. Thanks, but no thanks. And why would you do this? No matter how mad she'd be with me, she'd be ten times madder at you? Is that what you want?"

"What if it is?"

Parker paused. His marriage wasn't her business either, but she had a unique insight into his relationship with Sabrina that no one else had. He wasn't proud of that.

"Then I'd say you're trying to sabotage your marriage."

"Why would I be the one sabotaging it? Maybe this whole ridiculous party is her way of sabotaging it."

Parker laughed while standing up and peeling off her gardening gloves. "I'll grant three of your requests for this party without telling her. Then at least I can play dumb like I didn't know you weren't allowed any say."

"Three wishes?" Gus squinted, head cocked to the side. "Like a magic genie?"

She sighed and traipsed through the yard carrying a bucket full of dandelions. "Sure, like a magic genie."

"Do I need to rub you in a certain way for you to grant my wishes?"

"Mr. Westman—"

"Is my father, stop calling me that, *Parker*."

"I'm dating someone. You're married. There will be no rubbing." She opened the gate between their yards then turned. "Understood?"

"You hooked up with a guy that's filed, sanded, or done some weird shit with my dad's bunions. I'd hardly call that dating. And I hope you think of that *if* you do see him again."

"Three wishes. And I don't want your double hourly rate."

"No?"

"No. I want you to tell me how you met Sabrina."

Those verbal punches always came out of nowhere, turning fun moments into brutal reality checks.

He leaned his back against the wood fence post and folded his arms over his chest. "Her best friend married one of my friends from high school. Maid of Honor, Best Man sort of thing. Vegas wedding. Sabrina lived in Phoenix and invited me for a visit since I'd never been there. And the rest is history."

"But you fell in love and married her. Tell me that part of the story."

"For fuck's sake, you broke a glass in my kitchen when I mentioned the sex and you said you didn't want to know that, but now you want to know how or why I fell in love with her?"

Dropping the bucket by her feet, she mirrored his arms-crossed-over-chest stance. "Yes. I do."

"She was spunky and competitive, especially with her brother. Electricity is my thing, and she had this addictive energy that drew me in. I knew she'd take over the world someday. Her passion and confidence were so damn sexy, but she was never arrogant, except with her brother. And she loved me and my blue collar job, my Midwest upbringing, and my laid-back attitude. I suppose in some ways we were opposites, but the good kind that just ... worked."

"So what happened?"

He shrugged then adjusted his Cubs cap. "We just stopped working. And it's so fucking disheartening because I have no idea why. It's like one day she woke up and my existence in her life seemed to piss her off. It felt so out of the blue, but maybe it was gradual. Maybe I didn't see it because I so rarely see her anymore."

Parker nodded thoughtfully.

"Happy now?" Gus asked.

She grabbed the bucket again. "Not happy. It's a very sad story. But I'm satisfied."

"And why is that?"

Turning toward her house, she walked away. "Because I wanted *you* to remember why you fell in love with her."

Gus hadn't forgotten why he fell in love with his wife. He simply couldn't find her anymore. But he was determined to say goodbye to the stranger that had taken over her body.

"Jello shots. A piñata. And you stay until the party is over."

"What?" She turned.

"Those are my three wishes."

He waited and a few seconds later, she chased away the impending darkness with her smile.

"What flavor of Jello?"

"Cherry. Is there any other kind?"

Parker shook her head and continued home.

Chapter Fifteen

THE NEXT TWO weeks vanished. Parker planned the party to both Mr. and Mrs. Westman's standards—sort of. She also squeezed in two more dates with Mark. However, they didn't have sex again. She insisted he date her first if they were going to be anything more than a casual hookup.

Gus made it impossible to be around him with his lingering stares and suggestive comments that left her running for an underwear change. It felt like he had his eye on some prize and that it made his time left with Sabrina more bearable; Parker wasn't too sure she wanted to be his prize no matter how he affected her with his glances, smirks, and seductive pronunciation of her name—no matter how much she simply loved being in the same room as him.

Their relationship had been branded with a cheating stamp even though they'd never had sex. It would forever weigh on her conscience even if he divorced his wife. Parker didn't know if she could live with that. But she couldn't deny thinking about Gus when she was with Mark. That had to mean something.

"Why is there a fucking piñata hanging from the tree out back?" Sabrina charged down the stairs in her red, white, and blue dress fit more for an inauguration than a Fourth of July party.

Parker grimaced from the kitchen as she messaged the caterer to make sure they were running on time. "Uh ... Gus requested it. Did you two not discuss it?" She settled on the innocent-bystander role for the day.

"Of course not! How could you think I'd agree to something so juvenile? It looks hideous hanging there next to the tent." Under the stress of her meltdown, a few strands of blond hair sprang from her braided bun.

Parker's nose wrinkled. "Sorry. I assumed you two made some compromises."

"I have friends and colleagues who have flown in from Chicago, New York, and Miami; it's embarrassing enough that I live out in the sticks, but there's no way I'm going to allow them to see *that thing* hanging from my tree!"

Gus eased open the door to the garage. "Jesus, Sabrina ... I'm pretty sure the guys setting up the tent heard your whole hissy fit."

He blocked one exit from the kitchen while Sabrina blocked the other, leaving Parker stranded in the middle of Hell.

"Take. It. Down. Now." Sabrina stomped her bare feet against the tile with each word. A typical three-year-old move.

"If I take down the piñata, then I'm getting out the grill and throwing on some brats and a beer-butt chicken."

"This isn't funny. Do you hate me this much?"

"Wow, that's ironic. I thought the same thing when you replaced our close family and friends barbecue with this uppity party complete with strangers from *Chicago, New York, and Miami*, white table cloths, and a mandatory stick up your ass requirement to attend."

Sabrina slowly shook her head as tears filled her eyes. "Your jealousy knows no boundaries."

Gus rested his hands on his hips and looked at the ceiling, pushing a long breath out his nose. "And what exactly am I jealous about?"

"My success. The money I make. It emasculates you."

"No. No. And fuck no."

The caterer texted Parker back. "So …" She interrupted the silence. "The caterer is running on time. I …" She inched her way toward the back door, giving Gus the move out of my way look. "I'm going to see how the guys are doing with the tent and take Rags over to my place so I can do a final sweep for poop."

Gus didn't move. Instead, his eyes roamed along every inch of Parker like he hadn't eaten for days and she would be his first meal. With her back to Sabrina, she couldn't tell if his wife saw the same look. Parker hoped not because there was nothing subtle about it.

"Excuse me," Parker whispered.

He dragged his eyes up her legs and over her chest as if he *wanted* Sabrina to know. When he made eye contact, he grinned. "Of course, *Parker.*"

It was the Parker of all Parkers. The ultimate fuck-you to Sabrina and an I'm-coming-for-you warning to Parker. She'd hoped for an amicable relationship with Sabrina after quitting. Gus ruined it with one long look and one seductive word.

He eased to the side, giving her minimal space to squeeze past him. As soon as she shut the door behind her, Parker leaned against it and gasped for breath. The time had come to test Gus's theory. Was Sabrina ready to see her cheating husband or would her lack of readiness veil the obvious?

CARS FILLED EVERY inch of the Westmans' drive as well as Parker's drive and front yard. She rented two golf carts and hired a couple of kids on summer break from college to drive people from their car to the tent so the ladies wouldn't have to navigate Parker's gravel drive and grassy yard in heels.

The band played, the caterers served hors d'oeuvres and wine, and Sabrina fluttered around greeting guests while the piñata still hung from the tree next to the enormous white tent. It represented the Westmans' marriage—dangling by a thread or maybe dead, swaying in the breeze with a noose around its neck.

"Part of me is disappointed you followed Sabrina's dress code."

Parker jumped when Gus leaned over behind her to whisper in her ear.

"And part of me is so fucking hard right now because this tiny white dress of yours hides so little."

She swallowed hard and stepped forward a bit to distance herself from his dizzying warmth, minty breath, and nerve-wracking voice.

"You've been drinking." Parker gritted her teeth as she nodded, plastering on a smile for the couple entering the tent. It wasn't her job to guard the entrance, but it's where she felt most comfortable—a quick getaway in case World War III broke out between Gus and Sabrina.

"Not a drop. I like being one hundred percent sober when I look at you. No need to dull my senses when the *feeling* I have around you is pure *desire*."

Another pair of clean, dry underwear ruined by his words.

"August?" Sabrina waved him toward her, a painfully fake smile plastered to her face as her so-called friends stood in a circle around her.

"Duty calls." He walked toward Sabrina but glanced over his shoulder to give Parker a grin and a wink.

Her crimson skin nearly bled on her dress as sweat beaded along her brow, in her armpits, and even between her cleavage. Yet she still grinned because he was the only guy there wearing shorts and of course his matching Cubs shirt and cap.

Retreating to the house, she grabbed her phone from the kitchen counter and fled for refuge in their bathroom at the top of the stairs.

"Damn you, Gus!" She grumbled while shoving wads of tissue into her armpits. The screen to her phone lit up with a text from Gus and a missed one from Sabrina. She pinched her eyes shut and blew out a slow breath.

Sabrina: *Be a dear and bring me my lip gloss from my vanity. xo*

She wasn't livid with Parker. Gus's theory was right, at least with his wife.

Gus: *Where are you? I'm eating blah, triangular-shaped sandwiches. When I'm done, I'm going to cleanse my palate with you.*

"Not helping, Mr. Westman." She shoved another wad of tissue in between her cleavage and one in her panties between her legs.

After five minutes of sweat control and splashing cold water on her face, she hurried to the master bedroom to get Sabrina's lip gloss. There were five lip glosses neatly lined up on her vanity.

Parker: *Which lip gloss?*

Sabrina: *Clear. The rest are shades of pink.*

Parker disagreed. They were all shades of *clear*.

Sabrina: *Sorry. The one I want is in my travel bag. Drawer on the right side.*

The travel bag had a ton of zipper compartments. She froze after opening one of the side compartments filled with condoms. As bile climbed up her throat, Parker tried to reason. They had to be for when she traveled with Gus, except according to him, they never went anywhere together, and she knew Sabrina was on the pill because she had to pick up her refill two weeks earlier.

Sabrina: *Did you find it?*

Parker closed the side compartment and hurried to find the lipgloss. With shaky knees and the clear lipgloss in hand, she returned to the party.

"Thank you, dear." Sabrina smiled as she unscrewed the lipgloss. "If you see Gus, remind him to go feed Rags."

Parker nodded slowly. Every word an echo competing with her thundering pulse. "I'll … um … go feed him."

"Thank you. Hurry back before dessert is served."

Chapter Sixteen

WITH GUS NOWHERE in sight and Sabrina needing a favor, Parker jumped at the opportunity to make herself scarce.

After grabbing a cupful of his food from the mudroom, she slipped off her heels and walked through the cool grass to her property. "Rags!" She locked the fence gate and whistled for him to follow her to her house.

"Are you hungry?" She shut the door and grabbed a bowl from her kitchen.

His whole backside shook with excitement.

"I'm starving."

"Shit! Gus ... where ... how long have you been here?"

He chuckled. "I followed you and Rags inside. How did you not hear me behind you?"

She shook her head. "I'm just a little ... out of it."

"Where are my Jello shots?"

Her eyes narrowed. "In my fridge. You really think it's a good idea to take them to the party now?"

He locked the door behind him.

"W-what are you doing?"

"I thought we could have our own party. The kind where no one else is allowed in."

"Nope. Not a good idea. I already RSVP'd to the Westmans' party and dessert will be served soon, so … no way. No side parties. Unlock the door."

Gus stepped closer.

"Besides, you ate. I didn't. And I'm hungry. So I should get back before all the food is gone."

"The food is shit." He backed her into the counter and set a mysterious brown bag behind her.

Parker couldn't breathe, and like Gus she was sober and feeling *everything*.

"Don't leave your wife for me," she said so fast, six words sounded like one.

Even with the knowledge of Sabrina's likely affair, she didn't want to be anyone's mistress or a homewrecker. She didn't want to be with a cheater.

Gus flipped his cap backward and ducked down, kissing her neck while brushing her hair over her shoulder. "I'm divorcing my wife."

Parker hated how her body betrayed her mind. "Not for—"

"For *me*, Parker. Only me." He trapped her earlobe between his teeth as his hands gripped her hips for leverage, pressing his body to hers.

Her head fell back, eyes closed, as he dotted kisses along her jaw. She grabbed his biceps for support. "This is … wrong," she whispered as his lips hovered over hers.

"It's not wrong anymore. It just *is*." He kissed her hard, and she moaned into his mouth as their tongues tasted each other.

When his hands slid up her waist and cupped her breasts, part of her died of guilt while part of her came to life as she felt wanted, desired, and filled with hope for something of her very own.

She thought of the condoms and let him unzip the back of her dress—sin loved a good excuse.

"I-I don't..." her words came ragged and breathless as he worked his mouth back down her neck "...think we ... can do this."

Gus's lips, pressed against her skin, curled into a smile. "I disagree. I'm feeling *very* capable of this."

Her dress dropped to her ankles. The brush of his teeth against her bare nipples shot waves of prickly chills along her skin.

"Gus ..." She thought of the condoms as her eyelids grew heavy, and she arched her back as his hands held her breasts, thumbs ghosting over her nipples—sin loved justification.

Their affair started weeks before that moment. *Would sex make it any worse?* Hell was Hell. She could only be sent there for eternity once.

Releasing her breasts, he tossed his cap on the counter and clenched the hem of his shirt, removing it in one quick motion. So much for old man love handles and a beer belly. Gus had sexy muscles and a slender waist. Parker had seen it more than once, but each time it amazed her. There was no way Sabrina's possible affair had anything to do with her husband letting himself go.

It took her a few seconds to realize they were both staring at each other's naked chests.

He smiled. She smiled but hers faded a bit, and she covered her breasts with her hands.

"Uh ... what's in the bag?"

"Parker ..." He kissed her hard again. She released her breasts and threaded her hands through his hair. His hands began to unfasten his navy cargo shorts, exposing the hard bulge barely contained by his briefs.

"N-no …" She broke their kiss. "Not sex."

Gus's hands gripped the counter on either side of her as his forehead rested against hers. "Jesus, Parker … o-okay." His ragged breaths washed over her face. He nodded against her. "No sex."

"No sex." Her voice quivered as her hands clawed at his back. Those words were the only part of her that maintained control, which would have been great had they been in the middle of phone sex.

When Gus's hands slid under her ass, she sucked in a sharp breath. She wrapped her legs around him as he rested her butt on the counter and cradled the back of her head keeping it from hitting the cabinet.

Pressed to her lips, he moved his mouth with hers and rocked his pelvis into her. His erection rubbed against her clit. Two thin layers of cotton kept them from having sex.

"St-stop …." she murmured over his lips. Again, her hands clawed him closer. A complete mind-body disconnect.

Condoms. Sabrina had condoms in her travel bag.

"I will…" he said in a husky voice as he rocked into her again "…if you will." His hand made a firm claim to her breast.

Her arms and legs pulled him closer as her heels dug into his backside—every move greedy and mindless. Gus released the back of her head and slipped his hand under her bottom so he could thrust harder against her, each vying for more friction.

"I'm going to … stop …" She dropped her head to his shoulder and her teeth dug into his firm flesh.

He growled as she bit harder, returning the favor as he sucked the sensitive skin along her neck, rocking their bodies together over and over. "Me ... too." His fingers gripped her ass tighter.

"Ar-are ... you ... stopping?" Every muscle in her body contracted.

They kissed with more passion than she thought possible in a million lifetimes.

"Mmm-hmm ..." He moaned between them.

Parker's eyes closed to a galaxy of stars. Waves of euphoria rippled along her body settling between her legs in a hard, heavy pulse. She bit her lips together to keep from crying out.

Gus's hand slammed against the cabinet behind her as his hips jerked into her one last time. "Fuccckk!"

After a few moments of idleness and labored breathing, Parker feathered her hands down his back, inch by inch, as they continued to cling to each other. She let herself have a timeout from the guilt as she imagined a life where she could feel the contours of his body close to hers every day.

Gus ghosted his fingertips along her bare legs, leaving a wake of goose bumps behind them. Slowly, they pulled back just enough to look at each other.

He smiled.

She smiled.

At the same time, they looked down between them at her drenched panties wadded and shoved to the side, exposing part of her soft, pink flesh. A large dark spot stained his gray briefs as well as a wet streak above his waistband that had failed to keep it all contained.

"Why is this sexy as fuck?" Gus asked.

Parker giggled. "My mom would be having a mini vomit about now."

He chuckled as their gazes met again.

"Thanks for stopping." She rolled her lips together, but it didn't completely hide her grin.

"It was the gentlemanly thing to do."

She let out a toothy smile. It didn't stand a chance against Gus Westman.

"Best smile in the world." He kissed her—a quick peck at first, but their lips felt like two magnets with an attraction too strong to resist.

With the same effect as throwing another log on the fire, a new flame flared between them. An insatiable hunger.

Gus fisted her hair with one hand while his other hand slid between her legs for the first time. They may have gotten off on each other like two young teenagers, but they both craved so much more.

He teased her hypersensitive flesh with the pad of his finger, dragging his mouth to her ear as she began to pant. "I want to put my mouth where my finger is, *Parker*."

Rags scratched at the door. They ignored him. Parker was well on her way to a second orgasm. He scratched again and barked too.

"Rags ..." Gus groaned.

Parker pressed her hand flat against his chest. "Let him out."

Gus cupped the back of her neck. "When I walk away, you're going to jump down and put your dress back on, aren't you?"

Rags barked again.

Amusement ghosted across her swollen lips as she released him.

He stepped back but didn't fasten his shorts as he walked to the door. "Dog ... you have the worst timing." Rags ran out and barked a few more times.

"He's telling everyone at the party what we did." Parker's nose wrinkled as she pulled on her dress.

Gus frowned, watching his prediction come true. He fastened his pants and grabbed his T-shirt off the floor. "I don't regret it ... unless you do."

"Well, I'm not exactly proud of it." She zipped her dress and fixed her mussed hair. "My boyfriend cheated on me with my sister. I sabotaged her wedding day—"

"You what?"

Parker shook him off. "It's a long story." She grabbed the tray of Jello shots from the fridge. "The point is I should be the last person in the world willing to have an affair with a married man." Tipping the plastic cup to her mouth, she took a cherry-vodka shot. "It's like the worst case of karma ever. And if I say I don't regret it, then it's implied I'm not ashamed of it, but I am." She took another shot. "Yet I let it happen. I *wanted* it to happen. But there's no way in hell I'd tell any of my family or friends about us."

"You made these for me." Gus grabbed her wrist as she brought the third cup to her mouth. He redirected it to his mouth. "Mmm ... cherry."

"Is there any other kind?" She grinned.

He cupped the back of her head and pressed his lips to her forehead. A tender gesture that came at the exact moment she needed it most. She fought back the tears because Gus felt like home, but he wasn't her home, and he wasn't the guy she could brag about to her friends, or invite to dinner with her parents.

"I won't drag this out. Just promise you'll wait for me ... preferably without letting Dr. Good Feet in your bed."

She blinked back her emotions and pushed away, quickly

downing another shot. "I can't wait for a married man. That's the most pathetic thing ever. It ranks up there with turning down scholarships to play your favorite sport to follow some guy to his college of choice."

Gus double-fisted the shots and took them one right after the other. "I can't get a divorce overnight. But I'll pack a bag and leave tonight. I'll stay with my parents or at a hotel if it makes you more comfortable."

"I don't care where you sleep. It's none of my business."

He grabbed her arms and pulled her to him. "What if I *want* to be your business?"

"This isn't love, Gus. Not yet," she whispered.

"Love is stupid. So I don't care if it's love. You're the best part of every damn day. You're sunshine, and laughter, and the fucking oxygen in my lungs. If this life is a game, you make me want to play it forever, be damned who wins or loses."

Narrowing her eyes, she twisted her lips. "Hmm … compelling speech, but I don't buy it. You already gave me the speech on desire. We look like hell and smell like sex right now because of desire, not oxygen to your lungs. You're going to have to show me something more than an erection for me to believe I'm your sunshine."

He released her and turned her toward the counter. "Look in the sack, Sunshine."

She grabbed the brown bag and looked inside. "Mr. Westman—"

"I'm not your teacher."

"Too bad. I've always had fantasies about sex with someone of authority." She reached her hand in the bag.

"What subject do you want me to teach you?" He stepped closer like an animal on the prowl.

Parker giggled, pulling a sprinkled donut out of the sack. She took a bite then offered him one.

He shook his head. "You should eat the slice of pizza first before it gets any colder."

"My mom would not approve of you feeding my secret addiction, but I find it sweet."

"I thought I was your secret addiction."

Rags barked at the back door.

"I think Rags likes me more than you." Parker took another bite of the donut.

Gus let him inside, shaking his head as Rags ran past him straight to her. She grabbed the slice of pizza out of the bag and tossed Rags a piece of sausage.

"You feed him food scraps and turkey jerky, of course he likes you."

Her smile evaporated slowly as she set the rest of the pizza and donut on the counter, wiping her hands on a towel. "You're going to break my heart. I can feel it." Tears stung her eyes. "One month." She blinked back her emotions. "I let you ruin me in one month."

Gus tipped her chin up with his finger under it. "I won't break your heart. But you're breaking mine by saying I've ruined you."

With one blink, a lone tear trailed down her cheek. "I thought I was a good person," she whispered.

Offering a sad smile, Gus softly kissed her lips and then her wet cheek. "You're the best person. I'm going to prove it to you. I promise." The sincerity in his voice comforted her, but it was easy to feel a false sense of security when it was the two of them in their little bubble.

"If I asked you to, would you go announce to everyone at

the party that you just dry humped your wife's assistant?"

"Yes." He gave her a resolute nod. "And I'm pretty sure there was nothing 'dry' about what we just did."

A tingling swept up the back of her neck as her face felt impossibly hot. She thought of all the panty changes she'd attributed to him.

"So …" He took a step back and jabbed his thumb over his shoulder. "I'll go announce our recent physical encounter."

"No!" Parker lunged for him and fisted his shirt. "I just wanted to know if you would."

He chuckled. "I'm yours."

She shook her head, feeling an ache in the back of her throat and a sluggish heartbeat beneath her weighted chest. "You're not, and that's what I'm afraid of."

"I'm. Yours." He cradled her head and pressed his forehead to hers.

"It's only been a month. This is crazy."

"I happen to love crazy." He kissed her, and she gripped his arms, feeling weak in the knees.

She pulled back. "Don't say that word."

"More words … okay, Ms. Cruse, what word am I not allowed to say now?"

Parker cleared her throat and gave him a tight smile. "The L word."

"Love?" He laughed.

She nodded, nose wrinkled.

"I said I loved crazy. I didn't say I loved you."

"But it felt close."

"Close?" Gus nodded thoughtfully. "I see. Like I *love* your hair after my hands have thoroughly messed it up?"

Parker felt heart palpitations as he threaded his hands

through her hair, tugging it in different directions until he had her chin tipped up, neck exposed.

He kissed his way from her ear to her collarbone. "Or the way I *love* how your skin feels against my lips?"

She released a breath with a whisper of a moan.

"Or the way I *love* how you whimper under my touch?" His hands ghosted down her arms eliciting a full-body shiver.

"Gus …"

"Don't say my name like that, *Parker*." He lowered to his knees, kissing her body over her dress as his hands skimmed up her bare legs. "I *love* it so much it makes me want to do very dirty things to you."

"God …" Her head dropped, chin to her chest as she stared at him with glazed-over eyes.

He looked up with a sly grin as he pulled down her panties. His fingers ghosted up her legs again, pushing up her dress.

"Gus …" Her weak voice broke his name into fragmented syllables as her eyes drifted shut, hands fisting his hair.

He kissed the inside of one thigh and then the other. "If I can't love you, then I'm just going to love everything about you. And I'm positive I'm going to *love* how you taste." He kissed her, *tasted* her.

Sabrina had condoms in her toiletry bag. She didn't deserve Gus. Parker wasn't sure she did either, but she wanted him. What would her family think of her wanting something that was not hers to have?

Cheater.

Sinner.

Hypocrite.

Worst. Person. Ever.

Chapter Seventeen

"TELL ME HOW you feel." Parker tugged Gus's arm before he opened the door.

They had to get back to the party before he broke his promise not to have sex with Parker. Given what he just did to her, intercourse was not a big deal. At least that was a guy's perspective.

"I feel like a fucking elated disaster."

She blinked, looking down as her posture sagged. "That's an interesting way to feel."

"I have to end my marriage officially."

"You don't have—"

Gus cut her off with an adamant head shake. "I *need* you to remember that my marriage ended long before you came into the picture. Even the times Sabrina and I have had sex over the past few months, it's been nothing more than trying to resuscitate something that's too far gone. But there's still a part of me that feels like a failure."

He cupped the back of her head and kissed her forehead. "I don't feel guilty for how I feel about you or what just happened here, but I feel guilty for dragging you into my mess. I am a prick who said inappropriate things to you and did things that are despicable. My anger at my life—my wife—came out on you. Fuck …" He laughed while shaking his head. "I couldn't think straight. One minute I wanted you to hate me so you would run and protect yourself from me, and then next minute I just *wanted* you. And I didn't give a damn about the rest of the world. I've made you feel guilty and bad about yourself, and for that I am truly sorry."

She hugged him, resting her head on his shoulder. "You *are* the worst, and I've never met anyone more inappropriate. My standards should be so much higher."

"But?" he said slowly.

Her lips pressed to his neck. "That's it. No buts."

Gus leaned back, inspecting her through narrowed eyes. "I'm the worst and most inappropriate person you've ever met and the only reason you're giving me the time of day is because your standards are low?"

"Don't fixate on how pathetic we are." She grinned, slipping her hands into his back pockets. "Besides ..." Her smile faded. "I'm still not convinced you're not going to break my heart."

Releasing a heavy sigh, he turned and opened the door. "You're too busy busting my balls all of the time; my ego's too damaged to break your heart. Now, let's go crack open the piñata."

"WHERE HAVE YOU been?" Gus's dad rested his hand on Gus's shoulder as he walked into the tent a few minutes before Parker, who needed to thank the caterer's on the Westmans' behalf.

"Oh, you know..." Gus took a swig of beer as he watched Sabrina across the room throw her head back in laughter, clearly not missing him a bit "...feeding the dog, trimming my nose hair, and beating the shit out of the piñata."

Gerald laughed. "Can I give you some advice, Son?"

Gus felt sure it wouldn't help his situation at that moment, but he wasn't ready to tell anyone about his intentions until he had a chance to talk with Sabrina. He may have been despicable, but a part of him still cared for the woman he married.

"Go for it, Dad."

"Find happiness."

Gus's thoughts froze. He scratched his temple. "I'm not sure what you mean."

"You're miserable. I've watched the life drain out of my boy for months now. You were our kid who always had a smile on his face. Something has broken your spirit. If it's something between you and Sabrina, then fix it."

"Fix it," Gus repeated, void of all emotion.

Gerald leaned in closer, lowering his voice. "You. Fix you."

A numbness blanketed Gus. "I'm trying," he whispered past the emotions bearing down on his chest.

After a firm squeeze on the shoulder, Gerald walked away. Sabrina's eyes met Gus's, and her smile fell off her face like his mere existence robbed every ounce of her happiness. He grabbed another beer and made his way to his wife and her group of friends, not a one that he'd ever met.

Sabrina's jaw clenched as he approached, and when the two couples next to her looked from Gus back to her, she gave them a painfully fake smile.

"Sabrina, introduce me to your friends. Sorry, I've been MIA, some pranksters put up a piñata in our tree. The only way to get it down was to beat the shit out of it." He reached into his pocket and pulled out a handful of candy. "Candy, anyone?"

"We're good, August," Sabrina gritted behind her smile, which was nothing more than her lips curling like an attack dog. "Everyone, this is my husband, August."

He turned and shook hands with the two overdressed couples. They looked him up and down a few times before formulating their own fake smiles that seemed to be sympathy smiles for his poor wife.

"Did you get dessert, August? He has such a sweet tooth." Sabrina faked a laugh.

Gus's lips twisted as he cocked his head to the side. "Uh … yes. I did. Parker made sure I got my fix."

"Parker is my domestic assistant." Sabrina managed to form a genuine smile when mentioning Parker's name. "She planned everything."

Everyone nodded, and they too found genuine smiles. Gus couldn't begrudge his wife's *domestic* assistant. He too was very fond of every single inch of her.

"In fact, August, you should check on Parker. I messaged her over fifteen minutes ago asking her to bring me a light sweater."

"Good idea. I'd be happy to look for Parker. Nice to meet you. Thanks for coming." He nodded to their guests and made his way to the house.

Rags jumped up from his bed when Gus walked in, but then plopped back down as if he'd wasted his excitement on the wrong person. Parker wasn't in the kitchen, so he went upstairs. The light was on to their bedroom.

"Parker?"

Standing in the middle of their bedroom with her back to him, she turned slowly. Her body shook like the room was a deep freezer.

"What's wrong—"

Gus stopped, his feet unable to take another step as his pulse shot up with panic. The bomb-strapped-to-the-chest look on her face sucked the air from his lungs.

Swollen, red eyes.

Tear-stained cheeks.

Quavering lower lip.

"You just broke m-my heart," she whispered.

"Jesus, Parker, what are you talking about?" He managed to move his legs again, just barely.

She eased opened her hands fisted at her chest, revealing a pregnancy test.

He shook his head, taking the last few steps between them. "I ... where did you get this?"

Her brow pulled tighter. Gus didn't think she could look any more pained. He was wrong.

"I was looking for..." she swallowed and sucked in a shaky breath "...Sabrina's sweater."

He eased it from her hand. The display window was blank. "Has it been used?"

Parker shook her head.

"She's not pregnant."

Bloodshot eyes shot up to meet his gaze. "How can you say that?"

Gus continued to shake his head, willing the whole fucking nightmare to disappear. "Because—"

"NO!" Parker sobbed and yelled at the same time, running her hands through her hair. "You don't get to make up some excuse for this. You fucked her. You *told* me you fucked her!"

Every word hit hard and true. Gus couldn't undo his past, but he could hold on to his future—his happiness. "Parker, listen—"

"No! No more Parker. No more listening to you. I choose the wrong guy every time and it stops now." She shoved him enough to throw off his balance.

He used the wall to right himself and lunged for her, grabbing her arm before she got to the bedroom door.

"Let. Go," she growled.

He grabbed her shoulders and shoved her toward the bathroom, and she tried to wriggle out of his hold.

"Let me go!" She fell into the wall as he released her and shut the door behind him. "Locking me in the bathroom with you won't change anything."

He leaned against the door and crossed his arms over his chest. "Look in the trash."

"Move, Gus!"

Her efforts to shove him aside were met with his refusal to let her go mixed with desperate fear of losing his *happiness.* She'd have to kill him to get past him.

"Look in the trash."

"I'm not looking in your stupid trash!"

"Then I'm not moving."

She bared her teeth as a vein in her forehead popped to the surface. "Fine. Then I walk out and you never contact me again. If that means I have to move, then I'll move."

Gus swallowed hard. His eyes widened under furrowed brows. A painful tightness in his throat made it difficult to breathe. In one month Parker Cruse slammed into his life, shaking his entire existence, magnifying his misery, and cracking open the door to the freedom he *needed.*

After a few moments of silent, unbearable tension, Parker sighed, directing her gaze to the trash. She chewed on the inside of her cheek for another few painful moments, then she pressed the toe of her shoe to the bottom of the stainless steel bin and the lid popped open revealing wadded toilet paper and tampon wrappers.

"She's not pregnant," Gus whispered.

Parker kept her lifeless gaze on the trash. "It doesn't matter."

"The hell it doesn't!" He hated the wall she'd built between them.

"I can't see past the 'desire.' And it's going to ruin me." Regret-filled eyes shifted to meet his as she moved to Sabrina's vanity. "I have to fall in love with my eyes open this time." She unzipped one of the pockets of Sabrina's toiletry bag. "And maybe it's none of my business, but you need to open your eyes too." Parker tossed the condoms onto the vanity counter.

Gus blinked trying to focus. He hadn't purchased condoms in years. Thoughts scrambled to make sense, desperate to glean something that made sense. For a moment he closed his eyes, feeling a bit lightheaded.

"I'm sorry." Parker's words echoed as if she were miles away.

His body jerked, taking a few steps forward, fighting for balance as she turned the doorknob and pulled open the door. Every bit of strength and fight he had wobbled like the rest of him.

When he squeezed his eyes shut, he saw Sabrina on their wedding day, Sabrina in bed wrapped around his body, and long walks at Grey's Lake hand-in-hand with Rags tugging them in every direction. He'd been so blind. *Him.* When Gus opened his eyes to an empty bathroom and a sharp image of condoms on the counter, he turned and ran after Parker.

"Parker?" Sabrina called from downstairs. "Gus?"

Parker was halfway to the stairs when Gus covered her mouth with his hand before she could answer. He dragged her into the guest bedroom and farther back to the walk-in closet they used for storage. Her moans remained muffled behind his hand as her eyes bulged, fingernails digging into his arm.

"Shhh..." he whispered in her ear. "Give me two minutes, then I'll let you go. Please, two minutes."

Her eyes darted side to side a few times before she gave him a slow nod. An inch at a time, he moved his hand from her mouth and threaded both of his hands into her hair. Parker grabbed his forearms, but she didn't fight him. Instead, with one blink tears ran down her cheeks.

Gus leaned down until his lips hovered a few inches from hers. "I love you."

She pinched her eyes shut and tried to shake her head, biting her lips together.

"Yes, I do. You can tell me what to call you. You can make a million snarky comments about my age. You can break the news of my wife's affair. But you *cannot* tell me I can't love you. That's my choice, and I choose to love you because it's *all* I want to do." His emotion-choked voice struggled to keep to a whisper. "I don't give a damn about those condoms. That's not my life. So if you thought I would explode into some rage of jealousy, you were wrong. I don't want to fight with Sabrina. I don't want to beat up some guy she's sleeping with. I just ..." He pressed his forehead to hers as she shook with silent sobs. "I just want *you*."

Parker surrendered. She wrapped her arms around his neck and cried more. He held her tightly to him, not wanting to let her go or let her think a second beyond that moment. "You're a horrible, heartbreaking old man, Gus Westman."

A smile pulled at his lips. "I am. But you love me, right?"

She inched back, sniffling and blinking the tears from her long lashes. "Against my better judgment, but ..."

"But?" He grinned.

Her lips fought for a tiny bit of hope with the slightest curl. "Yes," she whispered.

"Yesss ..." He beamed, kissing her until he felt certain the only thing holding her up was his arms around her waist.

When they came up for breath, a touch of sadness stole her features again. "Don't," he whispered over her lips. "Don't give me that look like you're waiting for something bad to happen. Give me three days to work through everything with Sabrina before she leaves town again. Then come away with me."

"I ..." She shook her head. "I can't leave with you. My family will never understand how this happened. Not after Caleb and Piper."

"Then don't tell them. Not now. Tell them you're going with friends or to check out a job, or whatever, but just ... come away with me. Just for a few days. You, me, no clothes."

Parker laughed. "Such a guy."

"Your guy." He bit her lower lip then ran his tongue over it. "Come with me."

She nodded. "Three days and if I haven't heard from you, I'm hooking up with Dr. Blair again, and you're still going to rewire my house for free."

"Three days. I'll knock Dr. Stinky Feet on his ass if he steps foot onto your property. And I'll rewire your house after I spend a week buried inside of you." He kissed her again, leaving her breathless one last time before the longest three days of his life. "Now, go home. I'll deal with Sabrina."

With a dazed nod, Parker released him and took two steps before turning back around. "Are you going to tell her?"

"Tell her what?"

"That you know about the condoms?"

Their words were still nothing more than whispers.

Gus nodded toward the master bedroom. "She's probably already been in there and seen them on the counter."

Parker's eyebrows gathered together. "Are you going to tell her about us?"

The blank, indifferent look on her face gave away nothing. Gus wanted to do right by Parker, to make up for all the wrong that he'd done. "Yes. So … you're out of a job."

A hint of a smile graced her face. "Three days." On a slow turn, happiness walked away.

Chapter Eighteen

WAKING TO THE loud drone of a lawn mower, Parker untangled herself from the sheets and clicked on her phone. "Well done, me." She grinned at the time that read five minutes after noon. Before she released her phone, it vibrated in her hand. A picture of her mom lit up the screen. After contemplating answering it, she caved and pressed the green button. "Good morning, Mom."

"Morning? It's afternoon. Please tell me you're not still in bed."

Parker jumped out of bed and stretched her free arm above her head, arching her back. "Nope," she said with a yawn.

"How was the Westmans' party?"

"Um … good. What did you guys do?"

"Well, we had a little surprise."

"Oh?"

"Yes. I've made lunch. I'll tell you all about it when you get here."

"Mom, I'm—"

"See you when you get here. Don't be too long, we're hungry."

Tossing her phone on the bed, she headed straight for the shower. The events of the previous day still clung to her, and she wanted to wash it all away, not think about Gus for the next three days, and keep her hope at bay until things were truly over between the Westmans.

After a shower and quick hair drying, Parker stepped out onto her front porch closing the door behind her. "What the hell?" she whispered.

The lawnmower that woke her belonged to Gus. In his Cubs cap, headphones, tank top, and cargo shorts, he rode the big John Deere back and forth in his front yard making a perfect quilt of crosshatches. She fumed, feeling the rage of fire burn the surface of her skin. He should have been ending his marriage, fighting, dividing belongings, packing stuff up, calling his attorney, *not* mowing the lawn.

A flood of gut-wrenching scenarios played in her mind: Sabrina got drunk and seduced her husband; Gus chickened out after his wife broke down over their affairs and begged him to stay; she wasn't having her period, she was spotting at the beginning of her pregnancy. Parker wanted to run back in the house and hide from the big bad world, but she didn't. With as much confidence as she could muster, she threw back her shoulders, slipped on her sunglasses, and walked like a queen toward her parents' house, not sneaking a single peek in Gus's direction.

She was done being the disposable girlfriend. Done with succumbing to physical desire. Done thinking the best of people. Done. Done. Done.

As soon as she reached the other side of the road, finding shade and privacy behind a cluster of tall trees, her phone vibrated in her pocket.

Gus: *I can hear your thoughts from yards away, over the motor of the lawnmower, and through my noise-cancelling headphones. Stop thinking so LOUD. Sabrina got sick last* *night. She's still in bed. I have to mow the lawn before I leave town with YOU.*

Parker bit back her foolish grin.

Gus: *And just so you know, I slept in the guest room ... thinking of you.*

"Jerk," she whispered, no longer able to hide her smile. With slow steps, eyes stuck to the screen of her phone, she shuffled her flip-flops along the gravel drive toward her parents' front door.

"Hi."

Her momentum halted like a gunshot to her head. Parker closed her eyes. That voice, even years later, she recognized it. "Piper," she whispered.

"Aren't you going to look at me?"

On a deep inhale, Parker lifted her head to her twin. Piper's hand making small circles on her tiny bump drew Parker's attention away from the rest of the world.

"I'm five months along. We didn't tell anyone until I was almost four months because I was so sick."

Words required too much effort, so Parker stuck with a slow nod.

"It's a boy."

More slow nodding.

"Jesus, Parker, say something!"

A heaviness settled in her body, and her heart felt like it was shrinking. The right words didn't exist to express the mess of emotions that warred inside of her. "It's getting hot out here. We should go inside."

The painful smile on Piper's face said everything. Their relationship was severed in a blink, but it would take so much more to fix it. Every step Parker took toward her sister meant something. She could have turned and run back home, but she didn't.

"Aw …" Janey's eyes filled with tears as Piper and Parker walked into the kitchen. "My girls are finally back together."

Parker gave her dad a toothy grin. He returned a wink, and she knew it meant thank you.

"Let's eat." Janey gathered her composure and ushered everyone into the dining room.

Their parents sat at both ends of the table with Parker on one side and Piper and Caleb on the other side.

"Parker …" Caleb nodded at her but quickly averted his gaze to anything and everyone but her.

It took a few minutes of eating in silence for Janey to clear her throat and end the awkwardness. "Piper and Caleb are going to put most of their stuff in storage, but I told them since you don't have much furniture it might be a good idea to use their sofa and chairs in the living room."

Parker had trouble swallowing her bite of food. "So…" she wiped her mouth with a napkin "…you're moving in with me?"

"Just until our house is finished." Piper cut into her steak.

"I see." She knew they were waiting for her to object so they could threaten to make her sell the farmhouse.

"I'm surprised you want to live in an old farmhouse. There's probably much nicer places you could rent."

"If it's too much of an inconvenience, we could—"

Piper rested her hand on Caleb's arm, cutting him off. "It's hard to find places to rent for less than a year."

The pain of biting her tongue was excruciating. They could afford to sign a year lease and move out after three months.

Chump change for Caleb. Piper wanted to make Parker bend or break. It was too early to tell which one.

"Fine. When are you moving in?"

Four jaws dropped. Even her dad, the one ally Parker had, gave her an incredulous stare.

"Parker, I'm ... very proud of you." Janey's eyes filled with tears again.

How proud would she have been knowing what Parker did with a married man less than twenty-four hours earlier?

"Thanks, Mom. I'm going to be leaving in a few days for a trip with some friends. Feel free to move your stuff whenever."

"Where are you going?" her mom asked.

"Uh ... New York."

"Oh, Parker, do you know how dangerous that is? Do you realize how much political unrest our country is in right now? It's not even safe to fly, let alone go to a major city like that."

"For crying out loud, woman!" Her dad shook his head. "Something could happen to her anywhere. We can't be so damn paralyzed by fear. Let her go and live a little."

"New York City is the best!" Piper sat up straight with a ridiculous smile. "Caleb and I have been there so many times. You'll love it, Parker."

When the twins made eye contact, Piper's smile faded a bit. They used to be best friends and share everything with each other. Parker wondered if they would ever get that back. The scars of what had happened would never completely disappear.

"You haven't been working for Sabrina that long, I'm surprised she's giving you time off."

Parker glanced at her dad, silently cursing him for bringing up that subject. "Yesterday was my last day working for Sabrina."

"What happened?" Bart's brow furrowed.

She rearranged the peas on her plate with her fork. "Nothing. Just between us, I think they might be having marital issues and things are a little too intense around there for my taste. But don't say anything. Besides, I really do need to look for a career, not just a temporary job."

"You should have gotten a different degree." Piper couldn't keep her trap shut.

Parker glared at Caleb. He squirmed in his chair.

"Yes, a lot of 'should haves,' but here I am with a fabulous communications degree. I'm still paying off student loans, so I'm going to figure out a way to use my degree or die trying."

"We'll cover the utilities and insurance while we're staying with you." Piper rubbed her belly and gave Parker a pity smile.

"Thanks. Speaking of utilities, Gus has agreed to rewire the place."

"Ah …" Bart nodded. "That's good. What's he charging you to do it?"

Twisting her lips to the side, Parker hummed a bit. "I … I don't remember the exact price, but he's giving me a neighborly discount and I might … do some stuff for him, so we'll barter as much as possible."

Sex. They would barter with sex, or they would have sex and call it bartering. It didn't matter to Parker at that point. She wanted Gus. Period.

"Is he going to start the rewiring before you get back from New York?" Piper asked.

Parker pursed her lips to keep from grinning. "Not likely."

"Our stuff comes tomorrow. We'll stay another night or two with Mom and Dad until our bed arrives and we get it set up." Piper rested her hand on Caleb's leg.

His hand covered hers. Their love was disgustingly beautiful, maybe even *despicable.*

"Well, I need to get home, do some laundry and cleaning, and get packed for my trip. Thanks for lunch, Mom."

She gave her soon-to-be roommates a quick look. Piper didn't back down, but Parker wondered if the day would ever come that Caleb would look her in the eye like a brother-in-law and not like the cheating boyfriend. He probably wondered the same thing about Parker.

THE HIGH PARKER got from cleaning her house fell under the slightly obsessive category. Thinking of leaving town with Gus amped her up a bit more than normal. Her high fizzled the moment she started to pack for their trip to whatever unknown place, probably not New York. Everything in her PJ drawer resembled workout clothes or swimsuit cover-ups.

No silk.

No lace.

No satin.

No sexy.

Gus married a woman who refused to wear cotton. Parker owned nothing *but* cotton and polyester. Her wardrobe defined anti-sexy. She didn't have time to worry about it. If Gus didn't find her sexy in a T-shirt and soft, chunky socks, then he wasn't the guy for her.

After organizing a week's worth of random outfits into her suitcase, she brushed her teeth and collapsed onto her bed. Two more sleeps until Gus.

The next day had her a fidgety mess. The house was spotless and her stuff was packed. Drinking too many cups of coffee, she stood guard at her kitchen window hoping to see some sign of activity at the Westmans'. The pathetically insecure stream of what-ifs made their rounds in her head.

What if Sabrina was still sick and Gus still hadn't talked with her?

What if he decided he couldn't be with a cotton girl?

What if they chose to stay together for the dog's sake?

When the what-ifs obliterated her last bit of sanity, Parker decided to go outside and pull weeds, water a few plants that didn't need water, sweep the shed, and rake the gravel in the drive to an even level. Then she washed and waxed Old Blue, vacuumed the interior, and sat in the driver's seat like she had somewhere to go while she stared at the Westmans' house. After the sun had baked her to a medium-well, she clocked out for the afternoon and fled to the safety of the air-conditioned house to take a shower.

While eating dinner for one, a sandwich and green grapes, she texted Gus. It occurred to her that three days was a bit confusing. Would he come for her on day three or did he need three full days with Sabrina, therefore, he would come for Parker on day four?

Halfway through typing her request for clarification from Gus, she hit the delete button. That's not the woman she wanted to be with him. She had no plans, no job, and barely a life. She didn't need to be impatient or demanding. He didn't need a text in the middle of working out terms with Sabrina.

Parker could wait. She would wait. And she did wait with beer and leftover Jello shots.

Chapter Nineteen

*D*ING DONG.
    Ding dong.

Ding dong.

"What the hell?" Parker grumbled as she threw the covers off her bed and rubbed her eyes.

Ding dong.

Ding dong.

Ding dong.

She knew from the dim light filtering through her shades that it was early in the morning, barely past sunrise. Tying the sash to her robe, she navigated the stairs like a drunk person. When she cracked open the door, a dark wet nose tried to wedge it open even more.

Rags. Her heart tried to escape the confines of its cage as she looked up knowing it was Gus.

"Hey—" Her heart deflated a bit. "Gerald." Parker tried not to sound too disappointed that it was Gus's dad at her door and not Gus. She opened the door all the way.

Rags shot past her, straight up the stairs.

"Rags!" Gerald called.

Parker chuckled. "It's fine. He knows his way around. Came over during a storm one night and refused to go home when Gus came to get him."

Gerald nodded. "I uh ... hate to inconvenience you in any way, but could you watch Rags for a few days?"

"Um ..." She wasn't sure if telling him about her trip with "friends" to New York was a good idea. While she had no intention of telling her parents anytime soon about her relationship with Gus, it was possible he'd confided in his parents about them.

Gerald sucked in a slow, long breath and held it, his expression drawn in agony.

"Are you feeling okay?"

Nodding a half a dozen times, he released his breath and then shook his head. "Yesterday afternoon Sabrina and Gus ..." his voice broke and tears filled his eyes.

Parker's stomach hardened as a wave of nausea crawled up her chest. Her heartbeat slowed to the point she couldn't feel it or any other part of her body.

He continued. Each word choked with emotion. "It was a car accident." With each rapid blink, more tears filled his bloodshot eyes.

Parker took a step backward with a slow, disbelieving head shake. Every muscle in her body trembled.

"They didn't make it." He wiped his tears with the back of his hand and cleared his throat. "We need a few days to get things arranged. Can you—"

"Yes," she whispered.

He nodded once. "Thank you."

"Yes," she whispered. "I'm so ..." She couldn't breathe.

Gerald gave her a painfully sympathetic smile. "I know. Thank you." He turned and shut the door.

Parker covered her mouth to hold back her sobs as her body crumpled on top of itself, leaving her a broken pile of complete emptiness on the floor.

"NOOOOO!" She rolled onto her side in a ball and curled her arms around her head.

KNOCK KNOCK.

Ruff ruff ruff.

Something wet and warm slid along Parker's cheek.

Ding dong.

Ruff ruff ruff.

More wetness and warmth along her cheek and nose. Her swollen eyes protested almost as much as her pounding head as she peeled them open and sat up. If it hadn't been for the hyper canine's dog breath in her face, Parker might have convinced herself that it was all a nightmare.

She stood in a thick cloud of shock. Numb and drained of every tear. After brushing back her hair and straightening the tie on her robe, she opened the door.

"You heard." Her mom frowned and stepped inside, pulling Parker into her arms. "Your dad just heard about it from Roger. He was one of the first responders yesterday. They were pronounced dead at the scene." Janey released her daughter and cupped her cheek. "I knew you'd be very sad since you've worked for them for the past month."

Rags ran up and shoved his snout into Janey's crotch. She turned to the side and shooed him away. "Why is he here?"

Parker headed toward the kitchen, moving in slow, stiff strides like a zombie. "Gu—" She choked on the pain of trying to say his name. "Mr. Westman brought him over earlier and asked if I could take care of him for a few days." Her words came out flat and as lifeless as she felt.

"I can't imagine losing a child. It's my worst fear. Gus's dad must have been a wreck."

Parker nodded as she filled a glass with water. She closed her eyes, not wanting to see Gus's house out her window. Her kitchen, the spot on the counter three feet away, the chair where he sat across from her the night they had dinner … it all held memories that could never be anything more than painful reminders of *him*.

"What does this mean for your trip to New York?"

Her mom would never know how deep that question cut Parker. She grunted a laugh, the kind of laugh that was laced with pain to the point of near insanity. "I'm not going now."

Janey hugged Parker from behind and kissed her shoulder. "New York another time?"

Her mom could have seized that moment to say it was some sort of fate since New York was such a dangerous place, but she didn't. Parker gripped her mom's hand, giving a firm squeeze to say thank you.

"New York another time," Parker whispered, opening her eyes again to the big, beautiful, vacant house next door.

PARKER DOLED OUT her grief in believable doses. Her boss died. Her neighbors that she knew for a month died. A certain amount of grief was expected. Refusing to unpack her suitcase and sleeping until two in the afternoon was not an appropriate reaction for a professional or even neighborly relationship.

It took superhuman strength to get out of bed before noon. Feed Rags. Walk Rags. Smile on cue. Nod when someone asked a question. Any question. All she did was plaster on a fake smile and nod for three days after the news of their deaths.

"It rained yesterday. Maybe you should wear flats so your heels don't sink into the ground at the cemetery." Janey picked a few stray hairs on the back of Parker's black dress as she stared at her daughter's reflection in the bathroom mirror.

"I don't have flats that aren't flip-flops or Chucks." She pulled her hair back and then released it, then repeated the same thing two more times before deciding to leave it down.

"I bet Piper does."

Her sister and Caleb had been kind enough to give Parker a few extra days before moving in, but their moving truck was scheduled for the following morning.

"I'll be fine. If the ground is too soft, I'll shift my weight forward and walk on my toes."

"Maybe you should pull your hair back." Janey gathered Parker's hair and twisted it into a bun.

Parker turned, forcing her mom to release her hair. "I'm wearing it down."

Janey frowned. "You're looking thin in the skin. Come to dinner tonight."

"I'll think about it." She started out the bathroom door, and Janey followed.

"Do you have plenty of tissues? Inevitably someone will give a speech that will bring everyone to tears."

"I have plenty of tissues and a pair of sunglasses that practically cover my whole face." Parker grabbed her purse and the keys to Old Blue.

"Drive safe, honey."

"I will." Parker stepped out into the muggy humidity. It was only ten; everyone would be melting by the burial.

THE DOUBLE FUNERAL for Gus and Sabrina Westman packed the Evangelical church to capacity. Parker recognized Gerald and Tess Westman and Gus's nephew, Brady, but everyone else was a stranger in various stages of grief—hundreds of people who had no idea Parker was Gus's mistress or that Sabrina also had a lover who was not her husband. She wondered if he, too, was there repressing his true level of grief.

Parker zoned out during most of the service, replaying every moment she'd shared with Gus. He was incorrigible in so many ways, but her heart only remembered how it thundered to life in his presence. Her eyes missed seeing his smile peeking out of the shadow of that stupid Cubs hat that she loved almost as much as the man who wore it.

After an hour of various friends and family bringing the congregation to tears, the families followed the caskets out of the church. Parker inspected each one of them. The man she assumed to be Sabrina's dad hugged his wife to him, practically carrying the grieving mother out of the church. Janey's voice echoed in Parker's mind. *"I can't imagine losing a child."*

Behind Sabrina's parents walked a guy dressed for … something, but not a funeral. His bronze-shaded blond hair hung in his eyes a bit, ruffled like Brady's was the day he came to her house with Gus. It had to be Sabrina's brother. She mentioned him briefly once. However, she failed to mention his idiotic taste in fashion—a purple and yellow paisley dress shirt, eggplant dress pants, a canary yellow vest, and a purple and white striped bowtie. Parker strained her neck to see if he wore clown shoes to match the rest of his outfit.

Nope. White Chuck Taylor Converse high tops. Close enough—yet totally awesome in Parker's eyes. Her gaze worked its way up his solid body as he approached her row, desperate for something to make her laugh instead of cry. After his bowtie, she continued to run her gaze up to his face, but before she got to his eyes, his lips pulled into the hint of a grin.

Her brow instantly furrowed. Who would smirk at a funeral? At the last second, they made eye contact. He held her gaze, blue on blue, for the final steps until he passed her row.

She brought the tissue, balled in her fist, to her face to hide her own untimely grin. The fine line between laughter and tears faded with each passing breath. Parker felt drunk on grief. How could the urge to giggle coexist with such raw pain in her heart? Sabrina's brother was the piñata at her funeral.

It took forever to herd everyone out of the church. It took even longer to drive the five miles to the cemetery. Parker didn't have that many friends and family; her funeral procession would be much quicker.

At the cemetery, several men guided the vehicles through the open wrought-iron gates into rows to accommodate everyone. Total gridlock.

"No ..." She grimaced when they motioned for her to start the next row, landing her a parking spot close to the gravesite. After she shoved it into park, she took a deep breath and prayed. "Please. Please. Please. Not today. I'm begging. Just this once. I'll do anything." She had a full tank of gas, so she contemplated letting her truck idle through the ceremony. They weren't usually that long. But she also knew the exhaust was not that of a newer vehicle. And two deaths were enough for that day. So she turned off the ignition.

POP!

The throng of people walking to crowd around the caskets jumped and turned—a million eyes on the mistress in her grandfather's old truck that had recently started backfiring after shutting it off. Not all the time. Just sometimes and apparently at funerals. She cringed, sliding down in the seat, holding completely still, in case they couldn't distinguish which vehicle farted.

After a few seconds, attention returned to the two rectangular holes in the ground atop the small hill. Parker's door whined like an errant toddler being dragged out of the candy aisle as she opened and shut it all in one quick motion. "Gah! I should have been the one to die," she whispered to herself, body temperature rising exponentially, feeling all eyes on her again.

Waiting again for curious eyes to lose interest in her noisy truck, Parker grabbed a few fresh tissues from her purse and made her way up the small hill to the graves, passing a sun-blanched stone angel and several cracked headstones. The minister began to speak, but Parker was too far back to clearly make out his words. She observed the black-clad mourners and the many pictures of grief painted on their faces: anger, sadness, fear, shock, sympathy. Whereas Sabrina's mom seemed to be falling apart, slowly dying herself, Gus's mom stood at her son's grave with a lifeless expression, slack jaw and unblinking.

Parker knew that type of grief. She still hadn't unpacked her suitcase. Every day she waited for Gus to knock on her door. Every day she watched out the window for the white Westman Electric van. He was gone for the day, but he would return. Gone running errands. Gone to get the neighbor donuts and pizza. Not *gone*. Finality was a hard concept for the living to accept.

Her gut knew the worst days were yet to come. Someday she would unpack that suitcase. Someday she would stop looking for the white van. When that day came, she would have to accept that he was truly gone, and at that moment she would have to grieve the loss of the part of her he took with him.

Blotting a few tears, she sniffled and tried to focus on something less tragic, a place less suffocating. Why did so many people bury their loved ones instead of cremating them? She couldn't wait to get as far away from the empty bodies as possible. She didn't feel close to Gus, even with him a few yards away. That wasn't him. It was the worst reminder that he no longer existed in her world.

When her emotions bubbled past the point considered fitting for a neighbor who simply worked for the Westmans, she took slow steps in the opposite direction. Finding a shaded spot near Herbert Ross's grave, she slipped off her high heels and leaned back against the tree.

"Fuck you for breaking my heart, Gus," she whispered while wiping away a new round of tears.

Why were they in the car together? Sabrina was scheduled to fly out that day, but Gus never took her to the airport. Maybe that day was an exception. Maybe that's when Gus decided to tell her so she could get on a plane instead of sticking around to argue or make excuses for her own indiscretions. Maybe Gus did it to protect Parker. Surely Sabrina felt angry and betrayed if he told her about them. A million maybes that didn't matter.

"Parker?"

She turned, resting her hand on the tree trunk to slip back on her shoes. "Gerald, sorry I …"

He shook his head. "It's hot. I think that's why the minister sped through the ceremony." The smile on his face looked as painful as it did the day he brought Rags to her house. The day he shattered her world.

"I couldn't hear anything anyway, so I thought I'd take cover under a tree before I melted."

He wiped his brow. "Yeah. Life never checks the forecast before it just decides to … happen."

"Life …" She nodded. "Definitely makes you feel insignificant and vulnerable to its power."

"Come to our house. We're having a few family and close friends over to help eat all the food that's been delivered over the past few days. The church offered to host the reception, but Tess didn't want anything that big."

"Oh, thank you, but I'm not really family."

"Both Sabrina and Gus spoke very highly of you, and we took an instant liking to you the day you brought over the banana bread. Please, I insist. Come and stay for just a bit."

"Okay." Parker returned a small smile. "I will."

"Good. We'll see you soon, then." Gerald made his way back to the grave sites where Tess and Sabrina's parents remained.

Old Blue was blocking a whole row of cars, so Parker hustled in that direction, slowing for a brief moment to take a final look at Gus's casket. Her throat constricted and more tears burned her eyes as she slipped on her big black sunglasses. She didn't want to hear the motorized hum of the casket being lowered into the ground or the first fistful of newly turned earth clattering against it.

Good bye, Gus.

The couple in the car behind Old Blue gave Parker a look that said hurry the hell up. Fair enough, it was almost a hundred degrees that day. She turned the key.

Nothing.

She tried again.

Nothing. Not even the tiniest effort to rollover.

"No. This can't be happening. Not today. Not here. Come on!" She tried again while pounding her heel into the floor of the truck.

She jumped out and cringed, giving an apologetic look to the couple in the car behind her. He rolled down his window.

"My truck won't start. I'm sorry."

The man frowned as they both assessed the situation, which happened to be almost twenty cars lined up behind her, bumper to bumper. Zero wiggle room.

"I'll push it forward enough for you to get out."

The older man grumbled something as Parker went back to the truck and shifted it into neutral then hopped out again. The old bastard just sat in his car and watched as she wedged her body between the two vehicles and tried to push the truck forward.

"If it rolls backward, you'll be crushed."

With sweat dripping down her face and chest, she glanced over at the source of the deep voice. Mr. Funeral Clown offered a half smile while rolling up his sleeves.

"Step aside."

Parker moved out from between the vehicles. He pushed it forward with the effort of sliding a sofa several inches.

"Thank you."

He nodded.

The car behind them pulled around and exited the cemetery followed by the rest of the cars.

"It won't start?" he asked.

Parker wiped her forehead, wrinkling her nose. Her dress had dark sweat spots and clung to her sticky body in the most unflattering way. "Nah, it'll start. I'm just trying to be environmentally conscious by saving on gas."

He grinned, the same toothpaste commercial smile that Sabrina had. Same blond hair. Same soft blue eyes.

"Sorry." Parker shook her head. "Bad joke. Bad timing."

"No. Good joke. The timing ..." He shrugged; sadness stole his smile as he glanced back to his father practically dragging his mother away from Sabrina's grave, sobbing uncontrollably. "I need to go. Do you need a ride?"

"What? Nope. I'll call for a ride."

"Okay." He gave her a quick look with a barely-detectable smile and walked toward his parents. His mother released his dad and clung to him. He scooped her up in his arms and carried her to the car.

Parker had been to a handful of funerals in her lifetime but never had she seen something so heartbreaking as a son carrying his mother away from the casket of her daughter. She blinked back more tears as she pressed the wad of tissues to her nose.

Chapter Twenty

AFTER PARKER'S DAD rescued her from the cemetery, she took a quick shower and borrowed her mom's car to make an appearance at Gerald and Tess Westman's house. It was the last place she wanted to be, but she did it for Gerald, and in a small way, she did it for Gus.

They lived on an acreage with hayfields, horses grazing in the pasture, a few goats, and chickens wandering in the yard outside of their coop, pecking at bugs in the dirt. The ranch-style house was older but well-kept with recent renovations and a large addition to the back of it with a covered deck.

Parker knocked on the door, hearing voices inside. She looked out at the grain silos in the distance. When no one answered, she eased open the door. The "small" gathering was far from small, but admittedly much smaller than the funeral. Groupings of people filled the space, creating a narrow maze to move through. Aside from the high-pitched cry of two kids chasing each other toward the kitchen, everyone spoke in low voices, almost reverently.

As she wormed her way toward the kitchen, a hand gently grabbed her arm. "Parker," Tess said.

"Hi." Parker hugged her, fighting past the burning tingle in her nose of more tears forming. "I'm so sorry for your loss."

Tess pulled back and nodded once, a sad smile on her weary face. "Thank you. Please, make sure you eat something while you're here. There's more seating out back if you can stand the heat."

"Thank you." Parker continued to the kitchen where more people were packed wall to wall separated by counters of food. Tons of food.

"You made it," Gerald said, handing Parker a glass of lemonade.

"Yes, thank you." She took a sip.

"Come here. I want you to meet some of our family."

They stopped next to a table by the sliding doors.

"Bran, Tabitha, this is Parker. She worked for Sabrina and lived next door to them as well. Parker, these are my other two kids."

"Nice to meet you. I'm sorry for your loss."

They both said hi and nodded at her condolences.

"Have you met the Paiges?"

"Who?"

"Sabrina's family."

Sabrina was a Westman, so Parker never knew her maiden name. It was probably written on the memorial announcement that she shoved in her purse, not wanting another reminder of Gus's death. Thinking back, it was surprising that a career-driven woman like Sabrina didn't keep her maiden name.

They went out back where it was still suffocatingly humid, but facing east it put everyone in the shade, and they had a few big fans on the large porch circulating the heavy air. Trellis lined the sides with climbing vines of honeysuckle. A swing set with a yellow tornado slide sat next to a giant oak tree in the backyard.

"Joe, Stephanie, I'd like you to meet Parker. She was Sabrina's assistant and their neighbor."

Joe held out his hand as Stephanie looked up through dark sunglasses, no doubt hiding very swollen eyes. "Hi, Parker, it's very nice to meet you. Wish it were under better circumstances."

"Me too."

Stephanie clutched Joe's other hand with both of hers and swallowed hard. "Hi," she whispered like a single word could shatter her composure that hung by a thread. Her chin trembled.

"Where's Levi?" Gerald asked Joe.

Joe strained his neck. "I'm not sure. Probably in the kitchen with the food or chasing the kids."

"Hmm …" We'll find him and I'll introduce you two before you leave."

Parker returned a tight smile, having trouble focusing on anything but Stephanie's body visibly shaking as people passed by giving her hugs and whispering condolences in her ear.

"Where's the restroom?" Parker asked.

"Down the hall to the right," Gerald said.

Stephanie flinched when Parker gently slid her hand over Stephanie's, death gripped to Joe's.

"Come with me?"

Joe's brow furrowed, eyes flitting between Parker and his wife.

"Please," Parker whispered in her ear.

Slowly, Stephanie released her shaky hold on Joe and took Parker's hand. She deposited her lemonade on the counter then led Stephanie down the hall and past the bathroom. Looking left and then right at the two bedrooms, Parker chose the smaller one that looked like a guest room.

"In here."

Stephanie stopped at the doorway.

"Come on." Parker gave her hand a gentle tug.

With hesitant steps, Stephanie followed Parker into the room. Parker shut the door.

"Here." She motioned for Stephanie to sit on the bed.

Again, Stephanie hesitated for a moment then eased onto the edge of the bed. Parker slowly removed Stephanie's sunglasses an inch at a time. Her heart twisted in her chest. Stephanie's eyes were nearly swollen shut. But the moment Parker removed her glasses she choked out another sob that shook her body. Parker sat on the bed next to her and held her hand.

It didn't matter that Sabrina had an affair. Or that Parker and Gus had crossed too many lines. Two people, loved by many, lost their lives. Surviving the grief was all that mattered.

"I know you don't know me, but I know what it feels like to lose someone you love. My mom said no amount of pain could ever compare to losing a child. So I've taken my worst pain ever and multiplied it times infinity to try and get a glimpse of what you're feeling right now."

Stephanie released more sobs and Parker hugged her, pulling her back onto the bed where Stephanie curled into a ball on her side in front of Parker and continued to cry. Parker stroked Stephanie's long blond hair. "You don't owe anyone a second of your attention right now. You laid your daughter to rest today…" Parker choked on her own words "…it's okay to just close your eyes and wait for this day to end."

MANY TEARS LATER, Stephanie stilled. Her breathing slowed

into a soft, steady rhythm. It was the only sound in the room. Parker continued to stroke Stephanie's hair as she let her own grief have its moment to settle into some sort of reality. Nearly an hour later, the door to the room cracked open. Stephanie didn't stir an inch. Parker couldn't see any more than a shadowy outline of someone's head peeking in, so she eased off the bed, straightening her clothes and smoothing down her hair as she tiptoed to the door.

Sabrina's brother gave her a curious look as she stepped into the hallway, gingerly closing the door behind her.

"You." He cocked his head to the side.

"Parker." She held out her hand.

He smiled a little and took her hand, not really shaking it, just holding it. "Levi Paige."

"The brother."

"Yes."

She looked at their hands. Hers soft with delicate fingers. His brawny with a few callouses. He released it as if he'd forgotten that he'd been holding it. "Nice to meet you. I'm very sorry about your sister and G—" Would his name ever fall from her lips without crushing her heart to get there? "Uh, your brother-in-law."

"Thank you." He nodded toward the door. "My mom ..." He pointed toward the door, retaining the curious look on his face.

"She's sleeping. Don't wake her. Sleep is good. Peaceful. A break from reality."

"So..." he scratched his chin, and Parker's eyes went to his wrist where he had a tattoo on the inside of it, but she couldn't make out what it was "...how does my mom know you?"

"She doesn't. Well, not really."

He squinted one eye. "Yet, you were lying with her in bed."

"Correct."

Levi continued to question her in silence.

"Gerald introduced us. She seemed to be hanging from a cliff, so I found her a soft place to fall."

Keeping his gaze on her, he lifted his chin a bit then dropped it into a sharp nod. "I see. Uh, wow, that was very kind of you."

Parker shrugged. "Kind of a do-unto-others thing."

"Well, thank you. I don't really know what else to say."

"Say there's still some food left." She pressed her hand to her stomach.

"Tons. Follow me. I'll make sure you get only the good stuff. I've tried everything."

"Where did everyone go?"

"Home or out back." He handed her a plate. "Avoid all mayo-based foods. They've been sitting out too long."

Parker reached for a little turkey sandwich.

"Meat too." His nose scrunched up.

"What does that leave?"

"Vinegar and oil-based salads, crudités—skip the dip, way too much double dipping today—and desserts."

Parker's lips twisted as she inspected the remains. She grabbed a few carrot sticks and took a bite out of one.

"Healthy girl. That's good."

"No." She chewed the warm, dry carrot stick that had minimal crunch left to it. "I'm just waiting for you to go out back so I can raid the desserts in private."

Levi grabbed a plate and loaded it with a mix of at least a dozen different cookies, bars, and cake. Then he opened the refrigerator. "You driving yourself home?"

"Yes."

"Okay. Water for you." With his free hand he grabbed a bottle of beer and a bottle of water. "Come on. I hear they have goats in the barn."

She followed him out the front door, avoiding the remaining family and friends gathered in back. Since the funeral, Levi had shed his vest and bow tie. His shirt was no longer tucked in and his sleeves were still rolled up from helping her push Old Blue out of the way. He didn't have the tall, lean, Gus-like runner's stature. Levi was wrapped in well-developed muscles.

Parker opened the side door to the white barn for Levi and then flipped on the lights which amounted to three bare bulbs, one that crackled and flickered.

"Goats? Where are you?"

She snorted a little giggle that felt inappropriate for that day. Levi walked to the opposite end of the barn and turned.

"There's not a single animal in here. What kind of barn is this?"

Parker plopped down on a hay bale next to a wooden ladder leading up to a loft. "The kind that stores hay and other miscellaneous stuff." She glanced around at the hooks on the rough wooden walls holding tack, shovels, rope, and a few pitchforks. The stagnant air smelled like wood and moldering hay. "The animals are probably in the other barn."

Levi sat on the hay bale angled ninety degrees from hers and handed her the bottle of water and the plate of desserts.

"How did you know my sister and Gus?" He twisted off the top to his beer and took a long pull.

She studied him for a few seconds. His presence engulfed everything around them, sturdy like a mighty oak tree, unblemished, commanding yet gentle. Parker admired his air of confidence. Taking a slow breath, she willed herself to keep as much composure as possible. Direct questions about Gus and Sabrina were still too difficult even after days of endless crying.

"They are—" She cleared her throat. "*Were* my neighbors. And I was Sabrina's assistant."

He paused mid-swig and slowly lowered his bottle. "Is your last name Brock? I thought her assistant's name was Brock, and I was under the impression it was a guy."

Parker wedged half of a s'mores brownie into her mouth and chewed it while nodding several times. "Brock assisted her with her job. I was the B-team assistant."

He stretched out his legs and crossed them at the ankles, watching her shove food down like someone with tapeworms. "So you were Brock's protégé?"

She licked the chocolate off her fingers. "No. I did things like drop off and pick up her dry cleaning, dog walking, dandelion removal, grocery shopping, baking … just random stuff."

"Oh! You're the neighbor that I'm supposed to get Rags back from, aren't you?"

"Are you taking him?"

"Yes. It's stated in Sabrina's will. Fitting, I suppose, since I'm the one who gave him to her. He was just a furball pup then. Our parents never let us have pets when we were young. So I gave him to her on her thirtieth birthday."

Parker felt a pang of disappointment that Rags was leaving her too, even if she felt certain on some days that he was out to get her in trouble.

"You live in Arizona too?"

"Yes. Scottsdale."

"Wife? Kids? Other pets?"

"God no!" He grinned behind his beer as he brought it to his mouth. "That sounded bad. Let me rephrase: No, I'm not married, no kids, no pets. Did it sound less terrifying that time?"

"Much better." Parker took a drink of her water. "Are you a dog person?"

Levi twisted his lips to the side and narrowed his eyes. "Not really. I guess it's hard to say. I've never had a dog. Sabrina was the one who always wanted one."

"So how does this work? Do you fly him home? Drive him there? He can be loud, and he likes his freedom, so I don't know how well he would do on an airplane."

"Are you saying I've just inherited a loud, hyper dog?"

Parker set the plate of desserts on the ground and dusted the crumbs off her lap. "Truth?"

"Sugarcoat it." Levi grunted a laugh before taking another pull of his beer.

"In that case, Rags is basically an oversized lap dog. Very low maintenance. Rarely makes a sound. And never gets into trouble."

Levi nodded slowly, staring at his feet. "That bad, huh?"

"Let's just say I met him after he got out of their fence and into my cockleburs. He likes to destroy personal clothing items, totally freaks out during storms, and a few weeks back I found myself scraping *his* shit off my ass. Long story."

The barn echoed with Levi's laughter. "I'm screwed." His gaze met hers and both of their smiles deflated back to reality.

"It's hard, isn't it? And if it's not hard, then it makes you feel guilty."

Parker cocked her head to the side. "What do you mean?"

"The pain. The grief. For the first few days after someone

dies, it feels like you'll never smile or laugh again. Then something or *someone* happens, and it brings a smile to your face or a laugh escapes, and it feels so amazing … until you realize you're doing it, and …"

"And the grief rushes back in to steal it, or the guilt just …"

"Oh the guilt…" Levi pushed a long breath out his nose "…it's the worst. As if the grief isn't enough, guilt sits on your conscience asking you, 'What the hell are you so happy about?' But I think we should rebel. What do you think?"

"Rebel?"

Levi sat up straight. "Let's smile. Not the guilty, courteous one that we've been sharing with everyone else today. The kind that physically hurts your face after a few seconds. The kind that will leave all the muscles in our faces sore for the next hour. It will be our little secret."

Levi Paige was crazy. Nothing like Sabrina.

"You in?"

Parker gave him a suspicious look for a few seconds, and then she nodded.

"Okay. On three, smile as big as you can. I want to see your molars and gums. And hold it for ten seconds. Ready? One, two, three, go!"

Levi smiled so big Parker thought his eyes were going to pop out of his head to make room for his smile. She focused on showing him her gums and molars at the same time, which proved to be quite difficult. It felt like the world's ugliest, most ridiculous smile, but she held it. Levi slowly held up his fingers to count. When all ten fingers were up, they both exhaled, not realizing they'd also been holding their breath.

"Man, you have a shitload of chocolate in your teeth," he

said while massaging the muscles in his cheeks and jaw.

Parker cupped her hand to her mouth. "Oh god!" She grabbed her water and poured some into her mouth, swishing it around.

"Don't you carry a compact and a few toothpicks with you?"

A bubble of laughter caught in her chest and she spit out the water all over him. "Oh no!" With the water out of its way, her laughter erupted until tears—happy tears—filled her eyes.

"Clearly you were raised in a barn." He wiped his face. Then he shook his arms and brushed off his legs. "Zero manners."

"I'm…" she fought to catch her breath "…so sorry."

"My poor suit."

Again their gazes locked for a few seconds, and Parker's laughter fizzled as her smile vanished.

"Don't." Levi shook his head. "That's what I mean. For a few minutes, you forgot about the grief and guilt. I won't tell anyone. New rule. When we feel like crying, we put on a big-ass smile instead. Or we laugh and spit water and chunks of brownie at people."

"I think that might be frowned upon."

"The spitting?"

"All of it."

Levi shrugged. "Maybe. But I think Sabrina and Gus would want us to smile and laugh."

Parker didn't know about Sabrina. Gus painted her to be a much different person than she was years before. Did Levi know the Sabrina that worked all the time and traveled with condoms? But she knew Gus would want her to smile and laugh. In spite of his moments of being crude and inappropriate, Parker knew he wanted the best for her.

"Maybe. Speaking of smiling and laughing, do you need another beer before you can tell me about your fashion inspiration?"

"What do you mean?" Levi shot her a pointed look.

"Your funeral attire is a bit ... eccentric. Do you dress this way every day or just for special occasions?"

"Dress what way?"

"Like ..."

"Like?" His head jutted forward.

"Um ..." Parker fidgeted with the hay, plucking pieces out and tossing them on the ground. When she risked a glance up at him, a shit-eating grin resided on his face. "You're terrible!" She flicked a piece of hay at him. "Gah, I thought I'd really put my foot in my mouth."

He chuckled. "I wore this to an 'Ugly Suit' party years ago. Sabrina and Gus were there too. I bet her five hundred dollars that I'd win."

"And you won?"

"No. Believe it or not, there was an uglier suit. Sabrina hated it so much, I threatened to wear it to her wedding just to get a rise out of her. She said, 'Over my dead body.' So I responded, 'Deal. I'll wear it to your funeral.'"

Parker's jaw unhinged. "Oh my gosh! And you really did. That's ..." She shook her head.

"Crazy. I know. But it helped me get through the day. I'd rather laugh than cry. And I'm a man of my word, so really I had no other choice."

She inspected his paisley shirt, purple pants, and white Chuck's again. "A solid choice. What socks are you wearing?"

Levi pulled up his pant legs, revealing yellow socks with

white smiley faces.

"Nailed it."

He chuckled. Even in the dim barn light, his blue eyes shined with life. Had Sabrina's once shined like that for Gus? Was that the jovial person he married?

"Well…" she stood and brushed off her backside " …I should go."

"Yeah, I need to check on my mom again." He grabbed the plate of half-eaten desserts. "I'll come by tomorrow and get Rags. I think we're going to stay at their house for a few days and go through everything. I don't think time will make going through their stuff or selling their house any easier. Gerald agreed. He thought we should just get it done. Find closure."

Every muscle in Parker's body tensed, desperate to keep her emotions in check. Go through their stuff. Sell the house. Done. Closure. It all cut too deep, especially with the packed suitcase still on her bedroom floor at home.

"Yeah." She cleared her throat. "That's uh … probably for the best." She led the way out of the barn into the suffocating heat, still thick and hot even with the sun setting low in the sky. "I'll see you tomorrow." She held up her hand in a friendly gesture and started toward her mom's car.

"Parker?"

She turned.

Levi gave her a thoughtful look, brow slightly tense, smile barely there. "Thank you for what you did for my mom today. I'm still a little awed by it." He rubbed the back of his neck.

"It was nothing." She shrugged.

"It was everything."

Parker held his gaze for a few seconds and then nodded. "Good night, Levi."

Chapter Twenty-One

A KNOCK AT the door woke Parker again. For the rest of her life, early morning knocks at the door would always trigger a who-died panic attack. She sat up in bed, surprised by the instant burning of tears in her eyes, the pounding of her pulse, and the cold sweat seeping from her pores.

The waves of grief were unpredictable. After leaving the reception, she made it the rest of the night without shedding a single tear. Even looking at the suitcase on the floor didn't spark a reaction. Maybe it was taking to heart the comparison between her love and loss of Gus to Stephanie losing her daughter of thirty-eight years.

Rags barked at the door as Parker came down the stairs.

"Rags, shhh!" Parker opened the door. "Oh, hi."

It wasn't a bearer of bad news. Just bad news in general.

"Good morning." Piper's long lashes fluttered, hand on belly, pink sundress waving in the early morning breeze, long, dark hair braided over one shoulder. The perfect wife.

Parker stepped back letting her inside. "You're up early, looking awfully *perky*."

Piper laughed, slipping off her sandals then padding straight to the kitchen. "It's almost nine. What time do you usually get up?"

Parker started a pot of coffee. "Depends on the day. I'm

generally sluggish at the start, but by noon I'm killing it."

After a cheating scandal and a sabotaged wedding, everything settled into small talk. No apologies. No, *hey, we should discuss what happened?* In two years, the *You ruined my wedding day, I'm never speaking to you again,* turned into, *How's it going, I'm pregnant, who sleeps past nine?*

The pregnant princess took a seat at the table and petted the greedy pooch who perched himself right next to her. "We delayed our move to let you get through the funeral and all, but we'd like to have our bed, some other furniture, and few boxes of clothes delivered today. Does that work for you?"

"Well ..."

Another knock came at the door, sending Rags running to it in a flurry of barking.

"It's Saturday. Doesn't anyone sleep in?" Parker grumbled on her way to the door.

"Holy hell! When did you get so big?" Levi's head jerked back as Rags dashed out onto the porch making a few circles and a thorough sniff of Levi's crotch before running back into the house.

Parker frowned. "I'm always a little puffy in the morning. Some guy feeding me a bunch of desserts last night didn't help either."

Levi grinned. "Guilty as charged. And good morning."

"Hi. Come in. And please don't ask me why I'm still in my robe." Parker dragged her feet to the kitchen. "Coffee?"

"Now you're speaking my language."

"Cream? Sugar?"

"Black. And I'll reserve judgment on your attire."

"Levi, meet my sister, Piper. Piper, this is Levi. He's here for Rags so don't get too attached to him."

"Parker!" Piper narrowed her eyes.

Parker filled two blue mugs with coffee, internally snickering. "Relax. I meant the dog. Don't get too attached to the dog."

The twins shared evil glares for a few seconds.

"Nice to meet you, Piper." Levi narrowed his eyes a bit as his gaze moved back and forth between the two women.

"Nice to meet you too." Piper winked. "And, yes, we're identical twins."

Levi nodded. "That's cool."

"The coolest," Parker mumbled.

"Are you family?" Piper asked.

"Yes. Sabrina was my sister." He rubbed his forehead. "Or ... *is* my sister? God, that's awful. When you lose someone do they stop being what they were to you?"

Parker handed him the mug of coffee, playing with that idea in her own mind.

Gus was my lover. Gus is my lover.

"I think *was*. When we die, we are no more, right?"

Levi took a sip of coffee, brow furrowed in concentration.

"Well, I'm very sorry about what happened to your family."

"Thank you." The corner of his mouth twitched like a failed attempt at smiling.

When Levi wasn't looking at Piper, she gave Parker a wide-eyed look that said *LOOK* as she jerked her head toward Levi.

Parker ignored her. If they weren't going to discuss cheating and wedding day fiascos, then they weren't going to discuss the man in the kitchen who Piper found attractive in a not-for-me-for-you sort of way.

Piper rolled her eyes at Parker's lack of response. "I won't keep you two. I just wanted to give you a heads-up about the moving truck coming later today, Parker."

She gave Piper a tight-lipped smile.

"Oh ..." Piper stopped just as she reached the front door, slipping on her sandals. "Will you need help moving your stuff out of the master bedroom? Mom said your new bed is a queen and you only have one dresser. It would be crazy for Caleb and me to try and squeeze our king-sized bed, two end tables, and mammoth armoire into one of the smaller bedrooms."

Those were fighting words. It was one thing to move in, it was another thing to shove Parker out.

"You're moving in?" Levi asked, looking at Piper.

"Yes. Just until the house we're building is finished."

"That should be fun. I can help Parker move her bed and dresser before I leave. It's the least I can do after how awesome she's been with my family."

Coffee mug halfway to her mouth, Parker stood frozen in disbelief. Piper wormed her way into the house and managed to kick Parker out of her bedroom all because Levi showed up at the wrong time.

"Perfect! Thanks, Levi. Bye, puppy." She blew Rags a kiss. "Later, sis."

"Sis my ass," Parker grumbled to herself.

When the door shut, Levi turned toward Parker. "Twins. I love this. I don't know too many twins. It's great that you're so close."

"Mmm, so great." She took another sip of coffee before something venomous and snarky shot out of her mouth. "How's your mom?"

He sighed. "Terrible, but better. Does that make sense?"

"Perfect sense." Parker set her mug of coffee on the counter. "Give me five minutes to slip on some clothes…" looking down, she frowned at her robe and fuzzy socks " …brush my teeth, and then we can get going on everything."

He scratched the back of his head, ruffling his messy hair even more as he yawned. "Take your time. I'm going to finish this cup of coffee and steal another if you don't mind. My body refuses to submit to the caffeine this morning."

"Help yourself," she called on her way up the stairs.

"NICE, PARKER. WHEN did you lose your dignity?" She stared at herself in the bathroom mirror, face blotchy as if she slept on something other than a pillow that left indentations on her right cheek. A hideous rat's nest clung to the back of her head, and her teeth felt fuzzy like her socks.

Keeping to her quick five-minute promise, she combed through her hair, tied it back, rolled on some deodorant, brushed her teeth, and settled on a pair of khaki shorts and a plain white tee.

"Has that caffeine found your veins yet?" she yelled down to Levi. "If so, come on up and show me your muscles."

She heard his soft chuckle before she saw his grin as he cornered the kitchen to the stairs. He flexed his bicep while ascending the stairs. No surprise, it was huge, much like the rest of his physique. Seeing him in short sleeves and a pair of shorts confirmed her previous assessment: he had the body of a professional athlete.

"Well, if you've got it, flaunt it." She grinned, trying to ignore the fact that Levi had *it* more than any man she'd met in her life. Genetics had been very generous to the Paige family. She knew it the day she saw Sabrina naked in the closet.

Levi's arm dropped to his side. "You asked. I wouldn't dream of flaunting."

She motioned him down the hall. "What do you do that requires you to be able to lift a vehicle?"

His refreshing chuckle brought a smile to her face. "I pushed your truck. I didn't lift it."

"Are you sure?" She glanced back over her shoulder giving him a slow, building smile. "Because I could have sworn I saw the back tires off the ground for a brief moment."

His face turned a shade of pink. She couldn't fathom him blushing, yet when he looked away, she knew that was exactly it.

"I'm an architect."

Parker pulled out the drawers to her dresser to make it easier to move. "Well, that explains the muscles."

He laughed. "I like to work out … a lot."

"Yeah? Me too."

"Running?"

"Hell no." She unplugged her TV and lamp. "Tore up my knees with volleyball injuries. I do more interval training and tramping."

"Tr-tramping?" He cleared his throat.

Winding the cord around her lamp, she gave him a sideways glance with a grin. "Rebounding. Mini trampoline. But tramping gets a better reaction out of people."

"Ah, I see."

She stripped the bedding from the mattress. "What's your favorite workout?"

"In the gym?"

"Just in general. How do you like to work up a sweat?"

That's what she needed, random conversation—no one

cheated, no one died conversation.

Levi took the mattress off her bed. "Well, um …"

When they made eye contact, he bit back a grin and shot his gaze in another direction.

"What?" she questioned.

"Nothing. Which room is this going in?"

"The one on the left." She followed him with her arms full of bedding. "What were you going to say?"

He leaned the mattress against the wall. "About what?" Everything in the room demanded his attention more than her.

She attempted to follow his gaze so he would look at her. "You dance, don't you. Ballet?" Tapping her finger on her lips, she narrowed her eyes. "No, I can't see you doing ballet. Tap? Ballroom?"

Levi shook his head and walked back to the other room.

"Jazz? Lyrical?"

His head continued to shake as he tipped her platform bed on its side.

"Come on." She followed him to her new room. "What's your addiction? What makes you sweat?"

She helped him set the bed down and adjust it into place.

He glanced up. "Change the subject."

"No way! Now you have me too curious."

Levi stood erect, hands resting on his hips, chin tipped to his chest as he blew out a long breath. "Sex. Now can we finish moving everything?"

While Parker stood frozen in place, eyes wide, moving side to side, Levi made long strides back down the hall. It sounded to her like he said sex, but that didn't make any sense. His favorite exercise was sex?

"It's going to take two of us to move this dresser so we

don't scrape up the wood floors," he called from the other room.

Parker jerked out of her stupor and hustled to the other bedroom.

"Get this side so you can walk forward. I'll walk backward."

"Okay." Parker lifted her side.

As they maneuvered it out of the room and down the hall, he looked at her. "Stop looking at me like that."

"I'm not looking at you like anything." She curled her lips between her teeth.

They set the dresser opposite the bed.

"Anything else?" He gave her a lightning fast glance before looking around the room again.

"Nope. I can get the rest. Thank you very much."

He headed back down the stairs. "Give me the CliffsNotes on Rags."

"Do you really consider sex a workout?"

He groaned, hunching down to make nice with the dog by scratching him behind the ears. "Yes. Does he sleep on his own or in bed with someone?"

"I'm going to have to disagree. I don't think you can call sex a workout."

"Then you're not doing it right. How many times do you feed him each day?"

Parker sat on the second to the bottom stair, resting her elbows on her knees. "What could I be doing wrong?"

"I wouldn't know. How long can he go without being let outside?"

Pinching her bottom lip together, Parker squinted her eyes in contemplation. "I suppose you'd have to go through a lot of positions and have really good stamina and control, huh?"

Levi stood, rubbing his temples. "You asked me what my favorite exercise is, what makes me sweat, and the truth is sex. A truth you didn't need to know. But I have this terrible problem ..." He blew out a long breath. "I suck at lying. Worst fucking poker player in the world. A total narc as a kid. My parents figured it out quickly. Nobody else around me got away with anything either. It was always, 'Go ask No Lie Levi.' It was worse than acne, untimely erections, or walking around half the day with my shirt hanging out of my fly."

Parker blinked. It's all she could do. Who was this guy? A sex athlete and honest to a fault?

"Wow ... that sucks." She grimaced. "I'm not implying lying is a good thing or suggesting that I'm some pathological liar, but sometimes you need to lie to save face, relationships, and not look like a dick. No offense."

"Tell me about it. I go through a lot of friends. I have a select few who stick by me even with my *problem*. It's just inevitable; eventually, I will say something that is offensive—true, but offensive."

"Are you autistic? My friend's nephew has Asperger's, and he has no filter at all."

"I don't think so. I have no other signs of autism, and I think in that scenario he's speaking honestly without real recognition that what he's saying is offensive. Trust me, I know what I'm saying is offensive. It's why I'll do anything to change the subject or avoid certain topics altogether. But when people, like yourself..." he pinned her with an accusatory glare " ...just keep pushing me for an answer, I eventually crack and say exactly what I'm thinking, or I lie and start sweating, avoiding eye contact, and stuttering like an idiot. But I don't unsolicitedly say everything that pops into my head."

"Are you super religious?"

"No."

"Hmm …" Parker rubbed her earlobe between her fingers. "That's crazy. Sorry I pushed you for an answer."

"Are you really?"

She grinned. "No. I'm going to be thinking about your answer for the rest of the day."

"Thinking about sex?"

"No, just …" Her head tilted to the side. "Well, yes."

"Can you mentally multitask so we can discuss Rags now?"

"Yes. What do you want to know?"

Chapter Twenty-Two

AFTER ONLY THREE hours of having Rags, Levi questioned how the dog would fit in at his place in Scottsdale. For an eight-year-old dog, he had the energy of a puppy. It worked fine at the house in the country with a doggy door and huge, fenced-in yard, but Levi had neither to offer him in Arizona.

"He sure does bark a lot." Joe, Levi's dad, said as he carried another box down the stairs. "Your neighbors won't be too thrilled."

Levi took the box and carried it the rest of the way to the garage where they were sorting things to be sold, things to donate, and things family members wanted to keep. "Yeah, that same thought has crossed my mind. The barking seems excessive, and he keeps jumping on the fence and digging a hole by it like he's trying to escape."

Joe took a black permanent marker and wrote "donate" on the box. "I think he likes the neighbor better than you."

"Can't blame him." Levi grinned, looking out at the spastic dog.

"Down boy." Joe looked over his shoulder with a matching grin. "Your stay here is temporary."

"Just an observation. That's all. How's Mom coming along?"

"She's still sitting on the floor of the closet folding all of

Sabrina's clothes, hugging them, sniffing them, staining them with her tears ... basically breaking my goddamn heart. I've been able to fix a lot in her life, but this..." he shrugged, swallowing back his own emotion " ...I don't know if she'll ever be the same."

"She seemed to be better when Tess was here."

Gus's parents had loaded up the back of their vehicle with things they wanted to keep and said they would be back later.

"Rags!" Levi whistled, tired of listening to the nonstop barking.

"Sabrina won't know if you don't keep him," Joe said.

"*I'll* know."

"Looks like you're going to get some help." Joe nodded to Parker walking toward the gate. "I'll be upstairs. Don't say anything stupid." He chuckled.

"Me? Never." Levi continued packing things from Gus's workbench that Gerald said to donate, enjoying a reprieve from the barking, thanks to Parker on her way to save the day.

"Excuse me, sir, your dog is barking excessively."

He liked how she joked and the way she said as much with her squints, winks, and rapid blinking as she did with her words. Levi had never seen such expressive eyes.

"Sorry. It's been brought to my attention that he may like the neighbor better than he likes me. Which is crazy. I'm very likable." He focused on her hand where Rags was eating something out of it. "What's that?"

"Turkey jerky. He loves it."

"Clearly. You didn't mention that in your bag of tricks earlier."

"I'll hook you up with some before you go."

"I'd be forever indebted if it keeps him quiet." Levi took in her tan, sexy legs, curvy hips, narrow waist, and perky breasts. When his eyes met hers, she gave him a knowing look. He prayed she didn't ask him if he'd been checking her out or staring at her boobs.

"How's the packing going?"

"Um…" he returned his attention to the tools in the drawers " …good. For only two people, they sure did accumulate a lot of stuff."

"I was just thinking the same thing about my sister and her husband. They're moving 'a small amount' of their stuff in as we speak. I needed some fresh air. Although, I'm not sure the air is fresh here. It's weird being here."

"It's weird going through their stuff. I feel like I'm invading their privacy. Then there's the part of me that worries we'll come across something they don't want anyone to see."

Parker chuckled. Levi liked the innocence in her laugh as much as he liked how the resting position on her face was always a slight smile. Kind. Warm. Welcoming.

"You thinking drugs or sex tapes?"

He also liked how she read his mind, yet didn't seem to judge him.

"Both. And it won't be me who finds it. My mom or Tess will find it."

"My mom would not survive finding a sex tape of me. Drugs? Yes. But not sex. She has an aversion to it. It's a miracle my sister and I are here. If I'm honest, I think she's the Virgin Mary reincarnated. It might explain why we look nothing like our dad."

Levi laughed at her candor. "By the way, my mom is going through all of the stuff in Sabrina's closet. If we can tear her away from clinging to everything that smells like Sabrina, you're more than welcome to take any of her clothes or shoes. They're just going to be donated."

Parker stiffened, her natural smile pulled into a slight frown. "I'm ... uh ... good. Her clothes are too small for me. I'm certain everything is a petite size. Not fitting for my height. And I know her shoes are three sizes smaller than my tens. But thanks for offering."

"No problem."

Pulling out another stick of turkey jerky, she bit off a piece then tossed the rest to Rags.

"What are your job plans? Have you had a chance to think about it?" Levi asked.

"I have a degree in communications. I'd like to use it, so I think I'm going to submit my résumé to the local radio and television stations. If they're not hiring right now, I'll have to get another temp job, but at least it's a step in the right direction."

"What kind of position are you hoping for?" Levi taped another box shut and moved it to the pile.

She rocked back and forth on her heels, hands interlaced behind her back. "Sports reporter."

"Good choice. Not weather girl?"

"No way. I suck at geography, therefore I have no business pointing to a map on live television."

"I loved geography."

"Yeah?" She shrugged, looking around the garage with a slight grimace as if something caused her pain. "Then maybe you should be a weather girl. But ... I have to go. It's very weird being here with their stuff, his van ... just everything. I don't know how you're doing it."

Levi leaned his backside against the work bench. "I'm not

sure the day will come where it's easy. I just want to be done. Go home. And try to adjust to life without them. Sabrina and I didn't see each other as much since she took over the firm, but I still texted her every day. Sometimes it was nothing more than a gif of some guy's hairy ass, or a picture of me on the golf course bragging about taking the day off—on a Tuesday." He laughed.

Parker grinned, the kind of grin that made him want to do funny dances, tell his best jokes, and master the art of making her smile. Maybe he didn't want to be done. Maybe seeing her made enduring the house of memories a little longer worth it.

"I'm sure you know what I mean. I'd imagine you and Piper probably talk every day as much if not more than Sabrina and I did."

Her eyebrows gathered as she chewed on her lower lip. "Actually, we had a falling-out a couple years ago. They just moved back here from Kansas City. After two years, we're talking again, but things are still a bit … rough."

"Really?" He crossed his arms over his chest. "You haven't talked to your sister in *years?*"

Parker nodded, nose wrinkled.

"Must have been something pretty bad. You're twins so she couldn't have stolen your boyfriend, so—" Levi's eyes shot open wide as Parker's cringe revealed that *was* what had happened. "No. Not possible." He shook his head a half dozen times.

"Yeah."

"But that's not who she marri—" He bent forward as Parker's cringe intensified. "Oh, ouch! Who does that?"

"My sister, apparently."

"Your ex-boyfriend aka brother-in-law and your pregnant

sister are going to be living with you for several months?"

"So you see it too? It's weird and wrong, and just ...
well ... *wrong.*"

"You two seemed fine this morning."

"Given the events of the past few days, I'm too emotionally
drained to deal with her. That, and you were there offering to
help move my stuff from *my* room to the smaller bedroom.
You helped kick me out."

Levi fisted his hand at his mouth and snickered. "Oh shit. I
had no idea. Why didn't you say something?"

"And put you in the middle? Were you going to take my
side?"

"Probably not at the time. I would have slithered out the
back door with Rags before the claws came out. But had I
known the story then, yes, I would have marched up the stairs
and nailed you to your, or ..." he closed his eyes and shook his
head "...nailed your bed to the floor." Levi blew out a breath
of how-the-hell-did-I-say-that? "Your dresser too, but of course
not ... you." His voice was barely a whisper by that point.

Parker pinched her lips together, wide eyes fixed on him.

Levi held out his hand. "It's been a pleasure knowing you. I
wish the circumstances had been better. Now, I think it's best
if we part ways before my twisted words cause me any more
humiliation."

He blamed his sister's and Gus's deaths on the jumbled
state of his brain. Lack of sleep and not having taken the
opportunity himself to properly grieve also played large roles in
Levi's Lewd Comments Show.

"Thank you. It has been an unexpected pleasure and relief
from ... *everything.* And your offer to *nail* things was quite
flattering, but the wood floors were recently refinished, and my

bed is new so … no nailing."

His temperature rose a good ten degrees around her. He tugged on his shirt to pull it away from his sweaty body and circulate some air before he overheated.

"Here." She dug into her pocket and handed him several more jerky sticks. "For the trip home."

He took them and set them on the bench. "Thank you."

"Don't eat them." She squinted one eye with her head turned a fraction to the side. "Because they are so good and if you try one, you'll eat all of them, and then you won't have any when you need them for Rags."

He made a criss-cross over his heart. "Promise. I'll stay out."

"Take care, Levi Paige. And …" The happiness on her lips wilted. "Again, I'm very sorry for your loss."

It still didn't feel real. He figured the first time he went to text Sabrina *then* it would feel real and knock him on his ass. "Thank you, Parker. And … if you're ever in the Scottsdale area, look me up."

He wasn't listed in any phone book or directory. How would she look him up? It felt like the right thing to say at the moment, and part of him, hell, all of him meant it.

"Job first. I don't have the funds to travel anytime soon. But if I hit the Powerball, I'll definitely stop by on my way to California."

"What's in California?"

"The ocean. I've never seen it."

"You've never seen the ocean. How old are you?"

"Twenty-six."

"How is that possible?"

"Iowa is in the middle. No ocean."

"And you've never left Iowa?"

"No. I've ventured to a few other states, but those are in the middle too." She waved. "Tell your parents I said bye and safe travels."

He nodded slowly as he tried to comprehend her lack of travel for someone her age. High school. College. Where did she go for spring break? Summer vacations?

Chapter Twenty-Three

"HOW'S LEVI AND his parents?" The stealer of rooms, perched on her leather sofa with her feet up, book in hand, greeted Parker when she walked in the door.

"Piper." Parker needed to practice saying her twin's name without gritting her teeth. Old habits.

"Did you happen to notice anything about him?"

"Such as?" Parker hopped onto her rebounder and started jumping.

Piper fidgeted with the end of her long braid. "Um ... like that he's quite nice to look at."

"Caleb been letting himself go? Doesn't surprise me. I thought he looked a little flabby in the midsection. He should switch to lite beer."

Piper's lips pulled into a hard smile. "I mean you. Back before you disowned me as your sister, I would have been able to say, 'Holy shit, Parker! He's ridiculously hot. Sexy blue eyes, fluid and reflective like the ocean or sky or something mesmerizing, strong jaw, brilliant smile, and that body. Parker, his body! Did you see his body!?!' And you would have blushed like you always do because we both would have known you definitely saw his body. But ..." She shrugged. "Now you're just bitter, and apparently you have no radar for that anymore."

Parker saw Levi, but she *felt* Gus. Pieces of him lingered

everywhere. She could close her eyes and taste him on her lips, smell the hint of leather and spice cologne in the crook of his neck, feel every muscle of his back beneath her fingertips, and hear his "I love you" echoing over and over.

He was the wind. The moon sketching shadows. The shiver along her skin at night when she shut off the lights and whispered his name. He promised her everything and left her with nothing. How could nothing—a deep, hollow hole—feel like *something* so tangible, like her pain had its own pulse.

"I wonder how it happened." Parker kept bouncing, eyes fixed to a scratch on her newly finished floors, probably from Rags.

"How you lost your radar for hot guys?"

Parker shook her head, words slow and monotone. "How the accident happened. What caused it?"

"Oh," Piper's tone softened to match the gravity of Parker's question. "Dad heard it was a semi-truck driver. He fell asleep at the wheel. Twelve cars were involved. Five casualties total."

She rotated on the rebounder, her back to Piper. Drawing in a shaky breath, she wiped the corners of her eyes and *smiled.* Parker smiled as big as she could, until her facial muscles burned, chasing the tears away and soothing the throb of grief.

"When were you going to tell me?" Parker cleared her throat and massaged her cheeks.

"About the accident?"

"About you and Caleb."

"Moving here?"

"Screwing around behind my back."

"Parker," Piper said with an edge of pain laced in her voice.

Parker turned again, bouncing even higher. "Had I not caught the two of you, when were you going to tell me? I mean, surely you weren't going to wait until the rehearsal dinner, right?"

"We weren't."

Choking on a laugh of disbelief, Parker stopped jumping. "You weren't? What does that mean?"

Piper frowned, closing her book and setting it aside. "You were engulfed in your quest to find a job. Driving here, there, and everywhere for job interviews—sometimes gone for entire weekends. Obsessing over finding a house for you and Caleb. Talking marriage when he hadn't even proposed. And Caleb still hung around the house even when you were gone. Dad would cook up brats, and they'd eat and drink beer while mom watched some series upstairs. I'd go out and sit by the fire pit with them, but eventually Dad would get tired and go to bed. So Caleb and I would drink more beer and talk about stuff that didn't involve marriage or finding the perfect house."

She glanced over at Parker, a somber expression on her face conveyed more regret than Parker had ever seen before.

"One night we had a little too much to drink. Caleb helped me to my room. Then he was going to call a friend to come get him. A few hushed giggles turned into a kiss. We both stared at each other through glassy eyes like it was a complete accident. We didn't say a word, but it's like our minds shut off and something physical took over. My brain was so fuzzy, I just remember thinking over and over, 'This is so wrong.' But I couldn't stop. I felt so completely out of control."

Parker swallowed hard, expecting to taste bile, but she didn't. Piper's story was *her* story. She was Piper. Gus was Caleb. Desire. She knew the addiction. The power. The guilt.

"That wasn't the night I walked in on you."

Piper shook her head. "No. It happened again and again.

Like a drug." Her cynical laugh shook her shoulders a bit. "Remember when Mom told us giving up our virginity before marriage would basically make us sluts? We'd slip into a habit of casual sex. It wouldn't be a first. It wouldn't be special. Like after you commit a sin once, it's easier to do it again and again. That's what happened.

"The crazy part is we barely talked about it. We'd chat with Dad like we'd always done. He'd go to bed and we'd go to my room and ... do the same thing. Very few words. Just like rolling up your sleeve and plunging the needle into your vein. The guilt was there for two seconds, and then it disappeared while we 'got high' so to speak."

Parker thought about her sister's explanation. She had never asked for it before that moment, but she imagined it. However, in her imagination, it involved love and intense emotions. Feelings that couldn't be denied. It never involved too much alcohol and casual sex. "But you loved each other, right? I mean, you're married."

"I do love him, and he loves me."

"That's a weird answer. We're talking about the past. We're talking about why you had no intention of telling me, which makes no sense."

"It was sex," she whispered.

Taking a step down from the rebounder, Parker moved closer to the sofa. "As in *just* sex?"

Piper nodded.

"But you married him."

"I was pregnant."

"What?" Parker's head whipped back.

"A week after you caught us, I found out I was pregnant. No one knew, not even Mom. Caleb, being Mr. Responsible, proposed. Me, being scared out of my fucking mind, said yes. Two weeks later I miscarried."

"Jesus, Piper, why didn't you say something?"

"I was ashamed and embarrassed. I didn't want anyone's pity."

"You didn't love him."

"I cared about him."

"Not the same thing."

She blew a slow breath out of her nose. "I wanted it to mean something. I ruined you and Caleb, so I wanted something to come from it. Love justified it."

"But you didn't love him!" Parker ran her hands through her hair.

"You didn't know that!" Piper's hand went to her belly as she took a deep breath and sat back again.

"Me? Are you serious? You married him for *me*? Do you hear yourself? Can you see how ridiculous that was?"

"I thought if you could see that it was for love, it would make it easier to forgive him. You'd think his heart was in it and it wasn't just some random guy act of not being able to keep his dick in his pants."

Parker laughed, a crazy woman laugh. "He *couldn't* keep his dick in his pants. Why were you so damn concerned about him if you didn't love him? Why did it matter to you if I forgave him or not? He pissed me off, but you're the one who hurt me. Don't you get that? *You* cheated on me. *You* broke my heart. *You* destroyed us! I didn't need you to pretend to be happy. I needed you to 'for real' feel some remorse and make an effort to repair us, not ... marry some dick with legs that you didn't love and who would be like a fucking misspelled tattoo that you're too broke to have removed!"

"A dick with legs? A misspelled tattoo?"

Parker and Piper turned. Caleb stood in the doorway to the kitchen, hands in his pockets, a weary look on his face. Piper held out her hand. Caleb walked over to her and caressed his fingertips along her palm, then bent down and pressed a kiss to her lips and then her belly.

"I wasn't head-over-heels in love with the man I married." Piper's smile grew wider until it reached her eyes as she looked up at Caleb and his expression matched hers. "But I'm deeply in love with the father of my baby and the life we now have together. All it took was taking my conscience out of the equation, letting go of the guilt, and welcoming the chance at love while it was standing right in front of me."

That had Parker tasting bile. Too mushy. Too … everything. "You guys are messed-up. I hope all of your weird traits are recessive in my nephew. Otherwise, he is doomed!"

Piper stood and wiped some of her red lipstick from Caleb's lips. "I'm going over to Mom's. She had cookies in the oven when I last talked with her."

He perked up. "Then I'm coming too."

She shook her head and patted his chest. "I'll bring some back. You stay and explain to Parker why you cheated on her too."

Parker headed up the stairs. "I'm done talking for today."

Caleb started his own protest.

"Why did I bring it up?" Parker whispered, plunking down on her bed. "I need a job. I need to move out of Iowa. I need to forget my past before I drown in it." She ran her hands through her hair.

"Hey."

She looked up and sighed. "You're off the hook, Caleb. I

don't want to know. It won't change anything. I'm perfectly satisfied knowing the fairy tale between the two of you was a hoax."

"I love her." His shoulder rested against the doorframe as he slid his hands into the pockets of his white shorts.

"Well, you should. She's carrying your baby."

"I thought I was missing out on something." His brow tensed as his gaze affixed to his feet. "We'd been together for so long. High school. College. I'd lost my autonomy. Everything was a 'we' not an 'I.' I felt like my future was all planned out and the pressure began to suffocate me. But I liked your family, and I actually enjoyed being at your house the most when ..."

Parker sighed a small laugh, rolling her eyes toward the ceiling. "When I wasn't there."

He nodded. "Your dad would tell me about his life growing up and all the stupid things he did. Or we'd discuss sports or just random shit. Since I grew up without my father, I craved that kind of attention. And Piper would join us, and she never mentioned you either. I think she needed her autonomy too. You were the perfect twin. The one who had more friends. The one who was most successful in sports. The one who had her life together and all planned out. She was messy. You were organized. She was spontaneous. You lived by your planner."

Parker no longer had a planner—she no longer had plans. Her house was organized, but her life felt like a tornado ripped through it. She had no direction. No future. No Gus. Life knocked her flat on her ass, and some days she questioned if the effort to try and get up was worth it.

"I shouldn't have followed you to college."

"I told you not to." He looked up.

"You never told me not to! You went on and on about volleyball being my life and how I'd probably forget about you. You made it sound like I was making a choice. You or volleyball."

"I just wanted you to think I'd miss you."

"Are you kidding me?" She shot off the bed and paced the room. "A simple, 'Hey, I'm going to miss you, but this is an opportunity you shouldn't pass up. We'll make it work,' would have sufficed."

"I'm sorry. I was afraid of hurting you."

She scrubbed her hands over her face. "Wow, it's crazy how you've derailed my life in some grand effort to not hurt me."

"I'm sorry," he whispered.

Parker stopped her pacing and rested her hands on her hips. "I am too." Never did she imagine apologizing to Caleb. In the deepest recesses of her mind, she thought someday an apology to Piper for the laxative incident at their wedding might feel right.

Caleb glanced up with confusion etched on his face. He probably never imagined her apologizing either.

"I like organization. I like direction. I like feeling a sense of accomplishment at the end of every day." She lifted her shoulders. "That's who I am. So I'm sorry if my dreams weren't yours. I loved volleyball. I loved the idea of playing it in college. But I gave it up because I may not have been your dream, but … you were mine."

"Parker," Caleb whispered.

She moved to the door and pressed her hand against his chest, applying enough pressure that he stepped back. "I learned my lesson. I hope you learned yours." Her tight-lipped smile bid him a farewell as she closed her door.

Chapter Twenty-Four

SQUEEZING PAST THE lovebirds in the kitchen, making a huge breakfast and an even bigger mess, Parker grabbed some coffee and headed to the back door.

"Where you going?" Piper asked, breaking eggs into a bowl.

After two days of wallowing in grief that she couldn't share with anyone, Parker needed out of the house and something to distract her from life.

"It's overcast, so I'm going to paint the shed."

"Today?"

"Yes, Piper, today."

"By yourself?"

"Yes, by myself."

"Is everything okay? You've been moping around for two days. You don't seem like yourself."

Parker found it interesting that after no contact for two years, Piper thought she knew her well enough to know if she was herself or not.

"Surprise! This is the new me. I like to mope then binge on a major project like painting the shed. Later." She fled the house before any more questions were asked.

As soon as she stepped outside, Rags shot through his doggie door straight to the fence, jumping up and barking. Parker sipped her coffee and walked his way. "Hey, what are you still doing here? I thought you'd be in Arizona by now." She opened the gate, and he circled around her, his whole backside wiggling out of control. "Did you get left behind?"

Rags rolled on the ground. Parker squatted down and rubbed his belly. "Did Mr. Muscles eat your turkey jerky and leave? I bet he did," she said in a baby-talk voice.

"Mr. Muscles didn't go anywhere."

Parker grinned as she looked up at Levi approaching the fence. He too had a cup of coffee in his hand.

"The Mr. Muscles reference was to me, correct?" He winked with a twitch to the corner of his mouth.

"Maybe." She stood, taking another sip of coffee. "Thought you'd be gone by now."

"Me too." He watched Rags chase his tail until a butterfly lured him in another direction. "But he's been having accidents in the house and…" Levi's face wrinkled "…eating it."

"Oh, eww, why?"

"I took him to the vet yesterday. He said it might be anxiety from losing his …" Levi took a long sip of his coffee as if it could drown his emotions.

"His people?"

Levi nodded. "I'm not sure how he knows they're gone. What if they were just traveling?" He shrugged. "I don't know. Dog sense, I suppose. Anyway, the vet gave him anti-anxiety pills and said he should be better in a few days." He tapped his foot on a patch of dirt and loose sod by the fence. "His doggie door has been locked until this morning. I've been taking him out on a leash to do his business because he wouldn't stop digging holes by the fence. I think he's trying to escape."

"Rags." Parker frowned while shaking her head. "Levi, there's no shame in trying to find him another home."

"Are you offering to take him?"

She chuckled. "No. Not unless he comes with the house and a spending account. I don't have a new job yet. We'd both starve after a while."

"If I wouldn't feel incredibly guilty about not honoring my sister's wishes, I'd take you up on your offer."

She squinted at him. "My offer? I just said I couldn't take him."

"Unless you had the house too and a spending account. Right?"

"Ye-ah ..."

He grinned, and after a few seconds, she did too.

"You're real funny. What did you do? Steal my Powerball ticket?"

Levi scratched his head, ruffling his shaggy, bronzy-blond hair. "Something like that. So, what are you up to today?"

"I'm going to repaint the shed."

"Oh yeah? What color of paint did you buy?"

"I haven't yet. There's a recycling place not too far from here where people drop off leftover paint. I'm going to see if there's enough of one color to paint the whole thing. If not, I'm not opposed to using two colors. If they're coordinating colors, it might look cool."

"Okay, let me rephrase, what color are you hoping to find?"

"Well..." she grinned " ...it's been white forever, blue is my go-to color, but red is really the flashy choice, so I'd have to say red. But I'm not holding out for either one of those colors. It will end up being beige, gray, or some other earth tone."

"You never know, it could be your lucky day."

"Yeah, we'll see."

"Do you want some help painting it?"

She didn't, at least she thought she didn't until Levi offered and made her question if spending the day by herself with a ladder, buckets of paint, and the shed was what she really wanted. "Sure, but it's hot. Don't feel obligated. I can do this on my own. No problem."

"I have a quick errand I need to run. Then I'll change my clothes and go with you to pick up the paint. Say ... in about an hour?"

It was her chance to be alone. Write *fuck you, Gus, for leaving me* on the back of the shed and then paint over it. Therapy at its best. But maybe Levi needed the company as much as she needed to be alone. He lost his family. She lost a mistake.

"An hour sounds good. I'll mow and trim the grass around the shed and check my supplies."

He shot her a roguish grin, and she knew it was the right choice.

"DO WE TRUST Old Blue to get us there and back?" Levi asked when Parker managed to get it started on the fourth try.

"Yes. He's old but faithful." She put it in *reverse* and backed out of the garage.

"Except at funerals."

Parker shrugged. "It was an off day. Gotta give him a little slack. With all of those other nice cars parked close by, I think he felt pretty intimidated. Performance anxiety. It happens, right?" She glanced over at Levi and winked.

He perked a brow. "What are you implying?"

"Nothing. Nothing at all." She pulled onto the main road and gave Old Blue some gas before he tried to die on her.

"Where did you get the old clothes?"

Levi looked down at his faded blue Nike T-shirt and jeans with holes in the knees. "I dug them out of the trash. They were old clothes from Gus's closet, not worthy of donating."

Parker drew in a slow breath to mask any reaction.

"Is this weird? Wearing a dead person's clothes?"

"You offered to let me take some of Sabrina's stuff."

"Did you think that was weird?"

Parker laughed. Yes, she thought it was a little creepy. "No."

"Are you being honest?"

She shot him a quick sideways glance. "Asks No Lie Levi who doesn't like to be pestered for the truth."

"So, it is weird. That's all you had to say."

Levi's approach to life and death was refreshing. He showed glimpses of his grief with unfinished sentences and the occasional pull to his brow, but mostly he moved on like it was expected of him to keep living and not give the past too much energy.

"Are you good at painting?"

"Sure."

"Sure?" She grinned. "What's the last thing you painted?"

"A model of one of my designs in college."

"In college?"

"Yes."

"Oh boy ..." She sighed as they pulled into the recycling center. When she turned off the engine, Old Blue backfired.

Parker pressed her lips together and closed her eyes.

"He's just nervous." Levi chuckled. "That's what people do when they get nervous, right?"

Parker opened the door, cringing at the piercing moan of

it, then she shut it and walked to the building without waiting for Levi.

"Good morning." The young man behind the counter stood as she walked through the door. "What can I help you with today?"

Levi slipped his hands into his pockets and looked around at the shelves of used products.

"I'm looking for paint for my shed. It's really an oversized garage, so I'll need quite a bit."

The guy behind the counter kept glancing at Levi. When Parker turned to look at him, Levi smiled, lips tight to his teeth. An unusual smile that looked incredibly guilty.

"Any specific color?"

"Red is my first choice, but I'm sure that's not an option so—"

"As a matter of fact, we recently had someone drop off quite a bit of red paint. The wrong tint. Here, I'll show you." He lifted a gallon of it onto the counter and opened it.

Parker leaned forward. "Doesn't look like it's been used."

"Nope. Like I said, wrong tint." He dipped his finger in it and smeared in onto a scrap piece of wood.

"It's a great red." She grinned.

The guy nodded.

"How much?"

"Nothing. We only charge for large quantities of neutral colors." He set up gallon after gallon pails of red paint onto the counter.

"These are all full?"

He nodded, glancing over her shoulder again at Levi.

"Well, damn! We'll take them."

She grabbed two gallons. Levi and the guy grabbed the rest

and carried it to the truck.

"Can you believe it?" she said as they fastened their seat belts.

"It's your lucky day."

"I'd say."

Their last stop was the hardware store.

"What are we doing here?" Levi asked.

"I need an extra brush, a roller cover, and pan liner."

"Oh. I'll wait in the truck."

"What? No. It's too hot, and if Erma is working today, she'll talk my ear off. I need you to drag me out before she gobbles up my whole day."

Levi chewed the inside of his cheek.

"What's your deal?" Parker opened her door. "You're acting strange. Or maybe this is you. Are you just strange, Levi Paige?" She laughed.

His grin looked like the side effect of constipation as he got out of the truck.

"Parker!" Erma greeted her from behind the counter.

"Hey, Erma. Don't get up. I just need a few things for my painting project."

"Wasn't going to, honey. My hip's bugging me too much today. Getting old is a bitch. Don't do it."

Levi took a quick left down the first aisle.

"Erma this is Levi. He's helping me out today."

"Hey, Levi."

"Mmm."

Parker laughed at his hum for a response. She grabbed what she needed and took it to the checkout, looking around for Levi.

"Whatcha painting now?" Erma asked.

"The shed."

"God, I wish I had a fraction of your energy." She scanned the items.

Parker gave her a polite smile, trying to avoid too much engagement in conversation.

"Levi, let's go. Thanks, Erma." It was a new record. Erma's hip must have really been bothering her.

Parker waited by the door. Levi came out of the first aisle with his chin to his chest, head cocked away from Erma.

"Oh, hey, you again," Erma said.

Levi gave her a quick nod and sped up.

"Red's a great color for a shed, Parker."

Levi stopped with a cringe on his face.

Parker cocked her head to the side. "I didn't tell you what color I was painting the shed, Erma."

"But your friend was in here earlier this morning buying red paint. I just assumed ..."

"Thanks, Erma," Parker said while scowling at Levi. "Have a nice day."

She pushed through the door, stomping toward the truck.

"Don't be mad."

Parker jerked open the door to Old Blue and tossed the bag inside. Levi got in on the other side.

"Why would I be mad?" She tried to start the truck. It wouldn't start. She tried several more times then dropped her head back and sighed. "No Lie Levi lied to me."

"I didn't lie."

"Omission of the truth is a lie."

"I told you *that* kind of lie I can do."

She laughed and rolled her head to the side. "I see."

"Don't be mad. I wanted you to have a red shed."

"Why?"

Levi shrugged. "Because I like you. And when you're happy it's a pretty damn good day. I haven't had too many of those recently, so …"

She blinked owlishly. "It's the nicest thing anyone has ever done for me. Thank you." A crooked smile touched her lips.

He leaned over and turned the key. Old Blue came to life. "See…" he sat back with a huge grin of satisfaction " …it's a damn good day."

Chapter Twenty-Five

L EVI WAS THE salve to Parker's hurting heart. When they were together the grief was bearable. When she smiled and laughed with him, it felt good. No guilt. She wondered if he felt the same.

"Now *that's* a shed." Levi crossed his arms over his chest as they stood back a few yards inspecting the finished red shed.

"It's the perfect color."

He grinned. "I think so too."

Parker turned to him. "Thank you. That was several hundred dollars in brand-new paint." Her lips twisted to the side. "Weren't you afraid of someone else taking it before we got there?"

"I'm hungry. How about you?"

"Levi ..."

"I told the guy at the recycling center to hold it behind the counter for you."

"You told him?"

He shrugged. "With some cash, I told him to save it for you."

"You paid for the paint, and then you paid for someone to save it for me?" Her head jutted forward. "Wouldn't it have been cheaper to just take me with you to buy the paint in the first place?"

"Would you have let me do that?"

She thought about it. "No."

"Then there's your answer. Now, food. Can I take you to dinner after we change our clothes?"

"No." She looked down at her paint-splattered clothes. "Dinner is on me. But I'm starving too, so let's go." She started toward Old Blue parked by the fence.

"Where are we going?" He followed her.

"Get in."

He grinned as he hopped in. "We're a mess."

She got it started on the second attempt. "We are. Here." She tapped her finger on her phone. "When they answer, order a large pizza to go with your favorite toppings."

He took her phone as she pulled out. "What do you want?"

"I'll eat anything."

When they pulled up to Casey's General Store, she grabbed some cash from the glove compartment.

Levi laughed. "Great place to keep cash."

"I know. Right? Be right back. Don't let Blue die."

A few minutes later she returned with a pizza box and a twelve-pack of bottled beer.

"Where's the party?" Levi inspected the beer as she handed him everything.

"You'll see."

They drove back toward the house, but she pulled off the road into a field just before reaching her drive.

"What are we doing?"

She opened her door. "It's my field, nothing got planted this year. So we're going to eat, drink, and look at the stars."

Levi got out. "It's not dark quite yet, and we're under a sky full of clouds."

Parker opened the tailgate and climbed in back. He handed her the beer and pizza then climbed in beside her, their backs resting at the front of the bed, near the back window.

"That's why I got a twelve-pack of beer. By the time we're done, we'll think we see the stars." She grabbed a beer and twisted off the top then handed it to him.

"Did I mention that I really like you?"

She twisted off the top to her beer and clinked it against his. "I like you too."

"Twelve beers might not make us legal to drive."

She took a long swig. "That's why we're in walking distance from home." She set her bottle on the edge of the truck and opened the pizza box between them. "Have you ever had pizza and beer in the back of a pick-up truck in the middle of a barren field?"

Levi grabbed a slice of pizza and took a big bite then shook his head. "No," he mumbled, "never."

"Then you really haven't lived." She stretched out her legs and crossed them at the ankles, releasing a deep sigh after another long pull of beer. "Here's what you can expect. It's going to be a little rough going with the mosquitoes as the sun sets. But once we get enough alcohol into our systems, we'll be good. Mosquitoes? What mosquitoes?"

"Tomorrow we'll be hungover and itchy as hell, probably with some mosquito-transmitted disease settling into our bloodstream."

Parker giggled. "So you *have* done this before."

"No. Just an educated guess."

They drank more than they ate, which wasn't a good thing. By four beers Parker was slipping into her drunken state.

"So let me get this straight..." Parker leaned back flat to

look at the stars that weren't there "...you played lacrosse in college and you still play, but sex is your workout of choice? Maybe you're just a sex addict and you're trying to justify it by making it seem like it's heart-smart."

Levi spit out part of his eighth beer as he laughed. "Where did that come from? You asked me about college. How did my playing lacrosse turn into a sex addiction problem?"

She sighed then giggled. "I don't know. It's your problem, not mine."

He lay down beside her. "I'm so fucking buzzed right now, I can't even defend myself against your crazy accusations."

"It feels so good to not feel."

He chuckled. "That makes no sense."

"Is it the amount of time you have sex that makes it workout-worthy or the positions?"

"Fuck me ... your thoughts are so damn random." He slurred his words a bit as he laughed.

"Tell me! How much alcohol do you need before you can tell me what I want to know?"

"Fine. It's both." He rolled onto his side, head propped up on his hand.

She rolled over, facing him, mirroring his pose. "Favorite position?" Her body tingled from the alcohol, and her judgment was delayed, but her mouth asked the question anyway.

"For pleasure or workout?"

"There's a difference?"

"Of course." He wet his lips and let his eyes roam down her body.

Drunk Parker liked it. Sober Parker would be very disappointed in her.

"Workout," she said.

"Standing."

"Against a wall?"

"No wall. Just standing."

Parker let her eyes drift shut.

"What are you doing?"

"Imagining it."

He chuckled.

"So nothing? No wall. No desk. Nothing? Just you doing all the work?"

"Are you … imagining *me*?"

Her eyes blinked open. "No. Yes. No."

"Were you imagining you?"

"Yes. No. Yes." She giggled. "I don't know. Stop making me blush. I can't think right."

"You started this." He bent his leg and nudged hers.

She nudged him back. "Pleasure?" She bit her lip.

He reached over and pulled at her hair, removing some dried paint. "Don't you think this is a dangerous conversation after twelve bottles of beer? When my brain is fuzzy, and my eyes can't focus, and my hands feel like they want to wander a bit."

Parker sat up, a little wobbly. "I need more pizza. Did you eat the rest?" She spotted the box on the other side of him. "There it is." She threw a leg over his midsection and leaned up, stopping when his hands gripped her waist. "Oh …" Her gaze dragged along his torso as she sat astride him. She giggled. "Well, now you know my favorite position."

As she started to reach for the pizza, Levi sat up, bringing them face to face.

Shallow breaths. Drunken gazes. The lingering scent of whatever made Levi smell so fucking irresistible—like a crisp, cool day lost in a grove of pine and cedar wood trees. Parker couldn't decide if she wanted to inhale him or devour him.

"When's the last time you did something really stupid?" he whispered in a throaty voice, sliding his hands up the back of her shirt.

He could touch her or she could breathe, but the two couldn't coexist.

"I-I'm drunk. And this is ... wrong." Her words came out breathy as she gripped his biceps to steady herself or stop him. Maybe stop herself. She didn't know. But buying a twelve-pack of beer in an emotionally vulnerable state and drinking it with a man who looked like all kinds of trouble—*that* was the answer to his question.

Levi grinned. "So am I. And it probably is. But ... do you wanna do something stupid with me?"

Her eyes blinked slowly as her lips parted. "How stupid?"

With one flick, he unfastened her bra. "Pretty fucking stupid."

The screech of crickets and croaking of the toads by the pond across the road marked time while they both waited for Parker's next move. It hurt to think. So she didn't.

"I hope you're good at stupid." She lifted her arms.

Levi's eyes lit up the night. "You have no idea." He pulled off her shirt and then shrugged off his.

Her sluggish gaze shifted between his eyes and his bare chest. "Well, damn ..." She wet her lips and grinned.

He pulled her bra off her arms and tossed it over the side of the truck.

"Hey—"

He shoved her hands behind her back, clasping her wrists in one hand, tugging them down just enough to force her chest forward and her head back. "Shhh …" He ran his tongue down her neck. Cupping her breast, he brought her nipple to his mouth and sucked it so hard she jerked and moaned, head falling back even more.

In the half seconds of reprieve where his mouth moved with precision from one erogenous zone to the next—and he knew them all—Parker's brain tried to find sobering thoughts. But after that much alcohol, it was fruitless.

"Don't come …" she whispered, eyes fighting to stay open as Levi manipulated her like a rag doll, making her body bend and submit to him.

He released her arms, and she fell forward. He cupped her face in his hands and devoured the skin along her neck and jaw. "What did you say?" he whispered in her ear.

"I told…" she feathered her fingers down his chest "…myself not to come yet." She grinned when she felt his lips pull into a smile against her cheek. "I think it's a lost cause."

"God, I hope so." Levi pressed his mouth to hers, thoroughly exploring it. He tasted like beer and every ounce of *desire* she'd craved since Gus pinned her against the fridge.

Parker unfastened his jeans with clumsy hands then pushed against his chest, breaking their kiss. "Back." She beamed, feeling drunk, high, and overly-confident.

Levi grinned, inching back while she teased his abs. His eyes drifted shut when she scooted down, releasing him from his briefs, and did what she only did after four beers, a week from hell, an unexplainable death, the loss of something that was never hers, and a man who made numb feel like nirvana.

"God … damn …" Levi fisted her hair controlling her every move.

After a minute or so, he pulled her away, sat up, and lifted her hips like she weighed nothing. "Stand." He laughed as her legs buckled like spaghetti.

She giggled, grabbing his hair to steady herself. "The cars driving by see my headlights. Get it?"

He peeled off her jeans and panties, tossing them over the side of the truck too.

"Not cool." She frowned.

"Turn." Holding her hips, so she didn't trip over his legs, he helped turn her so her ass was level with his face.

"Ow! Did you just bite me?"

Levi licked the bite mark on her ass and grinned. "Down." He guided her into a squat.

"You could ask nicely." She laughed, falling back into him, not a shred of balance left in her body.

"I could. But I'm so fucking buzzed all I can feel is my dick, and all I can think about is where I'm going to put it."

"Thanks for your honesty, Drunk No Lie Levi …" She sighed a small laugh. "Hope you don't flub up."

He jabbed her entrance with the head of his cock.

"Jesus…" she gasped " …Christ …"

He pressed his hand to her back, pushing her forward until her hands rested on his legs.

"Flub up?" He chuckled. "I'm not that drunk. Hold on, this could be a rough ride."

He lifted her up a couple inches and jerked her back down onto him.

"Fuck!" Her chin dropped to her chest and the second his right hand slid between her legs, she saw the stars.

Chapter Twenty-Six

TOO MANY HOURS after the alcohol wore off and just as the sun started to edge its way into the morning sky, Parker eased off Levi's chest. Cringing when Old Blue creaked, she climbed out of the truck bed, shaky on her legs, searching for her clothes. She dressed as fast as one could with a painful hangover, walked the half acre to the fence, climbed over it, and clumped her way up the yard to her farmhouse.

She eased open the back door to the kitchen then closed it slowly behind her.

"Good morning."

Parker whipped around. "Caleb."

He smirked, nodding to the counter. "Coffee?"

There was no way to hide the guilt on her face. She felt the heat crawl up her neck. "Shower. But thanks."

Caleb continued to eye her with that stupid smirk. "Long night or early morning?"

"If only it were any of your business." She glared at him as she slipped off her shoes and walked toward the stairs, but he kept grinning as he returned his focus to his phone and sipped his coffee.

She carried an extra hundred pounds of guilt as she climbed the stairs, straight into the bathroom. After flipping on the exhaust fan and turning on the shower, she stripped down and stood in the middle of the bathroom with her face buried in her hands as she cried. There were no words to explain why she felt so incredibly guilty. Why she felt like a cheater again. Why she felt like a terrible person.

Gus was dead. He had been married. They never had sex. Levi wasn't married. They were two consenting adults. And for a few hours after too many beers, she enjoyed life again—emotionally and physically.

Sex. How could something that seemed to ruin everything one minute, feel like the exact thing she needed the next? And she did ... she needed to do nothing more than feel connected to another human without having to use words or make sense of it in her head.

Still, the guilt won over. It always did. Parker sat on the toilet, desperate to relieve her full bladder. "Shit!" She grimaced, leaning to the side. When she finished, she wiped the steam off the mirror and glanced at the refection of her backside. On her right butt cheek there was a red bite mark.

"Lovely." She closed her eyes and wiped a few more tears before getting in the shower.

"STOP LOOKING AT me like that." Parker laughed even as she hugged her nauseous stomach, sitting on the end of her bed, staring at the unpacked suitcase on the floor—*talking* to the suitcase. Maybe she needed to bury it too. That required saying goodbye and that was too much to ask. How could she say goodbye when part of her still waited for him to knock at the door?

Parker rolled her eyes when a real knock sounded at her bedroom door. She hurried and slipped on her shorts and tee then fingered through her wet hair as she opened the door.

"Dad," she said, narrowing her eyes, expecting to see her mom, if anyone, knocking on her bedroom door the morning after a drunken night.

He rubbed his chin. "Uh ... Old Blue is in the field ... with a half-naked guy in the back. Should I call the police?"

"No! I-I've got it. Don't call anyone." She shot past him to the stairs. "Especially—"

"Your mom?"

"Exactly." Parker slipped on her shoes, ignoring Caleb and his dumb-ass grin, and ran out the back door. She figured Levi would have woken up by then and gone home. If he wasn't careful, crows would be pecking at his bits and pieces.

As she approached Old Blue, a bare, hunched back appeared in the bed, moving stiffly. Levi was on all fours and lumbering to his feet. She stopped in her tracks, eyes flitting between the road with cars going by and the burly man standing in the bed of her truck, shirt off, hair a disaster, jeans unbuttoned and holding on for life low on his hips. He brought his fists up to his chin, elbows out, and twisted his torso side to side, mesmerizing her with the shifting and rippling of his muscles. Levi stopped when he spotted her.

"Morning." His face pulled into something between a grin and a grimace. Maybe a grin gone wrong or a grimace trying to redeem itself.

Parker swallowed hard then opened her mouth to speak, but nothing came out. The previous night replayed in her head. Her naked body pressed to *every* part of his. The flex of his muscles when he moved behind her, above her, beneath her. What she couldn't see clearly in her mind, she could feel along her skin. Those lips sucking her sensitive flesh. The slide of his tongue between her legs.

Those hands were not the delicate hands of an artist. They were large, strong, and controlling. Parker liked every single fucking thing he did to her with his hands—palming her ass like he owned it and fisting her hair so she knew it.

Levi fastened his jeans and pulled on his shirt. "You're not real talkative in the morning."

Old Blue whined when he jumped out of the back. "You have that look." He walked toward her.

"Look?" She managed a shaky word past her lingering thoughts and an enormous hurdle of regret.

He nodded. "The what-do-I-say-about-last-night look."

That was the look for sure.

"About last night …"

Levi grinned. "It happened." He shrugged. "It didn't happen. Totally up to you."

There was an option B. She liked that.

"What if it happened?" she whispered.

"Then we talk about it."

"And if it didn't?"

"Then … what didn't happen?" His lips twisted, concealing his amusement.

Before Gus, the answer would have been: the night before *happened*—once the previous night and another three times in her head that morning. But Gus happened, which meant the night before should not have happened.

"It didn't." Her gaze left his and settled on the clumpy dirt around her shoes. "I'm sorry."

"Don't apologize for something that didn't happen." The hard ground crunched beneath him as he walked past her toward the Westmans' house.

Chapter Twenty-Seven

P ARKER RE-CLEANED THE kitchen after the pigs made a mess and half-assed the cleanup. Their kids were doomed. Aunt Parker would be their only example of cleanliness and organization.

Normally she wouldn't have cared about the mess, but it required her to deal with the worst part of the farmhouse—the view from the kitchen sink. She needed to plant a blue spruce in front of it to hide the Westmans' house. It was like a gigantic tombstone staring back at her.

Would the day ever come that she stopped being mad at Gus? She knew he didn't die on purpose, but something inside of her blamed him for her broken heart. He could have died without breaking it, had he not been carrying it around. That's how things got broken. Even children knew that. Why didn't he leave it alone? Let it be. Mind his own business.

Just as she grabbed the last wet dishtowel, Levi walked out with Rags on his leash. He watched the dog sniff for the perfect place to lift his leg, and then he looked toward Parker's house. After a few seconds, he dropped his head and rubbed the back of his neck. When Rags finished, they headed back to the house. Just before he shut the door, Levi looked back toward the farmhouse. Parker took a step backward even though there was no way he could see her.

"Levi ... Levi ... Levi ..." She shook her head. "Pretty fucking stupid. Sex. No condom. No questions." Parker was on the pill, but he didn't know that. Didn't ask. She wondered how many Levi spawns might be scattered throughout the world. How many stupid moments he'd had in his past.

"I probably have HIV or herpes now. Great, Parker. Just great," she mumbled, taking the dishtowels to the laundry room. Aunt Parker needed to work on other areas of role modeling.

THE THREESOME ATE dinner together. Afterward, Piper and Caleb invited Parker to watch a movie with them. She planted herself on the opposite end of the sofa. The movie didn't hold her attention quite like the couple beside her. Caleb's hands covered Piper's, both resting them on her baby belly. Their presence made Parker feel lonelier than when she had truly been alone. Gus took their love to the grave with him. If she couldn't share what they'd had together or how much she missed him, then maybe it never happened. Maybe it wasn't real. Who would ever believe her?

"I'm going to bed." Parker stood.

The happy couple smiled. "Good night."

The wood floor creaked beneath her as she climbed the stairs. She turned left but after two paces, she sighed, turning the opposite way to her new room. The only thing constant in her life was change.

Somewhere between counting all of the memories of Gus in his Cubs cap and then feathering her fingertips over every part of her body he'd touched, Parker fell asleep. Several hours later she awoke to the crack of lightning and the roar of thunder. The war in the night sky flickered and flashed. Parker watched the shadows dance along the wall. She sat up, listening hard to a faint sound that grew louder and louder.

"Rags," she whispered, throwing off the covers and slipping on a pair of shorts under her baggy tee. Easing down the stairs, grimacing at each creak, she hurried to the back door, slipped on her black rain boots and a yellow raincoat.

Gusts of wind sprayed her with rain as the endless flickers of lightening lit her way to the fence. "Shhh ... quiet, you big goof. You can't chase it away." She opened the gate and whistled for him to follow her to the shed. The wind slammed the door shut behind them as she flipped on the light. Rags shook, sending water flying everywhere, not that it mattered. They were already soaked.

Retrieving a couple of old towels from the cabinets, she dried them both off. After sniffing every inch of the shed, Rags dropped to the floor, content with his new surroundings and the company.

"How did you get out? I thought you were on house arrest?"

He blinked at her.

"I can't take you in the house. You're too messy, and I have roommates now that might not like a middle of the night visitor."

Rags cocked his head to the side.

"I know. Who doesn't love a wet dog?" She crossed her arms over her chest. "If I leave you alone, you're going to freak out again, aren't you?"

His head cocked to the other side.

"That's what I figured." She opened several more cabinets and found an old plaid blanket that looked like it had been used as a paint drop cloth on more than one occasion. "This will have to work." She wrapped it around herself and sat down next to Rags. They waited for the storm to quit, but it had more stamina than Parker expected. After an hour or so, her body slumped to the side, head resting on Rags's belly.

"RAGS?" LEVI CALLED.

"Is he in the basement?" his dad asked, putting on a pot of coffee.

"No. That's just where I came from."

"He has to be in the yard," his mom said. It was the most she'd said in days. Even when Levi had been out all night with Parker, she never said anything.

Joe kissed her on the cheek and pulled her into his arms. Levi loved how his parents cared for each other after so many years. He questioned if that kind of love still existed.

"I'll check the yard again, but I didn't see him." Levi walked the parameter of the fenced-in yard for a second time, checking for holes Rags might have dug and making sure the gates were secure. He did a double take that time around as he tugged on the far gate. Footprints of both human and canine were on the opposite side in the mud, filled partially with water.

He opened the gate and followed them to the shed. Easing open the door, he peeked inside. The vision before him sparked an instant smile—Parker wrapped in a blanket, using Rags for a pillow. The dog glanced up at him, but didn't move, as if to say, "Shhh, don't wake the girl." Levi thought only one thing in that moment: lucky dog.

Inching his way into the shed, like stepping on broken

glass, he eased the door shut and sat on the ground opposite of her and Rags. Levi hugged his knees to his chest, resting his chin on one of them. Shifting slightly, she mumbled something that sounded like, "Don't go." Her eyes stayed closed, long lashes resting on her cheeks, lips parted, and hands balled together at her chest. Rags made his own noise as he sighed and rested his head against the floor.

Levi thought about their night together that no longer existed. It was just sex. It was stupid. It was all he could think about.

"What are you doing?" Parker opened her eyes in a few slow blinks, grimacing as she brought herself to sitting.

"You find a job yet?"

She yawned, stretching her arms above her head. "No." Her yawn ended in a chuckle. "We talked about this yesterday. I'm efficient, but not a magician."

"Then come back to Arizona with me." At that point, short of his sister resurrecting from the grave, there was nothing he wanted more. No explanation. No reasoning that made sense. It just *felt* right.

"What?" She narrowed her eyes.

"You don't have a job. Your sister and your ex-boyfriend slash brother-in-law just moved in with you and kicked you out of your room." Levi grinned. "Your truck is total shit. My newly adopted dog loves you. And I know I'll never find the right brand of turkey jerky without you."

Blink

Blink

Blink

"Uh ... I ... don't understand exactly what you're asking me. And I have ..." She frowned as if she had *nothing*. "You're crazy. I told you, I don't have money to travel. And ..." She stood and folded the blanket. "I've reached my lifetime limit of making stupid decisions." Her lips pulled into a sad, apologetic smile.

He knew she regretted what happened.

"I refuse to turn thirty and have nothing to show for my twenties other than a string of mistakes and missed opportunities."

"Don't think of this as a stupid decision; think of it as a missed opportunity if you don't go."

"Really?" She put the blanket in the cabinet and brushed off her clothes. "I think I need a real job."

"We'll look for you a *real* job along the way. If you don't find one, then you'll have my offer which is real."

"Along the way?" Parker perked a brow. "Is this fantasy trip of yours a driving trip or flying? Are we going to look for *Now Hiring* signs 'along the way' and dump me off as soon as someone employs me?"

"If it feels right."

"To who?" She could barely speak without laughing.

"To you. You'll know when it's right. Trust your gut."

"My gut is not trustworthy." She combed her fingers through her hair.

"Sure it is." Levi lumbered to standing and brushed off the back of his jeans.

"And how will I pay for this trip? Are you going to pimp me out? I'm not sure how good I would be at turning tricks."

"I'll pay your way."

"No, thank you." She reached for the door.

He pressed his hand to it. "I think ..." He sighed, eyebrows pinched together. For someone who excelled in the art of honesty, he couldn't find the words, truth or lie. "I think I need you."

Parker's eyes grew. "Excuse me?"

He weighed his words, but they didn't amount to much.

"Is this about—"

Levi shook his head. "It's not about anything *stupid*." It wasn't. As much as he craved their physical connection, he *needed* something more that only she seemed to possess, and he couldn't explain it because it wasn't tangible or easily definable.

"I think asking me to take off with you—no money, no direction, no thought—is not exactly *smart*."

Still, he didn't have the words. He thought if he stood there long enough looking at her, she might understand everything without having to say anything. A long shot.

"You need me for what? Rags?"

"Him too, yes."

"Like a dog sitter?"

"No. Like … just a person in …" His heart had a terrible time keeping up with his nerves. It beat erratically— desperately—in search of reprieve. Why couldn't her mind submit to his feelings the way her body had submitted to his touch?

Keeping her questioning gaze on him, she turned her head a fraction to the side. "Just a person in what?"

"My life." He took the leap, free falling with his stomach in his throat.

Parker pursed her lips, returning a very slow nod. "I … see. So, when my family and friends ask where I'm going and what I'm doing, I should say, 'I'm going to be *a person in Levi's life.*' Is this correct?"

He needed a better plan. Hell, he needed more time to sell

the deal.

"Yeah." He puffed out his chest and grinned, hoping confidence was a trait she admired.

Curling her lips between her teeth, she continued to nod. "Mmm-hmm ... I see. What's the contract on this highly unique position? And specifically what would be my duties? And I need more details on the pay and benefits. Is there room for advancement, or is this just an entry-level position with no place to go?"

"I think we can leave the contract open. And your duties are flexible, depending on your skill level and qualifications. You can pretty much set your own pay and benefits are negotiable." He scratched his chin. "It's definitely an entry-level position, but I think you could be eligible for promotions."

"Sounds like a dream job."

"I'd like to think so."

Shock and disbelief he expected, but not the pain. Within seconds Parker seemed to fade into some distant place as her whole body deflated along with her smile.

"Can we pretend I never said anything? Blame it on a toxic mix of grief and sleep depravation? What do you say?" A total chicken. He needed to find his dick. It must have fallen off in the back of Old Blue.

Chewing on the inside of her cheek, eyes cast downward, she nodded.

"I'm sorry. Again, just ... this never happened. I'm not even here. Rags, let's go." He led the dog out of the shed and back to the house. "You're an idiot," he mumbled to himself, angry for being so impulsive. "Of course she's not going to leave town with some guy she's known for less than a week. God!" Levi face-palmed his forehead as he went into the house.

He needed to find a way to deal with his loss that didn't involve life-altering invitations.

"I need to take your mom home. She can't be here anymore."

Levi turned to his dad's voice at the entrance to the kitchen.

Joe gave him a sad smile. "She's taken a handful of things, but she doesn't want anything else. If you want to stay and go through the rest with the Westmans, that's fine. If not, hire someone to auction it off, sell the house, and ..." He sighed, the previous few days hung in dark bags under his bloodshot eyes.

Levi watched Rags sniff around the kitchen. "I'm going to rent a car and drive him home. His meds seem to be working, so there's no need for me to stay much longer either. I'll wait a few days, but then I'm out of here too."

Joe rested his hand on Levi's shoulder. "I get it. And I know you don't need me to tell you this, but take your time coming home. You're still grieving, and I'm not sure where you were last night, but do whatever you need to work *that* out too."

"Yeah." Levi hadn't taken much time to grieve their deaths. Instead, he found a wonderful distraction. But ... he couldn't take that distraction with him, so the time to face reality had come. He swallowed past the thick emotion, turned his back to his dad, and he *smiled*. Big. Goofy. And soul-crushingly painful.

Chapter Twenty-Eight

I F PARKER STILL had a heartbeat, then it wasn't broken. That was the good news. Gus tried to break it. And for a few days, it seemed as though he had succeeded. Until ... Levi gave her an out. An invitation to live life for a while. She couldn't accept it for many reasons, or at least one: it was insane. Parker Cruse wasn't insane.

"Oh, god ... Caleb."

Not yet, anyway. At the top of the stairs, Parker cringed hearing Piper's moan behind their closed bedroom door.

"So ... fucking ... beautiful ..." Caleb's labored words twisted Parker's gut.

She scurried to her room, easing the door shut behind her. Visions of walking in on them years ago came into clear focus. Time hadn't faded a single part of that memory. With her back to the door, she slid down onto her butt, grimacing from the bruise of the bite mark. A few feet in front of her was the suitcase, still full of clothes, still full of memories waiting to be made.

Gus had shit timing. She chuckled out loud. Maybe she *was* crazy. Blaming him for dying at the wrong time didn't feel like the thought of a person with a sound mind. Was there ever a right time to die? Yes. The right time for Gus would have been after their trip.

After his divorce.

After marrying Parker.

After four kids.

After a dozen grandkids.

Maybe even after a few great-grandkids.

Was that too much to ask?

"Despicable to your last breath, Gus." She continued her one-sided conversation. "You could have at least left me your hat or a good referral for another electrician." Parker slapped a hand over her mouth to mute her laughter. The door at the opposite end of the hall squeaked as it opened. The lovers had finished their morning sexcapade. When she heard their distant chatter in the kitchen, she changed into her workout clothes and prepared to sweat out the crazy inside of her, like exorcising the demons.

DAYS OF OPERATION Get a Life ended in a string of calls and emails thanking Parker for applying but "the position has already been filled," or "we're looking for someone with more experience."

"You could go back to college, even technical training at a community college." Janey passed around a plate of pot roast with her family gathered at her dinner table.

Parker couldn't deny her mother had never looked happier—her whole family together again and on amicable terms. "Medical transcription. Dental Assisting. Massage therapy. Boring, boring, boring. I'd like to break into the media field. There's simply not a lot of options around here."

"Maybe you need to move to a bigger city."

"Bart!" Janey scolded their dad. "I just got my girls back

together again. Stop trying to send them away."

"He's right." Parker nodded, taking a bite of the tender, juicy meat. "A bigger city would mean more job opportunities."

"You went to Chicago after you graduated and didn't find anything there." Her mom had to remind Parker of her failed attempts at finding a good job after graduation.

"Maybe I should try again. Or be open to moving anywhere I can get a break. I need experience in this field, and right now I'm not in a position to be choosy."

"This is too upsetting. You're all trying to ruin my happiness." Janey slumped in her chair. "Sometimes I feel like nobody wants to be around me. I hope you girls both have kids someday that don't want to be around you either, so you can know how I feel."

Parker and Piper shared knowing smirks. At that moment, they weren't twins at odds with one another, they were sisters who knew how their mother turned everything into a violin-playing sob story of how nobody loved her. They'd watched her drag her blanket through the dirt many times over the years. Janey wasn't suicidal, but she craved the attention that came with "sometimes I think you'd be better off if I weren't around," or "sorry my opinions don't matter to you. Clearly I'm nothing more than a burden in your life."

"So in other news ..." Caleb interrupted.

Janey rolled her eyes. In spite of everything, she loved him as much as if he were her own son. And he could get away with far more than Parker or Piper.

"There's been another delay in starting construction on our house."

"Oh, god, you're living with me forever, aren't you?" Parker mumbled while blotting her mouth with a napkin.

"Sorry to disappoint you, but no."

"They just put the Westmans' house on the market." Piper's back straightened as she smiled on a deep inhale. "We're going to look at it tomorrow, and if we like it, we're going to make an offer."

"Oh my!" Janey pressed her hand to her chest, alight with excitement. "We're all going to be neighbors!"

"What?" Parker didn't recognize her own voice, but it was enough to silence the room, landing all eyes on her.

"Um …" Piper's eyes flitted between Parker and everyone else at the table. "I thought you'd be happy. If we buy their place, then we won't be living with you as long."

"But that's …" Parker lowered her voice, searching for an explanation that would make sense to them. She had to find one. She *had* to. "They died. Won't it feel weird living in their house?"

Caleb shrugged. "It's not like they died in the house. And we didn't know them, so I don't see what would be weird about it."

"I knew them." Her heart meant it as a plea, but she couldn't say it louder than a whisper and still hold it together.

"For a month. That's not that long." Her mom leaned over and rested her hand on Parker's. "I'm not implying that you don't miss them, but I don't think it would be weird for very long. I'm sure in ten years when Piper and Caleb fill that house with kids and our family memories, you probably won't even think of the Westmans."

Ten years was a long time. A month was not. But it didn't take Gus long to leave a permanent mark on Parker. Time couldn't erase that no matter how many kids and memories

Piper and Caleb shared in that house.

"We might not even like it." Piper shrugged with a flash of nerves curling her lips.

They would love it. It was well-built and stunning. Parker knew it wasn't a matter of if they moved in, but when.

EXCUSING HERSELF, PARKER walked home to have some time alone to process another bend in the road of her life. She held her hand up to her forehead, squinting at the Westmans' house. A white SUV with several boxes, a dog bed, and suitcase behind it occupied the driveway. Levi had to be leaving. It made her happy that he decided to drive Rags instead of putting him on a plane.

She removed her shoes and stood in the suffocating quietude of the farmhouse. Walking across the road wasn't enough distance between her and a life of lonely agony, joblessness, and ghosts only she could see. With the heel of her hand, she rubbed circles on her breast bone, trying to relieve the pain. The only time she could remember not feeling that crushing pressure was with Levi. His touch took it away. It was sunshine and oxygen. It was everything.

"Tell me what to do, Gus." Parker closed her eyes. A second later, she opened them to a dog barking. "Okay, I hear you." A grin stole her face as she ran up the stairs. Grabbing as many toiletries as she could carry in one trip from the bathroom, she threw them in the suitcase, latched it, and lugged it down the stairs. She snagged her purse off the kitchen table and shoved her feet into her blue Chuck's.

The second she opened the door, her lungs took their first breath since the day Gerald arrived at her door. It felt amazing.

Tears stung her eyes. "Wait!" she yelled, dragging her suitcase across the impossible rocky terrain of her drive, chasing the white SUV driving away next door. "WAIT! LEVI!" She waved her free hand. The torque of her purse and suitcase wrenching her shoulder made her grimace, but she didn't stop until Levi started to turn onto the main road.

Grabbing a golfball-sized rock, she pitched it at the vehicle. It pinged against the hatchback. Red brake lights illuminated. Her grin reappeared as she resumed her mad dash. The driver's door opened. Levi stepped out with a wrinkle of confusion along his brow as he moved toward the back of the SUV, staring at her for a long moment before inspecting the vehicle.

"You dented my rental." He ran his fingers over the small dent then looked back at her as she slowed to a stop, breathless.

"Sorry, you wouldn't stop."

His eyes shifted to her suitcase and then back to her. "Didn't know I needed to stop."

Parker adjusted the strap of her purse on her shoulder and tucked her hair behind her ears. "I like to cook. Most of the time I eat a healthy, balanced diet. But sometimes I need random junk food from a convenience store. I need you to accommodate my needs without judgment. Can you do that?"

A twist of the tiniest smile played across his lips as he wet them. "I think so. What does that have to do with you damaging my rental?"

She tugged her suitcase forward, dropping it at his feet. "I'm saying I think I need you."

Torturing her with nothing more than that barely-there smile, he inspected her and her baggage. Turning, he opened the back and put her suitcase on his, next to the boxes. Rags barked from the backseat, tongue out, tail wagging. Levi walked around to the passenger's side and opened the door, his grin growing bigger by the second.

Parker hopped in the front seat, unable to control the excitement on her own face.

"Being needed," he said. "It's a pretty amazing feeling."

She blinked back her tears. "It's indescribable."

THEY MADE IT a good twenty miles down the road without saying a word. Quick sideways glances and subtle smiles said all that mattered. When it sank in that she had in fact done the most spontaneous thing of her entire life, Parker fished out her phone and sent a text to her mom.

> **Parker:** *Please don't make this about you, but I've left to look for my life. I love you and you are needed in my life more than you'll ever know. TTYL xo*

She silenced her phone, knowing it would explode with texts in a matter of seconds.

"Letting people know where you are in case this turns into an abduction?" Levi grinned, keeping his eyes on the road.

"Hope you're not planning on demanding some sort of ransom. My family doesn't have that much money … except for my sister and her husband. But I'm pretty certain they wouldn't pay up."

"Damn! There goes my rent money." Levi grabbed his sunglasses from the drink holder and slipped them on.

"Are we going all the way?" she asked.

Levi shot her a quick sidelong glance then shifted in his seat while clearing his throat. "Um …"

"Oh jeez!" She laughed. "That sounded so wrong. I meant

are we driving straight through and just switching off driving, or are we stopping for the night?"

He massaged the back of his neck. "Oh, well, it's a minimum of a twenty-one-hour drive. We'll make several stops along the way. I'm in no hurry. Are you?"

"I'm just along for the ride. Once we get out of Kansas, it will all be new scenery to me. Drive as slow as you want."

"I don't drive slow, quite the opposite, but we might take a more scenic route."

"Fine by me." Parker said goodbye to her familiar surroundings one flat field at a time. "I have no job, no money, no direction, nobody—except my parents—missing me."

Chapter Twenty-Nine

LEVI LOVED BRILLIANT ideas, drawing tall buildings, racing down the interstate at insane speeds, and making Parker smile. He didn't know for sure what changed her mind, but he didn't wait to find out. The faster he could get her out of town—out of her head—the better. By the time they reached Wichita, it was past dinner time. It surprised him that she didn't say anything about being hungry. Parker didn't say much at all. She seemed content staring out the window, maybe watching the road passing, maybe reflecting on something he couldn't understand.

He had time to figure her out, but he didn't want to rush any of it. She would surrender those pieces in her own time. Everything given. Nothing taken.

"I thought we'd never stop. I'm starving." She unbuckled as they pulled into the hotel's parking garage.

Levi gave her a narrow-eyed look. "I asked you at least a half a dozen times if you needed me to stop."

"No." With stiff movements, she eased out of the car and stretched her arms over her head. "You asked me if I needed to use the restroom, not if I needed to eat. You let Rags out at two different rest areas, but never did you stop for food."

He got Rags out, attaching his leash. "I want to know what you need, even if I don't ask it in the correct way. Okay?"

She grinned, a little shy, a little foolish guilt as she shrugged. "Okay."

"Let's get checked into a room and then we'll grab some dinner."

They let Rags do his business then went to the front desk.

"We need a room for the night, please," Levi said to the gentleman at the front desk.

"Two beds," Parker whispered in Levi's ear.

"Two queen beds, please." He didn't give her a second glance. She asked him to forget about what happened so he couldn't use it as an excuse to assume it would happen again.

"Did you have a reservation?" the front desk clerk asked.

"No."

"We don't have any rooms with two beds. In fact, I only have two rooms available, and they're both suites."

"We'll take them."

Parker nudged his arm. "No. Don't get two suites. One is going to be plenty expensive. I'll sleep on a sofa or in a chair."

He twisted his lips, looking down at her. *She* would sleep on the sofa? He'd never allow it.

"There's an extra fee for pets."

"That's fine. We'll take one of the suites, thank you."

They took the elevator to the twelfth floor.

"We should stick to more affordable hotels for the rest of the trip." Parker grinned with a wrinkled nose. "And maybe plan it out tonight so we can make reservations and not get stuck with suites. You realize they probably had a cheaper room, but you were too agreeable. You really should have pushed him harder for a regular room."

"Hmm ... maybe." Levi twisted his mouth, looking straight ahead at the mirrored elevator doors and the reflection of the beautiful woman beside him with a shaggy dog in the middle.

They stepped off the elevator and made their way to the corner suite at the end of the hall. Levi opened the door and carried in their suitcases as she led Rags inside by his leash.

"Dang, this is a nice room. How much is it a night?"

"I don't know. He didn't say, and I didn't ask."

"What?" She let Rags off his leash to sniff the huge suite. "You just don't want to tell me."

"True. If I knew, I probably wouldn't want to tell you, but if you asked enough times, I'd either tell you or have to sweat through my lie."

"Oh …" She winked. "No Lie Levi."

"I don't love that name." He frowned.

"Sorry. I'll come up with something more original."

"Levi works." He sat on the purple velvety-looking sofa, arms stretched across the back. The simple-but-elegant furnishings had rich fabrics.

Parker followed Rags into the bedroom, situated in the corner of the building, showcasing two different nighttime views of the city. The king bed had an inviting, puffy, down comforter and equally fluffy pillows. White painted double doors opened to a spacious, marble walk-in shower and a separate soaker tub.

"Monogrammed robes. Yup, you're spending a fortune on this room."

He looked over her shoulder as she continued to gawk at the bathroom.

Parker turned, invading his space with hints of vanilla and lavender that still clung to her skin after hours in the car. Levi wanted to do very dirty things to her. The night in the back of the pickup wouldn't stop replaying in an endless loop in his head.

He took a step back to give her some space and so he could breathe. "I saw a McDonald's on the corner. We might want to eat cheap."

He eyed her suspiciously. "Do you like McDonald's?"

She shrugged. "It's fine. I don't usually eat fast food but in a pinch, it works."

"There's a restaurant downstairs. We could eat there."

"Probably pretty pricey. McDonald's is fine."

"I'll call down and order something to be delivered."

"What?" Her head jerked back. "Don't do that. Then we'll have a delivery fee. I'll go down and get it."

He sat on the edge of the bed and dialed down to the restaurant. "What sounds good?"

Parker shrugged. "Anything. I'm not picky."

Levi ordered two of their specials for the night and a bottle of wine. He covered the speaker to the phone. "Do you like wine?"

Another shrug as she stared out the window. "If it's good wine."

"What do you consider good wine?"

She laughed. "The kind that doesn't taste bad."

He removed his hand from the speaker. "Forget the wine. Two bottles of beer, IPAs, something local if you have it. Okay … thank you, bye."

Parker turned to face him, her hands behind her back, resting on the ledge of the window. He leaned back on the bed, fingers laced behind his head. His T-shirt rose up a couple inches, exposing some skin. Her eyes zeroed in on it for a few seconds before meeting his gaze.

"Comfy bed?"

"It's not bad." He patted the area beside him.

With a pensive expression, she studied the bed for a few seconds before walking over and easing onto it, keeping as close to the edge as possible without falling off. He wasn't so sure that she wouldn't fall off if he moved and caused the mattress to shift even an inch.

"Tell me what being a person in your life involves. My job description is a little sketchy."

"Well ..." He pursed his lips. "You travel with me if I want you to and if you want to. We eat together. Walk Rags together. Golf together. Go to concerts, movies, and Broadway shows. Attend car shows. Get coffee. Exercise—"

"Exercise?" She rolled on her side, head propped up on her bent arm. "And by exercise you mean?"

"Whatever you like to do. Interval training, rebounding, whatever."

"And *your* favorite exercise?"

Rolling toward the middle, he mirrored her. "What about it?"

Parker swallowed hard, cheeks blooming red. "Did you ask me to be a person in your life to have sex with me?"

The corners of his lips curled. She didn't say *again*. "No."

"Really?"

Levi cocked his head a bit, giving her a frown. She nodded once as if acknowledging his *truth*. It was a half-truth. After years of practice, No Lie Levi figured out how to give half-truths without breaking a sweat or fidgeting too much.

"Hypothetically, if a woman had sex with you, would she have to worry about anything like ... I don't know, maybe STDs?"

Levi grinned. "Not unless the last woman I had sex with gave me something."

Her eyes narrowed before giving him a sour smile. "Well, I hope for your sake she didn't give you anything, and I hope for her sake you didn't get her pregnant."

He trapped his lower lip between his teeth and nodded slowly. "Terrible assumption on my part, but I'd guess most single women her age are on some sort of birth control, but … I pulled out anyway, so the chances are pretty slim that she's pregnant."

"You did not pull out."

He chuckled. "How would you know? Were you there?"

She picked at invisible lint on the bed. "Well … no. But, I'm just saying if *I* were having sex with a guy, I'd know if he pulled out."

"What if you were too drunk? What if you were doing something so fucking stupid you couldn't remember *the end?*"

"Can we talk about something different?"

"You brought it up."

"Well, now I'm dropping it."

"Then we drop it."

"Show me your tattoos," she whispered.

"Tattoos? How do you know I have more than one?"

Biting her lower lip, her eyes roamed his body as if she was trying to figure out the answer. "Just a hunch."

Levi held out his arm. She traced the outline of a skyscraper.

"Explain." Her eyes shifted to meet his gaze. A toothy grin that he adored took over her lips.

"It's the first building I designed."

Her shiny eyes reflected depths of places he hoped to go

some day. "Where is it?"

"Right here. On my arm." He chuckled.

"No kidding. I mean where is the actual building?"

"On my arm."

She glared at him.

He laughed. "I'm serious. I designed it for an insurance company in Manhattan. Two other architects submitted designs too. Mine wasn't chosen."

He didn't want to move as Parker absentmindedly continued tracing it. Maybe if she touched him, she'd remember how it felt when he touched her. Because he wanted to touch her again so fucking bad.

"I've designed over a hundred structures, this one is still my favorite. I've brought out the blueprints dozens of times trying to figure out what I could have done differently—done better. But even now, eight years later, I still can't find a single thing I'd change. I think it will forever be my best design." He laughed. "And the only one that doesn't actually exist."

"I like that story."

He curled his arm across his stomach as if she'd punched him in the gut. "No! Don't say that. It's a terrible story. So tragic."

"Over a hundred of your designs are out there in the world, probably being occupied by all walks of life. I bet millions of pictures of your 'art' exist in cyber photo world, even blown up on peoples' walls in sleek frames. So what if the one you didn't get to share exists only on your arm. You get to see it every day, like a car you love, or a favorite coffee shop on your way to work, or the wet nose of *your* dog nuzzling your face before your alarm goes off."

Or the girl before me.

She tugged at her lower lip, but it didn't hide her grin—the grin he wanted to kiss off her face more than anything else at that moment. But ... she would have to give it to him. He would take *nothing* from her again. No more regrets.

"Think about it, Levi, it's pretty cool that you've made so many 'marks' on the world, but the one you love the most will be with you for the rest of your life."

"Nice spin." He smiled. "Maybe you're selling yourself short by looking for a job as a sports reporter. I think your ability to spin things would be a huge asset in the political world."

"Yeah? Well, we'll see how my current job goes. I need to make a good impression so I can have a glowing recommendation when my dream job calls me in for an interview."

"So far, I'm very impressed."

"Thanks, boss." She winked. "Now, where else are you inked?"

"My back. Surprised? As in nothing you have ever seen before?"

"I don't know what you're talking about. Sometimes people think they see things they don't. For example, if it's dark outside. Just saying ... So what's back there? Wings?"

He chuckled. "No."

"Buddha?"

"No."

"Serpent? Skull? Tribal markings? Wolf? Samurai? Angels? Jesus? Devil?"

Laughing, he rolled onto his stomach while pulling up his shirt.

"Oh, not what I expected."

Again, her finger traced it. He jumped, feeling her touch in certain places that needed to calm the fuck down.

"It's raised."

"It's over a scar."

"From what?" Her fingers ghosted along his side and lower back.

"Stab wound."

She stilled. "Someone stabbed you in the back?"

"Cowardly, huh?"

"A mugging?"

"Nope. Consequences of the truth."

"Someone stabbed you for telling the truth?"

"Yes. My best friend in high school got hooked on drugs and stole a car one night. When the police asked me about it …"

"You told them the truth," she whispered.

Levi nodded. "He found me before the police found him. Then my mom found me face down in our garage, bleeding out from a stab wound."

"*When life happened* …" she read the words that covered his scar.

When her soft, warm lips pressed to it, he stiffened—*everywhere*. He wanted to roll over and pull her to him. It pissed him off that his stupid scar got the kiss that his lips desired.

Rags barked when room service knocked at the door.

Parker leaped off the bed like a teenager caught with a guy in her room. Levi lumbered to standing at a much slower pace, the kind that gave his erection time to relax.

"Time to eat."

THE GRAVITY OF hopping in the car with Levi had yet to settle into Parker's conscience. She felt a what-the-fuck moment on her horizon; until then, she let herself explore life lived in moments instead of expectations. Her high-school sweetheart derailed her future. Gus did too. They promised her love and hope.

Levi promised her a job, even if it was the craziest job ever. Parker had no expectations beyond one day. If Levi changed his mind, she would go home, get a new job to pay the bills, and look for a different adventure. Comparing her life to anyone else's life wasn't fair.

So what if she didn't run an engineering firm before she turned forty? So what if her jobs never required more than Chucks and a Timex? High heels and flashy technology were overrated.

"This is the best salmon I've ever had." Parker closed her eyes as she chewed, savoring every bite. After a click, the air conditioner hummed to life.

They both sat on the sofa with their feet propped up on the coffee table, plates in their laps.

"I'm glad you approve." He took a drink of his beer.

"I wonder what rub they used on it? Maybe it's better than mine because they used a wood plank."

He chuckled. "I can't wait for you to cook for me."

On a sideways glance, she narrowed an eye. "You didn't mention cooking in my job description."

His gaze fell to her lips, it felt tangible. She shivered, adjusting her body to cover up his effect on her. It was the first time she put down her guard enough to let him have an effect on her without alcohol.

"Fair point. *I'll* cook for you."

"Stop," she whispered, her gaze finding his lips just as appealing.

"Stop what?"

"Being perfect."

"Ha!" He sat up, resting his feet back on the ground, setting his plate on the coffee table. "I'm far from perfect." Running his hands through his hair, he curled his fingers, scratching his scalp. "Has no man ever cooked for you?"

Parker shook her head.

"Well, you need better men in your life."

Agreed. One-hundred percent.

Rags eyed Levi's plate, a string of drool hanging from his jowl. Levi pushed the plate closer to the edge, silent permission for Rags to lick what was left, which wasn't much.

Parker inspected Levi's body every time he turned away from her. She'd seen it, touched it, tasted it, but only in the dark and under the influence of too much alcohol. Levi was a solid form built of defined muscles. She'd nearly self-combusted when he lifted his shirt to show her his scar and tattoo. Skin so tan and taut.

It felt crazy that he could want anything from her—a jobless girl in her twenties who had an affair with his brother-in-law. A truth she couldn't share, not without also sharing Sabrina's indiscretions. Why taint memories with truths that no longer mattered?

"Do you need a shower?"

Her eyes snapped to his as her neck and cheeks flushed. Levi gave her a caught-you smile, but he didn't say anything.

"Um, I usually shower in the morning, but if I smell—"

"No." He chuckled. "I'm going to shower, I was just going to let you go first if you needed to."

"Nope. You go ahead. I'm going to give my mom a quick call."

He nodded once then stood and headed to the bathroom.

"Shit," she whispered, fanning herself. It felt like one hundred degrees in the room, even with the air on. Parker coined it 'The Levi Effect.'

Her mom picked up on the second ring. "Parker!"

"Hi, Mom. I'm fine. Not abandoning you. I will return."

"Where are you?" Her words were clipped.

"Wichita."

"For a job interview?"

"Sort of, yes."

"When will you be home?"

"I'm not sure. I need some time away to clear my head. Find new direction. Maybe a week or two." A month or two. She had no idea, no expectations.

"Do you need money? Have you thought about where you'll stay and how to keep yourself safe? It's not smart for a young girl to travel alone."

"I'm good for now. And I'm not alone. I actually caught a ride with Levi. He rented a vehicle to drive Rags to Arizona."

"Oh ... well, you're not planning on going all the way to Arizona, are you?"

"Maybe, I just don't know yet."

"I don't like this, Parker, not one bit. Stay aware of your surroundings. Don't go out at night by yourself. Don't even leave the hotel room by yourself. And definitely don't use the stairwells in hotels. I know you like to use the stairs to exercise sometimes, but that's where people get raped and murdered."

She prayed the drama gene skipped a generation. "Really? Now I would have thought back alleys of bars where unsuspecting drunk women could wander would be a better play-ground for rape and murder."

"Parker!"

"Sorry," she laughed. "It's just crazy how your mind always jumps to rape and murder."

"Just …" Janey's voice deflated. "Be smart. Be safe."

"I will, Mom. Love you."

"Love you too. Call me tomorrow."

"I'll try. Good night." Parker grabbed her charging cord from her purse and plugged in her phone at the desk. Then she fished a pair of shorts and a nightshirt out of her suitcase. Listening for the shower in the bathroom, she hurried and changed before Levi came out.

There wasn't extra bedding in the closet, so she called down and asked for an extra sheet, blanket, and pillow. Within minutes, Rags barked at the knock on the door. Parker expected nothing less than timely service from the expensive boutique hotel.

By the time Levi emerged from the bathroom in nothing but a pair of jogging shorts riding low on his hips, Parker had her bed made up on the sofa. She stood and grinned, holding her tooth brush, toothpaste, and her breath.

Holy fuck!

Levi used something or sprayed something on himself. An intoxicating mix of sandalwood, warm spices, and patchouli radiated from his half-naked body. Every inch of her hummed in recognition. On their drunken night together it was faint along his skin, but she still recognized the scent that seduced her in the back of Old Blue.

He narrowed his eyes at the sofa. "You're sleeping in the bed."

"No way." She slid past him to the bathroom, holding her breath, one inhale away from begging him to reenact the pickup scene. "You're paying for the room. You will sleep in the bed."

When she came out of the bathroom, Levi was sprawled out on the sofa under the blanket, one arm tucked behind his head. The whole damn room smelled like his cologne, which had to be the brand called '*Fuck Me, Parker.*'

"Get up. Go to bed." She flipped her hip, resting her fist on it.

"I am in bed." He nodded to the light switch. "Mind turning off the lights before you get in bed?"

"You're making me feel terrible."

He flinched a bit. "Rags hasn't developed a love for sleeping with me yet. You two take the bed. Consider it part of your job."

"Sleeping with Rags? Seriously?"

Levi's white teeth peeked through his boyish grin. "Good night, Parker. Today's been a less bad day."

Parker returned a sad smile. A less bad day. Putting the previous two weeks into perspective, that meant something pretty great. She dragged her fingers through his wet hair, surprised by how much they ached to touch him, even more surprised by the way he released a quiet, deep moan. "Good night, Levi."

Chapter Thirty

THEY VENTURED THROUGH part of Oklahoma then into New Mexico. Parker couldn't stop gawking at the diverse landscape of red rocks and other wind-worn rock formations, pathways to deep forests, rivers, plains, and miles of sand dotted with cacti, acacia trees, and mesquite bushes.

Levi couldn't stop looking at Parker.

"I'll be quick." She cringed, hopping out of the SUV and jogging toward the brick building.

It was their third stop in less than two hours. To be fair, he did suggest she stay hydrated. Levi let Rags out to roam since they were the only people at that rest stop. Leaning against the door, he pulled out his phone and took a few photos of the shaggy dog. He flipped back through them, continuing to older photos. Sabrina's picture appeared on his screen like a knife impaling his chest. Living without someone didn't get easier, especially when that someone had been in his life since the day he took his first breath.

"Hey, what's wrong?" Parker asked.

Levi shoved his phone into his pocket as he closed his eyes and pinched the bridge of his nose. "Nothing ..." He shook his head. "Dammit! Not nothing, something ... uh ..."

Parker pressed her palms to his cheeks, and he died a little from the soft strength of her touch. "It's okay," she whispered.

"You don't have to tell me."

His heart raced, ready to explode. "I came across a picture of Sabrina." Levi opened his eyes.

Parker's eyes searched his. He had nothing to hide, no matter how deep she looked. What she didn't know about him yet were not secrets but truths waiting to be shared.

"Memories keep us grounded—give us an appreciation for life. Celebrate her life by living yours to the fullest. We're all going to die eventually."

He covered her hands with his, not wanting to lose her touch. With everything he had inside of him, he begged her to kiss him, to take away the bad and replace it with good.

Parker's thumb brushed over his bottom lip. His eyelids felt heavy, drunk from her touch. Rags barked as another car pulled into the rest area.

"We should get back on the road."

Levi eased his head side to side, holding her hands to his face.

Parker laughed. "No? You think we should stay here? Standing in the parking lot?"

Levi nodded.

The giggle that put all other giggles to shame, bubbled from her chest. "Levi Paige, what am I going to do with you?"

Both of his eyebrows shot up as a playful smile stole his mouth. He eased her hands off his face and held them behind her back like he had done that night in the back of Old Blue. Her breath hitched when he nuzzled his nose in her hair, lips at her ear. She arched her back like she too remembered that position and her body instinctively bent to his silent command.

"This is my favorite day," he whispered, releasing her hands and brushing by her. "Rags!" Levi whistled then looked over his

shoulder. Parker hadn't moved as if his words left her paralyzed. That brought another grin to his face. "Rags, let's go!"

No more drunken nights. He wanted her—completely sober and wanting him just as much.

The sliding door to the minivan, a few spaces down,
opened and out jumped a chocolate Lab. It shot off toward
Rags.

"Hershey!" A man and a woman raced out of the van,
sprinting toward the dogs.

The two dogs ran from the humans.

"Stop! Hershey! No!"

Levi and Parker walked toward the commotion, sharing a
confused look. Neither dog seemed to be aggressive. What was
the big deal?

"Rags!" Levi tried to get the dog's attention, but not with as
much urgency as the couple.

The man continued to chase the Lab. The woman turned
toward Levi and Parker.

"Oh my god! Oh my god! We have to stop them! Hershey's
in heat!"

"Oh, well, I'm sure Rags has been neutered," Levi said,
glancing sideways at Parker for confirmation.

She frowned and shrugged. "How would I know? You gave
them the dog. Did you have him neutered first?"

"You don't know if your dog is neutered?" The woman's
head jutted forward as her words sent spit in their direction.
"How can you not know if your dog has been neutered? What
kind of dog owners are you?"

"The new kind." Levi chuckled.

The woman threw her hands in the air and chased the man
who had disappeared into a wooded area along with the dogs.

Levi's nose crinkled as he bit his lips together. "I didn't have him neutered. I assumed they would do it."

"NO! NO! NO! NOOO!" A shrill screech echoed from the woods.

"Rags mounted Hershey," Levi said.

"Yup." Parker nodded.

A few minutes later, the couple dragged the dogs out by their collars.

Levi attached the leash to Rags. "Sorry about that."

"Sorry? Are you kidding me?" The lady's jaw dropped.

He wasn't privy to the proper way to apologize for his dog humping another dog. Some things they didn't teach in architecture school.

"If I find out he's not neutered, we're going to sue your ass." She lifted Rags's hind leg and then dropped it, stumbling back with her hand splayed over her mouth. "Oh my god! He's not neutered!"

"Are you sure?"

"YES!" She maneuvered Rags onto his side and then his back, spread eagle. "His testicles are NOT empty! See?"

Levi and Parker squinted for a second and then nodded.

"Hershey is a purebred Labrador Retriever. We're on our way to have her bred because she's in heat."

"Are you sure she's in heat?" Parker asked.

"Yes! Of course, I'm sure. Her vulva was swollen all last week, clear up to her pelvic opening, and her discharge was darker. She walked with her tail between her legs, and she refused to eat well. Now she's eating and her discharge is lighter in color. Did you see her tail? Did you see how high she had it? Fanning her scent for your stupid mutt."

Levi held up his hand. "Just calm down. He's not a mutt.

He, too, is a purebred—Old English Sheepdog. I have papers to prove it. Do you want to see them?"

"No, I don't want to see them. I want your contact information so my attorney can have you served with papers."

Levi laughed. "You can't be serious."

"Your dog raped my Hershey!"

"Whoa ..." Parker shook her head. "You just went on and on about her being in heat. Waving her tail in the air. Fanning her scent. Your slut mutt practically begged for it. I think we need to consider Rags was the probable victim here. Maybe *you* need to give *us* your contact information so our attorney can serve papers."

"That's absurd!" The man shook his head. "What grounds do you have for suing us?"

"Rape. Emotional distress and trauma. Rags recently lost his owners. The last thing he needed was a swollen vulva shoved into his snout."

They both gasped.

"Parker, take Rags and get in the vehicle while I settle this." Levi handed her the leash.

She flashed the couple a pointed look before pulling Rags back to the SUV.

"So what's it going to take?" Levi pulled out his phone and conducted a few internet searches. "Looks like the average number of Lab puppies in a litter is between six and ten. We can say ten. And," his thumbs continued across the screen, "two thousand a dog looks plenty fair. I won't even take out the cut you'd have to make to the owner of the other dog. Pad a little extra for your bitch's vet bills, and I think twenty-three grand sounds fair." He retrieved his wallet. "Here's my business card and a thousand cash. Go breed your dog. If in a couple months she gives birth to pups that look like a cross between our two dogs, then call me. I'll come get the pups and pay you the remaining twenty-two thousand in cash."

The couple stared at the ten crisp hundred dollar bills. "What if she isn't pregnant?" the guy asked.

"Then you have a grand to put toward your wife's therapy. Enjoy the rest of your day." He turned and walked to the vehicle.

"Did you tell them to shove their lawsuit threats up their asses?"

Levi chuckled as they pulled onto the main road. "Nah, we probably should've had him on a leash."

"Well, they should have had her on a leash."

"True. But if my boy knocks up some bitch, then I want to do the right thing. I gave them some cash and my card to appease them. If she has funny looking pups in a couple of months, I'll deal with it more then. But we're good for now."

Parker stared at him for a few moments. "Levi, you're going to be a wonderful dad someday. However, if you have a son, I hope he has more restraint than Rags." She grinned and when he glanced over, she gave him a flirty wink.

"Me too, but if some bitch with a swollen vulva chases him around, it's going to be hard to say no."

Parker snorted then threw her head back in laughter. "Oh my gosh, I can't believe how quickly our pit stop turned into a tutorial on dog breeding."

Levi chuckled, shifting in his seat, steering with his left hand while resting his right arm on the console between them. Parker nudged his elbow playfully with hers, leaving her arm next to his.

"I had no idea being a person in your life would be so

much fun." Her pinky finger brushed against his, and then she eased it over his, locking them together, keeping her head forward, eyes fixed on the road before them.

It was ridiculous. They'd had sex. Levi was achingly familiar with her body. Yet it was the simplest gesture that said a million things, sent ripples of euphoria coursing through his body and left him high on hope for something extraordinary in his life. All that from the locking of pinky fingers. However, he played it cool. The kind of cool that didn't move a muscle, not wanting to lose their physical connection.

"LET'S MAKE THIS our last stay before Scottsdale." Levi handed Parker the bag of fast food as he pulled out of the drive-thru on their way to the hotel. Traveling with a dog in the summer heat made eating anything but fast food an impossible challenge.

"Agreed. Anyway, I'm excited to see where you live. Are we …" She pulled her bottom lip between her teeth. "Or am I staying …"

"With me, for as long as you want. If you're tired of your new job in two days, I'll help you pack your suitcase, buy you a plane ticket, and send you wherever you want to go. Sound fair?" At that moment Levi made it his mission to make her want to stay for as long as possible.

"Sounds fair. You could tire of me before I tire of my new job. Promise you'll kick me out before you resent my presence in your life too much. Fair?"

"Fair." Never. No way. The woman brought him to his knees with her pinky finger. Tire of her? Hell no.

They let Rags walk around the perimeter of the hotel before going up to the room for the night—a regular room with two double beds, a desk, and a chair and ottoman.

"How old are you?" Parker asked.

They ate their burgers and fries on their beds. Levi leaned against the headboard. Parker sat in the middle of her bed facing him, legs crisscrossed.

"Thirty-three."

"But you've never been married."

Levi wiped his mouth. "No."

"Serious relationships?"

"A few."

"How serious?" She tapped her lips with a French fry.

"Not longer than six months."

"You ever propose?"

Levi laughed, shaking his head. "No. I'm not sure I'm cut out for marriage." He sipped his drink, gauging her reaction.

"Why not?"

"For the same reason I've had three 'serious' relationships that never led to marriage. Eventually, I say something stupid and they leave."

"The truth, isn't it? You say the truth or you're honest about something and they leave."

He nods. "Too many questions for which they didn't really want the honest answer."

"Like, 'Do these jeans make me look fat?'" Parker grinned.

"Like, 'Do you see us getting married someday?' Most guys could say 'maybe' even if they meant 'no, just enjoying the sex for now.' Me? Nope. My answers are much more blunt." Even *that* was something he didn't want to be honest about.

Levi wanted Parker in a way he'd never wanted anything in his life. There was a ninety-nine percent chance he'd fuck it up, but he still wanted to fight for that one-percent chance that *she* was the one for him—the woman who could forgive his honesty.

She shoved her trash in the bag and got Rags his food from the sack by Levi's suitcase. "The truth sucks most of the time. That makes you a natural bearer of bad news."

"Yep. Sucks ass." He wadded up his trash and shot it at the trashcan.

Swish.

Parker grinned and he gave her his best cocky wink.

"Do you wish you could lie easier? Or do you hate liars? I hated cheaters." Parker looked down as if she was ashamed of something. Lying? Hating cheaters?

"Sure, I wish lying was easier." Levi laced his hands behind his head. "Sometimes the truth doesn't serve any purpose other than hurting someone. Sometimes people lie to not hurt people then some lies are to cover your ass. And my 'honest opinions' are not always truths, just opinions. So ... of course I don't hate liars."

"Do you hate cheaters?" Her brow creased.

"Do you want me to hate cheaters?" He gave her a half smile, trying to lighten the mood.

"I'm serious, Levi."

"No. I don't *hate* cheaters. I'm sure there's a lot of gray area when it comes to relationships and why we do what we do to connect, love, and navigate this crazy life. Honestly, for many years I've questioned if humans were really wired for monogamy."

Parker nodded slowly. "And now?"

"I still don't know. My parents said I just haven't found the right person yet. The game changer." He averted his gaze so she wouldn't see that the game changer was standing a few feet from him. An impossible probability based on nothing more than a *feeling*. Levi wasn't sure if in that lifetime he'd ever be able to explain knowing something with such certainty in the timespan of a slow blink.

"I'm going to brush my teeth and change really quick so you can take your shower."

He lifted his arm and sniffed his pit. "Do I smell?"

"What? No, I just—"

When she caught his shit-eating grin, her eyes narrowed into revenge. "Ha ha! Stupid boy," she mumbled, disappearing around the corner.

Chapter Thirty-One

NOTHING LASTED.

Parker brushed her teeth, pulled her hair back, and washed her face. Who was the guy in the other room? And where had he been her whole life? The previous men in her life had messed with her head too much. She couldn't think about Gus without being reminded that nothing lasted. Don't get attached. When she thought about Caleb's recent revelations, it made her feel like a clingy, needy, stupid, blind woman who loved too hard, planned too far ahead, and in general suffocated everyone around her.

Maybe Dr. Blair was as good as it got. Sex. No attachment. No expectations. No future. How would she have a family? She ran the washcloth under cold water and pressed it to her teary eyes. The last thing she wanted to do was spook Levi. He seemed to like her. *Genuinely* like her—something more than the sex they did or didn't have.

The guy asked her to 'be a person in his life.' Weirdest request ever. Most flattering request ever. He liked her. She knew it, and she liked him too. A lot. It was the *a lot* part that worried her.

"Don't mess this up, Parker," she whispered to herself before opening the bathroom door. "It's all yours—" She gulped at the sight of him sitting on the end of his bed, no shoes or socks, no shirt, jeans unbuttoned, hands folded between his legs.

"Great." He stood.

After spending a few too many seconds staring at his unbuttoned jeans, her eyes darted to his.

Busted.

He brushed his knuckles along her cheek. "Feeling okay? You're a little warm."

Gulp.

"Um ..."

"Did you check your vulva? Maybe you're in heat."

Parker coughed out a laugh. Levi's pinky finger clasped her pinky finger. Her laughter faded as his touch held her captive. She looked down at their hands.

"I'm sorry," he whispered, "I just ... can't stop touching you. You're so fucking beautiful."

Her gaze worked its way up his body, pausing again at the exposed black waistband to his briefs then moving over each perfect cut of his abs. His beauty on the outside came close to what she'd come to know existed on the inside of Levi Paige.

"Levi..." Their eyes met and with one blink fat tears fell from her eyes, but deep down she knew they bled from her soul. "Where have you been?" She sucked in her quivering lower lip, searching for words that didn't exist. Parker didn't believe in fate. She barely believed in love anymore. But then ... Levi.

He made all thoughts inconsequential. Gus was wrong. Something existed between a man and a woman that went deeper than desire, lasted longer than loyalty, and didn't need to be nurtured like love. It simply *existed*. Levi was silence in the deafening noise of life. She couldn't explain *it*. But she felt it. And it was the only thing in her unpredictable life that she *knew*.

His other fingers threaded with hers as she stripped her emotions, baring herself to him, one tear at a time.

"Looking for you," he whispered, taking his free hand and pulling her into him—cheek to heart. It wasn't sexual. It was simply *beautiful*.

Rags whined at the door. Levi squeezed her hand and kissed the top of her head.

"I need to—"

Parker released his hand and stepped back, wiping her face. "Go. Just come back. Take the elevator, not the stairs, and stay out of the alley if there is one."

Levi grinned, fastening his pants then pulling on his shirt. "No stairs. No alley. Got it. Have you had a lot of people leave you and not come back?" He chuckled, tying his shoes.

She swallowed the boulder in her throat and fought like hell for a smile that hid the pain. "It happens."

He opened the door, tightening his grip on the leash as Rags tried to take off down the hall. "Life?"

Parker nodded. "Yes, life. It's on your back. It happens all the time."

RAGS HAD TOO much energy for eleven o'clock at night, so Levi ran him around the block a few times. By the time they got back to the room, Parker was asleep. He took a shower and brushed his teeth. Sitting on the edge of his bed, he watched her like a creeper. The one-percent chance of making it work with her weighed heavily on his mind, so did sex. But Parker was *it*. And he had no intention of ruining *it*.

They would have sober sex, and it would be mind-blowing. That would be the easy part. As much as he and every other guy in the world wanted sex to be enough—preferably everything—that reality didn't exist. Women were fickle creatures with delicate needs, invisible boundaries, and often times unrealistic expectations. Maybe Parker was the exception, but he had no way of testing that without risking losing her.

He couldn't lose her.

He shut off the light and pulled the covers up to his waist, knowing even the darkness wouldn't shut off his mind. An hour later, Parker tiptoed to the bathroom. Levi partially closed his eyes when she came back, not wanting her to think she woke him. She started to get back in bed then stood again, facing his bed—just looking at him. Did she know he was awake?

A good minute or so later, she sat on the edge of her bed, drumming her fingers on her legs. Again, she stood, taking a step closer to his bed, pumping her fists a few times then shaking them out.

He opened his eyes, not knowing if the shard of light through the slight opening of the curtains was enough for her to see them. But then her gaze locked with his. She knew then that he was awake, but still, she said nothing.

His heart pumped harder and harder, echoing to his ears. Taking a chance, praying he didn't breach that invisible line, he lifted the covers and scooted over a bit. Parker didn't move. It felt like agonizing minutes passed when in reality it was only seconds before she slid into his bed. He swallowed in relief.

"I'm not asking you for sex," Parker whispered.

He suppressed his grin as she nuzzled into his chest. The man who exhausted his bucket list before he turned thirty found a new experience—one that surpassed everything else. Levi hugged her to him, resting his cheek on top of her head while inhaling her. "I'm not offering it," he whispered on a slow exhale.

She scissored her legs with his, her hip grazing his erection. "Um ... are you sure?"

Levi didn't budge, didn't try to pull back and hide his attraction to her. "Ninety percent sure."

He didn't need to see her to know exactly what the smile, the one he *knew* she had on her face, looked like.

"WHY DOES THIS feel more intimate than sex?" Parker mumbled into Levi's bare chest, feeling content to never leave his arms.

"Good morning." He kissed the top of her head. "Because we haven't..." he cleared his throat to cover the lie " ...had sex, so you have no real comparison."

Of course, she laughed because ... Levi.

"I think it's because with sex you're trusting someone to make you feel good, but an embrace says you're trusting someone to make you feel safe."

"Safe from what?"

Parker traced the scar behind his tattoo. "From whatever: pain, embarrassment, anger, fear ... life. Sex says, 'I want you.' An embrace says, 'I've got you.'"

Levi didn't respond.

"You don't agree?" She leaned back, looking up at him.

His lips twisted to the side. "Does the embrace have to be reciprocated?"

"What do you mean?"

"Like a child hugging a favorite pillow, blanket, or stuffed animal. It's not reciprocated, but it still makes them feel safe."

"You're making fun of me."

Keeping his lips twisted, he shook his head, eyes alight with humor.

She rolled away and started to sit up. "I'm going to take a shower, maybe even listen to some music on my phone— maybe a ballad about an epic romance."

He grabbed her hand before she could walk away. "A ballad?"

Parker narrowed her eyes. "Yes. A ballad that makes you feel like you're the entire reason for another's existence."

Giving her a thoughtful look, he nodded and released her.

She guessed Levi didn't like ballads or hugs. It wasn't a deal breaker.

Parker showered to her favorite ballads, singing every lyric so everyone in the rooms around them could hear her. After drying her hair and applying a little makeup, she threw open the bathroom door.

"Shit!" She jumped.

Levi smirked around his toothbrush and mouthful of toothpaste foam, standing *right* outside the door. He squeezed past her to spit.

"How long have you been waiting to spit?"

He shut off the water and wiped his mouth. "Three songs ago. A Sia song, I think."

"I like to sing." She tipped her chin up.

"Really. Never would have guessed." He slipped past her again and put Rags's leash on him. "I'm taking him down to do his business. As soon as you're packed up, we can hit the road."

Parker couldn't read his mood. It seemed fine, but after her

spiel about the intimacy of hugging, and a karaoke performance in the shower, she questioned if maybe he was having
doubts about her being a person in his life, especially since
she'd taken sex off the table.

"Be right back."

"Levi?"

"Yeah?"

Her face scrunched. "Buyer's remorse is totally understand-
able. I really should come with a thirty-day return option. You
had no way of knowing about my love of singing or my
fondness for hugging. Don't sweat it. I'm not clingy, which
seems like a contradiction to the whole fondness of hugging,
but we can just shake hands and call it a crazy adventure."

Confusion washed down his face. "Who messed you up?"

"What?"

"Who made you feel like you should come with a thirty-
day return option?"

She folded her dirty clothes and tucked them in her suitcase. "It recently was brought to my attention that the reason
my boyfriend cheated on me with my sister years ago was
because I was sort of more than he bargained for." Parker
glanced up, hoping for some tell to his expression. Nope. Just a
poker face.

Levi crooked his finger at her. She dragged her feet over to
him like an errant child.

"His loss. My gain."

With a slight curl to her lips, she looked up.

"And for the record ..." He leaned down next to her ear.
"Today is my favorite day." When he straightened his stance,
pride danced along his curled lips.

"I thought yesterday was your favorite day?"

"It was. Yesterday." Levi surrendered to the dog at the other end of the leash, who jerked him toward the elevators. Two seconds later, the door slammed shut.

Parker finished packing and called her mom.

"I was starting to wonder if you were dead," Janey said without a hello.

"I texted you twice yesterday, even sent photos of New Mexico."

"Yes, I saw them. Nice of you to think of me."

"Mom ..."

"Sorry, I'm just frustrated with your dad today. He sprayed some crap on the yard early this morning, claimed it was 'natural,' but he failed to shut his window downstairs. Now the whole house stinks to high Heaven, and I have a headache which makes me question how 'natural' it was. I've already called Piper and told her to not come over here until the smell clears out, but I think that could take days. He never thinks before he does stupid shit. He just pisses gasoline everywhere and then walks off flicking a lit match over his shoulder."

"Well, that's too bad. Maybe you should go stay with Piper for a few days. My bed is empty."

"I don't know. She's been a little short with me and everyone else. Pregnancy hormones."

Parker set her packed suitcase by the door with her purse on top of it then sat in the desk chair. "Guess I'm even more glad that I'm not there to deal with that fun."

"When are you coming home? I don't like not knowing where you're going or what you're doing."

Perspective. Parker loved not being on her mom's radar. But she kept that to herself. "We're driving to Scottsdale today. I'm going to look for a job."

"Oh, Parker. Not in Arizona. The job market there is not great. It's crowded in the Phoenix area. It's oppressively hot most of the year. And you don't know anybody there."

"Thanks for the pep talk."

"I'm serious."

"You're discouraging."

"I'm realistic. The grass always looks greener on the other side. Which by the way, is another thing you won't find in Arizona."

"Then I won't need a lawnmower. And I know Levi, so you can't say I don't know anyone."

"A guy you really know nothing about."

A guy she couldn't stop thinking about. A guy who made her forget about losing love, losing her job, and losing her grip on life in general.

"I have to go." She winked at Levi when he and Rags came back into the room. "Love you."

Janey sighed. "Love you too. Call me when you get to Scottsdale."

"Yes. Or at least a text."

"A call—"

Parker pressed *end*. "Let's go. Just got the scoop from my mom on all the cons of Arizona. Totally pumped to see it for myself."

Levi sent Rags in her direction, slung Parker's purse over his shoulder, and grabbed the two suitcases. "Has your mom even been to Arizona?"

"Nope." Parker followed him out the door.

"It's hot and dry. When it rains the streets flood quickly. The traffic can be bad, but we have carpool lanes. And now that you're my person, I can take you with me everywhere and use the carpool lane."

"I'm your person? Or a better option for the carpool lane than a blow-up doll?"

"Both." He started toward the door. "And I mean that in the most endearing way."

Being anyone's person was a good thing. She was never Caleb's person, and she had a nephew on the way to prove it. Her occasional one-night stands didn't earn her a person badge either. And as much as it hurt to admit it, Parker wasn't Gus's person either. Even if he loved her—and she truly believed he did—he was married. That made her a mistress, a dirty little secret, not any sort of endearing friend to take in the carpool lane.

They loaded up their suitcases and the bitch humper and headed toward their final destination.

Chapter Thirty-Two

"YOU'RE HAVING SECOND thoughts." Levi rested his right arm on the back of Parker's seat, teasing the hair at the nape of her neck. In Levi's world, driving ninety miles an hour didn't require two hands.

In Parker's world, jumping in the car with a near stranger didn't take two thoughts ... until it did. She chuckled, keeping her gaze out her window while attempting to act unaffected by his touch. "Second? No. I had second thoughts before we made it out of the driveway back in Iowa. I'm on at least my hundredth thought."

They were less than a mile from Levi's place. Parker planned on asking him a million questions on the last leg of their journey, but the scenic drive demanded all of her attention. So did thoughts of Gus.

"Looks like my new job will be convincing you to stay."

"Levi ..." she whispered. "You don't even know me." The previous days felt like a vacation. Something to break up moments of reality. The hotels felt like neutral territory, even ground. Being with Levi. In his house. *In his life.* It overwhelmed Parker more than she'd expected.

"No. But I want to." He turned into a parking lot of a tall building that looked like a fancy hotel.

"What are we doing here?"

He pulled under a covered entrance. "I live here." He stopped.

A man in a suit opened Levi's door. "Mr. Paige, welcome home."

"Thank you."

Parker's jaw plummeted. "Holy shit," she whispered as another man in a suit opened her door.

Levi let Rags out of the back and then nodded toward the revolving door. "Coming?"

Parker grabbed her purse and gave the man in the suit, who greeted her with a nod, a small smile.

"Good afternoon, miss."

"Our suitcases?" Parker stayed by the vehicle, eyes flitting between Levi and the man in the suit.

"They'll bring them up."

Levi lived in a high-rise building with people who opened doors and delivered luggage to rooms—like living in a hotel. Parker couldn't make sense of it.

"But … you're … an architect." As she made her way to the entrance, she pinned him with a confused look.

He grinned. "Glad to hear you were listening. I thought we had a *moment* when I told you about my tattoos. The building *I* designed?" Levi cocked his head.

"Yes. I remember." Parker narrowed her eyes even more.

"Mr. Paige." The burly security guard with a close buzz cut and serious eyes nodded at Levi.

"Justin, this is my new dog Rags and Parker. She'll be staying with me until …" Levi looked over his shoulder as the elevator doors opened.

Parker's eyes widened, ping-ponging between the two men. "Um …"

"Welcome." Justin nodded, relieving Parker from the spot Levi put her in.

"Thank you." She returned a smile and stepped into the elevator with Levi and Rags. "Thanks for that awkward introduction." Parker nudged Levi's arm.

He beamed. "I love that you're here. I know you're having hundreds of second thoughts, but damn! I just love that you're here for however long."

No man had ever made Parker feel so wanted in a way that didn't feel strictly sexual. She took a hard swallow to hold back the emotions. Levi was well on his way to owning a piece of her heart, not only in record time, but without any expectations.

They stepped out of the elevator onto the fourteenth floor. Levi's door was the first on the right. He opened it and released the leash. Rags bolted inside. Parker stood at the threshold, another jaw-dropping moment.

Levi stopped a few steps inside and turned, crossing his arms over his chest. "You can come in. In fact, I encourage it." He shot her dead with his grin.

Parker knew from the first two-second glance that he lived in a sprawling condo with the nicest of everything. However, at that moment, all she could see was the man before her and how good he looked in cargo shorts, and the red tee that hugged his chest, and those red Chucks that accented her blue ones so well. For the tiniest moment, she let herself wonder if everything in her life to that point had truly led her to him. That's what took her so long to cross the threshold. Somehow she knew it would change everything.

Her heart ached, the yearning kind of ache, the pain that came with wanting something so much but being too afraid to believe it could happen to her.

Levi nodded. "Take your time. I'll wait. Can I get you a drink? Maybe a chair to set in the hall in case you get tired of standing? Are you hungry? I could make you a snack."

That was Parker's moment of impact. The one she would never forget. Timing wasn't her thing. She picked the wrong time to follow Caleb to college. She picked the wrong time to come home and find him in bed with Piper. She picked the wrong time to meet Gus, the married man next door. The timing in her life flat-out sucked.

And out of all the places in the world, she had to meet Levi Paige—quite possibly the greatest human God ever created—at a funeral. She had to meet him with a crippled heart. She had to meet him as a jobless hot mess with nothing to offer. She had to meet him while drowning in guilt.

Parker looked down to where the carpet in the hall ended and the stone floor of his entry began. "This is the worst timing."

"I disagree."

She slowly looked up as he took a step closer to the door.

"Meeting you has been the best." Levi shrugged. "So it was at a funeral. That just means life happened. Death is always untimely and the worst." He held out his hand.

"You're an architect." Her eyes left him to assess the luxurious condo in front of her—stone and wood floors, modern furniture, a royal blue sofa that made her lips twitch into a smile, and a chef's kitchen with miles of granite countertops. "Architects don't make this kind of money. Not unless you've designed lots of major landmarks. Have you?" Parker returned her gaze to him.

"No. I draw buildings because I love it. I own this condo because I designed and patented some virtual reality software in college. I've sold the rights to a large company, and my cut is ... generous."

"I see." Parker felt her eyes glazing over as her brain processed the real Levi Paige. "The first hotel room, it wasn't a huge splurge for you, was it?"

"No. Um ... is this, the uh ... money a huge issue for you? I can sell the condo. Downsize. If you want—"

"What?" Her head whipped back. "What are you talking about? Sell it? Downsize? For *me*? A girl you've known a few weeks? To what? Make me more comfortable? That's all kinds of crazy."

Levi shoved his hands into his pockets and stared at his feet. "I want you more."

"More than ..." She shook her head. Things like that didn't happen to people like her.

His chin lifted an inch at a time. "More than anything," he whispered.

No Lie Levi.

"I'm scared."

"Of what?" His brow drew tight.

"Of everything I'm not."

Keeping the intensity in his brow, he nodded. "Well, I'm afraid of everything you are because it makes me realize my biggest fear."

"Which is?"

"I'm afraid of having everything that means nothing and nothing that means everything."

Her brain exploded. It took too much effort to figure Levi out in her head. So she went with her heart.

Levi grinned, holding out his hand again.

After a few more seconds of contemplation, Parker reached

for it, hooking her index finger with his. He gave her a little tug, and she stepped into his condo—into his world. She took another two steps until the white toes of her Chuck's were touching the white toes of his.

She looked up.

"Welcome," he said as an infectious grin spread across his face. "Can I offer you the ten-cent tour?"

Twisting her lips, she nodded. "I think that's in my budg-et."

"Follow me." He turned. "Kitchen. One bathroom."

She laughed as he took long strides like the ten-cent tour was the ten-second tour.

"Office. Bedroom. Laundry. My bedroom. My bathroom."

Parker chased him. If she looked at a room longer than two seconds, he was already in another room.

"Main room." Levi opened the door to a huge covered bal-cony. "That's the canal. I live in the Scottsdale Waterfront district ... that's the water."

Resting her arms on the wide ledge, Parker looked over it. "A canal, huh? Well, it's not the ocean."

Levi leaned against the wall opposite the ledge, arms crossed over his chest, legs crossed at the ankles. "It's water. That's a huge deal around here. Desert."

"It's an incredible view."

"So is sunset over Camelback Mountain. But that's not for a few hours."

Rags brushed her bare leg with his wet nose. "I think you'll do well here, Rags. If you don't overheat. I don't imagine there are a lot of sheepdogs in these parts."

Levi chuckled. "I have air-conditioning."

Parker turned, taking another moment to admire Levi. She

wanted to run her hands through his crazy, blond hair, press them to his stubbly face, and kiss his perfect lips. But … guilt. Gus. Life …

"I left in a hurry. My refrigerator might be filled with rotten food. The good news is I live in walking distance of some really great restaurants. Can I interest you in dinner?"

Parker cleared her throat, hoping it worked on her mind as well. "Food. Yes. Mind if I change my clothes and do something with my hair before we go?"

"Not at all. I'll check for our suitcases."

She followed him inside. He opened the door to a neat pile of suitcases, a few boxes, and Rags's bed.

"They left it in the hall?"

"Yes."

"Aren't you worried about something getting stolen?"

Levi chuckled. "No. There are eyes all over the building. And no one can use the elevator without an access code. Also, I know my neighbors. They're not into stealing stuff." He set everything inside.

Parker grabbed the handle to her suitcase. "Which room?"

"Any of them."

"Yours has the best view."

"It does." He pursed his lips and nodded.

"But it's yours."

"Yes."

Her body buzzed, the unnerving kind that made her aware of every point of connection between her clothes and her skin. The kind that quickened breaths. The kind that made swallowing every five seconds mandatory.

Desire.

Even in death, she heard Gus whisper to her.

Parker didn't chase after Levi for desire. Even if at that moment it bubbled to the surface, it wasn't what she chased. No more quick fixes. No more weak moments. If Levi wanted her, he would have to steal her heart before taking her body. *Again.* It wouldn't take much, she felt certain he was halfway there.

"Where are you?"

After a few blinks, her gaze shifted from the floor to his face. "Thinking about us."

"Us?" He grinned. "I like *us.*"

"Yeah ... I ... I think I do too. Maybe more than I should. But I feel like we're very fragile, and I don't want to move. I'm so afraid of breaking us."

"I know," he whispered.

"So I'm going to use the room across from yours to change for dinner. Butterflies will invade my stomach as I put on my makeup and dot a small amount of perfume on my neck and wrists. Because ... I feel giddy thinking about going out with you. Then you're going to take me on our first date. I'll offer to pay, but you'll insist because you're such a gentleman." She smirked. "And because you know I don't have a job."

He clasped his hands behind his back, rocking back and forth on his heels, biting back his grin.

"You'll place your hand on the small of my back as we leave the restaurant. Then your hand will find mine and our fingers will entwine. A few more butterflies will stir to life. And we'll both think about the kiss that may or may not happen."

Levi swallowed hard. "What will I think when you step out of that bedroom? Will I feel underdressed in my shorts and Chucks?"

Parker brushed past him, leaving him with a flirty smile as

she pulled her suitcase to the bedroom. "Bring your A-game. I'm going to knock you on your ass in about fifteen minutes."

"I'm already there," he whispered.

Chapter Thirty-Three

"DON'T FUCK THIS up," Levi mumbled to himself as his hands wrestled with his blue tie tugging it in one direction and then another. He held out his hands. They shook. He fisted them and pinched his eyes shut. No woman had ever had that effect on him.

Parker thought they were fragile. Levi thought she was already cracked. Why? He didn't know.

Taking a deep breath, he finished tying his tie. She liked blue. He hoped she'd like his three-piece blue suit, crisp white shirt, and blue tie with white dots. It was his mom's favorite.

Levi ran his hand through his hair in three different directions; it did its own thing no matter what he tried. Why did he try?

"What do you think?"

Rags cocked his head to the side.

Levi brushed off his sleeves that had already captured a few souvenirs from his new furry friend. "We may have to buzz you down."

Rags turned and ran out. Levi chuckled, shaking his head as he followed him out. Just as he glanced up from one last tie adjustment, the door to Parker's room opened.

Knock. Out.

His lips parted but words were extinct.

Parker's eyes gleamed, inspecting him from head to toe before settling on his gaze. "I love blue." She grinned.

If he weren't already unconscious on the floor, that smile would have done it. "I think I knew that."

"Yeah?"

"Yeah. You ..." He pressed his hand to his chest and shook his head. Red looked stunning on her. The thinnest strip of material around her neck seemed to hold the whole thing from falling right off her. There wasn't much to lose. The simple, sexy piece ended several inches above her knees. The material kissed her body; it didn't hug it. It showed so much, yet left so much to the imagination—nothing short of perfect.

Parker tucked her silky hair behind her ear on one side as a small blush settled on her cheeks.

Beautiful. Stunning. It all seemed too cliché.

"The sunset here ... it's quite something. I would have said unforgettable. Until ..."

Parker rubbed her glossy red lips together, her nerves as palpable as his. "Until?"

"Until you opened the door." He sighed, giving his eyes permission to commit her to memory. "What sunset?" he whispered.

Parker pressed her hand to her stomach, a nervous smile beneath her tear-filled eyes. It wasn't his intention to make her cry.

She blinked them back, taking a deep breath. "So many butterflies."

Levi grinned, offering his arm. Parker took it, her matte gold high heels clicking on the stone floor.

Parker kept one hand pressed flat to her stomach and the other clasped to Levi's arm as they walked a short block to the restaurant. The sun slid behind the building on the other side of the street, giving them a little reprieve from the Arizona heat, but not enough to keep sweat from beading between Parker's cleavage.

"You're catching a lot of eyes in your dapper, blue suit." She glanced up at him.

"Only one set of eyes I'm trying to catch." He opened the door for her.

She jerked when he pressed his chest to her back and whispered in her ear, "Besides, I'm certain they're looking at you, not me."

Her hand gripped his thigh, steadying herself as she wobbled a bit on her heels.

"You can't grab me so close to my ..." He groaned in her ear as a cheery blonde approached them.

"Then stop breathing into my ear," Parker gritted her teeth in a low voice.

"Levi!" The fifty-something blonde smiled. "Where have you been, handsome?" She typed something into an iPad and then grabbed two menus.

"My um ..."

Parker's heart hurt for No Lie Levi.

"Uh ..." He cleared his throat.

The blonde's smile faded.

Parker slid her hand into Levi's and interlaced their fingers, giving him a reassuring squeeze.

"My sister and her husband were killed in a car accident, in Iowa."

"Oh no!" The blonde's hand moved to her necklace.

"I'm ... so sorry, dear."

"Thank you."

"Well, it's nice to see you again. Would you like a booth in the corner by the window?"

"Please." He tightened his grip on Parker's hand as they wormed their way to the booth at the far end of the restaurant.

Busy hands and clanging pans from the open kitchen caught Parker's attention. She liked watching the food preparation almost as much as she liked the dim overhead lighting and the sea of flickering candles on all the tables. The soft hum of evening conversations played like music in the background.

"Here you go. Mario will be right with you."

Parker and Levi said thank you in unison as they scooted into the booth.

"Are you okay?"

He looked at the menu. "No." Then he sighed and set the menu down, giving her his attention. "See ..." He tugged his tie a bit. "That's what I mean. When people say, 'How are you?' I should be able to say, 'Fine, thank you,' even when I'm not. When you ask if I'm okay, I should be able to say, yes even if I'm not. Because we are here on a date, and I just want to focus on the part of me that is okay instead of the part of me that's still standing over their graves thinking, 'How the fuck did this happen?' The truth doesn't always set you free, and lies are not always deception. But I don't have a choice."

Right there. Levi unknowingly gave Parker permission to never tell him the truth about her and Gus or Sabrina's affair. Parker could lie, but she didn't want to, not with Levi. She wanted something true in her life. Something untainted. Something *real*.

"Hi ..."

They both turned.

"Hey." Levi moved out of the booth and hugged his mom and then his dad.

"Where was our call that you got home safely?" His mom pressed her palms to his face.

She had a spark of life to her. A different Stephanie than Parker met in Iowa.

His parents turned their attention to Parker, eyes wide with recognition.

"You remember—"

"Parker, yes." Joe nodded, sharing a genuine smile.

"Nice to see you." Stephanie grabbed Parker's hand that was resting on the table. "I never got a chance to thank you for what you did."

"Oh, Stephanie, it was nothing."

"It was everything, dear."

Immersing herself in the Paige family wasn't comforting. It only flared the guilt.

"So … are you here for a visit?" Joe's lips pulled into a curious grin.

Parker's gaze shot to Levi.

"She chased me down the street when I went to leave."

Her jaw unhinged waiting for him to tell the truth. He couldn't lie. Then it hit her—it wasn't a lie.

"Parker's never been out of the Midwest, never even seen the ocean. Since she's between jobs, I invited her to come for a visit. Maybe she can find the right fit out here."

The truth. Every bit. The "right fit" was an interesting choice of words. Was it in reference to a job or a person?

"In my defense…" she kept her eyes on Levi for a few seconds before giving her attention to his parents " …he invited me before the 'chasing him down the street' part. I declined, but then I changed my mind."

The waiter cleared his throat. "Will you all be sitting together this evening?"

"Oh … no. We just wanted to say hi," Joe said.

"You should join us." Parker expected her comment to be met with a cringe from Levi.

"Absolutely," he said, gesturing to his side of the booth. When he glanced at Parker, she couldn't detect anything but gratitude.

If he didn't want them to stay, he would have said so. There was an upside to No Lie Levi.

When he sat next to her, she started to move over to give him more room, but he rested his hand on her bare leg, keeping her close and uncomfortably aroused.

After they had placed their drink and dinner orders, while chitchatting about the highlights of Levi's and Parker's road trip, Joe lifted his wine glass. "To Parker, may you enjoy your time here in spite of our crazy son."

Everyone lifted their glasses as clinking and laughter filled the space around them. Maybe she didn't need to clear her conscience. Maybe Sabrina's and Gus's memories were best left unmarred.

"IF YOU NEED help finding a job, just let me know. I've lived here my whole life, and I have plenty of connections." Joe hugged Parker as they said their goodbyes by the exit.

"Thank you. It's my first day here. I'm too overwhelmed to think about staying or going. But I'll let you know."

Joe ushered Stephanie out, and Parker followed them. Levi

rested his hand on the small of her back.

She grinned.

As they waved to his parents, who headed in the opposite direction, Levi moved his hand from her back and interlaced his fingers with hers.

She grinned even bigger.

"Thank you for inviting my parents to sit with us."

"They're really great." Through his family, Parker saw the Sabrina that Gus must have married. The Paiges were kind, funny, and welcoming.

"We'll have a redo first date tomorrow night."

"I don't know, I think this was a lovely first date." She took a deep breath, relishing the warm but not suffocatingly humid evening air.

"Dinner with my parents qualifies as a first date?"

"It became an irrefutable first date when I opened the bedroom door and saw you in this suit. This *blue* suit."

"I only have one blue suit. I might have to buy more since the bar has been set so high."

They nodded to the new guard on shift standing by the elevator to his condo.

"Dinner was amazing. The wine was too." Parker filled time with nervous chatter as end-of-the-date expectations drew near.

"So was my date."

The doors opened. Still holding her hand, Levi led her to his condo and opened the door. Rags made his best attempt at tackling them. Parker's gentleman of a date stepped in front to guard her against the attack that might have left her dress with a few snags and holes.

"Hey, buddy." Levi hunched down and scratched behind

Rags's ears so he wouldn't jump up anymore. I'm going to take him out. I'll be right back up."

"Okay."

He grabbed the leash then stopped at the door. "Leave that dress on."

Parker stepped out of her heels. "You worried about returning to me naked on your sofa?"

Levi's brows perked as his lips parted, tongue slowly wetting them.

"Go." She laughed. "I'll keep my dress on, but the shoes are staying off."

Chapter Thirty-Four

AFTER A LONG day in the car and then an evening cooped up in Levi's condo, Rags had energy to burn. Their quick trip outside turned into a walk. Levi shed his jacket and tie, but there was nothing he could do about the shoes. It was ten by the time they made it back.

No surprise, Parker, still in her red dress, was on the blue sofa, asleep. In all fairness, her body was two hours ahead; even Levi felt tired from their trip and life in general.

"Go lie down," Levi whispered to Rags. Then he flipped a switch that shut all the blinds.

That didn't wake her. Like at the hotel, he wanted to wake her. Their date wasn't over, but what was he supposed to say? *How about that goodnight kiss?*

Instead, like a true gentleman, he draped a blanket over her and went to bed.

After an hour and no signs of her waking and walking to bed, he fell asleep. Being in his own bed after weeks of other beds made it hard not to succumb to sleep.

The bed shook. He jerked up. Rags settled in beside him. "Shit, are you trying to give me a heart attack?" Levi glanced at his clock: 1:15 a.m.

After a quick trip to the bathroom, he started toward the kitchen to get a drink of water. The door across the hall was still open, bed made, red dress draped across the footboard. He turned on the lights beneath the counters to dim, but when he glanced over to the sofa, Parker wasn't there, just a folded blanket.

Levi checked the other bedroom and bathroom, then his office, and even the balcony. No Parker. Her suitcase was in the bedroom, so it didn't seem likely that she left for good. But it was after one in the morning, so leaving for any reason seemed crazy.

"Parker?" At that point he didn't care if he woke her from some hiding place he hadn't checked.

No answer.

She was an adult. The building was secure. There were no signs of a break in.

He tried her phone.

No answer.

Levi threw on shorts, a tee, and his tennis shoes then grabbed his keys. When he reached the lobby, he checked with the guard. "Have you seen a brunette—shoulder-length hair, tall, blue eyes, mid-twenties—come down here since ten?"

"Yes. Around twelve thirty."

"Was she alone?"

"Yes, sir."

"Did she happen to mention where she was going?"

"Asked if there was a twenty-four-hour convenience store nearby."

"Circle K?"

The guard nodded.

"Thanks."

"I'd take an umbrella, sir, it's starting to rain."

"Taking my car, thanks."

Levi drove toward the convenience store as the rain picked up. A block away, he saw her running down the sidewalk, hunched over, getting pelted by the rain. Making a quick U-turn, he pulled up beside her. She kept running, even picked up her pace. She had no idea what car he drove. All she'd seen was the rental. Of course, she'd run from some car with tinted windows following her at one thirty in the morning.

"Get in!" He cringed as the rain soaked his passenger seat from rolling down his window only an inch.

Parker ran faster.

"PARKER! DAMMIT! GET IN!" If he'd waited much longer, the street would have been completely flooded, and his car would have been floating down it.

She stopped, turned, and squinted, shielding her eyes from the rain with her hand.

"PARKER!"

She jerked up with recognition and hustled to his car letting in a few gallons of rainwater as she got inside—not that it mattered at that point because she was drenched, and so was his leather seat.

He swerved toward the middle of the dead street to avoid the water closing in from both sides. Terrible drainage.

"So … what's up?" she said casually.

How? He didn't know. The woman was drowned, hair matted to her face, water dripping from her everywhere, and a bag—or the remnants of a brown bag—disintegrating on her lap.

"*I'm* up."

She nodded.

He parked in the underground parking garage and got out. When he opened her door, she peeled her bare legs off his leather and stood. Shoulders back, chin up.

Splat!

They both looked down at the soggy mess that fell out of the bottom of her bag.

"Muffin?"

She shook her head. "Donut."

"You turned down dessert at the restaurant."

They continued to stare at the donut.

"I was full from appetizers and dinner."

"So you took off, on your own, in a new city, after midnight, looking for a donut?"

"Two donuts. I ate one before it started raining." Parker shrugged. "I woke up. You were asleep. I thought about waking you, but you looked too peaceful. By then I was really awake and hungry, so …"

He looked at her. "You were going to wake me to go with you?"

"No. For…" her face turned crimson "…*other* reasons."

"A goodnight kiss?"

"Maybe." She risked a quick glance up.

"Or more?"

She shook her head a half dozen times. "I don't know."

"But then you chose donuts over 'more?' And by more I mean me. Wow … major ego blow." Levi pushed a button and the trunk opened. He retrieved a towel. "Excuse me. I think there's a bit of water in my car."

"Sorry." Parker frowned.

"I can see that," he said with as much sarcasm as possible as he wiped down the seat and the inside of the door. "Let's go."

She followed him to the elevator. "Private garage. That's cool. So is your car. Red is my second favorite color."

As the elevator ascended, he glanced down at her, wondering if he'd ever figure her out. But even after she'd worried the hell out of him and soaked the inside of his car, he still wanted the opportunity. Maybe even more.

"Red sure was your color tonight."

Her lips pulled into a tiny smile. "Thank you."

When she stepped into his entry, a grimace contorted her face. "Sorry." She stared at the puddle of water on the floor as her clothes continued to drip. "I'm going to take them off before I do any more damage."

He glanced up from the puddle. "Oh ... I'll get you a towel or robe—"

She peeled off her shirt, keeping her eyes on him.

Levi blinked slowly as his lips parted.

As if she wanted him to watch, she held his gaze while tugging off her wet shorts, stepping out of them as she stood again.

Don't fuck this up.

He swallowed, scared out of his mind to let his eyes move from hers. She wore a nude bra and black panties. He didn't know the details of either. But he wanted to.

One step. Two steps. She moved toward him. Then she brushed past him, hooking her pinky finger to his, leading him down the hall. Making a right turn into his bedroom, she released his finger and continued to the foot of his bed, leaving her back to him.

Levi held out his hands. They shook. He fisted them. Wanting sex was nothing new. Neither was seeing a beautiful woman naked in his room. But *that* woman brought him to his knees. Because it wasn't just the body he wanted. Levi wanted the woman and all the little things about her that gave color to his world.

"I'm…" her voice shook as much as his hands " …not sure how many women have stood in this spot … w-wearing so little." She reached behind and unlatched her bra, letting it fall to his floor. "But if you don't understand what this means, then …"

Levi toed off his sneakers while he removed his shirt dropping it to the ground next to her bra. Parker's breath caught when he feathered his fingers down her arms.

"How do you do that?" she whispered.

"Do what?" He clasped her hands slowly bringing them above her head and then back behind his.

"Make me feel like you're the first man to ever touch me?" She fisted his hair and arched her back as he ghosted his hands back down, under her arms, around to her belly, teasing them just below the waist of her panties before inching up to her breasts. She moaned when he cupped them, and then she pushed them even more into his hands.

"Because…" he dipped his head and pressed his lips to her shoulder "…my touch is the only one that will ever matter."

Levi thought the night in the back of the truck was pretty fucking spectacular, even drunk. But touching her, knowing that she truly felt every bit of it, knowing that she wanted it with clear thoughts and no regrets, it left him teetering on the verge of coming undone.

She turned, pressing her hands to his face. "My heart is beating so fast it's hard to breathe."

A satisfied smile eased across his face while his hands traced her curves. "I'm not done taking your breath away." Lowering his body, he inched her panties down her legs.

Patient.

Methodical.

Threading her fingers through his hair, she hummed as he kissed his way up her naked body.

So. Very. Slowly.

"Today is my favorite day." Levi grinned. His lips a breath away from hers.

Parker's lips mirrored his. "You said that yesterday."

"That was *yesterday*." And when he kissed her, it put his imagination to shame. The real thing. Sober. Clear. Present.

She wrapped her arms around his neck as he lifted her legs, guiding them around his waist before lowering her to the bed. He underestimated his unquenchable thirst for her. The woman clinging to his body pieced together all the wrong and made life right again.

Levi couldn't tear his mouth from hers, so he kissed a hundred lifetimes out of her, taking his leisurely time while his hands set off on their own exploration of the rest of her body. Memorizing curves. Noting all the places that made her moan and even a few that made her lips grin against his as she squirmed a bit every time he brushed a ticklish spot.

Parker's hands released his hair and inched along his back, muscle by muscle, along his scar and tattoo and beneath his shorts.

He groaned into her mouth. That, too, made her lips curl into a smile against his.

"Take these off," she mumbled. "I want to see you. All of you."

He tore himself away and stood at the end of the bed, pushing down his shorts and briefs.

Parker leaned up on her elbows. Unhurried eyes moved along his body.

"You've seen it, whether you want to remember or not."

Her eyes snapped to his. "Nothing was clear that night."

"And now?"

Parker swallowed hard, a flash of pain ghosting across her face. "I want it to be clear," she whispered.

Levi crawled between her spread legs, kissing his way up her body. She played with his hair again like her fingers couldn't get enough as he tasted his way up her abdomen. Her lips parted, eyes locked on his. He hooked his arm under her knee as his mouth covered her breast. Watching her eyes the whole time, he pushed inside of her.

She sucked in a sharp breath, eyes heavy but still focused on him, as her hands curled into his hair.

Pulling back slowly, he plunged into her harder.

"Levi ..."

The bed jerked beneath them.

He kissed his way along her neck up to her mouth. "I think it's pretty clear," he whispered.

The bed jerked harder.

She arched her back, eyes drifting shut on a long moan. "Real ... I need something ... that's ... real."

Levi grabbed her other leg, guiding it behind his back, as he worked to find deeper penetration. "It's real. So fucking real." He devoured her mouth, making sure she felt him *everywhere*.

Chapter Thirty-Five

PARKER SLID OUT of bed early the next morning, wrapping a blanket around her as her heart and stomach did a happy dance together seeing naked Levi on his stomach.

"Shhh." She ushered Rags back toward the kitchen when he greeted her in the hallway, and then she grabbed her phone to call her mom.

"Hello, I wondered when I'd hear from my rebel daughter again."

Parker snorted a laugh, plopping down on the blue sofa. "Sure. I'm such a rebel. No tattoos. No piercings. No arrests. Not even a parking ticket. Try again, Mom."

"So where are you?"

"Levi's. He has a condo in Scottsdale, right in the middle of a shopping district. Lots of restaurants, art galleries … just a really cool vibe. We had dinner with his parents last night. And the view … Mom, it's incredible."

"You don't sound like my daughter. Who took my daughter? The grumpy one? The one who always had something smart to say?"

Parker chuckled. "What can I say? The desert suits me."

"And Levi? You're staying with him?"

Before Parker had a chance to answer, the man who took Janey's daughter shuffled down the hall in nothing but a pair of black boxers low on his hips, really fucked-up hair, and a life-is-good grin on his scruffy face. Her gaze followed him to the kitchen.

"Yes, I'm staying with Levi."

He grabbed a glass of water, giving her a quick glance over his shoulder and a wink at the mention of his name.

Parker wet her lips as her eyes continued to roam along his tan, muscled body.

"Is something going on between you two?"

She found her brain thinking, *What would Levi say?* "Yes. There's definitely *something* going on between us."

Levi leaned against the counter giving her a look that doubled her heart rate.

"Well … when are you coming home? Have you found a job? It's insanely hot there, isn't it?" Janey had a tendency to ramble when she got nervous. She was *very* nervous that her dream of having both of her girls living across the street from her could be ruined by a guy who lived in another part of the country or a job that wasn't in the Janey-approved radius.

"I just got here. I haven't had time to look for a job yet." Within seconds, the aroma of coffee filled the room. Parker took a deep inhale.

"Parker …" Janey sighed.

"How's Piper?"

"She's good. Tomorrow they're putting an offer in on the Westmans' house."

She closed her eyes and nodded slowly. "Of course they are."

"I thought you'd be happy. That means they won't be staying with you much longer. That means you can come home."

Grunting a laugh, she opened her eyes to Levi standing in

front of her, a mug of coffee in each hand. Parker twisted her lips. She had her phone in one hand, and her other hand held the blanket closed around her naked body. The smile on Levi's face said he knew that too. He shrugged as he started to pull the mug away. Without a second thought, she let go of the blanket. It fell open. Levi's eyes took advantage of her predicament.

"I'll come home when I'm ready." Parker snapped her fingers.

His eyes shot up to hers, a cocky grin pinned to his face. She gestured for the coffee. He handed it to her then sat on the coffee table in front of her, sipping his coffee with a front row view. Parker drew her knees to her chest. Levi frowned.

"But soon?"

"Tell Dad hi. I have to go. We'll chat later."

"Tonight?"

"Maybe. Or tomorrow."

Janey sighed. "You're killing me."

"Love you." Parker pressed *end* and tossed her phone aside. "How's the view?"

Levi sipped his coffee. "Spread your legs just an inch."

"You do realize this is really hot coffee. I could spill it and have severe burns. You should be fetching a robe for me or holding the blanket over me, but instead you're wondering what you might see if I spread my legs an inch. What does that say about you?"

He twisted his lips, keeping his eyes low just in case her legs drifted apart. "It says I can't think straight when you're not wearing clothes. It says I'm a guy and I want to fuck you so badly right now."

Parker's brows shot up.

Levi met her gaze and shrugged. "Anything else would be a lie. This is the point where you throw that hot coffee in my face or slap me and then grab your clothes and stomp out slamming the door behind you."

Most of his words held sarcasm, but a small part of his tone conveyed pain. He wasn't insulting her. Levi wanted her, even if his honesty made it sound a little crude.

They continued their stare-off for a few more seconds. Then Parker took another sip of her coffee and spread her legs a generous inch. Levi's eyes dropped to her legs, and he swallowed hard without taking a sip of his coffee.

"I like this sofa."

His tongue made a lazy swipe along his lower lip. "Uh-huh."

"So last night was good."

Levi chuckled, dragging the pad of his finger along his lip as he nodded slowly.

"I should go exploring today. Check out the area. Do you have a good bus system?"

His eyes lifted to hers. She grinned.

"I have a car," he said as if his mind were stumbling out of a daze. A naked Parker daze.

"I'm not taking your car. What if you need it?"

"I have a spare."

"A spare *car?*"

"Yeah." He took another sip of his coffee.

"One person needs two cars?"

"Yes. In case I need to loan one to you."

"Liar."

He grinned behind his mug. "Yes, I'm lying and not that well. I have two just because I can. There. I said it. Totally self-indulgent. Living in excess while people are starving."

She snapped her knees together. "I think I liked you better when I thought the boutique hotel was a splurge that you'd have to pay off over several months."

Levi's eyes locked on her legs, lips pressed tightly like he showed up to his favorite restaurant just as the sign flipped to *closed*.

"I'm pretty giving." His enthusiasm hit ten percent at best.

"Look at *me* and elaborate, please."

"I don't like to brag." He shrugged.

Parker brushed her lips along the rim of the mug. "I'm all for humbleness, but right now I think you need to brag, just a little, to redeem yourself in my eyes."

"I fund a few scholarships for kids wanting to go into the arts. I've designed buildings like libraries and community centers and also paid for part of their construction. Then just the normal stuff—veterans' programs, donations to charities for autism, clean water initiatives in third-world countries. Stuff like that."

"Stuff like that, huh? That's some good stuff, Levi."

He stared into his coffee. "I suppose."

"Well, my charitable contributions consist of volunteering to prepare and serve meals to the less fortunate over the holidays. I donate most all of my old stuff to Goodwill or The Salvation Army instead of selling it, and I give blood. Oh ... and I always buy Girl Scout cookies. But ... I think you have me beat."

He set his coffee aside and hers too. Then he kneeled in front of the sofa, palmed her ass, and pulled her to the edge of the couch. She wrapped her legs around his waist and draped her arms over his shoulders.

"I think you're amazing."

"Thank you. I think you are too." She teased the back of his hair. "Especially now that you've redeemed your humanity."

A small grin tugged at his lips. "I'm glad you're here," he whispered over her lips. "And by here, I mean in my condo. Not walking the streets in the rain after midnight."

Parker's hands went straight for his messy hair. "It wasn't raining when I left." She kissed one corner of his mouth. "It sorta came out of nowhere." She kissed the other corner of his mouth.

Levi bit her lower lip, dragging it through his teeth, and then kissed it. "That's how I feel about you. And now that you're here, I'm going to go out of my fucking mind if you leave me in the middle of the night like that again."

"Are you being bossy with me?"

"No. I'm just looking out for you. And now that your mom knows you're staying with me, I feel even more obligated to make sure you don't drown in a monsoon or get mugged in the middle of the night. And not answering your phone didn't help my situation."

She grimaced. "It died."

"Mmm, I see." He glanced over his shoulder at the kitchen clock. "I have a little bit of work to catch up on. We should get showered."

"We?"

Levi stood with her wrapped around him. "Yes, we." Wearing a playful grin, he carried her to his shower, turned on the water with one hand, then shimmied out of his boxers without letting her feet touch the ground.

She giggled when he stepped into the steamy walk-in shower with jets shooting at them in all directions. He consumed her with a kiss, deep and unhurried, as he pressed her back to the wall. After long minutes of exploring her mouth, Levi pulled back and peered at her with hooded eyes. He guided the head of his cock to her opening and slid in a fraction.

"Feel that?"

She nodded, still breathless from the kiss.

"How does it feel?" He guided her hips down another inch.

Parker closed her eyes and moaned. "Warm ... and ..."

"And what?"

Pressing her hand to her chest, she opened her eyes and waited for him to look at her. "Can I say something?"

He nodded, eyes narrowed a fraction as drops of water clung to his eyelashes.

"How I feel about you, it hurts in here."

The slightest flinch flashed across his face. Then he pressed his lips to her hand. "I'm going to take the pain away ... you'll see."

He plunged into her the rest of the way.

"Levi ..."

"How does it feel?" He kissed her neck.

"Levi ..."

Gripping her hips, he set the pace.

"Like a drug," she whispered just before her mouth crashed to his, catching the ultimate wave of addiction.

Chapter Thirty-Six

"SO THIS IS where you do your thing?" Parker inspected Levi's office filled with a fairly sparse desk, computer, drafting table, and his favorite designs tacked to the walls. They weren't in fancy frames, just randomly pinned here and there. It made them feel more personal and less showy.

He liked having Parker in his life. The big question remained: how would he keep her? Levi also liked how she feathered her fingers over things like she needed to feel her surroundings as much as she needed to see them. More than anything, he liked how she familiarized herself with his body using the same touch that left him caught between wanting to fuck her senseless and curl into a ball purring like a cat.

"Yes. I do my thing in here. I like the view." He nodded to the window and the sprawling city of Scottsdale.

She studied his designs on the wall. He studied her, shaking a proverbial head at how she managed to flip his world upside down. He knew it the moment he opened the bedroom door after the funeral and saw her holding his mom, stroking the hair of a woman she'd met only that day.

Raw humanity. It's not something one acquires over time. It's who they are to the deepest depths of their soul from the moment they take their first breath. *That's* what Levi's life was missing. Until Parker.

"I took your dog for a walk, unpacked your suitcase, sorted your clothes into machine wash and dry-clean only. If you tell me where to take them, I can do that for you too. And what about groceries? I can shop for you. Is there anything you won't eat? Allergies? Must-haves?"

"Why did you unpack my suitcase? And sort my dirty clothes?"

She turned to him, arms crossed over her chest. "Earning my keep until I find a job. I did that sort of stuff for Sabrina. I'm freakishly good at it. Efficiency is my middle name."

Levi leaned back in his chair, lacing his fingers behind his head. "Parker Efficiency Cruse. Interesting."

She rolled her eyes. "Might as well be."

"Why?" He chuckled. "What is your middle name?"

"Joy."

He bit his lips together. "That's ... uplifting."

"I think my mom lost a lot of blood during labor. It's the only explanation for giving identical twins names that both start with the same letter *and* vomiting the middle names Joy and Faith."

"Piper Faith?"

"Yup. So out with it. What's your middle name?"

"Joseph after my dad."

"Well, that's lackluster."

"Yeah, I'm pretty sure he was wearing Levi's Jeans that day too."

Parker giggled. "Shut up."

"I can't have you doing my laundry and grocery shopping. That doesn't feel right."

"Well, I'm not going to let you give me shelter and food without doing something to contribute."

"You are. My original offer still stands. I'll pay you to be a person in my life. You name the price."

Her eyes narrowed. "What does that mean? Tell me what a day as 'being the person in your life' might look like? I still can't wrap my head around it."

Levi shrugged. "You've been doing it since we left Iowa. You're great at it! A total natural."

"I haven't been doing anything."

"You've shared meals with me. Traveled with me. Conversed with me. Walked the dog with me."

"Had sex with you."

"Nope. I'm not going to pay you for that. Not a line I'm willing to cross. That you do for free or not at all."

"You're paying me to be a companion?"

"Sure."

"You have Rags. He's your companion."

"He sucks at carrying on a conversation. We don't agree on politics or religion."

Levi enjoyed watching her try to remain serious but fail miserably as she turned her back to him to hide her grin. "I'm going to turn my résumé into as many television and radio stations as possible. The market has to be much larger here than in Des Moines."

"Larger? Yes. Easier? No."

"Are you trying to discourage me?"

"Nope. Just doing my thing … spewing out shit that a better man would have the ability to *not* say. Maybe you should go shopping or something before I get any more real today. This is exactly why I can't talk about the serious stuff with Rags. I don't want to hurt his feelings. He'd probably start marking his territory all over my condo."

"You're scared." She plopped down in his office chair, propping up her bare feet on his desk as he swiveled toward her on the stool at his drafting table. "You're scared I'm going to ask you more questions. Probe you for honest answers. You're afraid of offending me, pissing me off. Aren't you?"

"Afraid? No. That word doesn't begin to cover it. Scared shitless comes closer, but even it feels too mild."

"What are my chances of getting a job around here in my preferred field?"

"Parker …"

"Tell me. If I didn't want your honesty, I wouldn't have asked."

Releasing a heavy sigh, Levi rubbed his temples. "With no experience?"

"Yes."

"Without having a prominent connection to someone with pull?"

"Yes."

He scrubbed his hands over his face and mumbled his answer.

"What? I couldn't understand you."

His hands flopped to his lap. "Zero."

Eyes wide, she nodded once. "I see."

"I have connections. I can get you—"

"No. I don't want—"

"My help. I figured."

"You think I should take your help?"

"Parker, let's not do this." He fisted his shaky hands. He'd had this kind of conversation too many times before. It always signaled the beginning of the end.

She dropped her feet to the floor and leaned forward. "I

want to do this. I want to have a conversation with you about finding a job. A real job. Not a hired companion job with no actual responsibility."

"Yes!"

She flinched.

Levi cringed. "I'm sorry. *That* is the truth. I don't want to have this talk with you, but if you want to, knowing I could say things you don't want to hear, then I have no choice. Yes ... I think you should accept my help. Not because we're sharing a bed, just because it's smart. In a perfect world, every résumé would stand a chance. But that's not our world. Your résumé will sit at the bottom of a pile and die. Even *if* it had twenty years of experience on it. The only way anyone in the industry will even read your name at the top is if someone tells them to read it. Fair? No. Life? Ab-so-fucking-lutely.

"I can't guarantee you a job. But with no experience, there's no way anyone will give you an interview even if they looked at your résumé. What I *can* get you is an interview. Then you'll have to sell the hell out of yourself. You'll have to give an Oscar-winning performance and make them see something worthy of taking a chance on. That's on you. We're all just looking for a chance to prove ourselves in life. I can't prove you to anyone, *especially* since we're sharing a bed. But I can get you a chance."

"It would still feel like I'm sleeping my way to the top."

Levi chuckled. "The top? Newsflash, you wouldn't be starting at the top. Even if you win the job lottery, it will be an entry-level position fetching coffee for some peon that's been there two years longer than you. Nobody's going to put you on live television tomorrow. Experience, that's what you need."

"And fetching coffee is what kind of experience?"

"It's character building."

Her jaw dropped. "Oh, so I don't have character?"

"You have the best character. But they don't know it. They want to see it for themselves. Patience. Hard work. Dedication. Coffee. Cream. Sugar. Pick up said peon's dry cleaning. Shouldn't be an issue, you already offered to do it for me." Levi smirked. He should not have done it, but he found her sexy as hell when she balled her hands and gritted her teeth.

"You're making fun of me. I see your stupid little smirk!" She stormed out of the room.

Any other man would have gone after her and made amends by lying through his teeth. Levi envied that man. He had no choice but to wait for her to come to him … or leave. That part made him ill to his stomach.

PARKER SPENT THE rest of the day exploring the Waterfront district, dipping in and out of boutiques for refuge from the relentless heat and grabbing iced cappuccinos at three different café's over the course of the afternoon. She checked her phone like a baby monitor, but Levi never tried calling or texting her. Day two in Arizona seemed premature for their first fight.

By five she headed back to the condo with no clue what she would say to him. Rags greeted her at the door and so did the aroma of Italian herbs, soft music in the background, and pans clanking in the kitchen.

"You cook?"

Owning every inch of his dark jeans and cornflower blue tee hugging his sculpted torso, Levi glanced over his shoulder. "Sometimes." He gave her the once-over with apprehension on his face as he stirred a red sauce in a copper pan.

"I'm sorry I walked out earlier. It was immature of me."
She moved behind him, pressing her chest against his back as
her arms wrapped around his waist.

He stiffened.

"But I'm not sorry I pushed you to be honest with me. I
needed to hear it. I just haven't decided what I'm going to do
with it yet."

"Where did you go?" His voice was cold.

She eased back from him, feeling like she'd crossed an invisible line he didn't invite her to cross. "Just walked around
the shops. Drank too much coffee. Gasped at the prices of
expensive shit I'll never be able to afford."

He kept stirring the sauce.

"Are you mad?"

Levi shook his head. "Don't ask if you don't want to—"

"I get it, Levi! I'm asking because I want to know."

He flipped off the gas and tossed the wooden spoon on the
counter. Sauce splattered everywhere, then he turned. "Yes! I'm
pissed off because I can't handle this shit. Waiting for the
answer all fucking day long. I had work to do, but I couldn't
focus on anything or draw with my goddamn hands shaking so
much!" He held out his shaky hands. Then he fisted them to
make them stop.

That familiar pain returned to Parker's chest as tears filled
her eyes. "Answer to what?" she whispered.

"The usual question. Are you leaving?"

"What?"

"Are you leaving? They all leave. They prod over and over
until I spill my guts and then they leave. Who stays with a
prick who can't censor a fucking thing? If you're going to leave,
then go. But don't leave your shit here and leave me in god-

damn limbo all day wondering when you're coming back—*if* you're coming back—or if I'm just going to get a call." He grunted a laugh as he raked his fingers through his hair. "Or my favorite ... sending the friend to pick up all your belongings. Just..." his voice cracked "...tell me if you're leaving."

"I'm not those other women."

"You pushed me like you wanted to know what I really thought, but nobody wants to know—"

Parker shoved his chest forcing him to back into the stove. "Now, I'm pushing you! Just so we're clear on that." She glared at him. "And if I ask you something, it's because I want to know what you really think. That makes me *somebody*, not nobody. If I don't like what you have to say, then I might leave to process it more, lick my wounds, and soothe my ego, but I will come back. If *you* don't want me here, then put my stuff in the hallway. Otherwise, I'm staying. Got it?"

Levi's jaw pulsed as he blinked at her, hands balled. "You unpacked my suitcase, but not yours. I don't think *you* believe you're staying."

Parker rolled her eyes, turned, and stomped toward her bedroom. Levi followed her, keeping a safe distance. She lugged her suitcase into his room and around the corner to his deep closet. Without any sort of discrimination, she removed the contents of the first two drawers she opened and shoved all of it into one—the bottom drawer. Then she filled the two empty drawers with her undergarments, shorts, and jeans. With one quick swipe, she pushed his neatly-spaced hanging clothes to the far side of the closet. In under two minutes, she had her shirts and dresses hung and perfectly spaced as his had been. A few pairs of shoes on the lower rack and her suitcase was empty.

With a long sigh, she turned to Levi blocking the entrance, thumbs in his pockets, a smirk hidden behind his twisted lips.

"I just marked my space. Don't invade it or there will be consequences. I'm. Not. Leaving."

"I love you," he whispered.

Whoosh!

Levi stole her moment.

"Don't say that."

He shrugged. "Okay, but it doesn't change anything. The sky is blue, water is wet, and the Earth is round, whether I say it aloud or not."

"You haven't known me long enough to love me." Her voice shook because the last time someone loved her ... he died. And he professed his love in a closet too. Closets were bad luck. Very bad luck.

Levi took a step closer. "You love me too."

The deafening pulse in her ears drowned out all other noise. "You're hungover from the sex."

He grinned. "True. But that's not why I love you."

"It is. It's desire. A very powerful thing. It's instinctual. Physical. *Carnal.* And when it wants its way, your brain shuts down ..." Gus's words poured from her trembling lips. "You say things you don't mean."

"I'm not afraid of not having sex with you again. I'm afraid of not seeing you smile when you think no one's looking. I'm afraid of not hearing you hum while you're doing mundane things like tying your shoes. I'm afraid of never seeing you hug my mom again or sleep next to Rags. I'm afraid of you leaving before I can figure out why you would risk your life for convenience store donuts in the middle of the night."

He took the final step separating them. "And for the record ... I never say things I don't mean. You know that. So fuck desire. I just want the girl for all the reasons every idiot before me failed to see."

Parker composed her speech in her head, piecing together the words that she would use when she told her family why she would not be returning to Iowa. It started with, "Levi is like ..." but Levi was not *like* anything or anyone. Levi was Levi—an entity all of his own, a phenomenon.

She was tired of crying. The past month had been an emotional marathon. Swallowing back the lump in her throat, she jabbed her thumb toward her hanging clothes. "I'm serious. That's my space. If I see your fancy shirts drifting toward my thread-bare sundresses, I'm going to lose my shit."

He hooked his index finger around hers and led her toward the kitchen. "Told ya."

"Told me what?"

"You love me too."

Yes. She loved him—so very much.

Chapter Thirty-Seven

L EVI DIDN'T NEED to work, but he did—a lot. When he wasn't designing something, he was surveying building sites and meeting with prospective clients and contractors. Parker had important stuff to do as well, like walking Rags and ... nothing. That was the extent of her purpose.

"Ugh." She sighed on the elevator, staring up at the digital readout. Their early morning walk still didn't beat the heat. "I'm not cut out for this, Rags. Are you?"

He didn't respond. He couldn't with his tongue dragging on the ground. Poor Rags.

"Yeah, my thoughts too. We might have to just play fetch inside for the next month or two." The elevator dinged, and they stepped out, sweat dripping down Parker's face.

She opened the door to Levi's condo greeted by a man with short, sun-bleached hair, jumping on a rebounder, that wasn't there when she left.

"You must be Parker."

Bounce bounce bounce

She nodded, giving him a wary eye. "If you brought that mini trampoline for me, then I think I may love you."

"I'm Ziek. And all the women love me. I have many gifts."

Bounce bounce bounce

Another slow nod. She released Rags from his leash. He

went straight to his water bowl.

"I'm only interested in the rebounder. Where's Levi?"

"Shower. Lacrosse was brutal this morning. So, Levi said you're from Iowa."

"Yes, I am." Parker grabbed a bottled water from the fridge.

"Corn. Tornadoes. And vast fields of … nothingness."

"Nailed it." She drank almost the whole bottle then sighed, wiping her mouth with the back of her hand.

"Were you born in a barn?"

"Yup. My mom labored next to our horse, Amazing Grace. I came out first. Went straight from her womb to suckling at the teat of Hilda, our goat."

Just as she gave Ziek a toothy grin, Levi walked down the hall buttoning his shirt. One corner of his mouth curled up as he eyed Parker with amusement. "Get off, Ziek. That's Parker's."

Ziek took one last big bounce before springing toward the sofa where he landed with a thunk. "We were just getting acquainted. Thought we should, since she already declared her love to me."

Her heated skin from the walk hid her embarrassment. "What I meant was—"

Levi backed her into the kitchen island, caging her in, hands gripping the counter. "What you meant? So you *did* declare your love to another man?"

Parker grinned while she finished buttoning his shirt for him. "He brought me a rebounder."

"*I* got it for you." He sank his teeth into her neck.

She giggled and squirmed away from him. "Not cool." Her eyes narrowed as she glared at Ziek.

"Baby, I'll buy you anything you want. Take you anywhere

you want to go. Just name it." He smirked, stretching his legs out onto the coffee table. His arrogance swallowed up his good looks. Such a shame.

Parker hopped on the rebounder. It was a hundred times nicer than hers. No squeaky metal springs. She imagined that's what bouncing in the clouds might feel like. "I want to see the ocean. Can you get me that, Ziek?"

"Fuck yeah! Done." He pulled his phone out of his pocket. "Pack your bag, baby … or not." He winked. "I prefer the clothing-optional beaches."

With an easy hook, like snagging a fish, Levi grabbed her waist and flung her over his shoulder.

"Hey!"

"Later, idiot," he called to Ziek as he hauled her down the hallway.

"Can I stay and listen?" Ziek laughed.

"Not if you value your life."

He turned into his office, not the bedroom where Parker had anticipated. "Where oh where to begin?" Levi sat in his desk chair with her on his lap, back to his chest.

"Stop!" She squirmed when he bit her bare shoulder by her sports bra strap, even harder than he did in the kitchen.

"I have a meeting in an hour. Can you stay out of trouble until I'm done? If you can, then I'll rearrange a few appointments and give you what you want."

Twisting her body to face him, she gave him a sexy smile. "I thought that's what you did about three hours ago."

"I did too." He kissed her nose and stood, setting her on her feet and then swatting her butt. "But thirty seconds ago you were ready to jump on a private jet with Rent-a-Dick just to see where water meets land."

"Private jet? Don't you think you're exaggerating a little? It was goofy banter, that's all."

Levi rolled up his design and slid it into a tube carrier then packed his laptop in his messenger bag. "Oh, my sweet little barn-born babe, I fear you may have suckled at Hilda's teat a little too long. There's a big bad world out there with guys like Ziek who have nothing better to do than wet their dicks all day."

Parker crossed her arms over her chest. "Really? That guy owns a private jet?"

"Yes." Levi continued to look around to make sure he had everything.

She blinked a few times. This wasn't her world. Parker didn't know people who owned jets. Caleb and Piper probably flew first class everywhere, but he didn't own his own jet.

"How do you know him? Is he just a teammate?" She followed him back out to the kitchen.

"He's a friend from college." Levi refilled his coffee cup. "There were four of us who hung out ... well, we still do. Techies. They went on to do even bigger things. I made enough money to do what I wanted to do, and then I focused on architecture."

"What did you want to do?"

"Travel the world."

Parker hopped back on her rebounder. "What do you mean? A bucket list?"

"All fifty states. All seven continents."

Her legs locked up and her body stilled with her mouth open. "You've been to all seven continents?"

Sipping his coffee, he nodded slowly.

"How is that possible?"

Levi chuckled. "Three crazy trips. I only got to see a tiny fraction of each place, but I just wanted to step foot on all of them. We went to Europe and Africa for our first trip. South America and Antarctica for our second trip. And Asia and Australia for the final trip—that one was a killer on the old body clock."

"Wow ... I ..." She shook her head. "I feel so ..." Parker dreamed of visiting the Four Corners Monument so she could say she'd been in four states at once. And the ocean ... she wanted to see the ocean, any ocean. Levi had seen all four. "And you went with Ziek and your other friends from college?"

"Yup." Levi rinsed out his coffee mug.

She stepped off the rebounder and plopped her butt onto it. They weren't in the same league. Not even close. He probably did believe she was born in a barn.

"Quick trip to the beach. Be packed by three." He slung his bag over his shoulder.

"Thank you for the tramp."

Levi beamed. "You're welcome."

Parker looked up, envious of the life he'd had. "Tell me, Mister World Traveler, what is your greatest memory, the one you'll never forget?"

He squatted down in front of her, resting his hands on her legs. "That's easy. Overcast sky. Barren field. Blue pick-up truck. Pizza. Twelve-pack of beer. And the woman who owns my world."

"Liar," she whispered as her heart nearly exploded.

He laid a sound kiss on her lips then grinned. "No Lie Levi." Standing, he walked to the door. "I love you. Don't you ever fucking forget it."

LEVI DIDN'T OWN his own jet. Parker kindly overlooked that flaw. Still, they took a private jet on loan from a friend.

"This isn't my life." She stared out the window as the jet made its descent.

"You've said that at least a dozen times since we took off." Levi glanced out his own window, but his eyes didn't hold the same wonderment.

"Does it ever get old?" She peeled her eyes away from the window.

"Sort of."

"Really? How can that be?"

"Destinations no longer become the experience. It's more about the people you're with." He shrugged. "So I've been to Malibu dozens of times, but never with you. That makes the trip new again. But if I were to come here with my buddies just to go to some party, it would get old. It *has* gotten old. At least for me."

"You've partied a lot?"

He fastened his seatbelt. "Some."

"Drugs?"

"No." He chuckled.

"Drinking?"

Levi squinted an eye. "I think you know the answer to that."

"Women?"

"Parker …"

"I'm not jealous. At least not in the way you think."

His skepticism remained firmly planted on his face. "Then in what way?"

"You did everything someone graduating from high school dreams of doing … and then some. College with your buddies;

you played a sport you love. Achieved financial success *and* got a degree that still pays well. Traveling. Parties. Fast cars. Sexy women. You've *lived*. I followed a guy and missed everything. But he didn't. He did those things without me, and now he's married, successful, and starting a family."

The most pitiful frown marred his face. "It's never too late."

Parker laughed. "It is. It really is. I'm not twenty-one anymore. I've become a little more levelheaded. My mom has branded too much worry and common sense into my brain. I think about kidnappings, date rape, infections, incriminating photos on social media. It's just taken the fun out of being young and stupid. Now, I'm only 'sort of' young and a little stupid, which makes drunk sex in the back of a pickup the craziest thing I can pull off."

Levi grinned.

She sighed. "And even then, at the time I wondered if we should get tetanus boosters since there's rust in the back of Old Blue. *That's* how my mind works now."

"For the record, I don't look back at all of the stupid things I've done with any sort of fondness. You know those people who say, 'no regrets'? That's not me."

The plane touched down.

"What do you regret?"

"Uh ... let's see ... getting arrested for public intoxication, three days in the hospital with a severe case of pneumonia because I'd spent almost a week partying, sleep deprived, and dehydrated. I had no immunity by the end of that week. Sex on the beach. Huge mistake—"

"What?" Her eyes popped out. "Why no sex on the beach?"

"Sand. Everywhere. In cracks, crevices, and *holes* sand

should never go."

Parker cringed. "Noted."

THEY RENTED A convertible and drove a hundred miles an hour to Malibu, or so it seemed. Parker kept thinking about the life that wasn't hers, but she embraced the experience and pretended for their quick one-night trip that it *was* her life.

"Holy ... w-what resort is this?" Parker craned her neck to see more of the luxury resort as Levi pulled into the circle drive.

"It's a house. Not a resort."

"Whose house?"

He jumped out and grabbed their overnight bags. "It's owned by more than one person."

"And you know the owners?" She almost stumbled over her flip-flop-clad feet as she followed him to the door.

He pulled out a key and unlocked it. An alarm beeped when they stepped inside. Levi typed in the code and it shut off.

"Yes. I know the owners."

The single-level home stretched forever in both directions with windows everywhere. Even the massive ceiling had windows, like a glass house.

White. It was the dominant color with a few places of bold red and aqua. Everything from the leather furniture to the chandeliers screamed money.

"Oh my god ..." Parker whispered as she edged closer to the double doors overlooking a long infinity pool and just beyond that—the ocean.

The girl from the Midwest ran right out of her flip-flops and sprinted to the beach.

"Oh my god!" She threw her hands in the air trying to capture it. Nothing was better than ocean air. All descriptions of it fell short.

Fifteen yards.

Ten yards.

Five yards.

Splash!

The second the brisk water swallowed her body, it drowned all of the warnings: Parker, watch out for undercurrents; Parker, beware of sharks; Parker, certain jellyfish can kill you.

WITH HIS HANDS deep in the pockets of his shorts, Levi strolled onto the beach. He may have been wrong. *That* was the moment he would never forget. It didn't matter how they got there—jet, bus, or hitchhiking. The color and quality of the sand didn't matter. The backdrop of multimillion-dollar homes stretching up and down miles of coastline didn't matter.

At age twenty-six, Parker Cruse saw the ocean for the first time, and he got to witness it like a miracle no one else would ever believe. The grin on his face pulled so tight it almost made his eyes water. Why did he traipse her through the desert when all her heart desired was to dive head first into an infinity of waves.

She splashed and squealed then waved him over. "Levi! You have to feel this! It's amazing!"

He stood there and watched, frozen in time, wanting to memorize each picture frame, the sound of her voice, and the way his heart ached with so much love for that woman.

"Now, Levi!" She flipped onto her back, arms spread wide, looking up at the sky.

He toed off his Chucks and grabbed the back of his tee to shrug it off.

Parker stood up in the water. "Don't take off your clothes. Don't think. Just dive in! You can't prepare for greatness—it just has to happen."

No truer words had ever been spoken. And every one of them summed up his feelings for her.

Don't think. Just dive in!

He jogged toward the water, fighting the wind. Parker splashed through the foaming waves, meeting him halfway, and jumped into his arms, wrapping her legs around him as they fell back into the water.

When they emerged, he shook his head like a shaggy dog, holding her close to him.

"Say it." She smiled so big he felt certain her face would crack.

"Say what?"

Parker kissed him, holding his face in her hands. Deep. Long. And filled with so much life. When she pulled back, she rested her forehead against his. "You know …"

"Today is my favorite day."

"Yesss!" She hugged him. "Thank you for this. Thank you so much," she whispered with her lips grazing his ear.

"ONE MORE TIME and then I'll quit." Parker traced the terrain of Levi's bumpy abs with her toe as they sat at opposite ends of a deep soaker tub next to a wall of windows with miles of the Pacific watching them as the sun set behind it.

He leaned his head back, closed his eyes, and grinned. "What's that?"

"This isn't my life."

"I disagree." He grabbed her foot and massaged it. "You're here with me. And we are *real.*"

"The jet belonged to someone else, the car is a rental, and so is this six-bedroom, eight-bathroom mansion. But I love that we are *real,* even if everything else is borrowed. And that huge body of water is real. In fact, I'm calling it mine for the rest of our short stay. It's the Parker not the Pacific."

Levi chuckled. "Works for me."

She teased her fingers up and down his calves. "So who owns this joint?"

"My friends from college." He kept his head back and eyes closed.

"That you travel with?"

"Yes."

"You said it belonged to four people."

"I did."

"Who's the—"

Levi peeked open one eye and looked down at her with a shit-eating grin plastered to his face.

"Oh my god!" She sat up ramrod straight sending water splashing over the sides. "This is your place? Are you kidding me?"

He brought his head up and opened his other eye. "A *fourth* of it is mine."

"Which fourth? Please tell me it includes this tub ... and the kitchen. I *love* the kitchen."

They both laughed as he sat up, meeting her in the middle, nose to nose. "I'd give you the world if you just asked me to."

Parker rubbed her nose against his. "I think you're more than enough for me to handle. The world might feel neglected." She slid her hand between them and *handled* him.

He sucked in a slow breath. "Let's get out. I want to show you which bed is mine."

She continued to stroke him as his teeth dug into his bottom lip. "Show and tell? I like show and tell."

As if it pained him, he slowly pushed himself to stand. Parker stood up on her knees and grinned.

"Let's start here. I'm going to *show* you something, and you *tell* me how it feels."

"Park—aw fuuuccck ..." He gently fisted her hair as she took him in her mouth.

Chapter Thirty-Eight

"I NEED TO call my mom."

Levi turned toward the door to his office and slid his pencil behind his ear. Since their long, sleepless twenty-four hours in Malibu weeks earlier, he'd had trouble focusing on work again. The bikini-clad Parker posed in the doorway to his office didn't help. His dick jumped to attention, sending not so subtle messages to his brain. They both needed a break from the monotony of drawing.

"Is your phone dead?"

"Look at me."

His eyes snapped from her cleavage to her face. "I am."

"My face." She gestured to her eyes with her index and middle fingers.

"I've been working for four straight hours, you've been lounging by the pool, and now you're standing there all sweaty and nearly naked, but I'm supposed to look at your eyes? Not fair, babe." His eyes returned to her breasts.

"I've been here for almost a month. There's a good chance I might stay a bit longer. She's a wreck because I have no job and I'm living with a guy who she doesn't know. I think she suspects you kidnapped me."

He crossed his arms over his chest, head cocked to the side. "A good chance you might stay *a bit longer*?"

"Maybe." She smirked.

"Come here."

"No way. I'll lose my bikini. You're giving me that look."

He chuckled. "What look?"

"That look you give me before my clothes end up on the floor and me on my back."

Levi adjusted himself. "You don't like that scenario?"

Parker dropped her chin and looked up with flirty eyelashes batting at him. "You know the answer to that. I just need to say something before the clothes come off."

He adjusted himself again with little relief because he was running out of room for adjustment. "Absolutely, but just to be clear … the clothes are coming off?"

Rock. Hard.

"Don't they always?"

"Three days last week—"

She rolled her eyes. "You mean my *five-day* menstrual cycle? By the fourth day, you had your way with me in the shower."

Painfully hard.

"Say what you need to say."

"I'm going to email my résumé tomorrow. You tell me where. You make the call. I'm ready to climb that ladder, even if I have to stand on your back to reach the first step."

"I changed my mind." Levi drummed his fingers on his leg. "I like lazy mornings with you in bed. Coffee on the balcony, talking about how you think you can 'kick my ass' at volleyball, even though I'm taller. I like lunch in the kitchen and post-lunch sex on the sofa. I like working my ass off all afternoon while you reorganize everything in this entire place a hundred times over before you head to the pool on the roof for the remainder of the afternoon. I like the click of your high heels on the stone floor, usually around six, knowing that you're starving and wearing something that will make me fall off this stool. I like taking you to a new restaurant every night and how you tear half of my clothes off in the elevator when we get back home." He shrugged. "I like this life. You getting a job would ruin it. Nope. Not going to be any part of that terrible idea."

Parker's head jutted forward, jaw reaching for the ground. "Are you serious?"

"Dead. If you wanted a job, you should have spoken up the day we discussed it. I've rescinded my offer. Sorry, babe. Now..." he crooked a finger "...get over here. Let's check out that tan line of yours."

She blinked. Waiting. Of course, she knew five—ten minutes tops—was how long it took to know if his words were truth or a shit lie. It didn't stop Levi from enjoying every second he could until his stupid conscience vomited the truth. His ability to hold out in the name of a good joke had improved over the years with practice.

"You're a selfish little rich boy." Then sometimes she went on the offensive. He loved that game too.

"Agreed. Bikini ... are you removing it or am I?"

"Levi Joseph Paige, if you're serious, then the only thing I need to tell my mom is what time my plane will arrive in Des Moines."

"I love how you not only ball your hands when you get mad but you curl your toes too."

Parker glanced at her feet and relaxed both her fingers and toes. Then she narrowed her eyes at him. The stare-off. Another favorite of his. He narrowed his a bit too; that usually made her grin against her will after a few seconds.

No grin. It was more of a smug smirk. She pulled the ties to her top letting it fall to the ground. Then she slid off her bikini bottoms and sling-shotted them at him. They landed on his drafting table.

"Are you going to give me a name? Then are you going to make a phone call?"

The girl clearly didn't know the rules. She played dirty. So dirty. Levi wasn't a pathetic schmuck ruled by his penis. Until … *the* girl.

"I'll message you the email address and make a call first thing tomorrow morning."

A huge, gloating smile stole her entire face. He unfastened his shorts as she prowled toward him.

"See…" her eyelashes fluttered " …that wasn't so hard, now was it?"

The girl had no idea how extremely hard it was … but she was about to find out.

TWO DAYS LATER Parker called her mom.

"I'm ready to disown you, Parker Joy. No job. You're living with some guy I've never met. And you've been ignoring my texts and phone calls for the past week. You could have been dead in a ditch and I would have no idea. How do you think that makes me feel? Someday, young lady, you're going to have kids, and I hope they hate you as much as you hate me."

Parker grinned, eyes closed, head back on the lounge chair by the roof-top pool. She had her earbuds in so the two other residents a few feet down couldn't hear her crazy mom going off on her typical rant.

"I have an interview in two weeks."

"Please tell me it's in Des Moines."

"Phoenix."

"Parker. You're killing me. Is that what you want?"

She laughed. "I'll say something to Levi. I'll tell him he needs to take me home for a visit. You're going to love him."

"Do you?"

Parker's smile grew even bigger. "Yes."

"Are you sure it's not just infatuation? Or maybe you're high on your little rebellion and you're mistaking that high for love because he's been your partner in crime."

"We're not robbing banks, Mom. Can't you be happy for me?"

Janey sighed. "I'm trying, but it's hard because I hate worrying about you, but it's impossible not to when you're so far away. And what about the house? Piper and Caleb are closing on their house next week. Are you selling the farmhouse? Renting it? This is something you and Piper need to discuss before she has a baby consuming her time."

"I know. I will."

"When?"

"Jeez, soon. I said I'd talk to Levi about making a trip back there."

"I miss you."

Parker rubbed her eyes. "I miss you too. I'll call you soon."

Chapter Thirty-Nine

P ARKER FROWNED AT Rags as she opened the door. The front corner of the sofa cushion had become his favorite humping spot. "Nice, Rags. That's probably a five-thousand-dollar sofa. We need to get you a stuffed animal from a carnival or something better suited for your *needs*."

He ignored her.

"Levi?" She peeked into his office. He wasn't there. She opened the door to their bedroom. "Damn," she whispered.

Muscles. Sweat. And shorts low on his hips. Levi was on the floor pumping out pushup after pushup with wireless earbuds in his ears. Parker walked up behind him and teased her toe over his back.

He didn't skip a beat. "I'm almost done," he yelled louder than he needed to.

"Sweet Jesus …" She sucked in her lower lip, admiring rolling muscles shifting along his taut skin.

"What?"

She plucked his earbuds from his ears. "I just wondered if you needed a little more resistance."

"Like what?" He breathed heavily.

"Me on your back."

Levi stopped at the top in plank. "I'm sweaty, but get on."

"I'm sweaty too." She lay on his back, legs on his, arms

around his torso.

"Count."

"One." She grinned, tightening her grip as he lowered his body. "Two. Am I hurting your back?"

Levi was a rock of muscle, but even rocks cracked under enough pressure.

"Count."

"Five ... sex ..."

He paused at the top. "Sex? Did you say sex?"

"Six."

"Sounded like sex."

She bit her top lip and grimaced. "I may have ... it's just that this is kinda hot."

He lowered, continuing with his reps. "Yeah?" His voice dripped confidence. Rightfully so.

"Is this what you meant when you said sex is your favorite workout?"

Levi grunted a chuckle. "Your body in that bikini pressed to my back is definitely sexy, but we're not actually having sex, so it's not exactly what I meant."

Parker slid her hands from his stomach to his shorts and slipped her hand down the front.

Levi paused again at the top. "Parker ..."

"Let's sweat together," she whispered, sliding her hand into his briefs and gripping his already hard cock, making slow strokes up and down.

"Fuuuccck ..." he groaned as he pushed through five more while she stroked him. "Don't say it," he grunted, "unless you mean it."

Sliding off his back, she giggled and scooted under him.

He paused at the top and grinned. "You're such a tease."

"A little." Parker traced his abs with her finger. "Do you ever wonder what we're doing? The rest of the world is making some grand contribution to society, and here we are just ... hiding out like the rest of the world doesn't exist."

He lowered down, hovering over her lips. "Today is my favorite day. Don't ruin it by suggesting other humans are inhabiting our world, expecting us to interact with them." Levi brushed his lips against hers.

As she started to nip at them, he pushed back up. "You and your favorite days."

He eased to his forearms, resting his lower body on hers. "We could go golfing? Would that count as a contribution to society? We pay, people make money. I'll even try to get a speeding ticket on the way; that would count as a contribution to the local law enforcement. Lunch? Maybe we pick a new restaurant that's trying to get up and going? I'll leave a big tip. On the way home, we pick up any trash we see and dispose of it properly. We already save water by showering together. We really shouldn't be that hard on ourselves. If you look at the big picture, we're doing quite a bit."

"Golfing?" She didn't hear anything past golf.

"Yes. Why? Do you golf?"

"I'm familiar with the game. I don't have clubs."

"Again ... we can buy some. Another contribution to socie-ty."

"Okay. Let's go golfing."

"Great. I love golf."

"More." She ran her fingers through his hair.

"More what?" He ducked his head and dotted kisses along her jaw.

"More Levi stuff. Things about you I don't know. Besides

drawing, golf, and impeccable taste in casual shoes, what do you like?"

"You." He trapped her bottom lip between his teeth.

"I'm serious." She released his hair and grabbed his ears tugging them gently until he set her lip free.

"Lacrosse. Action movies. Anything that goes fast. Memoirs. Riddles. Puzzles. Technology podcasts. String cheese. Popcorn. Anything with hazelnuts. And vintage Matchbox cars."

Parker closed her eyes as a soft girlish laugh bubbled from her chest. "More ... keep going. You're my favorite story."

Levi chuckled. "Corn fields. Volleyball. Convenience store junk food. Chucks. Random acts of kindness. Cooking. Rebounding. Organizing. Stroking my cock ... That's all I've got. I need more Parker stuff."

"What list was that?"

"Things Parker Cruse enjoys."

"Corn fields? Really, Levi? You're smarter than that kind of stereotyping. Now you sound like your idiot friend, Ziek. Just because I'm from Iowa doesn't mean I'm an expert on corn fields, or that I like them."

He scooted down her body, pressing his lips to her sternum. "Tell me something about young Parker. Like ... what was your first official job?"

Her hands moved back to his hair, eyes drifting shut as his thumb slid under her bikini top and teased her nipple. "Levi ..."

"Tell me." He tipped his head up, resting his chin between her breasts, as his thumb continued to tease her.

"I don't remember."

"Bullshit."

"Ouch!" She scowled as he held her nipple hostage between his thumb and finger.

He grinned, releasing her nipple and shoving her top to the side. His tongue made a slow stroke over it.

"Yesss … I … like your tongue on me." Clenching his hair, she tried to push him lower.

"I'll do anything you want with my tongue as soon as you tell me your first job."

"Levi …" She squirmed beneath him. Thinking of his tongue between her legs, but not having it there was its own special torture.

Scooting down her body even more, he spread her legs wide.

Parker swallowed hard, lifting her hips off the floor in search of him. Levi brushed his nose along her inner thigh on one side and then the other. She tugged at his hair.

"Tell me," he whispered, sliding the crotch of her bikini bottoms to the side. The warmth of his breath possessed its own touch against her sensitive flesh.

"God … Levi … yes … there …" Her heart pulsed in the back of her throat.

"What was the job, Parker?"

"Please." The second his tongue touched her, she would explode.

"I want to taste you so badly, but you have to tell me." He ran his tongue along her thigh stopping at the edge of her bikini bottoms.

"De - ta -s -ld co -r …" she mumbled, thrusting her hips off the ground.

Levi dodged her attempts to connect with his mouth, even with her hands on the verge of ripping out his hair. "I couldn't understand you."

"Detasseling."

He blew air on her sex.

"Dammit, Levi!" Parker lifted her head off the floor.

He grinned. "Detasseling?" He wet his lips and his eyes shifted from her face to the apex of her legs.

She was seconds from an orgasm just from his proximity and the memories of his tongue on her. "Do you want me to beg?"

He shook his head. "Just tell me what you detasseled?"

"Corn! I detasseled corn! Now—Oh ... my ... god ..." Her head fell back, mouth open, blurred vision from the world's quickest orgasm. He finished strong with fervor and precision. A man dedicated to doing the job right.

After her hips collapsed back to the floor, Levi pressed a soft kiss to her clit and sat back on his knees between her legs with a puzzled look on his face.

"That was ... fast."

Draping her arm over her face, she groaned. "Please don't talk about it. I'm ... *responsive*, that's all."

"Like a hair trigger."

"Shut up. You were touching me everywhere but ... and then you kept breathing on me right ... *there*."

"I see. Well, can we back up a second? I'd like to discuss the corn detasseling. Specifically your 'expert' knowledge about it, my very *responsive* Iowa girl."

Parker jackknifed to sitting, adjusting her bikini bottoms, then crisscrossed her legs. "The tassel is the top part of the corn—the male flower containing the pollen. When the wind blows, the pollen shakes loose, falling to the ear with the silk, the female flower, for pollination. But to ensure specific desirable qualities, seed companies and farmers work together to create hybrid corn. So machines detassel most of the corn, and then human crews go through to catch the tassels that didn't get removed."

Levi nodded. "They don't want corn inbreeding."

"Well, yes, sort of."

"I don't think I've ever met a corn detasseler."

"Gus probably did." Parker held her breath. She'd said his name out loud without crying for the first time since he died. It felt strange, and it hurt a little too.

"You think?"

She blinked a few times. What she had with Levi was so different than what she'd had with Gus. Levi gave her strength where Gus sucked the life out of her with promises that she never knew if he'd keep. She and Gus were almost real. But the man before her was the realest real that ever existed. Gus made a play for Parker's heart, but Levi earned it, waited for it, nurtured it, and she trusted him with it more than she had with any other man.

"Yeah …" Parker pulled in a deep breath, gaining a little more strength. "His parents have land and live in the middle of farm country. I'd be shocked if he didn't at some point during his teen years detassel for someone around there."

"Do you like farms?"

She shrugged. "Kinda. I like having space, but in spite of what I'm sure you've come to conclude, I don't love acres of corn and soybeans. I like trees, gardens, and a few animals. Maybe a meadow of wildflowers or lavender."

"So you're not into high-rises?" He rested his finger under her chin and tipped it up. "You can tell me."

"You live in a beautiful condo. It's huge and everything is

one hundred times nicer than anything I've ever had. And the view is spectacular."

"But?"

She returned a half smile. "But it sucks taking Rags outside all of the time. A doggy door is nicer. I think he misses chasing birds and squirrels. I miss grass. Where's the grass? I like the smell of fresh-cut grass or the feel of the cool morning dew on the blades when I walk through it in bare feet. However…" she lifted onto her knees and wrapped her arms around his neck "…I love the freedom of not living so close to family watching my every move. I love the change in scenery—specifically all the cacti that look like erections—this should be called the prickly penis state."

He chuckled.

"And I love the short walk to restaurants and shops. But mostly I love the man who has taken my heart hostage."

"Not giving it back either." He tugged one tie to her top and then the other.

"I don't want it back," she whispered over his lips. She closed her eyes and leaned in to kiss him.

He pulled back just an inch like he'd done earlier when she was so needy for him.

"Don't tease me again, Levi." Parker blinked open her eyes. The games were over. She saw nothing but love in his eyes. "Make love to me, Levi, but do it like—"

"Like you're the last woman I'll ever want for the rest of my life."

Parker couldn't breathe from the impact of his words. She was going to say "like we usually do," but he had to step in and remind her one last time that after twenty-six years, her heart had found its rightful owner.

Chapter Forty

"**D**O YOU PLAY here a lot?" Parker asked as Levi unloaded their golf clubs from his gray SUV.

"All the time."

"With your friends?"

"Yeah, but not on Fridays. Too crowded."

"It's Friday."

He nodded. "Exactly. We don't have to worry about running into them. You already met Ziek. Do you really want that personality multiplied by three?"

"Yet … they are your *friends*."

"Absolutely. Thick and thin. And for doing guy things, they are the best. But …"

He sped like a crazy man toward the clubhouse.

"But what?"

"They act differently around women, specifically women I date. It's like they lose all control of their mouths and just say random offensive shit. They wouldn't like you. No offense."

"Why? What's wrong with me?" She lowered her sunglasses to the tip of her nose, giving him a sideways glance.

Levi rested his hand on her bare leg, giving it a squeeze. "Nothing. You're perfect. That's why they'd hate you. Single guys don't like it when their buddies find the perfect woman."

"Because …"

"Because guys with perfect women in their lives don't usually want to hang out with their imperfect friends. That makes you the enemy to them."

"I'm not perfect."

Levi pulled to a stop by several other golf carts next to the clubhouse. "You are to me."

"Dude … our pussy-whipped friend has emerged from Vagina Land."

"Oh fuck." Levi closed his eyes.

Parker turned around.

"How's the trampoline?" Ziek asked, walking toward them, dressed in flashy golf attire, just like the two guys walking beside him.

"Bouncy." She returned a tight grin.

"Where was the call, buddy?" Ziek slapped his hand on Levi's shoulder.

"You guys don't like to golf on Fridays." Levi got out of the golf cart and nodded toward the clubhouse.

Parker followed.

"Where's the love?" One of the other guys said as they followed them inside.

"Sorry, Parker from Iowa." Ziek rammed the toe of his shoe into the heel of Levi's shoe. "*Someone* has forgotten his manners."

Levi turned, giving Ziek a shut-up look. "You're right. Parker, these are my other two friends, Trace and Kev. Guys, this is Parker. Now, if you'll excuse us, we're going to grab some drinks and tee off."

"We just got here." Trace, the one with black hair slicked back and his own impressive display of muscles, grinned. "So we'll meet you at the first hole."

"Not a good idea." Levi paid for two bottles of water.

"Why not?" Kev, the lankier one with male pattern baldness, asked. "You don't mind, do you, Parker?"

"Um ..." She shrugged, glancing up at Levi. "Might be fun."

Levi frowned. "Let's go."

"We'll be there in five," Ziek called.

"Now listen up..." Levi jumped into the golf cart "...stay close to me at all times. Especially if they get too nicey-nice with you."

"What?" She laughed at the seriousness of his voice and the absurdity of their conversation.

He nodded. "If they're nice to you, it's because they're trying to steal you away from me. Everything is a game to them."

"No guy code?"

"No. These guys are spoiled little rich boys like me." He winked at her. "They made their fortunes in college or shortly after. Total jerk-offs in their late twenties and early thirties with nothing better to do than waste their days golfing and taking private jets to fancy places for quick dinners and even quicker lays before flying back home to make their tee times the next morning."

"They sound like real winners."

They sped off toward the first tee. "Deep down, they're great guys, really. Their families haven't kept them quite as grounded as mine has."

Parker chuckled. "You're grounded?"

"Yes. I have a day job. That grounds me."

"Oh, right. The drawing thing."

"Yes, the drawing thing." He glanced behind them. "Here they come. No flirting. Don't smile too much. And don't bend over. That short-skirt thingy you're wearing is too fucking revealing for these idiots. And watch your nipples. It's ninety degrees out here, but I see they haven't gotten the memo."

Parker looked down at her chest. "Dammit. I hate this bra." She pulled her shirt away from her chest as much as possible.

Levi skidded to a stop at the first tee.

"Levi give you the watch out for us speech already?" Ziek asked. "He's afraid one of us will steal you away from him."

"You boys good at stealing girls from Levi?"

"Mandy, Elle, Veronica," Kev said with a wiggle to his brows.

"Monique, Deb." Ziek winked.

"Don't forget Haley." Trace shook his head and whistled.

"Haley," Ziek and Kev said at the same time and then sighed heavily.

"You guys are dicks. You know that, right? And you've never stolen a girl from me." Levi didn't wait for anyone. He teed up and killed it with his big dog, straight down the center of the fairway.

"Who was Haley?" Parker asked.

Levi slipped his club back into the bag. "Who's next?" He didn't look at Parker.

Ziek went next, followed by Trace and Kev.

Levi tapped his hand on the steering wheel of the golf cart like a smoker in need of a nicotine hit.

"You're up, hot stuff." Kev grinned at Parker.

"I'm going to shove your driver up your ass if you call her that again," Levi said, void of any humor.

"Relax, dude. It's a compliment."

Parker took a few practice swings. It had been awhile since

she'd played golf. Releasing a deep breath, she pulled back and swung.

"Are you fucking kidding me?" Ziek shook his head. "Levi, you brought a sandbagger. This is bullshit. She just out drove everyone but you, well ..." He squinted. "I can't tell. It's close. She might be ahead of you."

As Parker returned her driver to the bag and hopped in the cart, everyone—including Levi—gawked at her.

"What?" She shrugged. "We have golf courses in Iowa too."

FOUR AND A half hours later, they sat in the clubhouse drinking beer.

"We got our asses kicked by a girl today." Kev shook his head and tipped back the amber bottle.

Parker smiled at Levi. He rolled his eyes, but it didn't stop his grin from making an appearance. "I think she's been holding out on me."

She shrugged. "I may have worked at a golf course over the summers during high school and three summers in college." Volleyball was her first love, but golf quickly turned into her favorite hobby. However, it had been years since she'd played.

"Girls and their secrets. Levi, you really know how to pick 'em." Trace winked at Levi.

Levi frowned, avoiding eye contact with Parker.

"What am I missing?" she asked.

The guys all looked at Levi. He stared at the table. She recognized the fear in his face—the truth waiting to come out at the worst time.

"I don't need to know. I'm not used to being in the know anyway, so ..."

Levi cringed and looked up at her. She wasn't trying to guilt him with her past. But from the pain on his face, she knew that's what she'd done.

He sighed. "We used to golf at a private club, years ago. Until I had a relationship with a younger girl. Her name was Haley. She said she was nineteen. I was twenty-three at the time. I found out later that her father owned the club. The same day he threatened to have me arrested for statutory rape. His daughter was seventeen. He agreed to let it go after she told him that she lied to me and after I agreed that neither I nor any of my friends would golf at his club again."

"Kev gave Haley his phone number before we got kicked off the premises. Told her to call him on her birthday." Trace laughed. "She did too. We're pretty sure she's fucked most of the male club members by now ... maybe a few of the female ones too."

"Thanks, guys." Levi stood. "I'm so glad we ran into you today." He couldn't hide the anger in his voice, even behind the heavy dose of sarcasm. "Let's go." He held out his hand.

Parker took it. "It was nice meeting you." She smirked at his cackling friends.

"Wish we could say the same, but you kicked our asses today. So ... don't come back." Ziek grinned.

Levi led her to his SUV and opened her door. She hated the awkwardness that had been between them since the very first mention of Haley's name.

"Hey ..." she grabbed his arm before he shut her door.

He wet his lips and pressed them together, releasing a slow breath through his nose while looking at his feet.

"That was a decade ago. So what. I didn't need to know. I'm sorry I said anything to begin with."

Levi still wouldn't look at her.

"If it's any consolation, I was sixteen when Haley was seventeen. Had I met you then, I would have probably lied too if it meant being with you."

Levi stepped back, giving her a quick look. "It's no consolation." He shut her door.

Silence dominated their ride home. Parker couldn't figure out why it bothered him so much.

"I'm going to shower and then get caught up on some email," he mumbled, giving Rags a few quick pats on his side as the excited canine greeted them.

"Want me to join you?"

Levi walked toward the bedroom. "Would you take Rags outside?"

That was a no. Parker tried to not let it bother her. But it did.

WHEN PARKER AND Rags returned, Levi was in his office with the door shut. The door was partially glass so she could see him. But it was the first time she'd seen it closed. Instead of pushing him for answers, Parker took a shower and slipped into the red dress she wore for their first date. Foregoing the sexy high heels, she slipped on her navy Chuck's—the ensemble said sexy but playful.

"I'm thinking that tapas place tonight. What do you think?" She closed the door behind her, hoping it hadn't been shut to keep her out.

He closed his laptop and leaned back in his chair. "You should go without me tonight."

"Without you?"

Levi nodded, rolling his lips between his teeth, eyes set on the desk between them.

"Well, it's a nice restaurant. I think it will feel weird going there by myself. I'll just make us something here."

"No, you should go."

She grunted a nervous laugh. "Are we still talking about the tapas restaurant? Because you've been off all afternoon, and I don't want to push you to tell me anything you don't want to tell me. But now that you seem anxious to not be around me, I'm getting that backed into a corner feeling, and it's not a great one."

"What do you want me to say?"

"Well ... I guess I want to know what's wrong."

"Do you *need* to know?"

Parker had to remind herself that it was Levi. Had any other guy been that evasive, she would have been packing her bags. "I don't know, Levi. Do I *need* to know?"

"I don't really think so."

She nodded. Maybe she did need to pack, not everything, but just a few things for a visit back home—without him. "My mom wants to see me. I think it's time I go home for a visit."

He shrugged. "I can't stop you."

"Why would you want to stop me from visiting my family?"

"I didn't say I did." His jaw clenched.

It was still in the nineties outside but the air around Levi dipped below freezing.

"I'll see if I can get a flight out tomorrow or the following day."

Levi opened his computer. "I'll book it. You don't have the money."

"Jesus ..." she whispered, feeling the tip of his knife nick her heart.

He gave her a quick glance. "I didn't mean it like that. You know better."

"I have enough money to buy my own fucking ticket." She tried to keep from crying.

Levi pounded the keys for a few more seconds. "Done. You fly out at four-thirty-five tomorrow afternoon—first class." He shut his computer again and ran his hands through his disheveled hair, resting his elbows on the desk.

"I love you," she said in a small voice.

He kept his head down, hands fisted in his hair.

"I love you," she said again. Gus was right. Love required nurturing. Parker didn't care. She would nurture the living hell out of the love she had for the man sitting before her.

Levi nodded a bit as if that's all the acknowledgment she needed.

"I love you."

He looked up, frustration etched on his face.

"I love you." She had a point to make and nothing would keep her from making it.

"I heard you."

"I love you."

"What are you doing?" He sighed, releasing more frustration.

"I love you." She stepped toward him.

"Parker ..."

The pain in his eyes scared her. She wanted to turn and run, but she didn't. "I love you." She pulled up the skirt to her dress just enough to straddle his lap.

He swallowed, diverting his eyes to the other side of the

room. His hands moved to the arms of the chair.

"Look at me."

After a few seconds, he looked at her.

"I love you."

"Haley was pregnant." He waited for Parker to react.

She didn't.

"Those regrets from my past? This is at the top. I never told my friends because they didn't ask. They didn't ask how her dad found out we'd had sex. They didn't ask where I was the day her dad made me take her to the doctor to terminate the pregnancy. She asked me if I wanted her to keep the baby. I said yes. Then she asked me if I loved her." Levi cleared his throat, eyes red with emotion.

Parker knew the answer. She knew the outcome. It was all over his face. "I love you."

He shook his head. "Why do you keep saying that?"

"I love you."

"Stop it." He gripped the arms of the chair.

"I love you."

"I killed my child because I didn't love its mother!"

Parker blinked sending tears down her cheeks. "I love you."

"Jesus, Parker! What do you want me to say? What do you want me to do?"

"I want you to forgive yourself, and then I want you to love me back."

Gasping for his next breath, or maybe a shred of control, Levi narrowed his eyes and a blink later he grabbed her face and kissed her with the passion of someone drowning and grasping for that one lifeline.

He yanked up her dress, even more, probing his tongue into her mouth with an urgency like it pissed him off he couldn't kiss her any deeper. Keeping his mouth attached to hers, he pushed his computer aside sending a stack of papers onto the floor. Then he lifted her onto his desk. He fumbled for the tie to her halter top dress as she grabbed for the button and zipper to his shorts.

As soon as her dress fell below her breasts, he gripped them, kneading them until she arched her back, breaking their kiss. "Levi ..."

She released him from his briefs and stroked him. He hissed in a breath, leaving one hand on her breast. His other hand grabbed the crotch to her panties and pulled it to the side as she guided his erection to that very spot.

"Stop." He pulled back a fraction. His hand on her breast moved to the back of her neck, and he rested his forehead on hers. "I love you back," he whispered through ragged breaths. "I love you back so fucking much I'm certain it's the only thing I have ever done in my life that's one hundred percent selfless. But this isn't us. I don't want to have pissed-off-at-the-world sex with you."

"Levi ..." She panted, holding tight to his cock. "I kinda need this to happen."

He nodded, still leaning into her forehead with his. "Agreed." He laughed a little. "But it's I-love-you sex. I-need-you sex. My-whole-fucking-world-revolves-around-you sex."

"Agreed." Parker grinned and stroked him a few times, attempting to bring him closer.

"But, babe ..." Levi grabbed her hips and slid her off the desk to her feet. The pain in his eyes transformed into something feral. "It's still desk sex." He turned her toward the desk, pressing his hand on her back until she bent forward resting her cheek against the smooth wood. Her hands gripped the edge next to her head.

"Levi ..." she whispered breathlessly as her heart pounded in anticipation.

"Shhh ..." He eased off her panties, ghosting his lips along the back of her legs and over the curve of her ass.

"Fuck!" Her muscles clenched. "Did you just bite my ass again?"

He chuckled while his tongue glided over the spot. As he stood, he lifted her right leg and plunged into her. Bending over her back, he whispered in her ear, "My whole ... fucking ... world."

In a matter of seconds, Levi took something ugly and heartbreaking and turned it into something beautiful and soul-shattering.

Parker didn't love him for his perfections; she loved him for his flaws that begged for a second chance—that vulnerable part of his soul searching for its place in the world. She wanted to be that place.

Chapter Forty-One

RAGS CHEWED ON his favorite elk antler while Parker packed for her trip home.

"How long are you staying?" Levi gazed out their bedroom window, hands in his pockets.

"I don't know. I'll have to be back by the interview, so not longer than a week. You were supposed to go with me."

He turned. "I was?"

"Yes." She pulled several shirts from their hangers in the closet. "My parents need to meet you so they don't think you've abducted their daughter."

"You didn't ask me."

She shrugged, coming out of the closet. "I was going to ask you, then last night happened, and I thought you didn't want me here, and in that moment part of me didn't want to be here, so that's when I said something about going home. Before I knew it, you had my flight booked."

His eyebrows pulled together. "I meet with a client and their contractor tomorrow, but I could fly out after that. I'd love to meet your family."

"Yeah?" She glanced up from her perfectly organized suitcase.

"Of course. I'll see if my parents will take Rags for few days."

"Will that bother your mom? He's sort of a reminder of …"

Levi twisted his lips, observing Rags rolling on the antler for some weird reason. "I don't know. It's been over six weeks. The last time I talked to her, she seemed to be doing better. I'm not sure she'll ever be the same again. I mean … it's just been in the past few weeks that *I've* started to put things into perspective. Remembering things that were going on with them before they died. It's just still hard to wrap my head around everything that has happened over the past few months."

Parker's hands stilled, and she slowly looked up from her suitcase. "Past few months? What does that mean?"

He shook his head a few times. "Sabrina and I talked on the phone quite a bit. I knew she wasn't herself. We've never kept stuff from each other, but I knew she wasn't telling me something. Finally, she broke down one day and said she'd been having an affair."

Parker's world began to vanish along with the oxygen in the room.

"I was so mad at her. Gus wasn't just my brother-in-law, we were friends. He was the real deal—a hard worker, kind, honest, family-oriented, and he loved Sabrina. God … did he love her."

Slowly, Parker began to crumble inside, but she had to keep every single emotion hidden. It felt beyond unbearable.

"I don't know what happened to her. Maybe it was her new job or the guy she met, but … I didn't even recognize her. Everything she did seemed so desperate. I told her to tell Gus, to either save her marriage or let him go, but …"

Parker walked back to the closet, blinking away the tears, fighting to keep hold of her slipping composure. She didn't need any more clothes, but she continued to take things out of the drawer and off hangers.

"She was afraid and embarrassed to tell him. And just so you know, I'm not defending her actions—the cheating. I know how you feel about that." He walked toward the closet.

She kept her back to him. There was no escape. There was no longer any reason to not tell Levi about her and Gus. Parker knew she could lose him, but she refused to hold him with a lie.

He feared losing her with the truth. She feared losing him to a lie. The irony made her nauseous.

"Sabrina called me a few weeks before their accident. She said things were terrible between her and Gus, but that there was a 'silver lining.'"

"Hmm?" A hum was all Parker could give him without breaking down.

"She thought Gus had found his own distraction."

Parker froze.

"I called bullshit. Not Gus. The guy looked at my sister like the rest of the world didn't exist. The way I look at you."

One blink and the pain ran in endless trails down her cheeks. Her lips parted as she attempted to breathe instead of sob under the crushing weight on her chest.

"I stood over her grave, grieving the loss of my sister, yet part of me was still angry for what she did to Gus. How could she be so stupid to cheat on him and then think another woman existed that he could possibly want more than her?"

The end. They were over. He would never forgive her. If he still held resentment toward his deceased sister for what she did, he would *never* forgive Parker for the things she had done and the things she never told him. That was fine. She'd never forgive herself either.

Hugging the clothes to her chest, cheeks drowning in tears, heart buried in regret ... she slowly turned.

Levi's face tensed into instant worry. He took a step toward her and then he stopped.

When life happened, it did it in a heartbeat. That space between time. A first inhale, a last exhale. The dawn of realization, the eve of what was and never again would be. That's what Parker saw on Levi's face.

Parker waited for him to reach for his chest and pull the knife out while she stood there with blood on her hands, unmoving, at a loss for a single word, and feeling Piper's shoes on her feet. There was no way of imagining that mile in someone else's shoes. That understanding only came from lacing them up and taking the journey.

"Of course," he whispered, closing his eyes.

She knew Piper's shoes. She also knew Levi's shoes. So she said nothing. There was nothing Parker could say that would change anything. As much as she wanted to grovel, explain what really happened and beg for forgiveness as Piper had done, she knew it would only make things worse. It would only shove the knife in deeper.

Levi pressed the heels of his hands to his eyes. "What have you done?"

Silence. That was her parting gift to him. It was a greater apology than any words could ever have been. Silence acknowledged her guilt and respected his right—his need—to be angry. No one had respected Parker's right to be angry, and that only multiplied her toxic emotions.

When he dropped his hands and met her teary, red eyes, it hurt as much as the news that Gus had died. Love and life were every bit as painful as death.

He turned. She swallowed back a sob. Shoulders slumped, head down, he walked to the bed, pulled a piece of paper out of his pocket, dropped it on her suitcase, and then snapped his fingers so that Rags followed him out of the room.

Dropping to her knees, Parker continued to hug her clothes as she buckled over and started the all-too-familiar grieving process.

A ONE-WAY TICKET home. That's what Levi deposited on Parker's suitcase before he took Rags and left.

She finished packing—everything. Ordered an Uber. Got on a plane. And flew home.

A second Uber took her from the airport in Des Moines to home.

Home. Where was that? Twelve hours earlier she would have said Levi's arms. As she lugged her suitcase through the thick August humidity into the old farmhouse, she knew the creaky floor beneath her feet was home. It always would be.

"Parker!" Her mom weaved her way to the kitchen through the scattered cardboard boxes. "Why didn't you tell us you were coming home today?" Janey hugged her.

"I wanted to surprise you." Her enthusiasm died beneath the rubble of her broken heart, leaving lifeless words drifting from a hollow soul.

"We're packing up for the big move. Most of their stuff is in storage, but I told Piper she could have Grandma's china since you didn't show any interest in it. And it was just collecting dust in the attic."

Parker nodded, not really knowing what she was nodding

about.

"Welcome, home." Piper, with her hand on her belly, handed Caleb the shipping tape. "Where's Levi?"

"Uh …" She closed her eyes for a brief moment. Nothing seemed real. Voices were echoes in a dream where her worst nightmare crossed the line into reality.

"Dear, are you okay?" Janey brushed her hand along Parker's arm.

Her eyes shifted from her mom to Caleb and then Piper, and that's where they stayed. Piper held her gaze, the smile on her face faded into something sad and sympathetic, something only a twin could feel without having to ask any more questions.

"Just tired. I'm going to unpack."

"Need me to carry your suitcase up?" Caleb asked.

It was kind of him. Too kind. Parker didn't deserve anyone's kindness.

Parker shook her head.

"Unpack? Does this mean you're staying? Did you answer Piper's question? Where is Levi?"

Parker raced against her tears without actually running. She didn't want her mom to see them, nor did she want her mom to ask any more questions.

"He couldn't come. I'll explain later." Climbing the stairs, she held her breath and every emotion that waited behind hit, desperate to escape.

She dropped her suitcase and purse on the floor and dove into the bed, burying her face into the pillow to silence her grief. A million what-ifs pleaded their case.

What if Levi knew the whole truth?

What if she told him they never had sex?

What if she explained the condoms?

What if she told him Gus was going to leave Sabrina no matter what?

What if she could explain why she didn't tell him everything?

What if she would have told him everything that night in the barn?

She choked back her sobs, holding still as the bed dipped. Piper lay next to her with her baby belly nudging Parker.

"That's a lot of pain to bear by yourself. Why don't you let me take a little before it completely breaks you?" Piper whispered.

Parker sobbed harder. She didn't deserve that. Not from Piper. Parker had judged her unfairly. She ruined her wedding. She held an eternal grudge. And then she did the one thing she swore she would never do—she became the cheater.

The liar.

Despicable.

"Levi isn't coming," Piper whispered. Not a question. She just knew.

Parker shook her head.

"His loss." Her sister stroked her hair, the way Parker had done to Stephanie after the funeral.

"Mine..." Parker's voice broke between sobs " ...i-it's m-my l-l-oss."

Piper kissed the back of Parker's head. "I love you."

Parker turned to her reflection. Piper had the pregnancy glow and it looked so good on her. "I love you too." She sniffled. "But now I hate me." More sobs worked their way out.

"Oh, Parker ..." Piper wiped Parker's tears from her cheeks

with her thumb as Parker pinched her eyes shut.

"I'm a t-terrible h-human."

"No," Piper whispered. "If you want that statement to be true, then you need to remove the adjective."

AFTER CRYING HERSELF to sleep, Parker woke up in the middle of the night.

Crowded.

Hot.

And trapped. Piper sleeping on one side and her mom on the other side of her.

At that moment, she knew even if she never saw Levi again, she would be okay. She had people. The kind that loved her without judgment. The kind she could trust with her deepest secrets.

"I had an affair with Gus Westman."

Both bodies next to her stirred. She knew they were awake but neither said a word.

"We never had sex. And his wife was having an affair too, but it doesn't change anything. I fell in love with a married man, and he fell in love with me. It was wrong. I didn't tell Levi, and that was wrong too. No one will ever believe me, but I did it to not tarnish his memories of them. It was harder to keep it a secret than it would have been to tell him. It's been painful, confusing, embarrassing, and humbling. So very humbling. But I hope it's not what I've always thought cheating was..." she wiped a stray tear that rolled down the side of her face " ...unforgivable."

Piper took one of Parker's hands, and Janey took the other. Parker squeezed them, a silent thank you, an unbreakable bond. A love that would last forever.

THE FOLLOWING MORNING, the three women had breakfast at the farmhouse without Caleb and Bart. More tears were shed, apologies were given, and forgiveness was granted. Parker had to mend what she could and let go of the things in her life that were beyond repair. Letting go was a hard lesson.

"So what are you going to do for a job now?" Janey asked as she refilled their coffee mugs and juice glasses.

"I don't know. I'll find something. I know you want me to stay here but—"

Janey rested her hand on Parker's. "But you're an adult with dreams, and you need your freedom."

Parker raised her brows, glancing at Piper who shrugged with a grin behind her juice glass.

"Did aliens abduct our mom?"

"No." Their mom sat back in her chair. Something resembling a mix between love and worry warred along her face. "I want to be your lifeline, not your anchor."

"I don't know, Piper … she's bringing her A-game, setting the mom bar pretty high." Parker grinned.

"Mmm …" Piper nodded, rubbing her belly. "It's about time."

Janey faked a frown.

The back door opened. "Knock knock. The realtor just dropped off the keys." Caleb held them up. "Even though we don't close until one, we can start moving some stuff over now."

"Move all you want, peeps. I'll be here in the air-conditioning with my swollen ankles up." Piper blew Caleb a kiss.

"I could use the distraction and expend some energy. Let's get these boxes out of my kitchen." Parker stood and took her plate and cups to the dishwasher. She paused a moment, staring at the counter where she and Gus had been the night of the party. Grief was a sneaky little bastard, always hiding around the corner. Being back in Iowa, back in that house, and Piper and Caleb moving into Gus and Sabrina's house meant there would be a lot of corners in her life. She needed to find a way to get past them, accept them, and maybe some day those corners would disappear.

Chapter Forty-Two

"GO AWAY!" LEVI shooed Rags away from his face and then buried it under the pillow.

Rags barked.

Levi passed out after an unknown number of beers at an unknown time. He had one shoe on, one shoe off, shorts caught around the one shoe on, and his shirt stuck around his neck like a scarf. His mouth felt like he got into Rags's food by mistake. Rubbing his eyes felt like sandpaper. Had he cried? Levi couldn't remember.

Pissed off. That's the only emotion he recalled with any sort of clarity.

Pissed off at Parker, Gus, Sabrina, himself, life, and back again to Parker.

"Fuck you, Parker," he mumbled, easing from his stomach to his back, squinting against the morning light trying to stab his retinas. "I didn't want to love you." Levi rubbed his temples to ease the sharp throbbing in his head. "Fuck …" He hated that he couldn't even lie to himself. "Yes, I did. So damn much …"

Rags barked again.

"Okay, okay, you need to take a morning piss. I do too." He eased to sitting, frowning at his disheveled state.

In three hours he needed to have his shit together and his

ass on the job site. After piecing his outfit back together, he took Rags downstairs and then fed him his late breakfast, only four hours later than usual. A shower and seemingly endless piss later, he dragged himself into the closet to get dressed. Empty hangers and bare, half-open drawers taunted him reminding him of what he'd had and what he lost.

"Way to put your dick in my sister and in my girlfriend, Gus. That shit's just fucked-up." Levi ripped a shirt from its hanger. Being pissed off at Gus was a new experience and a little weird since he was dead. Just as well. Had he not died, Levi would have had to kill him for cheating on his cheating sister with a girl that was supposed to be his. "You're losing it, buddy." He pulled on his briefs and jeans. "Talking to yourself about dead people. Not good." Levi chuckled. "Ahh … the brink of insanity. It's a little creepy here."

He walked to the bed and sat down to put on his shoes. "Rags! Get in here so I'm not talking to myself."

Rags rushed into the room, tail in overdrive.

"Good. Now I need you to stay by my side when I'm here. Nod occasionally when I talk or at least do that head cock thing that you do."

Rags cocked his head.

"Exactly. So we're good?"

Rags cocked his head to the other side.

"Great. Good talk." He scratched the dog's head as he stood. "I'll be back by dinner. Time to settle back into the bachelor life again."

LEVI WASN'T FAMILIAR with the girl being the reason for the breakup. He tried to find some sense of pride for not being the one to ruin everything with his big mouth. But in reality, it was his honesty and oversharing that led to empty hangers and a big bed with a hairy dog beside him a week earlier, rather than the most spectacular woman ever.

He laughed at that thought as he bathed his liver in alcohol at his favorite bar down the street from his condo.

The most spectacular woman ever.

That thought alone pissed him off. How did his mind come up with that after everything that had happened? His brain needed more alcohol to think clearly.

He hadn't told his family or friends. He couldn't tell them. As much as he wanted to resurrect the dead, only to cuss them out and throw them back into their graves for being so stupid, he couldn't share that anger with his parents—taint their memories of Gus and Sabrina. They never knew about Sabrina's affair. Or Gus's.

At least a hundred times over the previous week, he'd typed a text to Parker then erased it. Sometimes the words were venomous. Sometimes they were questions he needed answered. Sometimes they were all the reasons he loved her, followed by all the reasons he couldn't be with her. The former outnumbered the latter, but the latter weighed heavier on his mind.

"Anyone sitting here?" a perky brunette asked. Perky eyes. Perky smile. Perky tits.

"Nope." He grinned.

She wedged her curvy little body between him and the guy two stools down who had his back to them. "I'm Talia."

"Levi."

"You live around here?"

"Yup." He took several long pulls of his beer. "You?"

She ordered a dirty martini without expecting him to buy it, which automatically earned her his full attention. As full as his half-inebriated state would allow.

"Just moved to Phoenix last week from Tampa. New job. I'm meeting friends here…" she glanced at her phone "…in about ten minutes. You by yourself tonight?"

"Nope. I have my beer." He held it up and grinned.

She smiled. It was a nice smile. Not a Parker smile, but living up to the smile of the most spectacular woman ever was an unrealistic expectation. He grunted.

Talia narrowed her eyes. "You okay?"

"Yes. Just had a disturbing thought. Keeps popping in my head. Won't go away."

Her perkiness dropped a notch. "O-kay …"

"I'm not mental or some psycho. Really."

"Says every psycho out there." She laughed, still a bit more reserved than when she first hopped up beside him. "So, Levi, what do you do?"

"I'm an architect."

"Really? Well, I'm a graphic designer." She was attractive. Friendly. Appropriately cautious. And shared his artistic talent. Talia was the exact type of woman he would ask out on a date or just take back to his place to see where things led, especially after that many beers.

"What do you know about corn detasseling?"

"Um …" She grimaced, biting her lower lip. "Nothing."

"You ever run to a convenience store in the middle of the night for a couple of donuts?"

Talia's laugh morphed into a giggle. "Definitely not. Do I look like the kind of woman who does that?"

He frowned, studying Talia but thinking about the most

spectacular woman ever. "No. You don't." Levi tossed a wad of cash on the bar. "I've got your drink." He smiled. "It's been a pleasure talking with you. Welcome to Arizona. I hope your new job goes well. Goodnight."

"Wait!" Talia called as he walked out of the bar.

He didn't look back.

DAY TEN. MISERY settled into Levi's life like battery acid. He couldn't work, eat, golf, sleep, or focus on a damn thing that didn't come in a bottle with a warning label. Parker turned him into a worthless drunk with a dog. He felt sorry for Rags.

"I'm gonna call her." He gestured to Rags with his half-empty bottle of beer. It was his sixth of the night. The fact that he was drinking only beer was progress.

Levi brought her up on his phone, frowning at the photo of her on the beach. "Fuck it." He pressed call.

After several rings, he contemplated leaving a drunk message, but at the last second, she answered.

"Hey." Her voice was barely a whisper.

Just the sound of it brought so much fucking emotion to him he struggled to find a breath, let alone a word. He put her on speaker and stared at the phone, watching the time tick away. She didn't say anything, but as long as the time continued its count, he knew she was there—waiting.

He waited five full minutes to respond, but she was still on the line. "You see the irony in what happened, right? Your sister and her husband. You and a married man."

"Yes."

He waited.

She remained silent after her one-word answer.

Pinching the bridge of his nose, he willed the stupid emotion to go the hell away, but it remained, burning his eyes. "Ask me something. I'm fucking dying to spill my guts, but I do it best when provoked. So ask me."

The time on his phone continued to count. One minute and thirteen seconds later she broke the silence again.

"Do you love me?"

"Don't ask me that."

"Are we over?"

"Yes ... No ..." He punched his fist into the sofa. "Fuck you! Ask me a real question, not this yes or no bullshit." Levi rubbed his temples, slipping into a place so dark and filled with anger he wanted to crawl out of his skin. He regretted his words the second he said them. Trying to break her only multiplied his pain. "This was a bad idea. I've had too damn much to drink. I shouldn't have called, I—"

"What do you want me to say, Levi?"

He swallowed hard as more emotion pooled in his eyes. "That I misunderstood. That you weren't having an affair with Gus."

"And after I tell you it wasn't a misunderstanding, what do you want me to do?" She sniffled.

He'd made her cry. Part of him hated himself for it and part of him wanted her to feel the twist of the knife too.

"Apologize?" she asked.

"I don't need your fucking apology."

"Fine. Real question—do your parents know about the affair? The *affairs*?"

"Another fucking yes or no question."

"I bet you haven't told them. Why? Why haven't you told them, Levi?"

"They don't need to know." He took another pull of beer.

"Bullshit! If you need to know, then they need to know! They *deserve* to know that their daughter and her husband were living a lie. They deserve to know their daughter traveled without her husband but always packed sexy lingerie and a box of condoms."

"Stop." He gritted his teeth.

"She treated him like shit."

"Goddammit! Shut the fuck up!" He threw his bottle across the room. Rags barked once then heeled while releasing a few whines.

More time ticked away. Three more minutes of silence.

"Go look in the mirror at that tattoo on your back." Parker's voice was controlled and laced with pain. "I'll take my share of the blame. I'm a terrible person for how I treated my sister and Caleb. I'm a terrible person for falling on the sword of my pride. I'm a terrible person for blaming the shortcomings in my life on everyone but myself."

She cleared her throat. "I could have stopped what happened between Gus and me. And I should have. But it would not have changed the outcome of their marriage. Had I known you knew about Sabrina's affair, I would have told you about my relationship with Gus."

"Bullshit. You never would have told me. You thought your secret was safe in the grave. Had I not said something about—"

"Jesus Christ! You have no fucking clue how much—" sobs ripped from her chest "—how *d-desperately* I needed to t-tell someone. I was *dying* inside. Heart ripped from my chest, soul c-crushing *dying* inside. But I couldn't tell anyone without tarnishing their memories, dancing on their graves, ruining more lives than had already been shattered! S-so I had to take all of my grief and hold it inside, showing just the right amount of emotion people would expect from a neighbor, an employee."

Levi fisted his hair and pinched his eyes shut, overwhelmed by the dizzying alcohol in his veins, the knife still lodged in his heart, and the sobs on the other end of the line.

"I should—"

"Stop!" He fisted his hair harder.

"Levi—"

"Not another fucking word."

"I don't regret not telling you."

"I said shut up!"

She kept going. "I should regret showing up to the funeral. Every conversation we had. The night in the back of Old Blue. Chasing after you. Every word. Every touch. Lov—" Her voice broke. "L-loving you. But ..." he could barely hear her whisper " ...I don't. I can't. So ..."

He fell to pieces right along with her, unable to speak as his body shook.

"Hate me. I'll still love you. Cut me with words. I'll bleed for you. Regret us. I'll vanish from your life. But don't ever ask *me* to regret us. If we weren't real, then I don't want to take another breath. And I want to live, Levi. For the first time in so very long, I don't feel like I'm drowning in anger, hiding from the truth, or in denial that this is my life. I'm imperfect like everyone else. But I'm also worthy of love and forgiveness and settling for anything less would be wrong."

Levi rubbed his red eyes and continued to grit his teeth to bite back all the things he wanted to say. He did it for her, even if she didn't deserve it. "You expect me to forgive you?"

"No," she whispered.

"You expect me to be able to love you?"

"No."

"Then what do you want from me?"

The time on his phone continued to tick.

"I'm not the one who called. I don't expect anything from you. But I wish you well."

The timer stopped.

Chapter Forty-Three

TRAMPING, TAYLOR SWIFT, and hours of endless yard work kept Parker from dying a little more every day. Two weeks without Levi. She had a Levi calendar with X's on it. On January 1, she would throw away the calendar and declare the end of her Levi detox. That was about four months away.

The phone call gutted her, but he needed it, and she understood that. Parker wanted to take his pain, and she took as much as she could without dying beneath the weight of it.

"We're grilling out in a little bit. You should come over." Piper handed Parker a cold bottled water as Parker pulled off her leather work gloves.

She was looking forward to fewer weeds in another month. "Not yet." Parker sucked down half of the water.

"I hate that we live in a house that holds such terrible memories for you. I really wish I would have known or that you would have spoken up before we bought it. We could sell it and we would. If that's what it will take."

Parker had helped them move, but every room held some significant memory of Gus. As much as she tried to ignore it, she couldn't breathe in that house. Every memory of Gus sparked a memory of Levi. Pain compounded by more pain.

She agreed to find temporary work until Piper had the baby, and if at that point the past still haunted her, she would move and look for work elsewhere.

"It's a great house. It really is. And you'll be glad Mom and Dad are so close when this baby comes and you feel over-whelmed, especially since Caleb travels so much. It's a smart choice."

"I don't care how smart you think it is. I just care about you."

Parker had her sister back. It meant everything. Maybe that's why Gus came into her life. Maybe he was a lesson, an experience she needed—and nothing more. But that didn't explain Levi. Parker worried her heart would never make sense of Levi's role in her life.

"Thank you for your concern, truly. But … I'm going to be fine. Eventually. Right?"

Piper nodded with little reassurance on her face. "I sup-pose. Have you heard from Levi?"

"Not since he called me to vent. We're done. It was pretty final."

"Why didn't you tell him? You know he thinks you slept with Gus."

"It was an affair. The lack of actual intercourse doesn't change that."

"It might in his mind."

"Well, it shouldn't. And … it's none of his business. I nev-er asked how Caleb kissed you and where and how he touched you. He cheated on me, that was all I deserved to know. The second he kissed you, he was no longer mine. Levi can think I lied to him if it makes it easier to hate me, but he can never say I cheated on him. I didn't even know him then."

Piper bit her lips, her eyes squinting. "Humans are so …"

"Human. Imperfect. Judgmental. Scared. Insecure. Easily

disappointed. Delusional. Impulsive."

Tugging on Parker's ponytail, Piper grinned. "Yes, but also … kind. Loving. Forgiving. Heroic. Truthful. Noble. Humble. Resilient."

Parker looked over at their house. "I'll come for dinner."

"You don't have to—"

"No. I do. I'll shower and be over in an hour."

Piper gave Parker's short ponytail one last tug. "You're a good person, Parker Joy."

"Thanks, Piper Faith."

DINNER WAS BEARABLE and what she needed. One slow breath at a time, Parker survived the close proximity to all the memories. A few times she even caught herself laughing at part of the conversation and forgetting about everything but the people who surrounded her.

After the final dish was washed and Piper found her spot on the sofa with her feet on Caleb's lap, Parker said goodnight. When she walked past Old Blue, she opened the door. It protested, and she grinned. Fifteen minutes and a slow drive later, she put it into *park* just outside of the cemetery. To her surprise, it didn't backfire when she shut it off.

The horizon was getting ready to put the sun to bed, but there was enough light left to guide her toward the back of the cemetery. As she climbed the last hill, a figure appeared by Gus's and Sabrina's graves. Her heart paused when she realized it was Levi. His back was to her, so she turned and ran back to the truck.

"Shhh …" She pleaded with the door when she opened it, but it paid no attention to her. Then when she went to start

Old Blue, he failed her again. He had a thing with the cemetery. "Come on! I didn't bring *you* here to die." She pumped the gas a few times and twisted the key.

Knock knock knock.

Parker dropped her head to the steering wheel in defeat. She knew whose fist rapped on her window. The door creaked again.

"I checked. They're still dead."

She didn't move. Looking at him would hurt too much, just his voice set her Levi detox back by a good month. But damn him for saying something as inappropriate and funny as the suit he had on the last time they were at the cemetery. Parker grinned even as tears welled in her eyes.

As quickly as it appeared, her smile faded. "I shouldn't be here," she whispered. Parker thought the same thing at the funeral, but at least then she was the only one who knew why her presence was inappropriate.

"Probably not. Yet here you are."

She raised her head and swatted away her tears. "Don't be a jerk."

"I need to be mad at you." His brow knitted tight.

Parker laughed. "You're doing a great job." She swung her legs around and hopped out, not waiting for him to say anymore and not shutting the door behind her before marching back into the cemetery. When she reached the top of the hill, she made a quick glance back.

Levi leaned his shoulder against the wrought-iron gate at the entrance, his back to her. She found the gesture odd. Was he giving her some sort of privacy?

Her attention returned to the graves in front of her.

August L. Westman

"Told you." She wiped away more tears. "I knew you were going to break my heart. You and that stupid Cubs cap." Parker squatted down by his headstone and traced his engraved name. "You've ruined my life." She laughed through her tears. "Even in death you just had to make sure I never found happiness."

Her breath caught and nearly two months of pent-up grief racked her body as she fell forward to her knees resting her head and hands on the cool granite, tears vanishing in the grass beneath her. "Why were you in that car with her?" she whispered through her sobs. "You were s-supposed to be with m-me."

Parker cried for every unfair thing that had happened to her in her adult life. She knew Gus would want her to leave it behind with him. He may have been despicable, but everything Levi said about him was true. August Westman was a good man, a hard worker, and he loved his wife ... he also loved Parker. That's how much love he had in his heart.

After the last tear, she sat up and drew in a shaky breath. She wouldn't visit him again. It was a final goodbye. "I knew you were too old for me." It hurt to smile, but that was the memory—the feeling—she most wanted to remember. "Rest in peace, Gus."

As she walked by Sabrina's headstone, she feathered her fingers over the top. "I'm sorry," she whispered. And she was.

Levi didn't move as Parker approached the entrance. She stood beside him; he seemed to be watching the last sliver of daylight disappear.

"Did you love him?"

Parker followed his gaze, admiring the splendid orange and blue sky. "Yes."

"How long had you been sleeping together?"

"We didn't." It wasn't a lie.

She and Gus road the line and even swayed over it on more than one occasion. But they didn't have sex. That was Levi's question.

"I need to know what happened between you two," the anguish in his voice cut her to the bone.

"Not all truths set you free and not all lies are deception," she repeated his own words.

"You're not going to tell me?"

They both continued to watch the horizon.

"No."

In life, there were truths and lies, and then there were intimate moments that stayed between two people. Even if what happened between Parker and Gus was wrong, it was still personal in the most private way.

Letting go of Levi hurt beyond words. But she couldn't apologize for the lie, and he couldn't forgive the truth.

Parker took a small step past him.

"I was on my way to you."

She stopped.

He breathed out the whisper of a laugh. "I think I've been on my way to you my whole life."

Parker's lips parted as she drew in a stuttered gasp, tears pooling in her eyes.

"I need you." His voice cracked, so did her heart.

One blink. Tears.

"I love you," he whispered as if the words were being ripped from his soul.

Parker closed her eyes. "I love you too."

"More than him?"

Her quivering lips pressed together as she swallowed past the pain and fear. "So much more."

Levi's pinky finger slid around hers.

And that's when life happened.

Epilogue

Four Months Later – Somewhere in the Middle of Nowhere

"I LOVE SURPRISES!" Parker's smile faded. "Well, the good kind. Please tell me this is the good kind."

"I think so." Levi gave her a sideways glance as they pulled into the drive. "No peeking."

"I'm not." She adjusted the blindfold. "Jeez, I just said I love surprises."

He turned off the car. Rags whined from the backseat.

She drummed her fingers on her legs. They'd been in the car for hours after staying at a hotel one night with the shades drawn the entire time. It had been a blind trip so far. Parker couldn't imagine what kind of surprise involved that much travel.

"It's the beach, isn't it. We're at the beach. Gah! I can smell the ocean air."

Levi chuckled. "Is that so?"

"What are you waiting for? Why aren't we getting out?"

"Really, babe? You *really* like surprises?"

"Yes! But not torture. This is torture."

"Hold tight."

"Where are you going?"

"To get your surprise. No peeking."

"Why do I have to stay here? You can't bring the ocean to

me."

"How many times have I promised to give you the world?"

She breathed an easy laugh. "God I love you."

"Stay put."

"But," she called to stop him, "seriously, why do I have to stay here?"

Levi sighed. "It's a *delicate* situation." He shut the door.

"What's that supposed to mean?"

A wet nose sniffed her hair.

"Is that your way of telling me to stop being so nosey?"

Fifteen minutes later, Rags barked, whined, cried, and danced impatiently in the back seat, even clawing at the window.

"Stop! What is it?"

The back door opened first.

"Hey! Why does he get let out?"

Levi opened her door next. "Because he's scratching my leather seats and doors."

Rags barked several times.

"What is his deal? When can I see? Come on! Come on!" Her hands clapped like a circus monkey as she jumped up and down.

"Here." Levi thrust something warm, furry, and wiggly into her arms.

"What the hell?"

He pulled off her blindfold.

The sun singed her retinas. "It's a puppy ... I think." Parker blinked several times as she giggled from the eager tongue tickling her face and neck. "You got me a puppy?" She squealed.

"You can thank Rags." Levi whistled to him.

Rags marked a few bushes lining the driveway to the house.

"What do you mean? Where are we?"

"The indiscretion at the rest stop … chocolate Lab … swollen vulva?"

Parker's eyes bulged out of her head, mouth agape.

Levi wrangled Rags back into the SUV. "It resulted in seven puppies. Six female. One male—the runt of the litter that didn't sell."

"This is their house? The freaky spastic lady?"

"Shhh …" Levi glanced back toward the house then tossed a nod toward the vehicle. "Jeez, woman. Get in. I think her front windows are open."

Parker hopped in the front seat.

"They named him Knutt. K N U T T." Levi retrieved a sack from the pouch behind his seat, pulling out a new dog harness and seat belt loop. "I think we should keep the name. I like it."

Parker stared at his secret stash of dog supplies. Levi was good. Sneaky, but good.

"Here."

She handed Knutt to him. Levi secured the soft, wiggly ball of brown fluff with the harness and seat belt.

"Knutt. Interesting." Her head cocked to the side.

Levi backed out of the driveway. "As in he's the result of Rags's nuts not being empty."

"Oh …" Parker snickered. "That's funny. Was she a bit calmer?"

"Barely. I'd say medicated. She called me right after the pups were born, frantic and demanding I bring a suitcase of cash in exchange for the 'hideous' puppies. I told her to see if she could sell them first. Come to find out, she sold them for more than she would have purebred Labs. Except…" he glanced at the review mirror "…the runt."

"Why didn't you tell me?"

"Because I wanted to keep my options open in case she called back demanding I come buy them from her. Actually, I was thinking of telling you just recently because I assumed she'd sold all of them, but then she called two weeks ago. Surprise!" Levi shot her a lopsided grin and a wink.

Rags kept to his side of the backseat while Knutt tried to squirm toward him.

"Two kids now. We have our hands full. Good thing I'm still unemployed. A puppy is a full-time job." She smirked.

Levi chuckled. "Indeed. Here." He handed her the blind-fold.

"What?"

"Put it on."

"Why?"

"Another surprise."

"I'm tired of wearing it."

"On. Or I'm pulling over and not moving another foot until you do."

With a heavy sigh and a pouty lip, she went back into the dark.

One Long Drive Later – In the Middle of a Barren Frozen Field

AT NEARLY TWO in the morning, Levi welcomed another favorite day, watching his world sleep in the passenger seat.

Never could he hate her.

Never would he cut her again with his words.

Never would he regret their love.

They were real.

Human.

And worthy of love and forgiveness.

Knutt rustled in the back then whined.

Parker blinked her eyes open. "Where are we?" She brought the back of her seat upright.

It had been a crazy trip that involved bathroom breaks with the blindfold coming off literally at the door to the ladies' room. He even helped feed her. A crazy and unforgettable adventure.

He pulled off her blindfold and hopped out.

"Levi—"

"I'll let the kids out to do their business."

"Levi—"

He zipped his coat. "Damn it's cold!"

"Levi!" Parker got out. "What are we doing here?"

Rags jumped out, nose inspecting the frozen dirt. Knutt followed his dad, marking and remarking their territory.

Levi shoved his hands in his pockets and lifted his shoulders up to guard his neck against the arctic temperatures. Parker hadn't even zipped her coat.

"Thought we should introduce the folks to their new grand dog."

She glanced over toward her parents' house just up the road. "And this couldn't wait? It had to be now? It had to be a surprise?"

"You love surprises." He hugged her to him, for totally selfish body-warming reasons.

"Yes."

"Why did you park here?"

His teeth began to chatter. "I like this field. It holds some really good memories."

Parker giggled. "It really does. But ... it's not as much fun in January."

"True." He whistled to the dogs. "Let's go, boys, before we all freeze our balls off."

They hopped in and drove the short distance to the farmhouse.

"Wrong way." She shook her head. "Old habits."

"Wrong way?"

"Man, you are tired." Parker laughed. "You need to go to my parents' house. See the sign in the yard that says 'Sale Pending'? The house is empty, and in a few days it won't even be mine."

"Then we should say goodbye."

"Fine. Tomorrow. I'm tired. And you need to sleep since you drove the whole way."

Levi shut off the engine. "Two seconds." He cupped the back of her head and leaned over, brushing his lips along hers. "Today is my favorite day."

After a brief stare-off, she smiled. Those five words always made her smile. "Two seconds." She nipped his lip, climbed out, and headed to the door. "And I don't understand *your* sentimentality for a house you've been in three times."

He jogged to the back door with Rags and Knutt chasing him. Parker retrieved the key from the lockbox then opened the door, flipping on the kitchen light. "Oh shit," she whispered. "Grab them before they go any farther! Someone is living here. I can't believe Piper let them move in before the papers were signed."

The house that should have been empty was filled with furniture.

"Thank God she did." Levi went back outside and returned a minute later with their bags.

"Why did you say that? What are you doing?" she whispered, attempting to keep the dogs in the kitchen while glancing toward the stairs with a cringe on her face.

"Come on, boys. I'm tuckered out." Levi moved past her, climbing the stairs. "Welcome home, Mrs. Paige."

He put both dogs in the bathroom for the night, knowing Rags would not like being in jail but Knutt needed the company until they could get him a kennel or housebroken.

Levi dropped their bags on the floor of the master bedroom, stripped down to his black briefs, and crawled into the new bed.

After a good five minutes, Parker appeared in the doorway with a blank face, lips slightly parted. She surveyed the bedroom, walls adorned with photos of family, Rags, the beach, and one shot from their wedding a month earlier.

"Are you sure?" Levi gave Parker a stern glare as they stood at the entrance to the white wedding chapel with the blue roof.

"Yes." She ran her hands down the fitted bodice of her white dress that fell just below her knees and covered her scars. "It's the Graceland Wedding Chapel. Do you realize how many celebrities have been married here?"

"Your mom already hates me for stealing you away to Arizona. I don't think eloping in Las Vegas, regardless of the chapel's notoriety, is going to score me any points with her."

"I've already told you, it's the only option. Piper and I have buried the hatchet, but revenge never dies. It just doesn't. If we have a wedding, she will poison me. I'm certain of it."

"You didn't poison her." Levi adjusted his blue tie.

"I'm pretty sure when she was buckled over in pain, vomiting

in the toilet while shitting down her dress, she felt like someone had poisoned her."

"We're your nephew's godparents. I think everyone has grown up since then."

"You're wrong. Trust me. This is best for everyone involved." She rubbed her glossed lips together. *"Just ... marry me, Levi."*

"That's my line."

She grabbed the lapels of his jacket. "Then say it."

Levi wrapped his arms around her waist ...

After staring at their Graceland Wedding Chapel photo for several minutes, Parker breached the entrance to the bedroom.

"It's temporary."

Her eyes shifted to him, sheets pulled up to his waist, hand cocked behind his head.

"We're ... living here?"

"Yes. But again, it's only temporary. Until we build on the lot to the north." He wiggled his eyebrows. "I'm going to design the house so the master bedroom is on the very spot where we parked that night."

A grin pulled at her lips. "In Iowa ... we're living in Iowa?"

"I think you once said something about liking space. Trees. Gardens. A few animals. Maybe a meadow of wildflowers or lavender. And a doggy door with a yard for Rags ... and now Knutt to run around. That wasn't going to happen in Scottsdale."

"But your job?"

"*But* your sister and your new nephew, who you cannot stop talking about. Remember them? And your mom who hates me because I stole you *and* took you to Las Vegas for our wedding."

"She doesn't hate you. I told you she adopted the whole

lifeline-not-anchor philosophy."

"Bullshit. She hates me … well, hated me. But now we're good friends. I might just be her favorite person right now because I brought you home to stay." He twisted his lips. "Clothes. Off. Naked. Now."

Parker took another step toward the bed. "I'm glad we're not living here forever." A twinge of pain etched her forehead.

"Memories?"

She nodded. They didn't have to have the conversation. He knew something must have happened between her and Gus in that house. Levi didn't like it, but he'd learned to accept the way their pasts had interwoven into something no one else would ever truly understand—including him. What Parker and Gus shared was before Levi. He left it at the cemetery the day he reclaimed the love that mattered more than illusions of lies or pasts buried beneath headstones.

No more questions. No more explanations. Levi just want-ed the girl for all the reasons every idiot before him failed to see. That was his motto. One of his mottos.

Parker pulled her phone out of her pocket, swiped her fin-ger over it several times, and tossed it on the bed as Taylor Swift's "This Love" started to play. She slipped out of her clothes, down to her white cotton bra and panties.

"Dance with me, Levi."

"It's late."

"It's our song."

He chuckled. "It's not."

She slipped off her bra letting the strap hang from her fin-ger for a second before releasing it to the floor.

He wet his lips and eased out of bed. She wrapped her arms around his neck, breasts pressed to his chest. His hands palmed her backside. They both grinned. Blue eyes locked on blue eyes. The lyrics told their story as they danced in a slow circle.

"Tell me what you said to me before we walked down the aisle at the chapel."

Levi ducked his head and brushed his lips along her neck. "I've said it a million times," he whispered, drawing her earlobe into his mouth.

Her fingers found their spot in his hair as she closed her eyes. "And I've loved hearing it a million times …"

"Marry me, Parker. This girl once told me that a ballad makes you feel like you're the entire reason for another's existence … "

Levi's hands slid up her back and into her hair, bringing her lips a breath away from his. "You're the ballad of my life."

The End

Acknowledgments

Thank you to my husband and three boys. I love our life together!

Thanks to my mom and sister for drudging through my words at their absolute worst and still seeing their potential—and for inspiring unbreakable bonds between mothers, daughters, and sisters.

Thank you to my best friend, Jyl, for keeping Jule grounded. :)

Thank you to Shauna, my queen of names and sharer of thinky thoughts.

Thank you to Jenn, my assistant, graphic designer, sounding board, and friend. You make me look and feel 100x more successful than I am.

Thank you to my Jonesies Facebook group. You are my people and I will forever adore you!

Thank you to my editor, Max, for your words of wisdom, even if they come in the form of "fuck you" at the plot twist.

Thank you to my beta readers and the rest of my editing team (Sherri, Monique, & Allison) for sacrificing your enjoyment of the story for the greater good.

Thank you, Sarah Hansen, for another beautiful cover. Once again, you nailed it!

Thank you, Jenn Watson and everyone at Social Butterfly for promoting this release. Your knowledge and patience has been invaluable.

Thank you to Paul with BB ebooks for always—ALWAYS—having the best customer service. It's a pleasure to work with you.

And last but never least, thank you to the readers, bloggers, critics, cheerleaders ... I still can't believe you let me take you on these journeys.

Today is my favorite day!

Also by Jewel E. Ann

Jack & Jill Series
End of Day
Middle of Knight
Dawn of Forever

Holding You Series
Holding You
Releasing Me

Standalone Novels
Idle Bloom
Only Trick
Undeniably You
One
Scarlet Stone

jeweleann.com

About the Author

Jewel is a free-spirited romance junkie with a quirky sense of humor.

With 10 years of flossing lectures under her belt, she took early retirement from her dental hygiene career to stay home with her three awesome boys and manage the family business.

After her best friend of nearly 30 years suggested a few books from the Contemporary Romance genre, Jewel was hooked. Devouring two and three books a week but still craving more, she decided to practice sustainable reading, AKA writing.

When she's not donning her cape and saving the planet one tree at a time, she enjoys yoga with friends, good food with family, rock climbing with her kids, watching How I Met Your Mother reruns, and of course…heart-wrenching, tear-jerking, panty-scorching novels.

Made in United States
Orlando, FL
07 June 2023

33892015R00257